Man on a Road
and Other Stories

Albert Maltz

Introduction by Patrick Chura

CALDER

CALDER PUBLICATIONS
an imprint of

ALMA BOOKS LTD
60 High Street
Wimbledon Village
London SW19 5EE
United Kingdom
www.almaclassics.com

Represented by:
Authorised Rep Compliance Ltd
Ground Floor
71 Lower Baggot Street
Dublin, D02 P593
Ireland
www.arccompliance.com

This edition of Albert Maltz's collected short stories first published by Calder Publications in 2025

For the publication details of the individual stories in this collection see the relevant note to each title.

© The Estate of Albert Maltz, 2025

Introduction © Patrick Chura, 2025

Front cover: David Wardle

Printed and bound by CPI Group (UK) Ltd, Croydon, CR0 4YY

ISBN: 978-0-7145-5098-5

All rights reserved. No part of this publication may be reproduced, stored in or introduced into a retrieval system, or transmitted, in any form or by any means (electronic, mechanical, photocopying, recording or otherwise), without the prior written permission of the publisher. This book is sold subject to the condition that it shall not be resold, lent, hired out or otherwise circulated without the express prior consent of the publisher.

Contents

Man on a Road and Other Stories
Introduction — vii

THE WAY THINGS ARE AND OTHER STORIES — 1
- Season of Celebration — 5
- Goodbye — 65
- Incident on a Street Corner — 77
- The Game — 85
- A Letter from the Country — 93
- The Drop-Forge Man — 103
- The Way Things Are — 119
- Man on a Road — 161

FROM AFTERNOON IN THE JUNGLE — 171
- The Happiest Man on Earth — 175
- Sunday Morning on Twentieth Street — 187
- Afternoon in the Jungle — 195
- Circus Come to Town — 203
- With Laughter — 219
- The Farmer's Dog — 237
- The Cop — 251

UNCOLLECTED SHORT STORIES — 269
- The Gentleman and His Son — 271
- The Piece of Paper — 279
- Husband and Wife — 293
- To Climb the Pyrenees — 321

Notes — 337

Other books by ALBERT MALTZ

The Cross and the Arrow

The Eyewitness Report

The Journey of Simon McKeever

A Long Day in a Short Life

A Tale of One January

The Underground Stream

Introduction

The rise of Albert Maltz – literary wunderkind of the 1930s who earned distinction as both playwright and story writer while still in his twenties – makes for a compelling narrative. Success came easily for the Brooklyn-born son of Jewish immigrants. The dark decade of the Great Depression was for him a period of action and adventure. As the years passed and times changed, so would his art – and his fortunes.

In June 1930, eight months after the stock-market crash and three months after his graduation from Columbia with a philosophy degree, the aspiring author enrolled at Yale Drama School to learn playwriting from the best in the business, Professor George Pierce Baker, whose workshops had been a training ground for major dramatists since 1905.

Maltz had come to New Haven with his closest friend from Columbia, George Sklar, a working-class radical who introduced him to Marxist politics and stoked his leftist leanings. They were warned that the Yale curriculum required total immersion in theatre, but they chose not to ignore the world outside the theatre, where there were 15 million unemployed Americans. Maltz and Sklar wanted to write about that world, and they got to work quickly. By January 1931, they had co-written *Merry Go Round*, a play about a gangland murder that exposed the human costs of urban political corruption.

When their professors said it was the best play ever done by Yale students, the two stopped attending classes in New Haven and took their script to New York, where *Merry Go Round* opened in April 1932. One reviewer called it "a play with a bite like an angry bulldog's". Maltz and Sklar were the talk of the town. They never went back to Yale.

A second collaboration with Sklar, the anti-war play *Peace on Earth*, opened in 1933 and was awarded the Annie E. Gray Peace Plaque as that year's "outstanding American work of art contributing most to the cause of peace". It was probably the first American play to present modern war as the inevitable result of capitalism. Maltz was twenty-three when he wrote it.

The Maltz–Sklar friendship would span decades, but in 1934 Maltz struck out on his own. He bought a beat-up Ford Model A and took to the road on a journey of four months and 10,000 miles, seeking "vital contact" with the downtrodden and the working classes.

Mainly, he wanted to show Mike Gold, the firebrand communist editor of *New Masses* and leader of the once-mighty movement for a workers' literature, that Albert Maltz was the real thing. Gold believed that a true radical writer should possess "the courage of proletarian experience".

This book includes nineteen short stories, the first nine of which were inspired by Maltz's epic deep-dive into "Depression Era" America. On his down-classing journey, Maltz intended not just to observe how the "other half" lives, but to suffer alongside it in the factories, mines and coal camps. Armed with press credentials from both the stodgy *New York Post* and the radical *New Masses*, he could operate on either side of the class divide – and he did.

On the day before Maltz started out, newspapers carried reports of a bloody strike in a General Motors parts factory in Ohio. He arrived in Toledo just in time to report on the inquest of a striker who'd been murdered by the National Guard. Later that day in the factory, he watched a teenaged "drop-forge man" at his gruelling work. Maltz shuddered at the homicidal force of the massive steam hammer, and made notes for a story.

He then drove directly to Pittsburgh, where he covered the tremendous efforts of labour agitators to unionize steelworkers. In the adjacent town of Monessen, he visited a girl whose brother worked in a nail factory and was going deaf at twenty-one from the extreme noise. In a story titled 'Goodbye', Maltz described the family and the home in which they lived.

In the nearby area of Brownsville, Maltz stayed a week in a coal camp, letting himself get filthy and trying to get a job working in the mines. He knew he was lucky not to get hired. Though he'd been a competitive swimmer and boxer, seeing real miners made him realize that he couldn't have handled digging coal. He wasn't miner-strong, but he was learning compassion.

While in Brownsville he got a letter from *New Masses* asking him if he would write an article on the farmers in South Dakota, who were organizing under the National Farmers Union to prevent foreclosures caused by the Dust Bowl drought. He wasn't farm-boy-strong either, but he earned the farmers' respect and was invited to speak at their rallies.

Just after he left the state, he heard about a danger he had barely escaped. Maltz's union friends had sponsored a dance that was crashed by vigilantes from the veterans' organization the American Legion, who swarmed in to break up the gathering, stopping cars on the road and beating up the union men and their families. In a bizarre twist, the mob dragged a dozen or so organizers into the legion hall. Except for the few who jumped out of windows, they were all tortured. Men and women, drunk, physically abused them, putting out cigarettes on their flesh and making them run the gauntlet.

This ungoverned savagery left Maltz emotionally scarred. He saw it as a direct counterpart to the Nazi phenomenon in Germany, and it convinced him that fascism could happen in the United States. Out of this atrocity, Maltz crafted the short story 'A Letter from the Country'.

From South Dakota he drove 1,300 miles to the Louisiana coast, giving rides to several hitch-hikers, then to Mississippi, covering an immense swath of the United States and absorbing as much life as he could.

From a rural sharecropping plantation came 'The Way Things Are', in which Maltz dissects with precision the race–class order of the New South. The central character is a white landowner and scion of the patriarchy who pretends to distance himself from the dirty work of racial oppression while he in effect perpetuates it. Also central to the narrative is the anguish of a young black worker threatened with lynching, whose assertions of manhood prefigure the motivations of the Civil Rights Movement.

Finally Maltz reached a mining area in West Virginia near Scotts Run, on the way picking up an unemployed miner. As Maltz's trusty Ford neared Gauley Bridge, the miner pointed to a tunnel and described shocking events: nearly 2,000 workmen had been employed for over two years to build the Hawks Nest Tunnel, an engineering marvel three miles long, one mile of it through solid rock that was ninety per cent silica. Almost as soon as the digging started, men began dying. Unaware of any danger, they'd been blasting into the rock without masks or respirators, inhaling with every breath a massive dose of deadly silica dust. Company contractors denied the hazard and conspired to subvert inspections. In the end, every man who worked in the tunnel for a significant time developed lung disease. It was profits over people, courtesy of Union Carbide and the State of West Virginia, who scandalously colluded in the worst industrial tragedy in American history.

'Man on a Road' tells the story of Jack Pitckett, whose lungs are ravaged by silicosis and who takes to the road because he'd rather die alone than be a burden to his family. On a rainy night, he hitches a ride with the story's narrator, who observes the sick man with compassion and stakes him to a meal, after which the barely literate miner asks the narrator to write a letter to his wife for him. The miner's simple missive elicits the narrator's "pity and love" and urges the reader towards social justice.

The tale first appeared in *New Masses*, and was immediately republished in *The Best Short Stories, 1936*. It reached a wide audience in labour journals and prompted a congressional investigation. On the morning the Hawks Nest Tunnel hearings opened in Washington, DC, every US congressman had on his desk a copy of 'Man on a Road'. Afterwards, Secretary of Labor Frances Perkins called a national conference on the dangers of silicosis.

Almost fifty years later, an ageing Maltz received an unexpected letter from Lorin Kerr, director of the Department of Occupational Health for the United Mine Workers of America.

The purpose of the letter, dated 21st March 1985, was to inform Maltz that the "storm of protest" generated by 'Man on a Road' had not been forgotten. "Today, the impact of your story continues unabated," wrote Kerr.

Appropriately, Maltz's book-length collection of 1938, *The Way Things Are and Other Stories*, included an introduction by Mike Gold, the dean of proletarian literature and gatekeeper of the radical left's artistic standards. Gold congratulated Maltz on stories that were "marked by a deep sensitivity and brooding pain". He also endorsed Maltz's proletarian journey, pointing out that "it was no mere slummer's pity" that motivated the author on his travels to the farms, factories and sharecropper shacks, but "a fraternalism that becomes an identification and a philosophy". Yes, Maltz was the real deal.

Just after *The Way Things Are* arrived in bookstores, 'The Happiest Man on Earth' was published in *Harper's* and won the O. Henry Memorial Award as the best short story of 1938. (Richard Wright and John Steinbeck finished second and third, respectively.) The central character is Jesse Fulton, a destitute father who has spent six years searching for employment in Kansas City. When Jesse hears that his brother-in-law is running a trucking company in Tulsa, he walks 250 miles to beg for a job, only to learn that the sole opening is for a driver of explosive nitroglycerine soup used in drilling oil wells. "Sooner or later you get killed," the brother-in-law warns. But Jesse, with a starving family and no other hope, decides for himself the outcome of his quest for dignity.

All of the stories Maltz wrote before 1940 show the degree to which he imbibed the politically charged aesthetic of communist art, which saw literature, in Leninist terms, as a weapon in the class war. But these stories of the Depression decade are just as apt today.

The peak of Maltz's fiction-writing career would come with *The Cross and the Arrow*, a deep analysis of a little-known phenomenon: anti-Hitler resistance within Nazi Germany. Upon its release in 1944, critics universally praised the novel, and 150,000 copies of it were handed out to American GIs fighting fascism in Europe.

Throughout the 1940s Maltz was a successful Hollywood scriptwriter. His screenplay for *The House I Live In*, a short film created to counteract an upsurge of anti-Semitic violence with messages of religious tolerance and inclusion, won a special Academy Award in 1946. The film starred Frank Sinatra, who wrote a congratulatory letter: "Albert, just for the record, I know that you're the best goddam writer around."

Four years later, Albert was in prison.

Summoned to Washington by the House Un-American Activities Committee, Maltz was asked under oath the defining question of the Cold War era: "Are you now or have you ever been a member of the Communist Party?" With a group of film-industry figures who came to be known as the "Hollywood Ten", he challenged the constitutional legitimacy of the very question. He was charged with contempt of Congress, fined, jailed for ten months and thwarted as a writer for almost two decades.

Those years were a dark night and a test of resolve – the opposite of Maltz's meteoric ascent in the 1930s. But during his time on the blacklist, he continued to develop as an artist. His short stories became less overtly political, but no less compassionate, and more nuanced.

'Circus Come to Town' was finished just before Maltz surrendered for his prison term in 1950. The Campbell brothers, seven-year-old Alan and twelve-year-old Eddie, get up early on a Saturday morning to meet the circus that comes to their Indiana hamlet every few years. Unable to afford tickets to the show, they earn their admission tickets by helping set up tents for the performance. The anti-capitalist lessons of this haunting tale are many, but they are implied rather than stated. Gone are the formulas of proletarian realism, overridden by a modernism characterized by a self-conscious break with the past and search for new forms of expression.

By the early 1960s Maltz was winning awards again, subverting the blacklist by using a pseudonym, but proving himself versatile in ways that would have shocked his 1930s fans. 'With Laughter', written under the pen name Julian Silva, tests the reader's perceptions of racial identity and prefigures Toni Morrison's daring experimental story 'Recitatif'. It won the *Southwest Review* prize for the best story published in that journal during 1960 and 1961.

'To Climb the Pyrenees', a riveting, tightly crafted morality tale, was rejected by the *Saturday Evening Post* in 1961, but resubmitted to the same journal in 1968, where it was published under the banal title 'The Spoils of War'. In this volume we restore Maltz's title. To appreciate this gem, all we need to know is the summary of its core truth that Maltz jotted down in his personal notes: "To respect himself a man must put principle above opportunistic considerations."

The previously unpublished 'Husband and Wife' was adapted for television in 1962 under the title 'The Great Alberti'. A candid two-character study of ageing and intimacy, this work was deeply meaningful to Maltz. In his notebook he framed its message as one of simple wisdom: "True love does not depend on the worldly achievements of one or another partner."

Maltz's diaries show that he struggled over 'The Cop', worrying the story through several versions. The central character, an Italian raconteur Maltz met during a 1968 trip to Rome, gently commands his American auditor, "Now, pay attention to what can happen to the human heart." We obey, and we learn the terrible price of trying to live for oneself alone.

The primary focus of Maltz's late-career stories is neither class war nor Cold War. In 1971 Liveright collected and published several of them under the title *Afternoon in the Jungle*. One reviewer asserted, "The humanity and sensitivity of Albert Maltz shine through like bright rays in a night of war and repression." In the *Los Angeles Times*, Robert Kirsch wrote, "Deep within us, Maltz is saying, is an instinct for humanity which if man is to surpass the jungle must be touched. These stories do touch that deep impulse."

– Patrick Chura, University of Akron

THE WAY THINGS ARE
AND OTHER STORIES*
(1938)

To my wife,
MARGARET*

Season of Celebration*

I

At Nine in the Evening

At nine in the evening Baldy White, nightman of the Hotel Raleigh, opened the door to Room B and poked his head in. He stood there chuckling. "Hey, Benson," he said, "here's someone wants to know if the beds is clean."

Except for a sick youngster, who was asleep in a cot further down the aisle, the man called Benson was the only one in the big room. He was lounging on the back end of his cot with his scraggly shanks hanging down loosely over the iron rim. Benson was a lank, ugly man of fifty, a farmhand and migratory worker. Thirty-five years of highballing over the forty-eight states from one job to another, from railroad jungle to Jesus flophouse, had lined and grooved his weary face into a steady bitter scowl. Now he sat grimly, hunched over, with an old newspaper spread on his knees to hold his game of solitaire. He ignored the nightman.

"Tell him, Bill, tell him," Baldy repeated laughing.

Benson sighed. He screwed up his face into a grimace that was weary, sour and impatient at the same time, jerked his thumb and sluiced a stream of saliva on the floor. Then he looked down at the cards again.

The nightman laughed and smoothed the top of his bald dome with a thick white hand. His mouth opened wide, and the gold-capped teeth gleamed yellow in the sharp light. He liked Benson. Benson was an old customer – a glum mutt with a cranky disposition, but no teeth left. Nice feller, Benson.

"Take a look," Baldy said. He closed one eye and inclined his head slightly towards the door.

A young man of about twenty-seven came into the room. He was shivering with the cold. His face was hollow and curiously serious with the brows knitted and the deep brown eyes, which were liquid and soft like the eyes of a woman, set in a peculiar stare. He wore only overalls and a scrappy sweater which had lost its buttons a long time ago. It hung down loosely from his angular shoulders, and he had it fastened at the throat with a safety pin. Under his arm he carried a brown-paper parcel – the suitcase and wardrobe trunk of a stiff on the bum.

Baldy watched him with an expressive grin on his face: a number-one boy – he knew the type!

The young man examined the long bare room with great care: the triple row of iron cots, the narrow lockers, the hanging electric bulbs encased in wire mesh. He took a long time for it. Then he rubbed one hand over the stubble of soft reddish hair on his face while a finger of the other hand played nervously with the string on his parcel.

"Ah cain't sleep if there's bugs," he announced finally.

Baldy laughed. He knew the type! He knew them all! He was sixteen years in the business, and he had seen the endless murky river of men with an old shirt on their backs and two bits in their pockets. Number one was the working stiffs out on their uppers – the scared, bitter stiffs floating from town to town with their teeth locked together and holes in their shoes from scraping the streets at six bells every a.m., trying to find them a job, trying to keep their poor schnozzles out of water. Yes, Jesus Christ, when Baldy looked at them, he thanked his aunt Lizzie he had this job. And the second was the bums, the boozers, the guys who had given up – two feet down already; tomorrow in a doorway or frozen by a kerbstone or keeling over in the street; the morgue boys waiting to be laid out; finished but still crawling, scratching, coughing, panhandling, hanging on they don't know why; buy 'em an' sell 'em for a nickel. And number three was the fish in between: the men on the skids with their guts dryin' up, stiffs with their juice runnin' out; you don't look for work so hard any more; you've given up tryin' for a job nowadays; you're startin' to get drunk on smoke when you get it – oh, the boot in the backside, but they don't know it yet; slidin' downhill, but they can't see the ground go past. Oh yes, Baldy had seen 'em all! Sixteen years of faces he had forgotten. New ones comin' up every day like somebody had planted them. Here was a number-one boy: a stiff with his nose for a job – but a boy with the trimmings; one of the specials... looking for a bed without bugs... banjo eyes like he just came out of the incubator, didn't know how babies were made... there were them kinds too!

"Texas," Baldy said, clapping the young man on the back, "Texas... you find a bug an' I'll eat it. Louse, bedbug or any kind of roach." He laughed again. "We kill 'em all with kerosene. There's none in here you don't bring with you."

"Ah'm from Arkansas," the boy said seriously. "Mah name is Luke Hall."

"That's fine, Mr Hall. I knew somebody from Arkansas. Fine feller! Bill," he said, "tell Mr Hall how you always come here on your business trips to New York."

Mr Bill Benson looked over at the gentleman from Arkansas, screwed up his face wearily and looked down at the cards again. Baldy wasn't as funny as he thought. Benson wished he'd get through and go wiggle his tail.

The nightman chuckled. He had a round, full, good-natured face the colour of fresh dough. The laughter made his fat cheeks shake. "Finest hotel on the gay white Bowery,"* he said. He waited for the boy to make up his mind.

Hall was silent.

"Unless you want a flop to yourself," Baldy suggested suddenly. The boss gave him a commission on the private rooms, and Baldy pushed them whenever he could. "You get side walls an' chicken wire on top, so nobody can't reach in. It's strictly private."

"What's the charge on that?"

"Fifteen cents more."

Hall shook his head. "Ah ain't got a job. Ah'll tell you, mista," he added confidentially, "that's why Ah've come t'New York. Ah'm hopin' t'get me a good job heah."

"You ain't got a job, eh?" Baldy wriggled his thick lips humorously. This son of a bitch was a daisy! "Most men come here got fine-paying jobs. They just like it here." He held out a hand that was like a cut of prime fatback. "That'll be twenty cents!"

Hall fumbled in his overalls pocket. He drew out a small woman's purse. "Anyway," he said, "anyway it's New Year's Eve, an' Ah'll be right glad to have company. Ah'm right fond of company."

"That's right fine," Baldy replied with a grin. He mimicked the boy's speech: "Mr Benson's right fine company. Regular entertainer. An' it's a cold night... this room'll fill up pretty soon. You'll have plenty of right fine company."

The stranger from Arkansas fished out two dimes. "That's good," he said. "Ehhh..." He felt hesitant about asking. "You don't have anything special on heah tonight, do you? Ah mean – like for your patrons?"

Baldy scratched his dome with exaggerated thoughtfulness. "Well, no... a'course," he said, "we have our regular New Year's Eve dinner – you know... soup, fish, duck, chicken, plenty of nuts... just the regular five courses... An' entertainment, a'course: some of the Park Avenue dames comes down for the dancin'."

Benson, four cots down the aisle, raised his ugly grinning head from the cards. "Don't miss it, buddy," he croaked in his hoarse voice, "it's a picnic."

Luke Hall looked doubtful. "It ain't free, is it?"

"Well, no," Baldy protested. "But it ain't so much either... four fifty a plate!"

"Four dollars an' fifty cents?" Hall smiled wistfully. "Ah reckon that's a little too steep for me, Mista White."

Baldy shook his head sadly. "It's too bad, Mr Hall." He held out a key which was fastened by wire to a piece of wood. "This is for your locker. There's a right smart toilet and washroom through the door on the other side."

Benson burst out into a snort of laughter. Baldy turned around with an appreciative grin on his face. Then he smoothed his bald dome and looked solemn again. "One more thing, kid," he advised kindly, with amusement, "don't leave your duds around loose – not if you want 'em again."

"Ah won't," Hall replied. "Ah know *that*. But thank you, mista." He walked down the line of cots searching for his number.

The boy who was asleep suddenly groaned aloud and flung his arm away from his face. Hall stopped, startled. Baldy lumbered over. "O'Shaughnessy!" he called.

There was no reply. The boy twisted in his sleep. He was muttering to himself.

"Is he sick?" Hall asked.

"He's all right," Baldy replied. "He's had ptomaine* for a coupla days."

"He looks turrible," Hall said.

"He don't look good," the nightman agreed. He called again: "O'Shaughnessy!"

The sick boy subsided. He slept quietly with one arm flung out and his head twisted to the side in a strained position. The bright lights overhead coloured the pallor of his flesh, giving it an unpleasant, wax-like appearance. His face was emaciated – the cheeks sunken in, the jawbones protruding; there were deep pockets under the eyes. He was breathing hard, but now the low muttering had stopped.

"Hey, Bill," Baldy requested, "call me if he wakes up, will you?"

"What's the matter?" Benson croaked. "You hafta blow his nose for him?"

"You call me, Bill!" Baldy said. "I'm worried! He owes me for a whole week."

"Aw, c'mon," Benson persisted, "you blow his nose for him. He ain't had it blowed all day."

"Say..." Baldy turned to Luke Hall. "Wanna buy an overcoat?"

"It's cold, ain't it?" Hall agreed. He rubbed his chin. "Ah didn't know it got so cold up heah in December."

"It'll get colder, son," Baldy warned. His tone became businesslike. "I know where you can get a good coat for a buck an' a quarter."

Baldy's rule was a coat or a hat for an unpaid bill. What the boss didn't know didn't hurt him, and there was a good turnover in it. Hell, Baldy only got twenty-five a week, an' he had three kids an' an old lady to support.

Hall shook his head. "That's too much for me, mista."

Baldy frowned. A bargainer, hey? That was fine. A bargainer an' cold sober. The drunks were better: they forked right over. "There's one for six bits I can pick up," he suggested confidentially.

Hall shook his head.

"You're gonna need one!"

"Ah ain't got a job yet," Hall explained.

"OK!" Baldy gave up in disgust. The Arkansas rummy must think overcoats grow on trees. "OK then!" Baldy turned quickly and left the room.

Hall sat down on his cot. He was wondering if it had been a mistake to let the overcoat go. That was a good offer Mr White had offered him. Still… he didn't have much money. It was more important to keep eating. He could buy one later, when he got him a job. Yes!

But how if he didn't get a job? The thought frightened the boy. But that couldn't be! It couldn't be! In a big city like New York there'd bound to be *somethin'* a man could do – if he was willing to take anything at all. Wouldn't there?

He felt reassured again. That was sensible! And prayer! Prayer would help too.

Luke shifted on the cot and began taking off his shoes. He wore no socks, and his feet were white with cold. He rubbed them slowly. He thought of the fine dinner that was going to be served at midnight. He wished he had the price of that fine dinner.

O'Shaughnessy twisted in his sleep. He was muttering to himself.

Luke watched him pityingly. It was turrible to be sick when you were away from home. It made you so lonely. Luke knew how lonely it made you feel.

He picked absently at the dirt that was caked between his toes. He hoped that the sick boy was a believer. It'd help him in his sickness if he believed. And it was good to be in a warm room. He could bathe himself here. When the disciples came back from a long journey, the first thing they did was to bathe themselves.

O'Shaughnessy subsided. The bright light was cruel on his white face.

The street noises of the Bowery drifted in. They sounded melancholy. They carried the dreary feel of a dark winter night.

II

As Blessy swung around the corner of Delancey Street onto the Bowery, walking quickly with his hard, hurried stride and his big head crooked down against the flurries of wet snow, he ran smack into a young girl. He was in a hurry to get up to the Raleigh and see how O'Shaughnessy was doing, and he hadn't been looking where he was going. The impact of his heavy driving body almost knocked the girl down.

Blessy grabbed her, and the girl regained her balance. She leant her head back against the plate glass window of the cigar store and burst out into an abrupt, foolish giggle. "Poosh poosh!" she said. She was very drunk.

"Did I hu-u-u-u… hurt you?"

Blessy flushed painfully. There he was – stammering again. Whenever he became excited, like a goddam ninny. How the hell did he get like that in the first place, he asked himself savagely. Since he was a kid.

"It's awright," the girl said. "It's a pleasure." She looked up at him and smiled drunkenly. It was a warm, free, abandoned, drunken New Year's Eve smile that meant nothing.

Blessy looked dumbly at the girl's red, smiling mouth. Then he saw her body. Her drab cloth coat had become unbuttoned, and she wore a gay party dress underneath. She was not a pretty girl.

Her face was dark and thin, and there were tired circles under her eyes. She looked Italian – like a factory kid, he thought. But her mouth was a warm red smear, and Blessy could see the flesh of her throat, naked and sensuously white against her dark face, and the slight curve of her breasts where the dress swung low, and the round, hard little nipples pressed tight and warm against the blue silk – and her youth, her warmth and her youth!

A keen, desperate desire for the girl swept over him. It had been so long since he had left home, and no one, not anyone, since then! A molten, quivering flame licked through the veins of his body. It tongued warm and bitter at his flesh, stripping away the lonely wall of security, leaving him weak and trembling and desperately hungry. A painful bubble of noise rose up in his throat. He felt choked. He stared at her – but he couldn't find words to speak.

The girl stopped giggling. For a moment she eyed the youth closely. Her head was swaying a little. He stood directly in front of her – a heavy, muscular, peasant-faced youth of twenty-four in an old lumberjacket and blue corduroys, without a hat on, standing there without speaking while the wet snow fell soft on his face and hair, standing there staring with hot blue eyes that stabbed into her. The girl stopped giggling.

Blessy's face was fiery red from the wind and the out-of-doors, and his features were extraordinary: big, thick, hard, with high, prominent cheekbones – a wide, hard, heavy jaw and a big, wide mouth with thick, firm lips. He looked as though he had been cut rough out of a quarry. And like a crown on his flaming face there was a wild, magnificent shock of yellow hair shot through by flecks of gold. He stood there, planted in front of her, gripping the earth like an inarticulate, powerful animal, and the girl could see the full tide of his desire – the humble, passionate, naked yearning written like script on his face.

If she had not been drunk, she might not have spoken to him. Her thin, dark face suddenly seemed full and soft, and she leant forward a little. "Well, so long," she said. She put her hand on his arm.

Then she stepped to one side and walked with stiff and drunken dignity to the kerbstone. On the other side of the Bowery there was an automobile crowded with young people. The girl crossed over. She got in. The car moved off.

Blessy walked again, more slowly now. His head had sunk down into the collar of his lumberjacket.

It turned colder. The snow became a dry, fine powder. It'd stick to the pavement now, and if it kept up all night, there'd be a couple more days' work. That was good. Blessy thought about it slowly. Snow was good. You made much more that way than selling the white sheets. If Jimmie hadn't gotten sick now, they could've cleaned up.

Blessy walked slowly – past the eating joints and the gin mills, past the pawnshops and the two-pair-of-pants joints, the Salvation Army flop and dark doorways where bums were sleeping, kept warm for a little while by smoke – but tomorrow morning they'd be picking up every third one with the sweat froze stiff on him.

In the instant that the automobile had moved off, Blessy had forgotten about the girl. Not really forgotten – she was just gone, that's all, the way a fire leaves you when it dies down to ash. You walk along the street and you can't hardly recall what it was like. It had happened to him before. He wondered why.

A bum see-sawed blindly across his path yelling "Hooray for the bums from Idaho" – yelling it at the top of his tinhorn* voice. Blessy stepped to one side. He stopped to look at a neon light winking first yellow and then green with the snow falling soft in front of it: "Beer, Beer!" It looked nice.

Perhaps, he thought, when a guy didn't have a job or a home or anything like that, he had enough to do just to keep alive. A man most always needed his belly full to start wanting a girl. Feelin' kind of tired all the time was about all the feelin' a man could have. Yes, you were always that way, always sort of half tired. Yet once in a while it hit you like a streak of lightning, and then it felt like somebody had poured gasoline all over you and struck a big match. That woman in the subway was like that.

The snow scuffed under his feet. He felt washed out. He wasn't used to heavy work any more. All day long shovelling in the cold. Better to have his supper first. No... no, he thought, Jimmie might be awake now. See him first. Poor Jimmie!

A current of emotion welled up in Blessy at the thought of his friend. Yes, God Almighty, there weren't many things he had left in life. You hung on, hand to mouth, a dog keepin' house in an alley. Outside people walking, you all alone in the dark countin' the cramps in your belly. If Jimmie hadn't been there to pal along with him, he'd 'a' gone crazy.

He thought of the future. Well, that was somethin'. Jimmie was trained, a mechanic. Two an' a half years in the state school. That prepared a man. One of these days they'd be needing trained men again. Jimmie'd get on, teach *him* something – maybe some day they'd have a machine shop together. I'm tired, he thought.

He passed a bonfire in the gutter. Half a dozen stiffs were hugging the flames. Something in the colour of it made him stop. Then he saw what it was: blue from a tar barrel. At home, when the rain came down, the coal dump burst into a hundred little fires. You'd see them just like that, flickering blue-red all over the side, way high up sometimes like ghost fires, with the odour of coal gas blowing down over the camp. Well, it was never so good in that lousy coal camp, but it was better than this – aw, what the hell, he thought. No soap in mining any more. So many machines coming in, five out of ten men were out, even the old-timers. It was better to be in a city. You could dig yourself a hole in a city.

Blessy crossed the street. A limousine touring car streaked past him like a black locomotive. A fat man in a college-boy overcoat leant out of the front seat and hollered, "Happy New Year, bud." The limousine shot hellbent uptown, and a burst of warm, careless woman's laughter rippled back to him.

They were waiting for midnight. Blessy had seen that headline in a newspaper: "America Waits for Midnight." A happy country was waiting for midnight.

A surge of bitterness rose up inside of him. What was he waiting for? Something, but not midnight. Sure, a job, a woman, a home. Christ, everybody was waiting for that. And tired waiting! Your bones were beginning to crack with waiting! O'Shaughnessy was sick from waiting. Free, white and waiting!

He entered the doorway of the Hotel Raleigh. A man was sitting halfway up the flight of stairs that led to the office. Blessy knew him, Jed Killifer, a bargeman from Boston. Jed was the one put him and Jimmie wise to the white-sheet racket. You wait till two, when the morning papers hit the stands. You buy 'em for three cents and then beat it over to Fourth Avenue, where the night-club traffic is scooting home to Brooklyn. You can always get rid of some at a nickel a piece, and that's the price of your flop.

"Hello, Jed," Blessy said. "How you doin'?"

Jed was blind drunk. He didn't recognize Blessy. He stood up and grabbed him by his lumberjacket. "I'm from ol' Beantown,"* he said belligerently, "an' a guy from ol' Beantown's as good as a guy from New York. Ain't that right?"

"Sure," Blessy told him. He removed his hand.

"They had fifty million dollars for the bankers," Jed announced fiercely, "an' not a goddam cent for me." He grabbed Blessy by the jacket again. "Ain't that right?" he demanded.

"Right," Blessy said. He sat Jed down and brushed past him. "You better turn in, Jed, you're loaded."

Jed burst out laughing and smacked his hands together. "Oh boy, oh boy," he whooped, guffawing. "Oh boy, what she did to me for a dollar!"

"How much was the dose?" Blessy asked. He walked up the stairs laughing.

"Happy New Year," Jed called after him. "Everybody's gotta have a happy... oh boy, oh boy!" He clapped his hands together again.

Blessy opened the door to the landing where the office was. There was no one in the cage. He crossed the floor and started up the corrugated-iron stairway that led to the rooms. Baldy White, the nightman, met him at the turn.

"Hello," Baldy said quickly. "I wanna see you."

"I'll be right down," Blessy told him.

"The kid's asleep," Baldy said. "No use in goin' up."

"Oh! Say, that's funny," Blessy speculated aloud in his slow, heavy manner. "He must be sure played out. He's been sleepin' all day."

"All day?" Baldy pursed his thick lips sarcastically. "Let me remind you somethin', boy: he's been sleepin' here *free* all week."

Blessy gestured impatiently. "I told you I'd pay you, Baldy."

"Awright, pay me!" Baldy snapped out his thick, white hand.

"I ain't got it now... What's the matter with you anyway?" Blessy asked suddenly. "You know I been working on the snow for three days, an' you know the city don't pay off right away. I told you, when I get it, I'll pay you. Jesus, we're good customers."

Baldy hooked both thumbs under his belt. For a moment he was silent. His plump, doughy face was flushed, and he was breathing hard and angrily.

"You make me tired," he broke out finally, "you stiffs make me goddamned tired. Who's doin' the favours around here anyway? Does O'Shaughnessy owe me, or do I owe him? For Godssakes," he burst out, "I don't own this joint. I been puttin' twenty cents in the till every goddam night your pal's been layin' around here. Why the hell should I do that for you?"

"I'm gonna pay you, ain't I?" Blessy insisted stubbornly.

"How do I know?"

"I'm tellin' you!"

Baldy snorted. "*You're* tellin' me! A lot of other guys has told me, but I had to pay for it, because I'm nothin' but a good-natured slob. Listen..." – he shoved his face close to Blessy's – "so far O'Shaughnessy's overcoat makes it even. I can take *that* in trade. But that's all! I ain't carryin' him a day more! Tomorrow mornin' he goes out!"

Baldy lumbered into his office: "Don't forget it!"

Blessy stood rooted. The nightman's threat was too unexpected, and it had come too quickly for him to comprehend it. Then his brain blazed, and he walked over to the cage with slow, heavy deliberateness. "You gonna thruh-thruh… throw him out even if he's still sick?" he asked.

"Listen," Baldy said, "I ain't no Rockefeller Foundation. There's a *lotta* sick people in this world. I can't carry him!"

"I won't leh-leh-leh-let you!" Blessy said. His body hunched down a little, and his thick neck became red and swollen. "I won't leh-let you!"

"Oh!" Baldy surveyed him calmly. "You gonna make trouble, I'll get a cop, that's all. If you want a month in the can, OK with me."

"Listen…" Blessy said thickly, "you be careful! You throw him out, you be careful!" The youth's face had suddenly become murderous. He shoved a big knuckled fist under the nightman's nose. "You listen," he said thickly in a voice that trembled with emotion, "you throw him out, I'm go-go-gonna *get* you. I'll… I'll…" – he searched for words – "I'll wait ten years, but I'll do-do it!"

Baldy slid out of his swivel chair and backed to the other end of the wire cage. He was scared stiff. This bull-headed bastard looked crazy mean. Baldy cast a quick glance over at his billy hanging by the cash register. No, it was too risky. Blessy was only a foot away. He couldn't make it.

"You be ca-careful," the yellow-haired youth repeated in a thick, choked whisper. He was still standing hunched over, with his big sledgehammer fist poised in the air.

Baldy's doughy cheeks quivered as though he were about to cry. "For Godssakes," he said in a burst of pleading, "what can *I* do?"

"I'll pay you," Blessy said. "But you got to luh-luh-leave him alone."

The nightman's head wagged exasperatedly. He started to speak, then stopped.

They stared at each other. Finally the youth straightened up. "Don't worry, I'll p-p-pay you…" he said. He walked out of the cage. "I'm goin' back to Dooky's – get some grub… You tell Jimmie if he wakes up, will you?"

Baldy sighed resignedly. Now, God help him, he was doin' favours again… "All right, I'll tell him," he said wearily.

The big youth nodded in his slow, heavy manner. He went out.

Baldy sat down. He wiped his forehead with his sleeve. This was a hell of a note. He wiped his forehead again. On the one hand… get stuck with an unpaid bill. Fine! He could hear his old lady hollering already. But, on the other hand, this big lug… hell, he was built like a bull and crazy enough to do anything. "Jesus!" Baldy exclaimed aloud. He wiped his forehead for the third time. But maybe the boy *would* pay. Baldy considered the prospect. He *said* he would. He wasn't trying to weasel out on the charge. It might be better to wait. Yes, he decided, he would wait. He could always grab the overcoat.

"Some job, hey?" he asked himself suddenly. He leant back in his swivel chair and swore softly with slow, keen relish. For twenty-five a week – him and J.P. Morgan.*

Blessy stepped out on the street and pulled his lumberjacket around him. It was brutally cold, and he felt the deep, long-time weariness heavy inside of him. It had been a mistake to come home without eating.

The holiday traffic roared past him as he trudged downtown. It gave him a lonely feeling. He wished Jimmie were well again.

III

Nine Twenty p.m.

Luke Hall came out of the washroom. He approached Bill Benson hesitatingly. Benson was still playing his solitaire with his face screwed up into its steady scowl. Now and then he reached into his pocket for a bottle of liquor. It was a smoky, white fluid, a bottle of murderous home-brew that he had picked up for two bits. It coursed down his insides like streaked lightning, and after each drink he coughed and spat on the floor.

"You want to play some cards with me, friend?" Luke asked in his soft drawling speech. He was holding a piece of toilet paper to a cut on his chin where his ancient razor had left its signature. Now that the stubble of beard was gone, his face seemed even more pallid and emaciated than it had before, but there was a curious softness to it, in the curve of his lips and the liquid expression of his eyes, that made him look wistful and young. Luke waited for the answer to his question.

Benson didn't reply. He kept his face down at the cards.

"Didn't you hear me, friend?"

Benson snapped his head up. He opened his mouth as though to speak, took a swift breath, clamped his wolfish-looking jaws together with an angry click and then looked down at the cards again.

Luke walked back to his cot. His lips were curved in a pout, and his face showed his distress. He hadn't expected to find people as non-sociable as this. He'd expected they'd feel different on New Year's Eve. They always did at home. They had fun at home.

The sick boy stirred in his sleep. He uttered a long-drawn-out sigh and raised his legs under the blanket. Luke watched him. He hoped this ptomaine wasn't catching. A fellow who got bad sick and didn't have a home was in a bad fix. The sick boy sighed again. His knees relaxed.

Luke stretched out on his side and pillowed his head in his arms. He felt lonely all of a sudden. Unhappy too. He wished he could do something to make himself feel better. Back home on New Year's Eve they used to sing songs. That was nice to do. Perhaps, if he did that now, it'd make him feel better. Yes, he decided, that was a *good* thought: he would sing a song and pretend he was home again.

He began quietly in a fresh, clear voice. It was a hymn:

> All people that on earth do dwell,
> Sing to the Lord with cheerful voice –
> Him serve with fear, His praise foretell,
> Come ye before Him, and rejoice.*

He rolled over on his back and began the second verse. He sang it tenderly, lingering over the notes.

Benson interrupted his solitaire. He glared over at the hymn-singing grease ball with savage contempt. New Year's Eve or no New Year's Eve, this was more than Benson could take. He gulped down a drink, spat a blob of juice onto the floor in bitter indignation, took another drink.

> The Lord, ye know, is God indeed,
> Without our aid He did us make...

An old man limped into the room. He stopped when he heard the singing. He was a small, round, plump little package of about sixty with rosy cheeks and a thick white Van Dyke beard* stained by dirt and tobacco drippings.

> ...We are His flock, He doth us feed,
> And for His sheep He doth us take!*

The old man smiled – the gentle, benign, foolish smile of senility. He commenced to sway his head from side to side in time with the music. With his tattered suitcase which had to be tied by cord to keep both sections together, with his tattered, cast-off clothes that were a mixture of rags and fancy patterns – the coat was brown, the trousers tweed, the shirt and tie green, the shoes had once been white – he looked like an unemployed street-corner Santa Claus who had, a long time ago, dreamt of becoming a band conductor. He stood beating the air with his locker key – a plump little pigeon of a man with an ancient derby balanced precariously on the back of his head.

> Abide with me! Fast falls the eventide...*

Bill Benson swung his body around. He was finished! For over four years now he'd been forced to trade an hour of Jesus singing for a mess of goddam fly stew. He was goddamned if he'd take it for nothing.

"Awright, Jesus," he burst out in his croaking whiskey voice, "awright, awright, that's enough! You can go to sleep now. It's time t'go to sleep!"

Luke flushed. "Why cain't I celebrate a little?" he asked. "It's New Year's Eve, ain't it? The lights ain't out yit, are they?"

Benson shot a stream of saliva between his shut teeth. "Yours is gonna be, yours is gonna be," he warned. "You wanna celebrate, get in bed 'n' have a good time with yourself – but shut your hole."

The old man limped forward. "Don't you mind him, boy," he broke in. "You sing fine. Go right ahead."

Benson glared at him. His face was drawn with rage.

The old man sat down on Luke's cot. "My name's Knox." He thrust out a plump, little hand. "Knox with an 'x', not 'knocks on the door'." He laughed gaily in his free, joyous, senile manner. His beard wriggled, and his round little belly rumbled with laughter. "Go ahead, sing something else."

"Where the hell do you think you are?" Benson demanded violently. "In a *hotel* or a goddam Jesus society?"

"Do you know this hymn?" the old man replied pertly. "It's a fine hymn." He began it:

> The birds without barn or storehouse are fed:
> From them let us learn to trust for our bread…

He smiled warmly at Luke. His face was amiable and rosy. Luke smiled back timidly.

> His saints what is fitting shall ne'er…*

Benson flung back his head. His voice exploded in the room, howling out an old, raucous, wobbly tune picked up somewhere in his fighting days:

> At the cross, at the cross,
> Where I lost my shirt and drawers,
> And the but-tons they all
> Rolled away, rolled away…*

Luke and the old man stopped singing. They stared at the man in amazement. Benson glared back at them. For a brief moment there was silence. Then the old man bristled like an angry little cock. He snapped his head up. "Come on," he urged Luke, "come on…"

> No strength of our own, nor goodness…*

Benson leant back, took a deep breath and howled again. He drowned the old man out:

> Scissor Bill, he is a little dippy,
> Scissor Bill, he has a funny face.
> Scissor Bill should drown in Mississippi,
> He's the missing link…*

Baldy White came racing through the door. He was breathing hard from the run up two flights of stairs, but he looked ready for trouble. His ugly little billy hung by a leather thong from his wrist.

Benson stopped singing. Baldy approached him crabwise. He scrutinized him carefully with the growing but unwelcome realization that poor Bill was slipping at last. "By God, Bill," he said in a low, concerned voice, "you ain't lost hold like this in the last five years. What in hell you *got* in that bottle?"

Benson sprang to his feet. "I gotta do somethin'," he cried wildly. "There's a couple Jenny Linds* you put in here – can't keep quiet." He pointed with majestic contempt. "Those blue-nosed punks're singin' hymns."

"Oh!…" Baldy stifled his desire to laugh. He knew this crotchet of Bill's. He swung around at the other two. "Now listen," he said severely, "no noise! Get it? No noise!"

"*Noise?*" Knox replied. "*Noise?*" He tugged excitedly at his beard. His round little face was swollen with insult. He tried fruitlessly to speak. Then he tugged at his frayed wing collar. And for the old man to tug at his wing collar was a sign of complete and final rage: because first Mr Knox had been a streetcar conductor in Brooklyn; and then the streetcar system had become a bus system and he had been laid off; and then (after refusing many offers), he had become a book salesman; and finally he had adopted a wing collar as a sign of respectability – and the more his fortunes declined, the more he relied on the morale which a wing collar gave him. The one thing he could never do was tug at it – it was too old to withstand tugging.

"Noise?" Knox repeated for the third time when his rage permitted him to talk. "*He's* the one who made all the noise. We was bein' *quiet*, *peaceful* and *gentlemanly*."

"Monkey nuts!" Benson shot a stream of saliva at the old man's feet. "You been eatin' so much beans you can't keep the wind from comin' out."

"You're a dingle-dangle," Knox shouted with his voice rising shrilly, "you're a low-down dingle-dangle."

Baldy burst out laughing. "Now, what in hell's a dingle-dangle?"

"Ain't we allowed t'do a little celebratin' on the New Year's?" Luke asked, sitting up. "We just bein' sociable."

"Well, you can't sing hymns," Baldy told him. "Bill here's got a grudge against hymns. Makes his pecker rise." Baldy's cheeks quivered with silent laughter. He smoothed his bald dome and shook his head weakly.

"We just bein' sociable," Luke repeated in a hurt tone. Luke hadn't expected things to be like this in New York. It wasn't nearly as friendly as at home.

O'Shaughnessy suddenly groaned and threshed his hand on the bed. He muttered something agitatedly. Baldy walked over to him. "How do you feel, kid?" he asked.

The boy's eyelids fluttered. He fell into his troubled sleep again. His lips were curved away from his teeth in a kind of snarl, and his forehead was wet with perspiration.

"You see," Baldy said, "you woke him up. No more singing now, or I'll throw you out."

Baldy left the room chuckling to himself.

Benson sat down and gathered up his cards. His ugly grinning face expressed the keen satisfaction he felt over his victory. There was one thing Benson knew: his rights. When *he* paid out good money, there was no Jesus singing allowed in the vicinity.

Luke Hall lay back on his cot. He felt lonely again. He wondered how many of the men in the hotel were going to be present at that fine dinner at midnight. He was feeling a little hungry. When he got a job, he was going to have a good dinner every night. With meat in it. And potatoes and beans. And a sweet cake. Yes!

The old man found his locker and stored away his top clothes. Then he opened his suitcase and began fussing over the contents. He had to be ready in case some business came his way. A good salesman was always ready, and Knox was a good salesman.

The room was quiet.

IV

Nine Forty-Five p.m.

The patrons of the Hotel Raleigh were beginning to usher in for their night's rest. From this hour until one in the morning men would be straggling up the corrugated-iron stairway to Baldy White's cage, to be shunted from there into one big room or another. On a cold night like this, everyone with the price would be heading for an inside bunk. It was a good night for business.

Two men entered Room B together. One was Charlie, a well-known figure on the Rialto.* It was he who had shouted at Blessy an hour before. He came in still yelling "Hooray for the bums from Idaho" – yelling it at the top of his tinny voice. Charlie was about forty-five. He was what Baldy called a "number two" boy. His unwashed hands and neck and face were so black with coatings of accumulated grime that he looked as though he had been crawling through a coal bin. Through the dirt on one side of his face could be seen the mottled flesh of a scarred and blistered cheek, at one time burnt by fire. It gleamed dully, making his face hideous. This cheek was the sign of Charlie's life. The fire, which had scarred his flesh, had seared his mind away in the same blinding moment. It had happened in a freight crack-up when Charlie, in another world, had been a railroad engineer. He lived now an idiot – a drooling, scratching, unwashed member of that great fraternity of men who are not born to this final glory, but are somehow nurtured to it, the forlorn, nameless herd who must once have sprung from women's loins as naked, unscarred babies, but who now would be recognizable neither to mother, father, brother nor God.

And so Charlie, arrived homeward for his night's lodging and shouting at the top of his voice "Hooray for the bums from Idaho", sat down upon the cot to which Baldy, the nightman, had directed him and issued the command of "Whoa, whoa!", as he might to a horse.

Baldy, chuckling with genial amusement, turned to Luke Hall and said: "What do you say, Arkansas? It's filling up like I told you, ain't it? Here's Charlie. He's right smart company."

And so, having successfully short-changed Charlie of four cents, Baldy hurried downstairs again – at the same time he made a mental note to get some candy for his kids, since there was nothing they liked better than penny candy, and since they didn't have candy very often.

As Baldy left the room, Charlie, with some strange urge troubling his maggoty brain, stood up abruptly and stepped away from his cot. He lost his balance. He tumbled backwards, clawed at the bed and slumped down to the floor. He lay for a moment, and then rolled over on his back. Sprawled out, with his body twisted and with one hand pressed convulsively to his throat, he lay quiet. His ruined mouth sagged open, exposing the broken stubs of teeth and the festered yellow gums. He slept, the sleep of the innocent and the good.

Only now did the man who had come up the stairs with Charlie decide to enter the room. He was a tall, swarthy man of forty with the solid, muscular body of a labourer. The skin on his pockmarked, clean-shaven face and on the thick trunk of his neck was tight and firm. He walked slowly, with dignity, carrying his cap in his hand, his heavy shoes scraping the board floor, and, as he passed the crooked figure of Charlie, he muttered a low "drunk bum" to himself, and his mouth twisted in contempt. It was the contempt of a sober, industrious man for one who was not sober and industrious – it was the contempt of a working man for a bum.

Methodically this man, Michael Zets, an unemployed labourer, set about preparing for the night. His overcoat came off and was hung in the locker, then the torn brown sweater, then the shiny blue trousers. He stood finally in his woollen underwear and bare feet, and began pulling small parcels from his overcoat pockets.

First he fished out a corncob pipe. He smelt it, tapped it on the bed rail, filled it and began to smoke. Then he opened a paper bag containing a rusty towel and a sliver of soap. Next came a crumpled newspaper. Carefully he smoothed it out and put it to one side. Finally he took out half a loaf of rye bread and an onion. Sitting down, he set the pipe on the floor, spread the newspaper on his knees and began to eat and read. He rubbed the onion on the bread before each bite.

Old Knox, who had been watching the newcomer with increasing interest, suddenly dug into his suitcase. He sorted rapidly through the contents and fished out a pair of horn-rimmed spectacles. Holding them behind his back, he limped across the room.

"*Pan, razuma Popolska?*"* he asked with a friendly wave of his hand, and thereby not only carried out Rule No. 3 of the book on salesmanship he had read in the Public Library in Cincinnati (a rule which advised all drummers to establish intimate relations with their prospects), but at the same time exhausted his entire knowledge of the Polish language.

Rule No. 3 worked. The man turned. One cheek bulged with a hunk of half-chewed bread. His sombre, heavy-featured face was flooded with warmth. He started to speak, stopped, chewed hastily and gulped down his mouthful. Then he broke into excited Polish.

Knox smiled benignly at him. "No spik Polish," he said. He offered the spectacles. "These are for your eyes. *Eyes...*" – he pointed – "help you read."

Zets looked at him bewilderedly.

"My name's Knox," the old man said briskly. He held out his hand. "Happy New Year! What's your name?"

Mechanically the big man shook hands with him. "You no Polish feller?" he asked.

"I have many good friends among the Polish race," Knox assured him, holding his hand and smiling at him warmly. "What did you say your name was?"

"Zets," the man replied. "Mike."

"A good Polish name," Knox told him. "Good Polish name."

The man took his hand away. "Zets is Rooshan," he said sullenly. His sombre face was a little flushed.

"All the same to me," Knox assured him. "I'm not prejudiced. Here's a pair of glasses for you," he continued. He displayed them rapidly from all angles. "A man of your age has to be careful of his eyes. Try them!" He shoved them towards the Russian's nose.

Zets drew his head back. "No want glasses," he said.

"Only a quarter, friend. Save your eyes!"

The big Russian champed his teeth down hard on a piece of bread.

Knox shrugged expressively. "All right, friend, but I've studied the eyes for forty years. Great specialists consult with me. How about you, son?" He darted over to Luke Hall and broke into a jargon he had carefully memorized: "Your pupils are distorted, showing eye strain and nervousness. Try 'em on. A quarter of a dollar."

Hall put them on. His gaunt face was illumined with excitement. The old man darted to his suitcase and hurried back with a handful of magazines.

"Here you are, son – take a look at these: the beneficial effect is immediate." He held one open.

Luke studied the print for a few moments. "Ah cain't see nothin' at all," he announced.

The old man laughed gaily. "The wrong pair, that's all, the wrong pair." He snatched the glasses off. "Now let me see…" He seized the boy by the overalls and peered closely into his eyes. Luke flushed in embarrassment and tried to back off.

"Ah yes… fifty-four forty… slight relativity and pupils a little to the oblique side."

He hopped back to his cot. The limp in his short leg scarcely seemed to interfere with his agility. He fussed through the suitcase like a plump little tomtit on the search for worms.

"Here you are, boy!"

Luke ignored the glasses. His eye had caught sight of the magazines. "What's that?" he enquired curiously. He was fond of reading matter.

"*That?* Ahhhhhhhh!" The old man screwed up his face, shut both eyes tight and stroked his beard. "That, m'boy, is a pamphlet…" – he drew a deep breath – "a pamphlet explaining the great mystery of life – love between the sexes! This one proves conclusively that love is caused by vapours. I have others… intended for men only… little spicy stories full of humour and situation, illustrated by pictures of many different kinds. Then…" – he added with emphasis – "then I have some religious pamphlets!"

Three cots down the aisle Bill Benson raised his eyes from his game of solitaire. His liquor bottle was half empty now, and the mellowing effect of the pint of rot gut in his belly showed on his face: the frown was still there, and the weary, acid mould had not altered, but there was a slight grudging smile on his lips and a shimmer of interest in his eye. He surveyed Knox with amusement.

The old man winked over at him in bawdy, senile suggestion. "Pictures of every kind," he repeated. "Ten cents."

"What's vapours?" Luke Hall asked.

"Vapours, my boy?" Knox put his hand paternally on Hall's shoulder. "Vapours is what passes between man and woman."

Benson spat a mouthful of liquor over the floor. "Sounds like crabs* to me," he said, snorting with laughter.

"Nothing of the sort, nothing of the sort," the old man sputtered. He thrashed his arms like a flustered hen. "A vapour's like air. It's a spark! Philosophical term is 'effluence'! You look at a young girl, a young girl looks at you, and a spark passes between."

Benson exploded with laughter. "What passes between?" he demanded. "What passes between?"

"A spark," the old man shouted. "A spark! It's a vapour!"

"If that's a spark, I'm a Presbyterian minister," Benson laughed. He leant back weakly on his cot.

Knox howled and shook his fist. "I speak twelve languages, and you're a fool! You're an ignoramus! You don't even know who I am! Some day you'll consider it a privilege to have known me." He pulled a little notebook from his pocket and thumbed the pages rapidly. "I'm writing a book! A book of life! Containing the meaning of all religions, a little humour, philosophy, poetry. It'll be published in every language in the world, a million copies in each language, and a hundred thousand free copies will be given away to my friends. You won't get one!!!" He turned to Luke Hall. "You'll get one! What's your address?"

Luke emerged from a daydream. "Have you got any writings on the Essanines?" he asked.

Knox clapped him on the shoulder. "My boy, I wrote fifteen books for fifteen years while I was a streetcar conductor in Brooklyn. They haven't been published yet, but I'll give you copies."

"Ah'm grateful t'you," Luke said. "Ah like t'read. You know Ah've been studyin' about the Essanines. Have you got any pieces on them?"

Knox cocked his head reflectively and stuck a stubby finger in his nose. "You mean Essenes… Essenes… one of the lost tribes of Judaea…"

"Oh no," Luke corrected, "they was in the time of John the Baptist. They—"

"Of course," said Knox, interrupting, "John the Baptist – 24 BC…"

"Oh no…" Luke began.

"I've been a student of the Bible for twenty years…" Knox continued.

"They believed that there should be no fornication between man and woman, unless it was to begat children," Luke said softly, dreamily. "They said you had to conserve your strength so you could wear the armour of the Lord and do the good work."

"Very interesting," the old man exclaimed. "I know all about it!" He clapped Luke on the shoulder again. "My boy, I'm interested in you." He darted to his suitcase. "Here's a little book soon to be published in which I take down notes of interesting people as I go along. You'll get one."

"Ah'd like that," Luke replied shyly. "If Ah had books, Ah'd read most all the time."

"I've visited every famous library in the world," Knox announced. "Known well in all of them."

"You know," Luke said dreamily, "since Ah've been converted, Ah don't have t'go to whores so often. Ah used to go for them turrible, but Ah got converted to the Pentecostal a while back, an' now Ah don't go to whores more'n two or three months at a time. Ah'm tryin' to conserve mah strength."

"You'll have to visit me," Knox stated emphatically. "We'll study religion together. I've lived eighteen years in Cuba. You'll spend the winter with me. I have hundreds of famous people from all over the world come and visit me every year. I'm working my way down there now."

"Ah'd like t'see Cuba," Luke said, smiling warmly at him.

"I'll be expecting you," the old man replied. "Ask for me anywhere."

"But Ah'm thinkin' of changin' from the Pentecostal to the Presbyterian," Luke confided. "The Pentecostals are too much for speakin' in the tongue.* Ah don't think that's necessary. Ah don't see that in the Scriptures."

"Here's the Gospel by Paul," the old man said with a sudden return of business zeal. "Eight cents – marked down."

"Ah'll take the one on vapours," the boy replied. He fished down into his overalls for his purse. "Have you got any hymns?"

Benson heaved himself up and see-sawed down the aisle. He was not quite steady on his feet. He buttonholed Knox with heavy joviality. "Hey, gran'pa, gimme a look at 'em."

"Which one do you want?"

Benson grabbed a magazine out of the old man's hand. "Not the hymns, hophead, I ain't a virgin." He flipped the pages and paused at the photograph of a girl who was lounging naked and seductive on a couch draped with a bear skin. His mouth split into a loose grin.

"Ten cents," Knox said.

Benson ignored him.

"Ten cents!" Knox repeated.

Benson grunted over the pictures, making little sensual smacks with his mouth and lips.

"Ten cents," the old man said, plucking at his sleeve.

"Some beetle!" Benson commented. "Ain't that somep'n, gran'pa? Some ham on it," he observed admiringly.

The old man hopped frantically from one foot to another. "Ten cents, please! Ten cents!"

Benson leant down with a genial grin and blew into Knox's face. "Poppa, I'm not that kind of a girl – an' besides I don't do it for ten cents."

The old man grabbed the magazine. "You can't look at it then. You can't—"

"Now listen," Benson said, "I ain't seen a good-looking dame like this in a year. Let me look at it, will yuh? I ain't got ten cents."

"No sir," Knox said. "If you can't pay, you can't look."

"Jesus!" Benson shouted in sudden flaming rage. "Jesus!" He tore the magazine from Knox's hand and flung it violently to the floor. "Jesus!" He strode away in a drunken fury.

Knox picked up the magazine and ran after him. "You can have it," he cried, "you can buy it. What do you want to pay?"

"Beat it," Benson ordered. He began shuffling his cards.

"Razor blades?" Knox offered, pulling a package from his pocket. "Five for fifteen!"

Benson uncorked his bottle of liquor and tilted it to his mouth.

The old man watched him drink, and his little blue eyes commenced to shine greedily. He sidled over to him. "Slip me a drink of the lush, hey, boy?" he requested.

Benson jerked his head and sluiced a mouthful of liquor into the old man's face.

"Tit for tit," Benson said. "Have another!"

Halfway down the aisle, Zets, the hulking, sombre-faced Russian, sat up abruptly.

Knox wiped his face and limped away, muttering. He looked like a hurt child wounded to the point of tears.

Benson regarded him with sour satisfaction. "Have another, Pop," he called. "It's good for that bush on your face. Keeps it growin'."

Slowly Zets got up from his cot. He set his pipe carefully on the floor. Then he walked over to Benson. His heavy-featured, pockmarked face was dark. The angry blood was pumping in it, swelling thickly in the veins on his forehead. "What for you spit in ol' man face?" Zets asked. His deep, slow voice had a leaden feel to it.

Benson looked up in amazement. "For Chrissakes," he said.

The big labourer repeated the question coldly, slowly. "What for you spit at ol' man?"

"Well, for Chrissakes!" Benson burst out angrily. "Mind your own goddam business."

Zets spat in his face.

Benson jumped to his feet swinging his liquor bottle. Zets flung him back furiously, and Benson toppled backwards onto the bed. The Russian stood over him with one huge fist, like a block of stone, poised in the air ready to smash down.

Benson lay inert.

Zets lowered his hand slowly. "You dirty sonabitch," he said, and then, in a tone of disgust and incredulity, "Spit at ol' man!"

He walked back to his cot and picked up his pipe again. He was finished. He had done what was right.

Old man Knox limped over to him. He shifted from leg to leg and finally pulled the pair of spectacles out of his pocket. "Go ahead," he offered, "take 'em."

Zets looked at him blankly.

"Free," the old man said. "Go ahead!"

"Never min'," Zets replied. He reached under the pillow for his towel and soap and turned down the aisle.

Knox ran back to his suitcase, snatched up a magazine and hopped after him. "Here," he offered, "something to read."

The Russian shook his head. "Never min'," he said. "You ol' man," he added seriously, "nobody spit at ol' man!" And, nodding his head slightly by way of ending the matter, he continued on his way to the washroom.

Knox looked after him. "Happy New Year," he called. He walked back to his place and stood thinking. His head was cocked at an angle, and his red lips were pursed thoughtfully. Abruptly he plumped himself down on his cot, took out his notebook, searched energetically until he found a pencil and then began to write. He wrote busily. Occasionally he stopped to scratch his beard or frown heavily in an attitude of profound reflection. He was adding to his storehouse of "Interesting Events and Characters", a compendium of life and philosophy soon to be published in all the countries in the world, a million copies in each country.

The room was quiet. Luke Hall sat absorbed in the pamphlet on vapours. A nervous finger picked absently at the dried cut on his chin, and one bare foot slowly massaged the other. Benson lay motionless, snoring. Both hands were fastened around his liquor bottle in an unconscious vice-like grip. And off to one side O'Shaughnessy slept fitfully. His slow, thick breathing was like a sigh in the room.

From outside there came the caterwaul of taxis and the occasional pound and rumble of the elevated trains heavy with holiday traffic. And now and then, from off the East River, there was the deep bay of a foghorn like a hound dog far away on a scent.

V

Ten p.m.

It seemed to O'Shaughnessy that if he could only throw back the blankets, he'd feel much better. Hot. He was hot. On a summer's day it was crazy to make him lie there with so many blankets on top of him so hot.

When I get a job, Momma, it'll be different.

It was obvious that the blankets were tied there with safety pins or a strong rope that went to both sides of the bed.

"Momma, Momma, Momma," the sick boy cried. But she didn't ever hear him! Never! I guess she's down at the stand. But on New Year's Eve it was foolish to have the stand open.

Oh God, it's so hot, Momma. If I can only push them all the way down to my feet, I'll feel better: I'll be able to sleep then.

And he was so thirsty.

If he could get the blankets down off his feet, then he could get up. But if things ever picked up, then he'd have a chance. A tool and die maker – they need them. Poor Momma, you've been workin' like a truck horse. Let it go tonight. Let's go to a movie and a burlesque movie tonight.

There was a spider as big as a cat sitting on his stomach. It had its claws in his flesh. Each claw was poisoned, and sent a pain through him. Right there!

And he was so thirsty from the hot blankets...

VI

The first thing Blessy saw when he came into the room was the little knot of curious men gathered at the foot of O'Shaughnessy's cot. It gave him a shock that was apprehension and anger mingled together, and he ran forward shouting: "What's the matter? What the hell's goin' on here?"

Zets shook his head soberly and wiped his face with a yellow scrap of towel. "This feller pretty dam sick maybe. He yell!"

"He's got ptomaine," Luke Hall announced, and then, in a murmur to himself, "It's catchin', Ah reckon."

"Jimmie," Blessy murmured, "Jimmie."

O'Shaughnessy didn't reply, but he stopped tossing. The whispered name seemed to calm him even in sleep. He lay quiet.

"You buddy wit' dis feller?" Zets enquired.

Blessy nodded. "When did he start yellin'?"

Luke Hall advised him: "Just now, mista."

Zets bent down and wiped O'Shaughnessy's wet forehead with his scrap of towel. He showed the towel to Blessy. "Boy bad sick maybe. You give him bicarb? Bicarb good for belly."

"He don't need that," Blessy replied. He rubbed his forehead reflectively. A troubled frown creased his big bony face. What the devil was wrong? Jimmie had been swell just that morning. He'd even gone out and shovelled snow for a few hours till he got tired. An' he was sure all cleaned out by now.

Old man Knox suddenly hopped at the big Russian like an agitated flea. He seized the towel. "Let me smell," he demanded. He pushed his little stump of a nose deep into the material. Astounded, Zets pulled it away from him.

"That's ptomaine all right," Knox chirped. "I can tell. Comes from poisoned food."

"You crazy," Zets said.

"Don't be ignorant," Knox rebuked him loftily. "All diseases have their smell. You just have to be trained."

"You crazy!" the Russian repeated. "Keep still," he added harshly. "No wake boy up!" He turned to Blessy. Blessy grinned at him. "You want tow'l?"

"I got one," Blessy said.

Zets nodded. He went back to his cot. Methodically he folded the towel and set it in its proper place in the locker. He stretched out on his back and lit his corncob pipe. He smoked and stared soberly at the ceiling.

Blessy began to undress. He needed a shower after the day's work, and there wasn't much time before they turned the heat off. By God, if there was anything colder than a flophouse toilet in winter, Blessy had never seen it.

The youth tossed his lumberjacket on the bed and unbuttoned his shirt. Then he stopped and stared absorbedly at the boy in the bed. It was bad. There was something the matter. Jimmie had been sleeping all day, and that was a good sign. But still… still, he just didn't look good. Worse than this morning.

O'Shaughnessy lay quiet. One knee was slightly raised under the faded army blanket. There was no curve or roundness to his neck any more, and the cords of his throat strained tight against the lined, waxy skin. His face was still wrapped in its ghastly pallor, and the sunken cheeks and the sharp lines that bit into the taut flesh made him look pained even in sleep.

Now, in an instant of sudden clarity, the truth slashed through Blessy's mind like a blow from behind. O'Shaughnessy looked terrible – like a corpse. He might be really sick now. He might be bad off.

The youth groaned. What should he do? A doctor. He didn't have any cash on him. But maybe Dooky… Or take him to a hospital?

A hospital? Jesus Christ, he wasn't as sick as all that. You don't take guys to a hospital for just a bellyache.

The youth rumpled his hair with blunt, nervous fingers. He sat down on his cot and put his head in his hands. He had to get straight on it. Jimmie looked bad now, but God – there were reasons. Even the drugstore man said he'd be knocked out for a while. No grub… all that castor oil… it'd make anybody weak.

The thing was to wait. When Jimmie waked up, then you could see. If he wasn't no better, sure, get him a doctor. There'd be two bucks comin' from somewhere, even if he had to roll* somebody.

Blessy stowed his lumberjacket in the locker. He felt better now. The thing was to wait an' see.

A hand plucked diffidently at the youth's arm. He turned around. Old man Knox was standing behind him with a bottle of pills balanced in the palm of his hand.

"Young man," Knox said hastily, "I have a vast medical knowledge. I have something here" – he displayed it – "get rid of that ptomaine by morning."

Blessy grinned and shook his head.

"Nature's remedy," Knox advised. "Don't cost much."

"No!" Blessy reached for the chunk of kitchen soap in his locker.

"Why don't you give it a try?" the old man persisted plaintively. It'd be awful if he couldn't sell *anything* in a place like this. He could get a turkey dinner with stuffing for twenty-five cents tomorrow if he could make one more sale. "If it don't work, you don't have to pay me," he offered.

"No, listen, Pop," Blessy explained patiently, "he's had about a quart of castor oil since Monday night. He don't need any more of that."

"But this is Wednesday," the old man argued.

Blessy burst out laughing. "What do you think he is, a gah-gah-goddam elephant?"

O'Shaughnessy groaned aloud and awakened. He threw back the covers on his bed and raised up on his elbow. Then he sank back on the pillow again. He looked around with glazed eyes.

Blessy ran over to him. "Hello, kid," he whispered. His tone was full of warmth and affection, and the love he bore this comrade of his was written unashamedly on his hard, coarse-grained face.

For a moment O'Shaughnessy didn't reply. He was awake, but his mind was still clouded by the sick nightmare he had been having. Then he recognized Blessy. He smiled. It was a tired, drowsy smile. The skin wrinkled back from his mouth, and his teeth jutted out like the teeth of a cadaver, making his young face look piteous and ugly.

"How do you feel?"

O'Shaughnessy drew a deep, tired breath. "I feel better, I think." His eyes dropped shut again. He muttered to himself.

"What did you say?"

"Water," O'Shaughnessy mumbled.

"Do you want some water?"

The sick boy opened his eyes. "No, I don't want any water."

Blessy was puzzled. "You *said* 'water'," he told him.

"Before. I wanted water before," the boy replied. His voice took on a weak, complaining tone: "I wanted water this afternoon, but there was no one to give it to me."

"Gee, I was out shovelling, kid," Blessy apologized. "But I brought you a sandwich to eat. Do you feel like eating it?"

"I'm still kinda sick to my stomach," O'Shaughnessy answered.

"Can't you eat it? We don't wanna—"

"Stop worrying about money," Blessy ordered. "It's snowin' again. We're gonna have a coupla more days' work."

"I guess I shouldna shovelled this morning," O'Shaughnessy reflected drowsily. "But I felt better. I thought I was all cleaned out."

"Sure you are," Blessy said heartily. "But you're pooped, that's all. That's why you need sleep."

"Sleep is nature's remedy," Knox interposed from the foot of the bed. "Sleep and vitamins." He looked over at Blessy to see if the comment had registered. He was still trying hard for his turkey dinner.

O'Shaughnessy moved one hand laboriously under the blanket. He was feeling for his belly. When he touched it, his face twisted in an expression of disappointment and despair. "Gee," he said, "my stomach's still puffed up the way it was. It hasn't gone down at all."

Blessy touched the blanket over the boy's middle. He wanted to say something to comfort the kid, but he couldn't think what.

"That always goes with the ptomaine," Knox advised. "Dropsy's the same way. And elephantiasis. Elephantiasis too!" He looked over at Blessy significantly. "I have a whole medical library. Keep it in Cuba."

O'Shaughnessy tossed his head. "Aw," he said confidently, "I'm gonna feel all right in the morning. You wait an' see. That castor oil cleaned me out. I'm all right."

"Sure you are," Blessy agreed fervently. "Listen, kid," he promised, "tomorrow night you're gonna be over at Dooky's peelin' spuds—"

"That's the trouble," O'Shaughnessy interrupted. "We peel spuds for him, an' he don't feed us right. Gives us garbage." He squirmed restlessly, fretting. "He oughta feed us better, oughtn't he? He don't hafta pay us in cash."

"Now, don't worry about that, kid."

"Did you go?" O'Shaughnessy asked suddenly.

"Where?"

"To the burlesque?"

Blessy laughed. "Forget it, kid. I wouldn't go without you. We're gonna go together... celebrate New Year's."

"When's New Year's?" the boy asked drowsily. "Ain't New Year's tonight?"

"No!" Blessy laughed. "New Year's is when..." He stopped talking. O'Shaughnessy had fallen asleep.

Old man Knox frowned. "I'm afraid..." he began.

"Sh!" Blessy jerked his thumb for the old man to beat it.

Knox sniffed. He walked off with an offended air. "That man won't take my advice," Knox whispered loudly to Luke Hall. He looked pityingly at Blessy. "He's a fool!"

"Are you a doctor?" Luke enquired.

"Never practised," Knox replied briskly. "But I consult very often."

Blessy got up and tiptoed over to them. "Hey, for Chrissakes, shut up, will you?" he whispered. "I want him to sleep." He went back to the cot alongside of O'Shaughnessy. He took off his shoes and lay down on his stomach with his head pressed into the pillow.

Luke Hall rolled up one leg of his overalls. "Do you know what this bump is?" he asked Knox in a whisper.

Knox peered at it. He scratched his beard thoughtfully. "I never make a diagnosis without an X-ray," he replied, "but that type of symptom often indicates a serious tumour necessitating operation."

Luke laughed uncertainly. "Why shucks, Ah've had this all mah life," he protested. "Ah don't think it's more'n a birth mark."

Knox probed one nostril with a stubby forefinger and regarded Luke with disdain. "M'boy," he said, "there's many a dead man thought that." He turned away, ending the matter.

Luke stared after him. His brow was furrowed, and his soft brown eyes were suddenly anxious. It'd be turrible if he had to have an operation. Where would he go? And he wouldn't be able to work for a long time. What would his folks do? Luke sat down on his cot and stared gloomily at the bump on his leg.

A newcomer entered the room. He was a small, comic-looking man of about thirty-five. He wore dungarees and a sailor's pea jacket. His head was massive, bulging and partially bald, and he had a thin, sharp-featured, over-serious face. One eye was swollen, and the injury gave his serious face a blinking, cock-eyed expression. He crossed the room quickly and went into the washroom. In another moment he returned with a wet handkerchief pressed to his eye. He found his cot and lay down on it. His name was Reynolds. He was a ship's cook out of a job.

Out on the street, an automobile sputtered and then backfired loudly. Blessy started up out of his doze. He glanced over at O'Shaughnessy. The boy had not been awakened. Blessy lay down again.

Bill Benson, who had been lying inert from the moment the big Russian flung him down in their quarrel, now pulled himself to his feet. He yawned, rubbed his eyes, took a drink. He had forgotten all about the incident. He looked around the room and then see-sawed down the aisle into the toilet.

Blessy pushed his head deep into the pillow. He knew he ought to be taking his shower, but he was too tired. He'd rest a little while first. He caught the strong oniony odour that came from his perspiration. In the mine it was different: you smelt like coal gas, you and your pit clothes and the house. But that was a good smell. An image of the girl on the street corner came back to him. It was almost gone now, her face was almost gone, but he could see the faint outline of her body, the white flesh and the little warm nipples pressed hard against the dress. Blessy stirred. He felt a twinge of weary, lonely desire. God, what a different New Year's for a guy who had a job and a girl. God, you could go crazy year after year, year after year. It had to stop sometime. A man couldn't... all the time.

He fell asleep.

VII

Ten Thirty p.m.

As Benson came back from the toilet, a boy with a pack on his back came in through the open door. They met in the aisle.

The boy was no bigger than a lad of sixteen, but his face could have belonged to a man of sixty. It was old, dead white and cold.

Sharp lines like little scars ringed his thin, cruel mouth. Under his blue eyes there were greyish baggy pockets. His shoulders were hunched, and his head was shaven clean except for a stiff brush of straw hair at the front. He carried his head erect, and on his lips there was a thin smile – self-assured, sneering.

He came in slowly, coughing, looking at the numbers on the cots, eyeing the men in the room. His eyes were knowing, distrustful – the slight smile was steady on his lips.

His name was Hunchy. On the box-car highway some called him "Coughy". He didn't care. He knew what he had to know. He knew how to take care of himself. He was seventeen years old by a week and three days, and he knew how to get along. He had been learning since he was twelve. He didn't want any help. He wanted to be left alone.

As Hunchy came up the aisle, Benson hailed him with drunken joviality. "Hello, punk," he said, "where'd you blow in from?"

Hunchy stopped walking. "Don't you call me 'punk'. I ain't anybody's punk." His voice was slow and coldly venomous.

Benson laughed. "Okay, Hunchy, I ain't after you. I ain't no goddam wolf. Whenja blow in?" he asked. "You look like hell. You look like you been in the coop for six months."

The boy's thin lips twisted into a sneer. "Listen..." he said slowly, "don't be such a friggin' pal. Go suck somebody else."

Benson stared at the boy with rising anger. "Well, for Chrissakes," he burst out, "you're a snotty little pup, ain't you? I oughta fan your tail for you." He took a step forward.

Hunchy stood where he was. Leisurely he removed his right hand from his pocket. A knife blade snapped open. Benson leapt back.

The boy held the knife low down in front of him. The short, thick blade gleamed in the sharp light.

"Keep away from me," he said slowly.

"Well, for Chrissakes," Benson exclaimed. "Why," he said, surveying the boy, "you're what I'd call definitely *anti-social*." He stepped between two cots. "*You certainly are!*"

Hunchy held the knife loosely in his hand. He sauntered down the aisle looking for the number on his locker key. He found the place and sat down with the open knife blade resting snug at his side.

Benson shook his head, swigged a mouthful of liquor and teetered back to his bunk. He shuffled his cards and resumed his game of solitaire.

Old man Knox limped down the aisle. He planted himself a few feet away from Hunchy and coughed politely. Hunchy ignored him. He was busy peeling off his clothes.

Every so often he coughed. At those times he would remain still, holding himself tight, while the cough racked up through his chest. Then he would spit and pause wearily for a moment before continuing to undress.

Hunchy's clothes were odds and ends, patched, worn. His overcoat had evidently belonged to a full-grown man and had been sliced off to bring it to size. The ends hung down now frayed and uneven. Beneath the overcoat he wore a thin sweater, then a layer of newspaper wrapped around his body and tied in place by twine, then another sweater. He stood finally in a dirty white summer shirt from which his scraggy elbows protruded, and carefully folded up the newspaper. He would use it again the next day.

Old man Knox coughed politely for the second time. "Happy New Year!" he offered. He smiled warmly. "My name is Knox – Knox with an 'x', not 'knocks on the door'." He chuckled, with his round little belly rumbling with laughter.

Hunchy ignored him. He fished a paper bag out of his pack. There was half a coconut pie inside. He wielded his knife, deftly cutting an enormous chunk.

The old man's eyes glittered. He watched the boy wolf the first mouthful. "Got some for me, kid?" he whispered. He glanced around cunningly to make sure no one else in the room had seen the pie.

Hunchy looked up coldly and crammed another slice into his mouth.

"Where'd you get it, eh?" Knox asked. "Lifted it, eh? Off a baker's truck! You're young," he said enviously. "Got t'be young t'do that."

Hunchy sighed. "Listen," he said, "you ain't gonna get any, so stop hangin' around."

"I'll trade you, sonny," the old man whispered. "Just gimme a little taste." He looked around hastily. "Some magazines! Got pictures in 'em! Young girls with nothing on! Give you two!"

Hunchy paid no attention to him.

"Want some razor blades?" Knox asked. He pulled a little box out of his vest pocket. "You need this all right: Nature's laxative! Always handy to keep around. Here. Here!"

The old man dropped the bottle on the cot and made a grab for the pie. With the speed of a young adder Hunchy struck out hard, rapping him on the knuckles with the flat blade of his knife. The old man retreated with a cry of pain and surprise.

"You make me tired," Hunchy said wearily. He flipped the bottle of pills to the floor.

The old man picked it up. "I wanted to trade, didn't I?" he complained.

Hunchy got up, coughing. "For Chrissakes, go away," he said angrily. "How can I eat with your stink around me?"

Zets turned around to see what was occurring. Luke Hall raised his head from his magazine.

"I don't stink... I don't stink," the old man cried. "You oughtn't to say that."

"Sure you stink," the boy snapped. "I'm smelling you, ain't I?" He took a step forward. "Get away from here!"

Knox retreated. "I don't stink... I don't stink," he wailed. He shook his fist. "You lousy bum, you dirty little—" Knox stopped! From O'Shaughnessy, the sick boy, there had come a sudden, heart-rending, nightmare cry. It was shrill, frightened, incoherent – a cry of sick agony that paralysed the room.

In an instant the quarrel was forgotten. Hunchy stood still, and for a moment his face was convulsed. Old man Knox pawed at his throat and turned, trembling and sweaty, to look at O'Shaughnessy.

And all over the room men jumped up in a start of fear.

VIII

Eleven p.m.

When men lose their sense of security, fear waits inside of them. To each man in the room O'Shaughnessy's cry of agony was the touchstone of his own fear: in that moment, fear coursed the room like a living thing, thrusting deep into each man there, turning the flesh clammy, gripping the heart and the nerve. And for a moment no one could be sure who had screamed – himself or another. Each man waited to find out, crouching, waiting to be told: "It was you: your time has come!"

Then it was gone. Now they stood clumped together, watching the boy in the bed. They were safe now. For a time they were safe. It was someone else.

And O'Shaughnessy didn't know either. When he finally heard Blessy speak to him, when he saw his friend's anguished face and saw the men clumped together at the foot of his cot, he became aware that the scream had been his own, that it was only in a dream. And then he knew that he was sitting up in bed and that Blessy's big hand was on his shoulder.

O'Shaughnessy groaned and fell back on his cot: his stomach was on fire.

The nightmare was gone. O'Shaughnessy could scarcely remember it, but it had left its sick feel with him. He had wanted something – and he had lost it. He had wanted something with such terrible, concentrated need – and someone had wrenched it from his hands. And at the moment of loss a hot, sharp needle had been thrust deep into his flesh, and somewhere far off a voice had screamed.

And now, as he lay still on the narrow cot with that burning fire in his belly, he thought of his life, the loss and the waste of his life, and slowly his head turned on the pillow, and the weak salt tears trickled out of the corners of his eyes. The pain and the struggle – the long, bitter years of pain and struggle... useless! His mother had tended the paper stand, and she had been up at six and never had been back till one – she had given pennies for candles, and never once accepted the wafer with false heart... useless! All their hopes, the years of effort... to no good! None! And now he was lying in a flophouse, and the pains had started again, and he must be bad sick now, and his mother wouldn't be there to help him, because he was far away, and she was dead. And he lay weeping.

IX

"It's all right, Hal," O'Shaughnessy said. A few minutes had passed, and he had become quiet. "I had a pain, that's all."

Blessy drew a deep breath of relief. "You got no business with pains," he told the boy in an awkward attempt at humour. "You're all through with pains."

O'Shaughnessy didn't reply.

Sam Reynolds, the little ship's cook with the swollen eye, enquired softly what the matter was. Luke Hall answered him. Old man Knox scratched his belly and explained the matter loudly: "It's the toxins. They pass through the corpuscles and stop the circulation."

"Ptomaine?" Reynolds echoed softly. His Adam's apple jiggled sharply as he spoke, giving him a comic quality. "Ptomaine?" he said again. He looked into the face of each man there. His glance was hot with challenge. He seemed to be questioning, probing their thoughts. "Well," he said finally, "it's fine, ain't it? Fine!" He paused. When he spoke again, his voice was soft, but fiercely, tremulously passionate. "I'm a ship's cook," he said. "*I* know what gives men ptomaine. I've dished out swill myself." The little man choked with repressed fury. He rubbed his mouth with a red, calloused hand that seemed strangely big for his thin wrist and arm. His deadly serious face, his bald hen's egg head were comic to look at. "Ain't God's food clean?" he burst out. "Ain't it?" He fixed his gaze on Zets. The big Russian looked back at him sombrely. "No, I guess it ain't," Reynolds answered himself bitterly. "I guess it damn well ain't. Not for us!"

O'Shaughnessy groaned and pressed his hand to his swollen belly.

"What's the matter?" Blessy leant down over him.

"I got another pain," O'Shaughnessy said with a sigh.

"Like Monday?"

"No," the boy said, "it's worse now."

"For Godssakes!" Blessy wiped the boy's brow with a towel. "I don't understand it, kid. You're sure all cleaned out."

"It's all right," O'Shaughnessy said. Then suddenly he groaned again. The blood drained out of his face, and he ground his teeth together. The sweat was pouring out on his forehead.

"Jimmie, Jimmie," Blessy cried. He grasped the boy's hand feverishly. He wanted to help him. His mind was racing wildly, trying to think of something to do. It was terrible. It was terrible to watch him. Jimmie was just a kid. It shouldn't happen to a kid like that.

The attack passed. O'Shaughnessy closed his eyes and rested back on the pillow. His breath was like a deep sigh in the room.

Reynolds cupped a hand over his injured eye and peered at O'Shaughnessy. "This boy had a doctor?" he asked. "Looks to me like he needs one."

"*I* can treat him," Knox said. "I've got some pills here. Special!"

"Shut up!" Zets ordered harshly.

"I don't want a doctor," O'Shaughnessy told them. "It's a waste of money."

"Jesus, kid," Blessy begged, "forget about the money, will you? We'll get it."

"We can take up a collection," Reynolds suggested. "We can go through all the rooms."

Hunchy, who had been standing off by himself, spoke out abruptly. "You'd better get an ambulance!" His voice was cold, matter-of-fact.

"What for?" Blessy demanded. The suggestion frightened him. "It's just some cramps. He don't—"

"Get an ambulance," Hunchy repeated.

O'Shaughnessy opened his eyes. "No," he said. His voice trembled. "I don't want no hospital."

"Get out of here," Blessy said to Hunchy. "Shut your face. Beat it."

"OK!" Hunchy sneered and walked away. He got into bed, coughing. He turned his back to the others.

"Hal," O'Shaughnessy pleaded, "I don't wanna go to a hospital. I'm afraid of them."

"Don't worry, kid," Blessy assured him. "You'll stay right here. I'll crack that little bastard in two," he muttered to himself.

O'Shaughnessy raised his head. "You know what they do?" he said. "They give you the Black Bottle. When you're a charity patient and can't pay, the nurses give you the Black Bottle. They gave it to Mary Croggins when I was a kid."

"That's *right*," Luke Hall offered. "Ah heard that too."

"Lay down, kid," Blessy pleaded. "You don't wanna get excited."

"There's more ways'n one a *poor* man gets screwed," Reynolds said softly. "A poor man gets screwed every day in every way. There's only one thing protects him…" He paused and looked from one to the other, blinking his swollen eye. "Organ-eye-zation." He spoke the word with difficulty, but with a strange flavour, with a sense of love, like a lonely man speaking of a woman. "Organ-eye-zation" – he repeated it, and he raised his head in a gesture of pride and dignity. He looked from one man to another, searching for their response.

The others were silent.

O'Shaughnessy stiffened. His pains were commencing again. He murmured something, and then suddenly pushed himself up in bed. A frantic, bitter cry burst from his lips. "Ain't we tried to get along?" he cried. "Ain't we been tryin' to get work?" He clutched at Blessy's arm. "Peelin' spuds – hustlin' the white sheets. Goddamit, we tried, we tried, didn't we?" He was choked with sobs.

Blessy pushed him back. "For Godssakes, Jimmie," he said, "you gotta lay down. You gotta keep quiet."

The boy fell back. The sense of loss that had been present in the dream swept over him again. What was there in life, anyway? No place to sleep… no job… couldn't have a girl. They ought to have a right to *something*, he cried to himself. Didn't they have a right to *anything*?

O'Shaughnessy's anguished body writhed under the blanket. "Hal, Hal," he cried, "it hurts me… it's hurting again."

Blessy jumped to his feet. "I'm gonna geh-geh-get you a doctor." He stammered with excitement. His big, hard face looked tortured with pity.

"No," O'Shaughnessy said. "No doctor." He was suddenly delirious. "Toilet. Gotta go toilet." He sat up in bed and tried to lift his feet from under the blanket. His eyeballs were glazed, and his glance was the glance of a blind man.

"Wait a minute," Blessy cried. "*Jesus Christ!*" He lifted O'Shaughnessy from the cot.

O'Shaughnessy stepped down. His heavy woollen underwear was unbuttoned, leaving his belly exposed. It looked enormous against his thin body. "Toilet," he mumbled.

"Let's carry him, for Godssakes," Reynolds said agitatedly. "He can't walk!"

"Can you wah-wah-walk?" Blessy asked O'Shaughnessy. "Wah-wah…"

O'Shaughnessy started to answer. There was a loud gagging noise in his throat. His legs buckled under him. He pitched forward.

Blessy grunted and caught him. O'Shaughnessy was bent double. His body hung grotesquely over Blessy's arm, like a misshapen sack of meal.

"Jimmie," Blessy cried in a sudden stricken tone. "Jimmie!"

O'Shaughnessy didn't answer.

Reynolds ran over and lifted the boy's legs off the floor. "Take'm t'bed," he ordered.

Blessy didn't move. He stood panting, looking down at the body in his arms. His face was stupid, stricken.

"C'mon, feller," Reynolds said. "What's the matter with you? *For Godssakes!*"

An inarticulate little cry burst from Blessy's lips. He came to himself. They carried O'Shaughnessy to the cot. "I'll call an ambulance," Reynolds said. He ran out of the room with one hand cupped over his swollen eye.

O'Shaughnessy's head lolled to one side. His eyes were half open. His breathing was slow, tortured. With each breath his chest heaved and his mouth sucked hard for air. When he exhaled, there was a hard, cruel rasp in his throat, like phlegm rattling. Then he was silent for a long time. Finally he would breathe again, his chest heaving, his open mouth sucking for air, his lips drawn back from his teeth in a snarl.

Zets bent over, slipped his hand under the covers and felt for the boy's heart. Blessy stared at him with the same stricken look on his face. The big Russian took his hand away and stood up.

"You feel sah-sah-somethin', don't you?" Blessy whispered.

"Maybe get hot-wat'r bottle!"

"He's not *d-dead*!" Blessy burst out in frantic, unreasoning anger. "He's *breathin'*! Can't you feel him breathin'?"

"No, no, boy – he no dead," the big labourer said reassuringly. "Just hot-wat'r bottle good."

Old man Knox tugged at his wing collar. "Not for this, not for this," he put in excitedly. "An ice bag!"

Reynolds ran back into the room with a red-knuckled hand still cupped over his eye. "The ambulance is comin'," he said. "How is he?"

The men looked at O'Shaughnessy. He was deathly still, not breathing. His young face was a muddy grey, the skin drawn tight over the bones with a thousand fine wrinkles to it.

"Is he daid?" Luke asked.

"What's the matter with you?" Blessy cried, turning on him. "What do you mean, 'dead'? He's br-br-breathin', ain't he? Ain't his eyes open?"

"He ain't breathin'," Luke said.

"He's breathin', he's breathin'," Blessy shouted. "Shut your goddam face."

Baldy came running in. "The ambulance'll be here right away. How is he?"

No one answered.

O'Shaughnessy's chest heaved, and he sucked for air. The ugly rattle sounded in his throat.

"Jesus!" Baldy exclaimed. "He looks like an old man." He rubbed one hand over his bald dome. "I'll be goddamned!"

The men were silent.

Hunchy got out of bed and walked slowly down the aisle.

"Have you got an ice bag?" Knox asked. "That would fix him up."

"You crazy!" Zets said. "Hot-water bottle."

"I ain't got nothin' here at all," Baldy replied.

Hunchy spat between his teeth. "I told you," he said. "An ambulance won't do no good now." He spat again and went back to his cot.

"I'll wait in the office," Baldy said. He walked down the aisle. He spied Charlie, the bum, lying asleep on the floor, and jiggled him with his foot. Charlie snored with quiet unconcern.

"Hey, Arkansas," Baldy called to Luke Hall, "comm'ere – help me a minute."

They lifted Charlie onto his cot.

"There's always a cop comes in with the ambulance," Baldy explained. "Nobody ain't supposed to sleep on the floor."

"Do... do lots of people die in this heah hotel?" Luke enquired timidly. It was a bad omen to be near death this way. Luke wouldn't have come here if he had known all this was going to happen.

"They do an' they don't," Baldy replied angrily. "What do you expect?" He turned on his heel and stalked brusquely from the room. Luke remained where he was in an attitude of gloomy foreboding.

"Kid take long time for breathe, hey?" Zets said to Blessy.

Blessy nodded nervously. "Ain't it time for the ambulance?"

"They said ten minutes," Reynolds told him. "Don't worry," he added, "they come quick." He blinked sympathetically at Blessy with his good eye. He started to speak, then stopped and muttered to himself. He wanted to say something to take the big fellow's mind off his friend, but he couldn't think what. Jesus God... "Organ-eye-zation," Reynolds muttered to himself. His Adam's apple twitched in his stringy neck. Then, "He'll be all right," he said aloud. He raised his hand as though to pat Blessy, but dropped it to his side.

O'Shaughnessy's mouth opened. He sucked for air with a dry, harsh rattle, sounding long and thick in his throat. He lay still again with the bright light cruel on his muddy face.

"Goddamit, why d-d-didn't I get a doctor earlier?" Blessy burst out bitterly. "Such a gah-goddam fool... But he was all right this morning," he said, turning to the others in pleading and explanation. "He was shovelling snow this morning."

"I think he's dead," Knox stated abruptly.

"Shut up!" Blessy said.

"That was a death rattle," Knox persisted.

"You're crazy," Blessy shouted furiously. "He's been breathin' like that right along. His eyes are open, aren't they?"

They waited! They were half a dozen men in a flophouse waiting to see if James O'Shaughnessy, a blond lad from Pittsburgh, who was a good Catholic and a good tool and die maker, would breathe again. And within each man there was a secret fear that waited in company with him. Within each man there was the fear that came in the still pause of the night when he lay on his cot alone and wondered when *his* turn would come, and how, how! – pushing it off, next week, next year, the man alongside, not me, please, not me, not that way, not my number yet! And to each man the young blond boy with the muddy face was himself.

And then Benson said it, into the silence at the foot of the bed his tongue, thick with drink, blurted out the word "me". "Me," he said, "that's me!" He swayed drunkenly, Bill Benson, a seamed, ugly man of fifty, and his voice rose in a strange, mournful cry of bitterness and defeat: "I'm the best goddam harvester mechanic in the whole United States," he cried. "I've got a pair of hands can handle machinery like a goddam newborn baby. But they turned me into a bum," he cried. "An' I let 'em. I let 'em!" He stood swaying. His mouth hung open in helpless anguish.

No one spoke to him. Reynolds cupped his hand over his swollen eye and muttered to himself.

"Pray for me, Jesus," Benson suddenly cried. He lurched forward and struck Luke Hall on the shoulder with his clenched fist. "Pray for the Lord inside Benson! Look at me, Jesus. The Lord's inside me, inside you, inside each and every backhouse* in the world."

He stumbled blindly, drunkenly from the room.

There was a moment of silence.

Then Luke spoke up fervently. "That man's lost," he said. "You look to Jesus, Jesus helps you. Ah don't know what Ah'd do without Jesus. When a man's hungry or lyin' out in the rain, he's got t'do *somethin'*." Luke's voice trembled. "Ah'd hold up somebody, or rob a bank, if Jesus wasn't there to stop me. It's Jesus keeps me safe."

"It's Jesus keeps you weak," Reynolds burst out fiercely, "keeps you down, keeps you from fightin' back – talkin' pie in the sky while you got wind in your belly. My God, when—"

Blessy swung around angrily. "Shut up, you guys. Can't you keep quiet a minute?" He turned back to O'Shaughnessy and resumed his fixed stare at the still form.

"There's too much keepin' quiet," Reynolds muttered in a low voice. "That's the trouble." His Adam's apple twitched in his throat.

There was silence. They waited.

X

Eleven Twenty p.m.

Baldy White came in calling, "This way, here!" A bulky, middle-aged cop followed him in. He had his nightstick clamped snug and ready under his arm. "Somebody get knifed?" he asked.

"No," Blessy cried. He ran past the cop to a young intern standing in the doorway. "Over here, doctor. There's a sick kid here. He's very s-s-s-sick."

The intern followed him in walking quickly. He was a young man, small, with warm, dark Jewish features.

Blessy ran to the cot. "Look out now," he said, "leh-leh-let him through. He's a doctor."

"C'mon," the cop bawled, crowding the men, "out of the way."

The intern bent over swiftly and felt for O'Shaughnessy's pulse. He paused – his eyes were intent on the boy's face. Then he dropped the hand and reached into his bag. He cast a quick, sharp enquiring glance at Blessy.

"He's not d-d-dead, is he?" Blessy whispered.

The intern was silent. He pulled down the covers and put the stethoscope to the boy's chest.

"I'll bet he *is* dead," Knox remarked loudly.

"Shut up!" the cop bawled.

Blessy watched. His shoulders were hunched, and his big bony face was agonized.

The intern removed the stethoscope from his ears and pulled the covers down, exposing the swollen belly. His mouth twitched a little.

"Is he dead?" Blessy asked.

The intern nodded. He stood up with a slight sigh.

"Can't you do nothin'?"

"No!"

"I read in the papers... there's an injection in the heart..." Blessy pleaded feverishly.

The intern shook his head. "Not for this. He'd die all over again. It's been hopeless for the last twenty-four hours. Before that it would've been easy."

"*T-t-twenty-four hours?* But he was b-b-better *last night*!" Blessy cried. "He was better all day! *Jesus Christ* – he was all right till just now!"

"I know," the intern said. "That's the way it acts – but he's dead now," he added gently.

Blessy turned away. Tears welled into his eyes and streaked down his big, hard face.

The intern pulled the covers up over O'Shaughnessy, hiding the body from view. He began writing his report.

The cop took out his notebook and thumbed the pages. "Death on arrival, hey, doc?" he asked.

The intern nodded.

"Wasn't I right?" Knox enquired loudly. "I have forty-five years of medical experience."

The intern looked up with a startled glance.

"Great specialists consult me," Knox told him.

"Shut up, you," the cop bawled.

The intern nodded at the old man and returned to his report.

"You'll leave him here for the morgue wagon, huh, doc?" Baldy said.

"Yes."

"I sure hope it don't take as long as usual," Baldy said mournfully. "This is a big night for me. I can fill up every room. But not with him here. It'll all go down the street."

The intern shrugged.

Baldy went out with a heart full of bitterness. It was a hell of a break to get. It always had to come on a night like this.

The intern touched Blessy's arm. "What was his name?"

"James O'Shaughnessy," Blessy said. His voice was hoarse.

"Irish, huh?" the cop observed. "How old?"

"Twenty-one, I guess," Blessy replied. His head was turned away.

"Where's his home?"

"He didn't have any."

"Parents both dead?" the cop asked.

"His mother is," Blessy replied. "The ol' man's on the bum somewhere."

"Occupation?"

"Tool an' die maker," Blessy said. "But he didn't have a job."

Sam Reynolds edged over to the intern and tapped his report. "He had a job," he remarked. He blinked his swollen eye. "Tryin' t'keep alive. That's a big trade nowadays."

The cop chuckled. "Guess that's true enough. Make it 'unemployed', doc."

The intern stopped writing. "It's too bad," he said gently to Blessy. "If the boy had had medical attention soon enough, we probably could have saved his life."

"That's fine," Blessy answered.

"Where was he born?" the cop enquired.

"Oh, what the Jesus difference does it make?" Blessy said irritatedly.

The cop shrugged and jotted down a memorandum. "Cause of death?" he asked the intern.

"He didn't have a job!" Reynolds said.

"The devil with that," the cop replied. "What did he die from?" he asked the intern again.

"He died from not having a job," Reynolds burst out savagely. "He died cos he couldn't eat right an' he couldn't live right, an' cos he didn't have sense enough to fight. An' that's the truth!"

"Oh, so you're one of *those*?" the cop observed contemptuously. "Now, you just keep your mouth shut till we fill out these records, or I'll shut it for you good."

Reynolds spat on the floor. "I'll talk till I'm blue in the face," he announced flatly, "an' you or nobody else won't stop me. There's one fink hit me already tonight, so you can try the other eye."

The cop stepped forward. The young intern put his hand out. "Peritonitis," he said pointedly, "probably ruptured appendix."

The cop stopped. "Appendix, eh?" He made the memorandum. "I figured it was ulcers, doc. Lots of 'em go by ulcers."

"That was no cause," Reynolds muttered savagely. "That was a result."

The intern looked up. He smiled. "The medical professors wouldn't know what you were talking about," he said.

"Then they're goddam dumb," the little man replied.

"I wouldn't say you were wrong," the intern answered. He patted Blessy on the arm and walked down the aisle. "Goodnight, Lehane," he called back to the cop. He went out.

Under the flesh of Blessy's cheek a nerve quivered, beating a tattoo against the skin. His eyes were dry now, the tears on his face were dry; his look was stony. He sat on his cot and stared, without moving, at the floor.

The cop put his notebook away and opened the dead boy's locker. He examined the contents.

Zets walked over to Blessy. His pockmarked peasant face was sombre with pity. "No feel bad, boy," he said. He sighed. "Goddam life no good." He shook his head. "For poor men no good."

"Say, buddy," the cop called to Blessy, "if you're this kid's pal, you can take his stuff."

"I don't want it," Blessy said.

Knox scurried over to the locker. "I'll take 'em," he cried. He reached inside.

The cop shoved him back. "Wait a minute. What's the matter with you?"

"It'll just go to waste," Knox cried petulantly. "What do you want to waste it for?"

"Take your time," the cop barked. "You old stinkpot," he added humorously, "you're a goddam gravedigger."

Luke Hall approached Blessy hesitatingly. He wasn't quite sure how to begin. "Mista," he said finally, "Ah'm a God-fearin' man all right…" He paused. "But Ah ain't got no overcoat, an' if your buddy had an overcoat an' if you ain't gonna dispose of it… Ah sure could use it awful well."

Blessy kept his eyes fixed on the floor. "Go ahead. Take what you want."

"Thank you, friend," Luke replied softly.

"Awright, you goddam ghouls, fight over it," the cop told them. He stepped aside and chuckled out loud.

Knox leapt to the locker and began feverishly sorting over the contents.

"Ah can have the overcoat," Luke cried, rushing over. "The overcoat's for me."

"Jesus," the cop laughed, "it's like the war. A guy'd kick off an' then they'd strip him… Well," he announced, stretching himself and yawning, "I ain't got anything to do now till the morgue wagon comes, an' that's liable t'take an hour or two. If you boys'll keep an eye on him, I can go out an' get a beer." He sauntered down the aisle. "Don't let him run away," he added jovially. He went out.

Hunchy got out of bed. "Cops stink!" he observed loudly in his cold, metallic voice. "If everybody in the world turned to Jesus Christ overnight... cops'd still stink."

Hunchy walked down the aisle until he came to O'Shaughnessy's cot. He looked down at the rigid form hidden beneath the blanket. He commenced to laugh softly. "Well," he said, "he's dead! He's dead, an' they'll take him down to the morgue an' make out a little slip for him. Then they'll pump the blood out of him, an' when he's all pickled proper, they'll hang him up on a hook that'll hold him nice an' steady right through the ear."

Blessy sprang to his feet. His face was sick with pain and rage.

"An' it'll be the happiest day of his life," Hunchy finished bitterly. "Hallelujah!"

"You shut your face," Blessy cried, choked.

"Hallelujah!" Hunchy repeated. He went back to his cot and crawled under the covers. Then he buried his old man's face deep into the pillow.

XI

Blessy sat crouched over. Hunchy's remark festered in his brain, stabbing his mind like a delicate, poisoned needle. He thought of O'Shaughnessy... his friend... the kid he had stuck with for over a year now. Dead! Hanging on the wall by a hook through his ear. Dead! "Oh God, Oh God Jesus," Blessy cried to himself. "Oh my God Jesus."

Blessy had been a miner. Death was no stranger to the routine of an eight-hour mine shift. He had seen men crushed by a fall of rock; he had seen death on a picket line; he had in his eye the image of his stoop-shouldered uncle caught between a slate car and a wall – crushed bloody like a soft bug between pincers.

It was not just death. No, Blessy knew that. What was it, then? It seemed important to know, and the youth's mind groped painfully for the answer.

He was not a thinking man, this Blessy, this huge, rock-faced miner's boy, brought up in a coal camp, learning what life was in a shack by a smoking coal dump, going into the mine at fourteen. He had never formulated his views on life – or wanted to particularly. He had never done more than grow up and work – and now, more lately, try to keep alive.

But this was different. It required thought. It was not just the death, the dying...

Yes! It was clear now. The waste! It was the waste! Yes, Jesus God, the useless, crazy waste! Good coal on a slate dump. Jimmie O'Shaughnessy junked for nothing. Good for so much, and now he'd hang by a hook through his ear – for what?

"God," Blessy cried aloud, and he didn't know he had spoken. Zets walked over to him. "No cry, boy," he said. "No good cry."

Blessy heard the soft, deep tone. No, he thought, he wasn't going to cry. What for? What the Jesus for? You cry, an' they get you down. He wasn't gonna lay down. You lay down an' they step on you. They turn you into a bum.

A bum! God Almighty, was that what he was gonna become? A bum like Benson? A blind, scratching, panhandling stew bum? No! Jesus Christ, no! Not him. Not in a million years. He'd turn the whole goddam world upside down! He'd tear it to pieces first!

The youth jumped to his feet. The long, bitter years were flaming blindly within him. He felt choked. In one moment he had become on fire with a thousand days and nights – the cold and the loneliness, the horror, the unspeakable indignity. And there flamed up in him a blind, unreasoning, overwhelming need to strike out, *now, now, at this moment, now!*

He screamed! It was like the cry of a beast. He seized a cot and flung it over. He grabbed a shoe out of Knox's arms and smashed an electric bulb. He flung the shoe violently at the wall. "*Not me,*" he yelled. "*They don't make no bum outa me. Not me! Not me!*"

He raged through the room, smashing everything he could get his hands on, tearing at the bedclothes, flinging down the lockers. His big bony face was flaming, his mouth was open, his hair was like a wild crown on his head.

The others stood speechless, backing off before him, frightened by this stricken, inchoate fury.

Baldy, the nightman, ran shouting into the room. "What the hell's goin' on here?" he demanded. He grabbed Blessy by both arms. "Stop it, you son of a bitch! You gone crazy?" He shook him violently.

Blessy became still. The change was abrupt. He stood limp, his body spent. His hands were trembling, and his face was haggard from rage and pain.

"For Godssakes, boy," Baldy said, stepping away from him, "you gone loony? What's the matter with you? What you tryin' to do?"

Blessy didn't answer. He stood hunched over, breathing heavily.

Reynolds walked over to him and put a hand on his arm. "I know what you want to do," the little man said softly, "but you don't know how to do it. Not the walls! You don't wanna fight the walls!"

"I'm a son of a bitch," Baldy observed, "I'm runnin' a nut house." He rubbed his hand over his bald dome. "You gotta pay me for everything you spoilt, Blessy, you hear?"

Blessy went to his cot. He picked up his cap and lumberjacket. Baldy caught hold of him. "Where you goin'?"

"It's all right," Blessy told him. "I ain't runnin' out. I ain't r-r-runnin' out on anything!"

"I'll see you tomorrow," Reynolds said.

Blessy shrugged his shoulders and went out.

"He'll learn," Reynolds said softly. "He's got good stuff in him, that boy. He'll learn."

"You too, eh?" Baldy observed. "You're crazy too?"

"Go ahead an' laugh," Reynolds told him. "You get hit hard enough, you'll find out too."

"Me an' Morgan," Baldy said. He yawned... "Listen, you stiffs, I'm gonna turn out the lights... Happy New Year, an' for Godssakes nobody else kick off tonight."

"Do we have t'sleep with him in here?" Luke asked, pointing to the body.

"Well, I can't keep him in the office with me, can I?"

"Ah sure don't like him in heah," Luke said.

"Too bad about you," Baldy told him. "Go to sleep. They'll pick him up in an hour anyway. Hey!" – Baldy noticed the mackinaw on Luke's arm. "Where'd you get that coat?"

"It was given to me."

"O'Shaughnessy's, isn't it?" Baldy demanded.

"Ah reckon so. What about it?"

Baldy grabbed it. "He owes me for a week's rent. This stays with me."

"You can't take it away from me," Luke protested fiercely. "*He* gave it to me. That man."

"Let go of it... For Chrissake, I'll run you in for stealing."

Luke's hands dropped to his sides. "That ain't fair," he said.

Baldy grinned. "Happy New Year, Texas." He went out.

Zets suddenly spat on the floor. "Whole goddam world no good," he said.

Reynolds laughed softly. He cupped a red-knuckled hand over his swollen eye and blinked happily at the big Russian. "That's the first lesson," he said. "That's where I began too. The second's to know why. Do you know why?"

Zets looked at him soberly.

Reynolds laughed and pointed to his swollen eye. "Look at this," he said. "A subway guard socked me for sellin' a newspaper, a *working man's* newspaper. You know why?"

Zets regarded him blankly.

"C'mon," Reynolds said. He took Zets by the arm.

"Where you go?" the big labourer asked.

"C'mon in the toilet," Reynolds said. "I wanna talk to you." He led him by the arm. "There's more'n one thing you can do in a toilet," he added happily. He cupped a hand over his eye and laughed.

They went inside.

The lights switched out.

Luke Hall approached old man Knox. "Do you mind if Ah sleep by you?" he enquired timidly. "It's New Year's Eve, an' Ah'd sure like some company."

"Certainly, certainly," the old man replied politely. His voice dropped to a whisper. "I'm sure glad that man didn't see these shoes." He had the dead boy's shoes clasped tightly, one under each arm.

"Ah'm goin' t'sure miss that overcoat," Luke said mournfully.

"You know something?" the old man exclaimed with a sense of discovery in his voice. "I've had a hard life! Yes sir! It's New Year's Eve an' I can say it: I've had the life of a dog!" He smoothed his beard. "Now, I always wanted to be a doctor," he reflected, "but somehow I couldn't ever get the schooling. First I was on a farm with my folks, but they couldn't send me. Then I was a streetcar conductor in Brooklyn, but that didn't seem to pay either. Nothing ever seemed to pay." He paused. "I guess it's just too late now," he finished sadly.

"Ah wish Ah could get rich," Luke joined in, "but Ah nevah get anythin' that pays enough either."

"Yes," Knox observed, "come to think of it, you might say God has been hard on *all* of us in here. Now, personally I feel I had the makings of a successful man in me, but somehow I never could get ahead. The harder I worked... the less I got. Still... I'm trying. Maybe I'll succeed yet."

"Ah'd like to tie up with a big business in Wall Street," Luke said. "Ah understand *that's* the way t'do it."

The old man rubbed his eyes with both knuckles, like a sleepy child. "I'm all tuckered out," he complained. He crawled into bed. He put the dead boy's shoes under his pillow. "I don't even trust the locker with these..." he said. "Not good shoes like these." His head touched the pillow. He fell asleep.

Luke moved his things to the cot beside Knox. He took off his overalls and lay down. It felt good to have the blanket tucked up around his chin.

The room was quiet and dark. The street noises from the Bowery drifted in.

Luke turned to the old man. "Do you want to sing a hymn with me?" he asked. "Ah feel lonely. Ah wanted to celebrate the New Year's."

Knox didn't reply.

"Are you asleep, friend?"

The old man snored.

Ah'd like to have sung some hymns at least, Luke thought sorrowfully. It's New Year's Eve. We always used t'do that.

He sniffed a little and turned over. That good dinner would just be starting upstairs now. And he was hungry. He wondered how it was at home. Maybe his folks were hungry too.

He was quiet for a few minutes. Then, softly, he began to sing to himself. He sang in a whisper:

> Count your blessings,
> Name them one by one…

He paused, then went on:

> Name them over,
> See what God hath done –
> Count your many blessings,
> Name them one by one…
> Count your many blessings,
> See what God hath done!*

"That's a good hymn," he remarked to himself.

But what if he didn't find a job?

A sob rose up in his chest. He pushed his face into the pillow and wept quietly.

"Oh Jesus God," he prayed, "Ah need a job bad. You got to give me one before Ah die like that poor man heah tonight. You'll help me, Jesus, won't you? Please God?"

XII

Twelve Midnight

The room was still.

The men slept.

Benson staggered into the room. He found his cot and lay down on his back, staring up at the ceiling. Hunchy turned over and coughed. Old man Knox slept soundly – he was snoring. And Luke lay curled up like a child with his face still wet with tears.

In the toilet a little man with a swollen eye and a comical Adam's apple walked up and down with a pockmarked Russian labourer. The little man was talking, and the big man was listening attentively with his swarthy face serious in concentration.

And the city lay waiting for midnight.

Outside, the sound of horns and bells and shouts broke out in a sudden, mad, abandoned tumult. The church bells pealed, and the taxis honked, and men called to one another and embraced.

It was midnight.

It was the eve of the New Year.

It was the season of celebration!

Goodbye*

Olga Bakovchen sat in the crowded room and stared at her father. She wanted to cry. It was important to cry. Her mother was watching, and her brother, Charlie. All the neighbours, the church people, the priest, Marty Kristoff, Uncle Raditch, everybody crying, everybody with one eye on her father and one eye on her.

"If only he looked different…"

Over her father the tall candles burned. The room was hot and stuffed to the corners – everybody praying and blowing their noses. Behind the coffin the priest was swaying, pouring out the words like a stream.

Olga looked at him. His dark eyes were fixed on her, and his thick beard was wriggling with the words pouring out. She squirmed in her seat. "What was the sense of all the praying? It didn't make any difference. It didn't really make any difference."

The priest kept looking at her, and she turned away. "Goddam him," she thought to herself. "What's he keep lookin' at me for? Maybe if I got out in front of him an' did a wiggle of my own or tore off my dress or something, he'd have somethin' real t'look at."

"Poppa," her brother Charlie cried out suddenly in a wail of grief, "Poppa."

Olga felt angry. A big feller like that calling out "Poppa"!

"If only he looked different…"

The candles burned, and the room was hot with people. "Why don't you cry?"

"I wanna cry," she tried to say. "Poppa's dead, I wanna cry."

An' the priest was talkin' Polish so fast, but Poppa couldn't hear it. Poppa liked to talk Polish. Poppa talked – songs sometimes down by the river. He was a big man, but he had a soft voice for a big man.

Olga raised her face. Everybody was looking. "Why don't you cry?"

"I can't," she said, "I can't. If only he looked different…"

And a knot twisted in her chest, and nobody heard her.

How would it be if she got up all of a sudden and played the phonograph? Everybody would jump. They couldn't play it any longer anyway. Uncle Raditch was gonna give them six dollars for it. Uncle Raditch was making money now. He opened a saloon right after Prohibition stopped. He wanted to give Charlie a job, but what good was it when Charlie was going deaf? Anybody who wanted a beer would hafta yell. That would be swell for the customers. So he was buying the phonograph, and the six dollars would come in handy. "Why don't you cry?"

The wail rose in the hot room, and Olga turned her face, mute and twisted. "I wanna cry, Momma." She pressed her hand to the tight knot in her chest. "I wanna cry, Momma… Momma, you look terrible."

Her mother's face was all screwed up. It was a million wrinkles, with the tears in a steady flow. She looked at Olga and shook her head. All eyes on Olga and the prayers for the dead pouring out like a stream!

"If only he really looked like Poppa… But it's a different face."

Her father's face had been broad and thick, with a copper-red skin as far back as she could remember – fiery red, sometimes, when he came back from work. Twenty-eight years of looking into a blast furnace in a steel mill, but now his face was white like a sick baby's, and the skin was all shrunk down over the bone. "That damn embalmer should have done something," Olga thought. "That damn embalmer."

The priest was silent. His lips moved rapidly. The thick beard wriggled, and the service was almost over. They would tell everybody what a bad girl she was. First she wouldn't cry…

Over the priest's head hung the old marriage picture of her father and mother. A million times she had looked at it. Taken in the old country with the oval frame and both of them standing so stiff. Her father was in dress clothes, her mother had on white – silk, maybe. Her father was straight with… and so tall… and… her father… her poppa… so tall… in an old box… in an old box… in an old box, and they couldn't even show him below the chest, because when the steel beam fell it cut him in two, and all the blood ran out of him… her father…

Olga's breast heaved, and the blood coursed up like hot fire into her face, and a great cutting sob tore up from her chest, and then she was crying with hot, bitter tears pouring down over her hands and dropping hot and fast into her lap.

And the wax dropped from the candles, and the priest swayed, and everyone looked at old man Bakovchen with the white skin drawn down over the bone and the face like a sick baby's and the big body cut straight in half by a steel girder. And Olga was on her knees crawling to the coffin, crying out, "Poppa, Poppa, come back, Poppa" – and then the service was over.

They came back from the cemetery late in the afternoon. The crying was over now, and the mourners would be crowding into the house to eat.

Olga walked alone. It was cold, and the streets were deserted. She walked slowly, her shoes scraping soft on the bare ground.

Down in the mill yard, a Bessemer furnace* was blowing flame into the sky, painting the dark clouds. Olga stopped to look at it. After a moment her lips twitched, and she turned away.

She started up the hill. A sharp wind whistled and flapped her coat. She shivered and bent her head. Inside her there was a cold, dull lump, heavy with the pain of the long, unending day, heavy with the service and the fevered cries, heavy with the dull clump of earth when the shovels swung and the grave closed and her father remained behind. "I feel dead all over," she thought. "Inside of me."

She bent her head and climbed the hill. Inside the house they would all be standing around her mother, crying and waiting to eat. They would eat up the six dollars for the phonograph and more besides. And the next day and the next, for weeks they would cry, until they forgot about it or until Charlie slipped and left his hand in a roller and they brought him home too. She quivered a little. "The hell with it! The hell with it."

A stone caught her heel, and she cursed. Ontario Street! Her Ontario Street! Born there, went to school there, worked there, but she'd be goddamned if she'd die there. Not on a street that wasn't even paved! Not in a steel town! Not married to a dumbhead like her brother Charlie, twenty-three years old and going deaf in a nail mill for three days' work a week! Not walking the rest of her life from an unpaved street up forty-eight steps to a three-room wooden shack the company built and forgot about! And her man to get hit by a crane or laid off one week and kicked around the next. Not on your life!

She started up the steps to her house holding on to the rickety handrail. Six, seven, eight, nine, ten, eleven – not on your life! There was a twelve o'clock bus, and she was gonna take it. "Why not? Why the hell not?" Twenty-two, twenty-three, twenty-four – "Why the hell not?"

At eleven o'clock Charlie came into Olga's room. He was a big boy, and he filled the narrow doorway. He stood silent, watching her, his big bony face creased and angry.

Then he jerked his head. "C'mon out. Everybody's goin' home."

Olga turned around sharply with her back to the bed.

"Whatsamatter with you anyway?" he asked. "Gettin' snooty, maybe? What'd you stay in here all the time for?"

Olga looked away from him. "They don't need no help," she said. "They can go home without me."

"What?" He bent his head, his hand cupping his ear. "What did you say?"

Olga flamed with sudden rage. Inside her there was a blind rush of hatred that always came when Charlie couldn't hear. "What?" she said. She bent her head in savage mimicry. "What did you say?"

Charlie waited a moment, uncertain. "Whatsamatter with you?" he asked. "Aintcha got no respect for Poppa?"

Olga stood silent, her lips pressed together.

"C'mon out. Momma's goin' away too. She's gonna stay tonight with Uncle Raditch."

Olga didn't move. Her face was hot. If he kept standing there, she'd tell him. The dumb fool. "You damn, dumb, deaf fool. You dumb bastard, do you hafta work in a nail mill?"

Charlie started to speak again.

"All right," she burst out. "I'm comin'. Can you hear that? I'm comin'!"

She went to the door.

Charlie looked at the bed. "What're you doin'?" he said. "What're you packin' that suitcase for?"

"Mind your own business."

She went out.

Charlie looked at the suitcase again and followed her.

The priest was the last to go. Mrs Bakovchen offered him a final glass of wine. He drank it and blessed her, murmuring a word of comfort. She burst into tears. In these last days she had gotten to look much older. Now, with her face all wrinkled with crying and her thin back bent, she looked like an old woman.

Uncle Raditch helped her into her clothes. The priest looked at his watch, sighed a little and went out.

Charlie hovered over his mother, trying to comfort her, straightening the thick shawl on her head. She leant against him and wept. He caressed her clumsily, his big hand fumbling over her body. Then she kissed Olga. Olga stood stiff, her eyes dry, her lips tight.

They went out.

There was quiet in the room. After a moment the auto sputtered below, and Olga turned and went into her room. Charlie looked stupidly after her – then suddenly his hand jerked up and he ran to follow her.

She was at the bed packing her suitcase.

He filled the doorway. She saw him there, but didn't stop. He watched her, biting his lips, his brow creased, the fingers of one hand rubbing his thigh. Then he took a quick step forward. "What're you doin'?" he demanded.

Olga didn't answer.

"What're you doin'?"

She turned around. "I'm goin' away."

"What?"

She flared up. "I'm goin' away!"

"Where you goin'?"

"I dunno."

"When you comin' back?"

"I ain't comin' back."

He stood for a moment, breathing hard. Then he burst out at her frantically. "You're crazy! What're you talkin' about? Where you goin'? What the hell's the matter with you?"

Olga faced him bitterly. "I'm goin' to New York! I ain't comin' back! I'm goin' right now! Tonight!"

He was silent, furious, holding his breath in the intensity of his anger. Then he grabbed her arms. "What's the matter with you?"

She swung her body and broke free.

They were silent, glaring at each other. Then his face twisted, and he stepped back. "Olga!" His hand gave a little jerk, and his voice was low and full of pain. "What's the matter?"

She didn't answer.

"What's the matter with you? What about Mamma?" There was a pause. "What about Mamma?"

"I'm goin' away." Her voice rose in a sudden scream. "I'm goin' away! I'm goin' away! I'M GOIN' AWAY!"

She stood face to face with him, sucking in her breath in deep sobs.

Charlie stared. He was frightened now. His hand jerked again. "Olga, you can't do it."

"You dope!" Her voice rose hysterically. "You dumb dope. You deaf bastard. Go to hell, you deaf bastard."

Charlie's face flushed with shame, and his hand swung up hard as though to hit her. She jumped back. He looked at her bitterly. "You don't hafta talk. You don't hafta say it to me."

She was silent, panting.

"Is that somethin' t'say? You think I like goin' deaf like a dummy? You think I wouldn't work somewhere else if I could get a job?"

Olga put her hand to her breast. She felt sick now. The weight of what she had said had come down on her, and she felt sick at the shame in his face.

His voice rose. "You think I like t'work in a nail mill? You think anybody likes t'work in a nail mill? You little bastard, I'll crack you in the face." He took a step forward. "I'll crack you in the face."

Olga's chest caved in, and she burst into tears. Charlie watched her, his face dark with hatred.

Suddenly she cried out violently and flung herself blindly against the bed. Her head hit the iron bedpost, and she screamed with pain. She slid to the floor and lay there weeping and beating her heels up and down.

Charlie watched her, his face twisted with bitterness. Then he turned to leave the room. But at the door he hesitated. It took him a long time to speak. "You gotta stay here," he said. "You can't talk about goin' away."

In silence Olga raised herself up and leant her head back against the bed. She was exhausted, but she still wept. "I can't stay here any more," she said. "I can't work here."

"What?"

She strained herself painfully to talk so he could hear. "I can't stay here any more. I can't work for the steel mill any more."

"Why not?"

"I can't!"

"What're you gonna do?"

She flung her head back with a sob. "I don't know. I don't care."

"You're crazy." His face was distorted with pain. "Where you gonna get a job? What you gonna do? You wanna starve?"

"I don't care." She cried out in a wail of passion and grief. "I don't care."

"You don't care?" he cried. "You don't care? You'll end up as a two-bit whore somewhere! You don't care!"

She shook her head and wept. "I can't work here any more, Charlie."

"Why not?" Then suddenly he looked at her with quiet, deadly concentration. "Why not – because of Poppa?"

She nodded her head, gulping. "I can't."

He was silent. His face creased with pain. Then his head weaved a little, as though he was trying to shake off what was troubling him. His mouth fell open, and his breath came in long, deep breaths of anguish and pity for her.

He went to the bed and picked her up. They sat down, and he cradled her. She leant close against him, folded in his arms. He was a big man, and she was small against him. "I can't," she said again.

He put his head down against hers. "Sissie," he said, "sissie." He stroked her arm. She quivered and wept, her face pressed to his chest.

And inside her there rose up the image of a time when he had called her "sissie". He was a young boy running in a back lot. She saw him so quick and alert, waving his hand and hooting at her, calling her "sissie" in derision, calling out the clumsy affection of a young boy to his sister – and she pressed her head against him, knowing that the quickness was gone and her brother was twenty-three, heavy and awkward, bending over to hear, with his hand cupped to his ear like an old man, because the noise in the nail mill had made him deaf – and her father was dead, and this was her life. "Oh Charlie," she said, "Charlie, Charlie, Charlie!"

He stroked her, and she leant against him and wept. And finally she became quiet.

Wearily Charlie raised his head. "You wanna go away for good?" he asked.

"Yes."

"You can't do that," he said, without belief.

Olga didn't answer.

"You'll come back maybe?"

"Maybe…"

Silence!

He looked at her dumbly, pleadingly… "You've got a good job, Olga. You're makin' sixteen a week. You stay here, maybe you'll be a private secretary. You'll get more."

Olga shook her head.

"We gotta take care of Momma."

She didn't answer.

There was a long pause. Then… "When you goin'?"

"Now," Olga said.

"Stay till tomorrow."

She shook her head.

"You can get some other job here."

She shook her head.

Charlie took his arms away from her. "You're crazy," he said sullenly. "You're crazy. You won't get along there. You won't even get a job."

She didn't answer. After a moment she shrugged a little.

Silently he got up, looking at her… He went into the next room.

Olga sat for a while, dully, and then lifted herself up. She started packing again. Her face was blotched and puffed from weeping, but her mouth was fixed in a tight line. Once during the packing she went to the door to look at Charlie. He was sitting in a chair biting his nails. She went back again.

When she had closed the suitcase, she made up her face and put on her coat. Then she went into the other room.

They looked at each other hesitantly, averting their eyes.

"You're crazy," he said.

She stood dumbly.

"Do you need any money?"

She shook her head.

"You can't go without money."

"I got last week's salary." She raised her voice so he could hear. "I got my salary."

"You goin' t'see Mamma?"

Her lips twitched, and she blinked her eyes as the tears suddenly welled into them – but she shook her head.

She walked to the door.

Charlie jumped up. "I'll carry your bag to the station."

Olga shook her head.

He took the bag from her.

"Put on a coat," she said. "It's cold outside."

He got his coat and cap. They went out.

Down the long stairway, Olga counted each step, checking each one off, one to forty-eight – the broken ones, the creaking ones, the loose ones. Forty-eight steps.

It was late, and the way was deserted. They walked quickly, silently, with tight lips, not speaking one to the other. The night was cold and heavy with darkness.

Near the station Charlie stopped. He stood biting his lips. Then he took her arm. "You're a young girl... You gotta be careful." He hesitated. Olga kept her eyes on the ground. "You gotta be careful... You gotta watch out for men."

With a sudden, swift movement, Olga lifted her lips to his ear. "I'll be careful."

Charlie looked at her. His bony face was twisted. "You're a pretty girl."

They stood like that, Charlie with his big body bending down to tell her something. They stood close, Olga looking at her deaf brother with her lips tight and no word to speak. And behind her, behind the hill, behind the covers of an old box, her father lay dead, his big body cut in two. And she wanted to tell him, but she found no word to speak.

Suddenly, quickly, she flung her arms around him. She raised her face and rubbed it against his. They stood close together in the open street, and she kissed his face with little, swift kisses. "Poor Charlie," she whispered, "poor Charlie" – but he didn't hear.

Then they parted. They walked again.

When they came to the station, the bus was ready to leave. They stood awkwardly, not speaking.

Finally, with stiff formality Charlie held out his hand. They shook hands.

Olga got in and sat down. She turned around to look for Charlie, but he was already gone, with the darkness all around.

The bus started. It left the station and went down the main street to the highway. And as they passed the open yards of the mill, Olga could see the great Bessemer furnace blowing the whole sky red, lighting up the yards and the mill and the houses around. She stared at it as they came up to it... and then they were even with it... and then they were passing beyond... and a great, hot, bitter wave surged up through her body, and a choking sob convulsed her. "Goodbye, you bastard," she said. "Goodbye, you bastard."

Incident on a Street Corner*

It was a Sunday afternoon in January. A wet mist hung heavy on the dark street. And although there seemed to be few passers-by, a small crowd gathered quickly.

The young man was very drunk. His face was set in a dull, thick mould, with his eyes almost shut, as though he were asleep. And his movements were sleepy, slow – but strangely stubborn, persistent, with the steady, stubborn purpose of a drunken man set upon doing something.

He wanted to get away. But the two policemen wouldn't let him.

The policemen were young, strong men. One was about thirty – he was handsome, with a white, bony face that had a small scar over the lip. The other looked more seasoned: his face was meaty and red, as though he had been out in the wind for many years.

Each held on to one arm, and as the drunken man tugged heavily, persistently, from side to side, they swung with him slowly, heavily.

The policemen wore dark oilskins. These bore them down and seemed to restrict their arms. Occasionally they tugged at one of the clips in an effort to free themselves. But each time the drunken man pulled, and then they had to hold on to him again.

The men in the crowd watched in silence. Some had a look of vague fear about them. Others held their lips in the curve of a smile. But all of them watched intently, waiting.

Suddenly the drunken man fell over backwards. The policemen had caught him off balance. He was not hurt when he fell: they had held on to him, and so his fall was broken.

Then the red-faced one stood up. "Hold him a minute," he said to the other. He began to undo his raincoat.

The drunk would not stay still. With his eyes shut and his blond hair falling over his young face so that he looked like a sleepwalker, he kept on with his fixed purpose.

The red-faced one got his coat off. He turned to one of the bystanders, a little man in a derby. "Hold this, will you?" he asked. The man took the coat and folded it over his arm. The policeman stepped back.

And as he stepped back, the drunk twisted his body, curled his legs under him and got to his knees. It seemed as though the whole struggle was to begin over again.

With a sudden, explosive movement the red-faced policeman crooked his leg and brought it up. "Awright!" he said.

The bone of his knee clumped against the man's face. It broke his nose. As though released from a floodgate, the blood spurted out in a thick red stream.

From the spectators there came an instantaneous muffled cry. It was low – a sucking-in of breath.

Then there was silence. The policeman stood up.

The drunk was leaning forward on both hands, no longer making any attempt to get away. His head drooped down too heavy for him to carry. Beneath the white skin of his neck, the muscles were limp and trembling.

The hot flow of blood was over. Now the thick, red drops bubbled out slowly and dropped in large drops to the pool on the ground.

A minute passed. Passers-by crowded to the scene. Searching for a place from which to see, they edged around and around, until in a few minutes they had made a solid ring about the man on the sidewalk.

The policemen looked down at the drunk and up at the curved wall of people and down again. They moved in as the thick wall moved closer.

Suddenly the drunk flung back his head and cried aloud. "Oh," he said, "Oh! It hurts me. Oh!"

There was a ripple of quick movement in the crowd, and voices buzzed out. A young man pushed forward, his face flushed. "Do something," he said, "you can't leave him like that – do something."

The policemen looked up quickly, their faces vacant, bewildered. The red-faced one made a half-gesture with his hand. "We been arguin' with him half an hour," he said.

The drunken man moaned again, his cry full of pain and shock. His head sagged back, and the blood clotted thick and cold on his mouth and dripped down to his worn coat.

A man called out from the crowd: "Lay him down. Put somethin' under his lip."

The one who had stepped forward bent over and put a handkerchief to the drunk's nose. He pressed him back until he was lying full length on the sidewalk. The policemen watched awkwardly, their brows furrowed.

For a moment again there was silence.

A woman turned the corner and came up to the crowd. She was about thirty-five, with a shrivelled, hungry little body and ugly teeth that pressed out beyond her lips. With her pinched, bony face lit up with curiosity she pushed through the wall of bodies like a thin wire through glue. She looked at the man on the sidewalk. Her face turned white.

Then, as though a shock of electricity had passed through her body, she began to scream. "I know you," she said. "I know you cops! You beat a poor man up. I know you."

The young policeman swung around. His face was flushed with rage. "What do you know about it?"

"I know," she screamed back at him. "You'll get beat up some day! You'll get this some day!"

"Go home," he said to her. His voice was ugly. "Go home – you better go home."

The woman kept on, her shrill voice rising higher and higher, her body trembling. "You brutes, you dirty brutes! Two dirty brutes arrested me once too."

"Go home," the cop said. "I know your kind – go home, go home." His face was ugly. He was crouching with his head pulled in against his shoulders.

The red-faced cop pushed into the crowd. His voice took on the familiar tone. "Break it up," he growled. "C'mon, you're blocking the street. Break it up there."

The crowd opened before him. He cleared a lane and walked back. The curved wall closed again. The ring was solid once more.

The cop stared. He gestured with his hand. "We been arguin' with him half an hour," he said.

No one answered.

The woman who had screamed looked down at the drunk. He was quiet now, stretched out on the ground with the blood matted on his face and coat.

She spoke evenly, with sudden calm. "Just wait! You'll get beat up some day too."

Then, as quickly as she had come up, she was gone.

There was silence again.

The policemen looked at the crowd. It was mostly composed of men. They looked like working men of one sort or another – Irish – all of them dressed in their Sunday clothes. They stood locked together, thickset, heavy-featured, with a sullen look to their faces.

The red-faced policeman jerked his thumb. "She don't know what she was talkin' about," he said. His tone was apologetic. "She don't know what happened."

A woman standing in the front line burst out in sympathy with the policeman. "Sure," she agreed, "everybody knows! A drunk is worse than a crazy man."

There was a silence again. The men looked on with the same cold, sullen stare.

"A drunk is worse than a crazy man," the woman repeated.

One of the men took a piece of paper and a pencil out of his pocket. Looking at the cops he started to write.

The young cop stepped over to him. "What are you doin'?"

The man didn't answer. He kept on with his writing.

"What are you doin'?" the cop asked again. "You want me to run you in?"

"You can run me in if you want to," the man replied. "I'm takin' down your number."

He put the paper in his pocket.

The cop was silent. He remained where he was.

A passer-by came up and asked in a loud voice what had happened. A man in the back row answered him: "Some poor guy got drunk – so these cops kicked the crap out of him." The answer was loud, challenging.

"What do you know about it?" the red-faced policeman said. He stuttered a little. "We been arguin' with him half an hour. What do you know about it?"

"We know about it," the voice replied calmly. "You're cops, aintcha?"

"What're you sayin' that for?" the policeman asked. "What's that got to do with it?"

"You're cops, aintcha?" the voice repeated.

There was silence.

"Do you know he tried to hit a woman here before?" the young policeman said.

"What about it?"

"What about it? What about it?" the cop asked. "We've got to keep order, don't we? We're guardians of the law, ain't we?"

"Like hell you are!"

"Who said that? Who said that?" The older cop stepped forward belligerently.

"I did." A stocky, middle-aged man with a big head and a powerful set to his body stepped forward. He stood with his feet wide apart and his hands behind his back. "I did."

"Oh, you did?" the cop repeated. He stuttered. "You want me to run you in?"

"I don't give a damn what you do."

"You don't, eh? You don't?" the cop repeated. "What's the matter with you?" There was a pause. "What do you come around here for, tryin' to make trouble?" He turned to the others. "Why the hell don't you all clear out of here?"

"We ain't gonna make trouble, officer," the stocky man answered softly. "We're just gonna see you don't beat him up no more."

"That's right," someone else said.

"Well, for Chrissakes!" The older cop burst out laughing. He turned to his fellow. "Did you hear that? Well, for Chrissakes."

The younger cop chuckled.

The crowd was silent.

"You talk like we was apes or somethin'," the older cop said bitterly. "I'm an Irishman an' a Catholic. I've got my dooty an' I do it."

"I'll tell you somethin', brother," the middle-aged man replied, "as one Irishman to another: it was a good Irish Catholic like you who cracked my skull in the dock strike of 1914. When an Irish Catholic puts on a cop's uniform, he's a cop. He's no Irishman or Catholic any longer."

"I oughta run you in, you Mick," the older cop burst out, swearing. "I oughta book you right now."

"Go ahead."

The policeman looked over the crowd of faces. The men looked back at him.

"Get an ambulance, you upstanding Irish Catholic," the middle-aged man said. "You're leavin' a hurt man lie on the ground."

The policeman glared at him.

"Go on, get an ambulance," several men repeated.

"I'm gettin' it, I'm gettin' it," the cop said. "Take your goddam time. I don't need you to tell me my business." He moved towards the crowd.

"Get it before you need one yourself," someone said.

The cop stopped. He put his hand to his gun.

"Take it easy," the middle-aged man said.

The ring opened. The cop walked through to the telephone box on the corner.

The ring closed again.

The little man in the derby who had been holding the cop's raincoat on his arm stepped forward and put it on the ground.

"What's the idea?" the young cop asked. "What are you puttin' it on the ground for?"

The man didn't answer. The crowd opened for him. He walked away quickly. The solid ring closed again.

It began to rain harder, but no one moved. It was quite dark now. They stood there waiting for the ambulance.

"What's the matter with you?" the young cop burst out suddenly. "What the hell's the matter with you?"

No one answered him.

The Game*

"Then I jump up on the wagon—"

"You forgot something!"

"What? No, I didn't!"

"Yes, you did," the man said. "What's the matter with you?"

The boy wrinkled his brows together. He was young, about ten years old. His peaked, pointed little face was slightly blue from the cold. He blinked his eyes to get the sleep out of them.

"Come on now!"

"I can't remember."

"You little fool – do you want to get caught?"

"I won't get caught. Jeez, I've played *games* like this. I can do it."

"How can you do it? You can't even tell me what you're *supposed* to do."

"Well, you just watch me."

"I won't watch you. We'll go home now – that's what we'll do."

"Aw, for Chrissakes!"

"What are you swearing for? That's not going to help you remember. I've told you a thousand times I don't want to hear you swearing. You'll grow up to be a hoodlum – that's what you'll do."

There was silence between them.

The man sighed. "I usta just be getting up now," he thought to himself. "I usta be getting up to a hot breakfast and walk down to the trolley car with a lunch pail swinging from my hand."

He brushed the snow from his thick, black moustache. "You poor little monkey," he thought, "it's too early for you. You ought to be back in bed."

"Well," he said to the boy, "have you remembered it yet?"

The boy shook his head. His face was screwed up into a sullen little point.

"What are you gonna do now – cry?"

"I ain't crying," the boy said. "What do you think I am, a baby?"

"You act like one. You can't remember anything I tell you."

"Aw…"

The boy stepped out of the doorway and scooped up a handful of snow.

"Well, what's that for?"

"I'm gettin' some snow."

"I ain't blind. You don't hafta tell me. What are you getting it for?"

"I wanted to make a snowball."

"Is that all you can think of? I thought you said you wanted to help your sister?"

"Well, I am, ain't I?"

"No, you're not. Not when you have your mind on everything but what you're supposed to do. Come in here now."

He took the boy roughly by the arm and pulled him into the doorway. "You forgot the bag! You forgot the most important thing. How can I trust you to do it right when you forget the bag?"

"I didn't forget it, Pop," the boy said. "I got it in my pocket, ain't I? I didn't think you meant to tell about the bag."

"You got to tell me everything. I got to be sure you know everything. Take it out now. I want you to have it ready."

The boy took a crumpled paper bag out of his pocket. He opened it by blowing into it.

"Then what do you do?"

"Then I wait till the milkman goes around to the back of the house."

"Which house?"

"That one over there."

"The green one?"

"No, next door."

"Why not the green one?"

"Aw, gee… I know all that, Pop," the boy said. "I don't hafta go over it again."

"If you don't tell me, we're going right home."

"Because he only goes to the side door at the green house, an' he goes all the way into the back for the other one. Gee, I can do it, Pop, you don't hafta be afraid."

"I know you can," the man replied, "but we just got to be as sure as we can. Are your hands cold?"

"Not much."

"Hold the bag under your arm."

The man took the boy's small white hands between his own thick red ones and rubbed them slowly.

"Then what?"

"When he turns the corner at the back of the house, I run out and grab a bottle. Then I put it right in the bag and walk the other way."

"Do you run?"

"No, I only walk."

"And if he sees you and runs after you then you run, don't you?"

"No, I keep on walking. I let him catch me and then I just start crying."

"You sure you're gonna be able to cry?"

"Sure. I been practising. I made Jenny think it was real." The boy laughed. "I made believe I was getting a licking."

"Sh! Don't make so much noise."

"My hands are all right now, Pop."

"Put 'em in your pockets. I'll hold the bag. Then what happens if you're caught?"

"I just keep crying, and you come up and say you know me and I'm a poor boy…"

"Sh!"

The man put his hand over the boy's mouth. "Someone's coming. Make believe there's something in your eye."

The boy squinted one eye and opened the other. The man pretended to be examining him.

A homeless man shuffled past them, pushing blindly through the swirl of falling snow. His head was wrapped in a burlap bag.

We're better off than he is, the man said to himself.

They watched him until the snow blotted him out.

"It's comin' down harder now," the boy whispered. "That milkman won't see me from away across the street. I could take more'n one bottle."

"One's enough! And after I tell him I know you... what happens then?"

"Then you say I'm just a poor boy with a sick mother, and I'm taking it because of her, and if he'll let me go, you'll see that I don't do it no more... That's all, isn't it, Pop?"

"That's all." The man sighed and brushed his moustache. "You hungry?"

"Kinda."

The man squeezed the boy's arm. "It's awright. I am too. What you gotta do is spit and pat your stomach." He spat out into the snow and patted his stomach. "C'mon."

The boy imitated him. They laughed.

"That proves you just finished eating and your belly feels good," the man told him.

"Sure, I just had two eggs and some cereal," the boy said.

They laughed again.

"Well, we'll have something when we get home."

The man stiffened. His big body was crouched over. "There's the milk wagon. Take the bag. Don't go out till I tell you."

"I won't." The boy's face flushed with excitement. "Wait till you see. I'll do it right. I've snitched apples already."

"Here's somethin' else to remember. If something goes wrong, you listen to what I holler. If I holler 'run', you run. You run no matter what I'm doing, you hear?"

"OK."

"You promise me?"

"I promise."

"No matter what happens to me, remember!"

"OK."

The milk wagon slowly made its way up the street. The man and the boy crouched down in the doorway.

"When it reaches the hydrant! Don't be nervous now! Awright, kid. Awright! Go ahead now."

The boy stepped out. He walked slowly down the street, lifting his feet high in the soft snow.

"I shoulda told him to pull his cap down. The snow'll get in his eyes," the man thought. He breathed with his mouth hanging open. His chest heaved, and each breath felt strangely painful.

The milkman disappeared around the back of the house. The boy's body seemed to leap forward. He jumped up on the front of the wagon and reached inside.

"It's taking so long," the man said to himself. "Oh, Jesus Christ, it's taking him so long…"

The boy jumped down into the soft snow. He shoved the milk bottle into the bag and walked off quickly down the street. The milkman was just coming down the alley. The man watched him. He turned down the street to the next house. It was done. It was all right. He was safe.

The man brushed his moustache. He swallowed and then sighed deeply. He set out after the boy.

The boy was waiting for him on the next block. His little face was radiant. "I made it. I did it, didn't I?" he demanded.

"Sure, son, fine," the man said. He patted him on the head. "I'll carry it."

"I can carry it," the boy replied.

"Awright."

"Jeez, it was easy, Pop. I coulda taken another one easy." He followed his father down the street, running and sliding in the soft snow. "Can I take two of them tomorrow, Pop? Can I?"

The man didn't reply.

"Hey, Pop!" The boy tugged at his coat.

"What?"

"Can I?"

"Can you what?"

"I just told you."

"I didn't hear."

"Can I take two tomorrow? It's just as easy. I can snitch them."

"No."

"Aw, I could take two."

"No."

They walked in silence.

"I wish I could tell the fellers," the boy said.

The man stopped. "You tell anyone an' I'll break your neck. I'll break your neck!"

"Sure, I know. I won't tell. I was just wishing."

"This is stealing," the man said. "It's stealing!"

"Sure, I know. Gee, let's go, Pop, I'm cold!"

They walked again. Their heads were bent against the snow.

"Are your feet wet?"

"Kinda."

"When I get a job, I'll get you rubbers. I'll get you boots. Hip boots. You can walk in the snow all you want without getting wet."

"Maybe the relief'll give you some rubbers for me," the boy suggested.

"Maybe. I asked them already. I'll keep asking them."

"I ain't afraid to get my feet wet."

The man suddenly stopped again. "You know stealing's wrong, don't you?"

"Sure, I know, Pop."

"You know we're only doing it because of your sister!"

"Sure, I know."

"I never stole in my life," the man said. "I worked hard all my life. I'm a good worker. I always provided. You can ask your mother."

"Gee, Pop," the boy said, "you don't hafta feel bad. I ain't gonna grow up to be a thief. I know stealing's wrong."

"You said you snitched apples."

"Well, gee, Pop, a feller wants something like that once in a while."

"Yeah, I know," the man said.

"But I ain't gonna steal. I'm gonna grow up strong like you an' get a job. Honest, Pop!"

The man looked down at his son's face. "Like hell you are," he said to himself. "When I was your age, I was a head taller than you. You poor little monkey, they're not giving you the chance to grow up."

"Gee, Pop, I'm cold," the boy said.

They walked softly through the fresh white snow.

A Letter from the Country*

...Well, that answers all your questions, I guess. Now I'll tell you why I didn't send you any letter before this, like I said I would.

I got hurt pretty bad about a month after you left here, and will now tell you the whole story from the beginning. If my handwriting skitters around, don't you mind it, because my fingers are stiff and I ain't been able to hold a pencil till now. And anyway I am still laying on my back, with Sarah bringing me vittals* like I was her prize heifer that she was nourishing for the state fair. Ha! Ha!

After you left us, everything was going fine. The effect of our winning the trial, after we were arrested for stopping Mogens Petrie's eviction, was that we had a big increase in the union. The farmers all learnt we could stop foreclosures if we all get together, and get us seed and feed loans also, and a moratorium on foreclosures, etc. And old Mogens Petrie was the happiest man in South Dakota, because we stopped the sheriff from throwing him off his farm, where he homesteaded forty-six years ago. He was the first homesteader out here, and Mogens works for the union now, hard as a beaver.

To give you just an example – we took over Sulky, which is the county seat you know, for a whole Saturday-afternoon celebration. We had a wagon opposite Milket's department store for our speechmaking, and our boys selling the *Farmer's Weekly* through the crowd. By God, we had every farmer in the whole blessed county who had enough gas to run his buggy into town. Julius Bosco made a wonderful speech, I can tell you, and there wasn't nobody in the crowd chinning* the women or doing anything but listen to Julius. There was about two thousand listening – half our people – and we got seventy-six new members into the union, including two Indians, who we were glad to get because we ain't reached them much, and there's many of them hereabout, because, as you know, this is reservation territory. It was a big victory. I guess you would have been glad to see something like that. Our union sure growed in the month you was gone.

Well, a week later we got a surprise package nobody expected. I guess it took us off our perch all right. We were all of us riding too high, and confident that the trust company would be too scared of us to venture any more evictions. The only one had his eyes open being Henry Plut. He said, "You're all so puffed up like turkey cocks you think there ain't nothing to do now but drink soda pop to glory. The fight's just beginning," he told us, "and they're agonna hit back at you." And we didn't a one of us believe him. Well, things is sure different now.

Saturday night, a week after the celebration, we had a meeting in a schoolhouse out near Belleville. Coming back, between Sissebel and Sulky, we stopped on the road. There was about five autos all stopped in the middle of the road. And a big crowd. It looked like an accident, so we stopped to see couldn't we help some. We were on our way to a farm dance. Everybody was feeling fine, because there was a big turnout at Belleville. We had with us Julius Bosco, Curt Wallace, old Mogens Petrie, Clarence Shipley and Mogens's boy, Jasper, who just got engaged to Emma Skarnagel, you'll be glad to know. You'll laugh when I tell you I had on a brand-new panama I paid eighty-nine cents for. Because I sure made a mistake wearing that. It was a sin of vanity.

Well, we never got a chance to get out of the car at all. Soon as we stopped, there was about thirty men on all sides of us pointing guns. Not saying a "God liveth" thing. Just silent and pointing.

Well, I sure don't know what to think. A few of them I know well. Not friends, but well. Like some farmers from Huk county – like John Babec. Some of them I didn't know. They were from neighbouring towns, I found out later. And some are loafers from Sissebel, Sulky, East Britters, etc., fellows who you see loafing on the corner or always with one foot raised in the gin joints and shooting pool. But there was some big shots like Major Paulson, head of county relief, and Peter Tiffler, secretary of the Legion* in Sissebel, John Sondegaarde, the grain-elevator man, etc. It sure was a mixed crowd, and when I see it, I don't know what to make out of it.

Then I see Emil Sutter, sheriff of Black Rock county. I figure then maybe there was a bank hold-up and they were a posse.

Well, there we were – them saying nothing, and we not knowing what to say.

Suddenly someone in the crowd yells, "Come on out from that car, you red b——"

I want to tell you there was two seconds there when no one breathed, we were so surprised. Finally Julius says, "What's the matter, Johnny, you drunk?" (Julius was correct there. Everybody is drunk to glory. They must have been guzzling all day to prime their stomachs for that dirty job. Johnny is a clerk at East Britters Trust Co., so you can see why he is in that bunch.)

Well, we still don't know what's up. But right off they tell us all we need to know. Sondegaarde walks over and swings a big hickory club he carries, and smashes the windshield. The glass goes over everybody, but fortunate it just got Jasper Petrie. He had a piece round as a quarter stuck in his cheek.

And at the same time everybody hollers, "Come on out – how do you like that?" One guy yells, "Give them a shot of tear gas." (They even brought tear gas. Got it from the sheriff.)

Well, Julius jumped right out of the car. Nobody can't scare him. And he's been so respected since the war he couldn't believe anybody was after him. Me, I knew better. I was plenty scared.

I guess you never met Julius, because I recollect he was on a speaking tour when you were here. Well, Julius is a big, husky fellow. He's about forty-five years now. When he come back from the war, Black Rock county was so proud of him they wanted to name the Legion hall after him. He got two medals and a personal letter from the president, etc. But Julius said no. He said, "Name it the Liberty Post of the Legion." (Just wait till I tell you about later.)

And Julius walks with a limp in his right leg, his four toes being shot away in the war. Did you ever hear Emmet, his daddy, talk about it? It sure is good. Emmet says, "The govinment gave Yoolyus (that's how he calls him) a medal in swap for his toes, but Yoolyus – the damn fool – he don't think it was such a good bargain." Ha! Ha! Emmet's against war like hell. Julius wasn't when he went, but he is now.

Well, Julius jumps out of the car and grabs Sondegaarde by the shirt. "What's the matter with you, Pete?" he says. "You gone crazy?"

Sondegaarde spits out his tobacco and says: "Julius, we're some of the good citizens of Black Rock county, and we decided we don't want any more Bolsheviki ideas around here. We're a law-and-order committee, and we're out to see there ain't no more interference with the law." How do you like that? "Some of you farmers," he says, "think all you got to do is laze around and not pay taxes or meet your honest debts, and then you just interfere when the sheriff comes to do his duty. Well, we don't like this red socialist and anarchist union of yours, and we're gone to bust it up."

"Oh, you are?" says Julius. "It seems to me like you must have been collecting some mortgages on the side, Pete. That's why you're so burnt up about our union."

Then Sondegaarde shoves Julius back then, and hollers at him mad as six hornets. "I ain't gonna argue with you, you red b——" he hollers. "We're here to make law-abiding citizens out of every goddam one of you."

"How you gone to do that Pete?" Julius asks him.

"This is how," Sondegaarde says, and he hits Julius twice. Later we found it cracked six ribs right then, and at the same time he slams Julius with his right fist on the neck, and Julius goes down like a head of beef. I sure thought I was gone to bust to pieces inside of me when I see that.

I just wanted to kill that big b——.

Julius is a big man, but Sondegaarde is bigger. He is about two hundred and sixty pounds. Like a tree trunk. Once I seen him bet

Nils Nielson he could stun a heifer with one blow. Did it too! Hit her on the front of the head. She just caved in and flopped over like she'd been hit with a sledgehammer.

Well, when we seen that, we all made a break to get out of the car, but someone shot off a gun and everybody pointed their double barrels at us. That stopped us.

Then that son of a b—— Sondegaarde steps to Julius, where he's laying on the ground, and kicks him between the legs, and Julius screams. I sure felt like Sondegaarde had kicked me, and we sure forgot about their guns then. If they had been holding machine guns at us, it would not have made no difference. We piled out fighting – even young Jasper with the piece of glass still sticking in his cheek, and blood running out all over like a stuck hog.

But they was three and four to one, with clubs. They shot their guns off, some of them, but I guess it was only to scare us, and they were nervous. I guess they ain't ready for killings yet.

That was when I got my nose broken so you wouldn't recognize me. It's like a young squash, Sarah says. Ha! Ha!

And my back got hurt from being kicked, so that's why I have been lying in my bed for two weeks, taking it easy like a banker. You know me.

Well, pretty soon they had us all laid out and hog-tied. They had potato sacks, which they covered our heads with. Also, they burned our auto, which was Curt Wallace's, that he loaned to the union. Turned it over and rolled it into a ditch. Then they took us into their cars to East Britters, to the Legion Hall there.

They didn't do much to me on the way. But a lot of name-calling. I told one of them they was all yellow b——, and he fetched me back a kick in the jaw for it. After that, I kept my mouth shut like I should have done in the first place. They were drinking a lot though. I guess you sure got to drink to go through with a dirty job like that.

So I lost that nice new panama hat, and it sure served me right for trying to be a turkey cock, but who could a knowed we were going to get kidnapped? As a matter of strict truth, I was celebrating, because Sarah and me been married ten years now. (Sunny has just come over to me, and I asked her did she remember you, so she says sure, you gave her the "onkey". She means the monkey you won at the Sissebel fair for throwing baseballs. I guess she don't talk good enough for a speech-maker yet. What do you think?)

Well, let me tell you, the shock of a thing like that is even worse than being beat up. Old Emmet says Julius acts like he was in a daze still. He just can't believe anyone would do that to him, and I didn't really feel so hurt till after it was all over. Most of all, I just felt boiling with wanting to kill them. But lying in the bottom of the car on the way over to East Britters, the blood kept running from my nose into my mouth, and my head felt like someone had taken a hand axe and swung it into my skull, where it was sticking just to give me a good time every time the car bounced. Sure wasn't no joyride that trip.

I want to tell you I never knowed I could hate so much. I kept remembering what Julius's face looked like when Sondegaarde kicked him. He didn't have pain in his face, although it must have hurt him simply terrible. It is a terrible thing to hear a man scream, I can tell you. But it was a look on his face kind of one like surprise. Well, no wonder. Him and Sondegaarde has known each other since they been kids.

We was on that damned ride of theirs for over an hour. I guess they were just riding around enjoying the cool of the night, but me, I sure would have chosen other ways to spend my free time. My busted nose ached me like sixteen devils, and was swollen so big I almost couldn't see over it, but more important you couldn't help from being scared of what was going to happen. I guess feeling scared and helpless is about the worst feeling a man can have. It sure seemed like they had to be done now, and let us go. It didn't seem like you could stand any more beatings, and you thought you would better take a load of buckshot and be done with it than have them start hammering at you with their clubs and gun stocks again.

But they rode us into East Britters and took us down to the basement of the Legion Hall. When we got in there, I sure thought I was having just a nightmare. Because I heard music and singing and laughing, and all around us you could feel people dancing.

Well, let me tell you something now. They stretched us out on the floor and took our potato sacks off. And there was a *fancy party* going on, and there was *women* there.

I want to tell you, when I saw that, I felt my head was going to bust inside and send me crazy. There was women, and they were dancing and laughing and yelling, and all drunk to glory, and they didn't stop one second when we came in. Everyone had masks on, and it was easy to judge they were expecting us. There was Julius, getting beat up in the Liberty Hall they wanted to name after him.

There was a woman, looked to be young, came up and bent over me. She asked me did I want a cigarette, like she was sorry for me. I said yes. Then she shoved the lighted end of her cigarette against my mouth. Can you imagine that? I tell you, it was the only time for about twenty years I felt like crying. Then she went off laughing like it was a Charlie Chaplin picture.

I been laying here on my bed for the last two weeks, trying to figure out where all that hate comes from that could make women act like that, let alone men. Of course, some of them were rich men, and they and our union are enemies. And some were just grub worms that anybody can buy for a pint of whiskey. But there was others who are good people just gone wild, I guess. I guess they been as much driven down by the last ten years as we have, and when somebody tells them it's the union at fault for things, they believe it, because they have to blame somebody.

But once I heard a couple of them yelling off in a corner, with one man hollering they ought to let us go. So I guess some of them were sorry – and two days later Julius got a letter from two farmers, who said they were in the bunch went to beat us up, and they was ashamed now. They have resigned from the Legion, they said. And Emmet said their eyes is opened now, and in a couple of months he bet we'd have them in the union.

Well, they only kept us there about an hour, but that was sure a long time. I started to feel my hurt there beginning bad, and I couldn't breathe easy. Also, I kept being worried lest I be hurt real bad inside, and can't tend the farm no more, with Sarah and the four kids still young. But it turned out I ain't been – so the doctor says. It sure was good news to hear. And all the time them saying they were going to throw us in the lime pits out by Sissebel, and knowing you couldn't do nothing to help yourself but lie there like a trussed animal. And hearing old Mogens groaning, and thinking, "I can stand anything they do to me, unless they kick me between the legs, like Julius. I can't stand that," I think. But then saying no to myself. "By God, I will stand anything they give me, and more. I just will never give in to them." But it sure was a long hour, I can tell you.

They seemed to hate Julius the most, calling him names, and kicking him, and bringing people over to introduce them to him, like it was a game. I guess because he was a real war hero and wouldn't have anything to do with their Legion, after the big boys started to run it. But they had a lot of people there who weren't members of the Legion. A lot of kids, also, trying to be tough because they had guns. Strutting around, calling us dirty reds and pouring liquor on our heads, and every once in a while kicking somebody with their hobnails, or jumping full weight on your hand and then running back and saying "Oh, excuse me mister", like it was an accident. And that is how both my hands were hurt.

Well, finally they took us out to a side alley, and Sondegaarde hollers at us: "Well, you going to leave the union now, you Bolsheviki b——?" And Julius, who couldn't stand up he was so hurt, he says, "You go to hell." And Mogens says, "Sondegaarde, I wouldn't use even one of you rats for garbage for my hogs. You'd make them all die of poisoning," he says. (He is going to be in the hospital for a long time. They ripped all the muscles attaching his shoulder blade, the doctor says, and he is bad off.)

Well, they made us walk a gauntlet then, with fellers standing on both sides of us, hitting us. I guess I didn't feel any more by then, but I kept looking at Julius, who could only crawl between the lines, and them clubbing him all the time.

And then they took us in the cars out of town and dumped us there. Well, we would have been there all night maybe, being still tied up, but it was Saturday night. Pretty soon some car came along, and Jasper crawled out on the road and lay there. It was one of our boys too – Saul Anderson – and he just started to cry when he saw how we looked.

Well, this is how things have happened since you have gone, and I guess it learnt us all a great deal. For one thing, we have found out who are the stickers and who are the quitters in our union – and it would surprise you. There's some been scared by this, and they have stopped coming to meetings or give excuses, and others come, saying we ought to lie low and not fight for relief for a while, or try to stop the trust company from evicting anybody. But there's others, who you would never suspect, have come through fine. Real men, like Pete Bubnis, who would never work much for the union before this, but does now. Others too.

And since then meetings have been held regular, but everybody brings guns. And there's been four men on guard day and night where we live (the ones who was beat up). They been dropping their farm work to do it, even though it is harvest season – although, truth to say, there is not much to harvest, the drought kept on so bad even after you left.

Yes, the very next day we decided to arm ourselves for self-protection. It was fair day in Culleyville, and the governor was there. We sent him a telegram demanding the state take action, because we knowed we could expect nothing from the sheriff, when he was right there with them. And the governor answered us it was out of his jurisdiction. How do you like that? I guess we sure are dirt farmers all right. Dirt to him.

So we sent men to every store for sixty miles to buy shells, because some of the towns like East Britters wouldn't sell to us.

By God, you know what Saul Svenson did? He went right into East Britters Monday morning, and he says, "I want a whole case of forty-four* shells." They all know him there for a union member, and there was some of that bunch hanging around, including Hanky the store owner, who is one of the worst. Hanky says, "What are you needing forty-fours for?" Saul says, "To shoot jackrabbits." Hanky says, "Nobody uses forty-fours for jackrabbits. They're too big." Saul says, "That's all right, Hanky, the jackrabbits is growing big out my way." How do you like that? And Hanky was so surprised he went and got them – but later they wouldn't sell to nobody.

So there we are. This is the longest letter I ever wrote, but I will tell you the truth. I wrote it because I am hoping you can maybe write this up to a story, to let people know concerning some of the things that is happening in this good old USA. Not one of the newspapers in any town here would print a blessed line about any of this, although everybody knows it and is talking about it.

Well, it just shows that we farmers have got to make our union like the thistle out here, that never stops growing no matter how hard you try to get rid of it. Not good to look at, but hard to down. Ha! Ha!

Sarah says you come out here and visit again next year – maybe there won't be drought, and we'll have some fresh things to feed you this time. She says you must have thought we were trying to make you diet. And Sunny says the same thing, only it sounds like she's got store teeth* in her mouth which is interfering with her talking.

Well, you tell me how things are going with you, and how they are in the big city. I sure appreciate the magazines you sent, and I am going to figure out a leaflet now, because there is a lot of work to do with six of us on our backs.

Your friend,
LESTER COOLEY

The Drop-Forge Man*

I

Sure enough, when Leeman came into the room, there was Bob sitting in his woollen underwear and Ella perched on his lap. "Hi, Lee," Bob called heartily.

"Ain't we bad, Mr Hayes?" Ella giggled, the way she had giggled yesterday and the day before that, and would again tomorrow.

"Shucks," Lee responded with a sinking heart. He closed the door and set his lunch box down.

"You let me go now," Ella squealed coyly to Bob, without meaning it. Ella rose up a head taller than Bob, and she was twenty pounds heavier, but Bob, as usual, seemed to be managing fine.

"Feathers! Stay right where you are," Bob commanded. He linked his fingers together and held her down by squeezing his palms against the soft bulge of her bosom. "Lee don't mind – do you, Lee?"

"Shucks no," Lee replied, trying to hide his misery.

"Supper'll be ready in two minutes, Mr Hayes," Ella chirruped. She was only sixteen, in spite of her womanly girth, and she could never feel quite at ease in the presence of anyone else. Even knowing Leeman from back home didn't make any difference. "I've made us a meat stew," she added, giggling.

"What's your hurry?" Bob asked. "He ain't even started to bath himself yet."

"I like Mr Hayes to know it'll be ready when he wants it."

"Lee knows that. Don't be a ninny." Bob took Ella's ear between his teeth and bit her delicately. Ella shivered, screamed, burst out laughing. "Lord God," she burbled, "I'm sure Mr Hayes don't know what to make of all this carryings-on."

"Now, Ella, stop that," Bob ordered, becoming irritated. "You're just being flirty now. Lee ain't no mamma-sucking-sugar-tit. Lee's a grown man. How old are you, Lee?"

"Eighteen." Leeman was behind the curtain that enclosed his cot from the rest of the room. He was stripping off his clothes.

"You see?" Bob said. "Lee's old enough to know what a man does with his wife – ain't you, Lee?"

There was no response from behind the curtain.

"Ain't you heard me, Lee?"

"Uh-huh."

"You see?"

"Tell me when you want your water, Mr Hayes," Ella called.

"Reckon now's all right."

Ella jumped off Bob's lap and filled a washtub with hot water. She pushed it half under the curtain, and Leeman pulled it the rest of the way. "Oh my," she burst out, "are your feet dirty! Bob don't get dirty feet like that." She ran back to her husband and tweaked his drooping black moustache. Bob drew her onto his lap again. "Tell me when you want your back washed, Lee," he called.

"Uh-huh." Leeman stepped into the tub. He felt too dejected to be grateful for the water, even though his feet ached and his stomach, as usual, felt all caved in from the forge. Mechanically he scrubbed his body with a brush. It took real rubbing to break down the surface cake of foundry grime, oil, perspiration. Factory dirt was different from farm dirt, he thought mournfully – everything was different in the city.

"Ooop-hah-oh!..." Ella screamed. There was the sound of a slap, then a series of playful kisses. Leeman groaned. It was getting so he hated them. And he didn't want to. Bob was as nice to him as a man could be, looking after him, giving him advice. And Ella was all right too, though a little foolish, like most women when they've just been married and their man is fussing over them. In the summer, when Bob had proposed that they go up to Detroit together, he had been grateful. A man needed a friend when he was in a strange place. If not for Bob, he might not have had the courage, in spite of the good money. And then Bob had suddenly married, just one week before they started out. At first it had seemed all right – living would be cheaper and better with a woman to do the cooking. Even the first month had worked fine. But then he had been switched from night to day shift, the same shift as Bob, and then this terrible trouble had begun. And prayer nor hard work nor anything else made no difference.

"You ready for your back yet?" Bob called.

"Reckon about," Leeman murmured.

Bob came around the curtain and patted him playfully on the buttocks with the back of the brush. "You're losing weight, Lee," he warned. "You don't eat enough."

"I'm afraid Mr Hayes don't like my cooking," Ella warbled.

"Shucks," Leeman protested, "it ain't that. You cook just dandy, Ella. It's just that ol' hammer cramping my stomach so's I don't want to eat."

"I don't like that job of yours one bit," Bob commented seriously. "I talked with Bill Watts today. He knows the whole plant. He says more men has sprung their insides at your job than any other."

"Shucks, I ain't worrying about that," Lee said. "I'll get used to it all right."

"Bend down, you big galoot," Bob ordered affectionately. Bob was two heads shorter than Lee, and bow-legged at that, which cut his reach further. He took pride in Lee's being so big and only eighteen. He felt real warm towards the boy, quite apart from that they were second cousins.

"You stop being such a turkey cock," he went on, adopting his serious tone again. "Bill Watts tells me when that steam hammer comes down it hits your biddy piece of steel with more'n five thousand pounds' worth of pressure. That's a powerful lot! That's too much for one human to take!"

Leeman laughed suddenly, feeling proud of his strength. "I can stand it," he said. "It can't down me. But Lordy, when that old hammer hits my tongs, I feel just like *I'm* going up in the air. The old floor all around just trembles like it's going to crack in two."

Bob soaped the brush and shook his head. "Nossir," he advised. "That machine is too much for one human. You ought to request for another job."

"Oh no," Leeman cried out in a startled tone. "Oh no!"

"Yes, you ought," Bob persisted. "I'm worried about you. That talk with Bill Watts has scared me."

"Why, I couldn't do that," Leeman said. His gaunt, youthful, big-nosed face looked down at Bob with a sudden, almost terrified expression. "Why, if I did that, they might fire me."

"No, they wouldn't."

"Oh, I couldn't risk it, Bob. If they find out you're not satisfied, they don't change you, they just pink-slip you."

"An' what if they do, Lee? Ain't that better than getting your insides sprung?"

"Oh, no," the youth replied. "Why, I couldn't go home now without the money Pa and Ma is expecting. Why, I'd be ashamed."

"Yes, but you watch yourself," Bob advised. He stepped out from behind the curtain. Ella was at the stove fussing over a pot of meat stew. "Well, hello, Ella Wella," he exclaimed in jovial surprise. "I ain't seen you in a coon's age." He pulled the front of her dress away from her body and peered down. "You're looking right smart," he confided.

"Go away," Ella cried, pushing him. "Stay to your own side of the patch."

"A hog roots where he can," Bob explained, rumbling with laughter. He smacked her softly on her fat rump and stood regarding her proudly as she fussed over the meat stew.

Leeman listened to their intimacy with a feeling of growing despair. It was the end of the second week now, and it was getting harder to bear, not easier. It was only November – there was one week more in this month. Then there was December and all of January. How could he last till April? He didn't know. He just didn't. For the hundredth time he agonized over the problem of taking a room by himself. But how could he do that without hurting Bob's feelings? Bob counted on him to pay part of the rent.

Everybody from down home doubled up when they came to work in the auto factories – that was the way you made it worthwhile. The Ainslees from Fulter's Run were up here just this month with six in two rooms. And worse than hurting Bob's feelings, if he went off by himself, Bob would say he could go eat by himself too. That would mean double for room and more than double for food. Ella wasn't so smart as he might want his own wife to be, but there was no mistaking she could cook better than any Greek Coffee Pot. And there'd be no hot water ready neither when he came home just aching to bath himself. Or a cheery word, or someone to talk to after the long day. Why, if he did something foolish like leaving them, come lay-off time in the spring he'd go home with a third less money saved up than otherwise. How could he do that?... But Gosh Almighty, he groaned to himself, how could he bear up night after night, week after week, under all this turtle-doving?

"You dressed yet, Mr Hayes?" Ella called.

"About."

"Supper's on."

Leeman pulled back the curtain and dragged his cot closer to the table. With two beds and a stove and a bureau there wasn't room for more than one chair. Ella sat on a box, and he always used his cot.

Bob was spooning up his stew already, fast as he could. Leeman could tell from the noise he made that it must be good: when Bob enjoyed his food, he was like a young hog sucking in his mash. As Leeman took the first mouthful, he prayed that it wouldn't be like always, with the filled-up sense as soon as he had just begun and the knotty cramp in his stomach. But it was. He downed part of it slowly, with effort – then he stopped. He knew without looking up that Ella and Bob had stopped too, that they were watching him, but he just couldn't go on. "I'm sorry, Ella," he said finally, "I just don't know what's the matter with me these days."

Bob shook his head. Ella sat silent – the plump cheek on the left side of her face was throbbing with suppressed emotion.

Whenever life became too difficult for Ella, her left cheek commenced this throbbing: the surface flesh visibly moved – a mechanical ripple extended up the full length of her stubby nose. Leeman saw it now – it made him feel awful. He knew it was his fault for treating her meat stew so bad. Finally Bob took up his spoon again, but silently, filling his mouth automatically, without any of his former relish. Seeing this made Leeman feel even worse – and mad, too. He wished somebody would say something, but nobody did. He fixed his glance upon the sharp peach stone of Bob's Adam's apple as it bounced and jiggled and quivered unpredictably in his thin, reddish neck. He knew he was looking at the peach stone so that he shouldn't have to face Bob's eyes.

"Why, fire and damnation," Bob burst out suddenly, "there's no call for *you* to feel bad, boy. Why, all *you* have to feel bad about is that old steam hammer making it so hard for you to eat."

Bob's sympathy confused Leeman. He had almost rather Bob had burst out swearing a blue streak or something, and then they could have had mean words with each other. This way, all he could do was feel mad at himself, because all day in the foundry he had been fixing in his mind how he was beginning to hate Bob, and now he was bound to feel grateful – it left him all fuzzled up. "I reckon I'll go out and walk a piece," he said.

"Lordy God," Bob said, pausing with his spoon in mid-air, "what do you want to walk for every night?"

"Oh…" Leeman answered nervously, "I just like to walk."

"Where do you walk to?"

"Just walk. I like to look at the city."

"I declare," Bob expounded, turning to Ella as though Leeman weren't there, "this cousin of mine has sure got queer since he came north. Just like a jack-in-the-box. Up and out. Never stop. Don't even wait to pick his teeth."

"Now, I'll tell you what, Mr Hayes," Ella announced in a tone of maternal firmness, "you just stay home tonight, and we three will play us a game of cards."

"Oh, no," Leeman replied instantly, seized by terror.

"Why not, Lee?" Bob asked.

"Oh, no!" Leeman jumped to his feet. The one thing he didn't want was to stay around now so that all three of them would go to bed at the same time. This way they might be asleep when he came home. "I just got a big *need* to go out," he said, desperate for an explanation.

"Oh!" Bob paused suddenly, significantly, looking up at Leeman with his baldish, egg-shaped head cocked to one side. "Why, sure, boy – why, sure," he agreed, with understanding coming into his voice. "Well, I declare, of course," he added heartily. He gave a merry, confidential little chuckle and leant over to pinch Ella softly on the breast. "Let him go, Ella, let him go – you mustn't stop him now."

"Lord God strike me dead," Ella pronounced, "I don't know what in sin you're talking about."

"That's right, Ella," Bob responded, roaring with laughter, "some calls it sin and some don't care."

Ella blushed. "I declare," she said hastily, "I do think you're getting soft in the head. Have a nice *walk*, Mr Hayes."

"That's right, Lee, have a nice *walk*," Bob echoed, laughing. "Say," he leant forward confidentially, "watch your money now, boy."

Leeman nodded. He was delighted that Bob had gone off this way. It would give him a good excuse in the future. It made him feel real elegant, too, like one big-time man talking to another.

"Say, Lee…" – Bob swung one bony knee over the other in an excess of excited interest – "does it cost much up here?"

"I declare, I don't know what you're talking about," Ella said.

Leeman found the question pleasing, but highly embarrassing. He wished Bob wouldn't ask such things before Ella. "Two dollars," he said with a slight flush, thinking back to what a straw boss* had remarked one day. "Two dollars and up," he added, recalling the exact phrase.

Bob's little blue eyes popped. "Two dollars?"

Leeman nodded knowingly. "An' up! It shore God costs more'n down home," he stated, with the flush rising higher in his thin cheeks.

Bob stroked his moustache in bewilderment. "Two dollars and up," he repeated. "Cracky, Lee..." – he stiffened, interrupting himself – "you ain't spending two dollars *every* night you go out, are you?"

"Shucks no," Leeman said hastily. "I ain't that crazy. I just roam around, Bob."

"Oh! Roam around, eh? See what you can find, eh?"

"Uh-huh!"

"I declare," Ella broke in, "I just don't know—"

"Now, hush you up, Ella," Bob ordered severely, "you do too know what we been talking about. Anybody'd think you and me were on natural together the way you talk. You know what a grown man does with his evenings when he can – or what he wants to do if he can't. Now, hush up!"

Ella blushed violently. The flesh of her left cheek commenced to throb, and a nervous ripple travelled the length of her nose. "Well, have a nice *walk*, Mr Hayes," she murmured stubbornly.

Bob jumped to his feet in a rage. He took a few steps over to the window, swung around, strode back. Then he pointed a forefinger at Ella and shook it violently. "Ella, goddamn it, will you stop calling him 'Mr Hayes', before I lose my temper? Ain't you known Lee from down home? Ain't you been living together with him for almost two months now? You've heard him snore, you know what he smells like – you damned near know what he looks like from root to hair. Are you goin' t'stop acting like a minister's wife, or am I goin' t'bash you in the head?"

Ella howled as though she had already been bashed. Her body shook with the intensity of her resentment, and the tears poured from her eyes like water from a high-pressure tap. Leeman decided to "git" – he had caused enough trouble already. He bolted for the door just as Ella, without warning, leapt to her feet. They collided. His clumsy elbow resounded off the top of her head like a piece of wood banged on rubber. The next thing he knew, Bob was rocking around the room on his bowed legs, laughing fit to choke, and Ella was throwing herself around on the floor, beating her fists and screaming. Leeman ran out of the room, and four mules and a horse pulling the other way couldn't have been enough to hold him. He heard Bob's guffaws and Ella's yowling all the way down the flight of stairs, and it wasn't until he was out on the street that he stopped to put on his lumberjacket. "Lordy God," he murmured aloud. "Lordy God..." He started to walk.

II

At about eight thirty Leeman found himself in front of a store, far down on Michigan, that he had often noticed on his way to work. Unconsciously, he had been tracing the trolley route he took each morning to the plant. He had been spending the evening as he spent all his evenings: whenever he came to a store, no matter how shabby, he paused in front of it to gaze slowly, to wonder, to possess. A whole street lined with shops was a thing of delight, and sometimes he would try to calculate beforehand how long he might dawdle on the one block, finding reward if he could stay longer than he had estimated, taking extreme pleasure in competing with himself. As usual, too, his heart would leap each time some unattached girl approached him on the street. When that happened, he would straighten up to his full height, thrusting his hands with nervous awkwardness into the pockets of his lumberjacket, and look down boldly over his big nose into the face of the girl, hoping that she would be transfixed by his glance, hoping that the next moment, by some magic alchemy, might find them amorously locked in each other's embrace. And when the girl passed without pausing, without smiling, without winking, he'd know that she was a nice girl and not anyone to be picked up just like that. And then, especially if she was in the smallest degree attractive, he would dream sweetly about her for a few minutes, thinking how if she was his girl they would walk together arm in arm, thinking how he would tell her the whole story of what happened at the plant – how the boss picked him out from thousands of others, how a thousand times a day he took all that steam-hammer pressure without blinking an eyelash – and then he would look down at her, and her sweet face, her sweet eyes, would be glowing with lover's pride... And his heart would be humming too... But then the dream would pass: only the shabby street would be left, a lamp-post for company, the smell of coal gas so different from the smell of a brown meadow in fall, or the sweet smell that comes squirting from the udder of a cow – then his heart would ache, his hands would slip from his pockets to hang loosely by his side, then he would groan aloud as he thought of Bob in his long underwear, with Ella sitting plump and rosy, bouncy and willing, like a proper wife on his lap...

As Leeman peered into the store window, his tired senses stirred with interest and curiosity. He had paused before many store windows this night, and was surfeited with all he had seen – and left behind. But this was different: it was something he had never seen before. The display was meagre: a phrenologist's head,* a bloody-looking affair with naked blue veins squirming like snakes over the skull and a small white sign with gilt letters that said "I TELL FORTUNES!" Beyond the raised level, where the store itself began, there was an armchair that was turned towards the street – a massive, ancient hulk with the seams split and the white batting squeezing out. But beyond the chair, shutting off the recesses of the store from his greedy gaze, there were some colourless, grimy curtains – and these, in spite of their squalor, suggested with thrilling suddenness all of the mystery and intrigue that he associated with witchcraft and things occult. He pressed closer to the window, trying to discover some rent in the curtains through which he could see. His memory leapt back vividly to the time, as a boy, when he ran for the croup poultice to Black-Sally-Gone-to-Hell in her witch's hovel on Stony Hill. Most people didn't believe in witches – and neither, really, did he. But you couldn't help having some thoughts when you saw your grandmother carefully sweep up her pared nails and throw them into the fire, or when… Without warning, with startling, dramatic suddenness, the dark curtains in the store parted! Before Leeman could gather his senses, a Gypsy woman strode from the hidden recess, and in an instant was seated in the chair, directly in front of him, looking up into his eyes with a fixed, challenging stare. For a second they gazed at each other. Leeman had never seen a Gypsy before, and the sight of her electrified him. He stared back with unabashed curiosity while the thrilling thought rushed through his mind that, sure to God, he was the only man in all of Tennessee, or Sweet Grass county anyway, who had ever seen a real, live Gypsy face to face. Her clothes fascinated him. He had never seen colours like that, or a woman who wore bangles and bracelets all along her arm, from her wrist to her elbow, like a dancer, or a vampire, or something strange in a book. Almost instantly, however, curiosity was submerged by burning embarrassment. He felt as though he had been caught snooping outside the window of a private home. He turned, crimson-faced, to escape. Something made him pause, he didn't know what – a gesture, perhaps, that the woman seemed to make at the moment he turned his head – but the urge to look once more was irresistible… His mouth gaped open in astonishment: the woman seemed to be beckoning to him. He watched her, gazing directly at him, toss her head towards the inner room. Her full lips were clearly framing the words "come in!" Stupidly he gawked at her. Again she gestured. In disbelief, Leeman turned around to see if there was anyone behind him. No, there was no one. He turned back again, this time to discover, with a sense of shock, that the Gypsy was laughing at him. It made him angry. Then subtly, swiftly, his feelings began to change. He felt his anger go… and then the sense of mystery… And now suddenly, through laughter, she was becoming a woman for him – foreign-looking, unfamiliarly swarthy – but female-fleshed, darkly handsome, with intense black eyes that were like magnets to his latent desire. Still once again she gestured with her head, this time with lowered eyelids and a soft, whorish movement of her lips that said "Come in – why don't you come in?" Leeman felt himself beginning to tremble. He wanted to go in, but he was deeply uneasy, filled with vague fears and uncertainty. Was this something she always did? Was the fortune-telling a blind or... How did he know what lay behind the curtains – a knife, a drug? And the woman herself was strange... unfamiliar to the senses... but a woman – and handsome, yes, like a glistening ripe olive.

As if she understood his conflict, the Gypsy laughed again, showing white teeth, her eyes unveiling to full brilliance... Leeman burst through the door.

There was a moment of pause. The Gypsy had risen to meet him, but stepped back, startled by the violence of his entrance. They stood in silence, each with his gaze riveted upon the face of the other. Now that he was so close to her, Leeman felt nervous, and vaguely but distressingly anxious. It was all so unusual. How should he act? Should he put his arms around her? He couldn't: they were in full view of the street. Maybe he had better wait for her to make the first move? But...

"I tell you fortune," the Gypsy said, stepping up close to him. Her manner gave the lie to her words. Her full lips were moistly parted as she smiled up at him, her eyes were bold and cunning at the same time, alive with sexual promise. She seemed older when he saw her up close – in her thirties at least – but he didn't care about that. He could guess the fine mould of her body in spite of her shapeless skirts, and Bob had told him never to worry about age. It wasn't that which counted, Bob said. He repeated that to himself now. And a woman like this would be more willing than an average woman. She would have Eastern passion in her blood. She wouldn't care that he was inexperienced, or laugh at him.

"I tell you fortune, come in," the Gypsy repeated, making the whorish movement of her lips again. She spread the curtains and waited for him. She knew he would follow.

Leeman peered over her shoulder cautiously. She waited, smiling. He stepped in, and she let the curtains drop softly behind him. He glanced around quickly. The room was strangely bare, illumined by two dismal naked bulbs that hung from the ceiling. At the far end there was a door, and, close by them, along the wall, there was an overstuffed divan in the same rotting condition as the chair outside. There were no fine rugs, there were no soft cushions in blue and red. It was just a big, bare, dirty room. Even the smell seemed ordinary – a musty, bad smell. Leeman felt disappointed.

"Give me you hand," the Gypsy said softly. He looked at her, wondering and startled. Why did she want that? He hadn't come in there to get his fortune told.

"I make you good wish," the Gypsy said. She reached down and took his limp, red-knuckled hand in her dark, soft, delicate one.

"I... I don't want my fortune," Leeman stuttered. He was burning with embarrassment.

The Gypsy smiled up at him slowly. Her thumb was gently caressing the palm of his hand. "You think I not know what you want?" Her eyes were cunning, bold. They made him tremble. "You wait, I give you what you want."

Leeman remained passive, drunk, completely obedient. "Put odder hand on you heart," she ordered.

He did so, slowly. His eyes were on her bosom. Her bodice swung low at the centre, revealing smooth brown skin and, faintly, the fluent line of her breasts.

"You fadder, you modder, you sister," the Gypsy recited. "I make good wish for them." She repeated the words, "You fadder, you modder, you sister." Then "Whooo..." she blew warmly on the palm of his hand. "Whoo."

Leeman bubbled with nervous laughter. "Whoo," he echoed. He blew down the front of her dress. The Gypsy twisted her body slightly and smiled at him. He tried to take hold of her, but she slipped away. "Oh, please," he said, "come on, please."

"You give me three dollar?" the Gypsy asked in a sudden, businesslike tone.

Leeman was aghast. "No," he said, "no."

"Oh," she observed scornfully, "you no want I give you big happiness?"

"Two."

"You come to me for something, no? You want I give you what you like?"

"But I can't spend three dollars," the youth cried unhappily. "I got to save my money. I got to take it home."

The Gypsy tossed her head scornfully.

"Here!" He offered two single bills. She saw his wallet. She saw his trembling hand. "No," she said.

Leeman groaned. He was agonized by the decision he had to make. The woman placed her hand on his arm in a sudden change of manner. "I know what young feller want," she whispered. "I do big good for you." He yielded silently, taking out his wallet again with such clumsy haste that he almost dropped it. But, as he offered her the money, she shook her head. "You put here," she whispered. She pointed to her bosom. "Bring good luck for you." Leeman felt the blood rush to his head. He moved closer to her. They were almost touching. He was frightened, yet something in his breast made him want to laugh out joyously. But the moment the bills reposed safe in her bodice, her hand flashed up and caught his, thrusting it away.

"Oh, please," the youth cried out in agony. "Oh, please."

"Now I give you what you want," she said. She grasped his hand and led him to the grimy, rotting divan. "Sit down," she ordered. He obeyed her. She sat next to him and he tried to embrace her. She evaded him. "Wait," she said. "I know what you want."

"Lordy God, what's the matter?" Leeman groaned. He felt dizzy – his stomach was twisted into a knot.

"Put you hand on you heart," the Gypsy said. "You make big wish now!"

"Goddamn it, I don't want to wish," Leeman exploded. "You know what I want."

"You don't want make wish?" the Gypsy enquired in a shocked manner. "You no want I wish for you nice girl – she make you happy, she give you big love?"

"Oh, please," Leeman pleaded.

"You pay me for wish you good girl," the Gypsy asked, "no?"

"No, what are you talking about?" Leeman cried.

"What *you* talk?" the Gypsy said. "I make you good wish. You get fine girl now."

"What?" he stammered. "What?"

"Sure, you have good luck now. Maybe you girl stand outside, right now!"

Something cold, like a pinpoint of ice, seemed suddenly to congeal in Leeman's heart. For a moment he couldn't breathe. Then he saw the cunning in her eyes, and he knew what she had done to him. "You can't do that," he said. His throat was so constricted that he could hardly speak.

"What you talk?" the Gypsy enquired airily.

"You got to give me my money back," Leeman whispered hoarsely. Instantly the Gypsy leapt to her feet, chattering in her foreign tongue. Leeman rose slowly – he followed her. "I got to have my money," he said.

"You don't worry," the Gypsy told him as she backed away. "You get fine girl quick, tomorrow maybe. She have black hair."

Leeman leapt at her. She turned to flee, but he caught her by both arms. She cried out at the pain from his hands. "Give me my money before I tear the goddamn dress off you," he shouted.

"Oh, I shamed for you," the Gypsy cried severely. "I give you better wish than just three dollar. How you think I make my living – I give everybody his money back?"

Leeman seized her dress at the neckline. He gave one violent, raging jerk and ripped the garment down to the waist. She was too stupefied to do more than gape at him. Her black eyes bulged from fear and shock. He stood glaring at her. She was naked. Then suddenly she burst out with a violent scream. He bent down swiftly and snatched the crumpled wad of bills on the floor. Then he ran from the room.

III

Leeman stood on a street corner trembling, sweaty, consumed with bitterness and rage. He cursed the Gypsy, he cursed himself for almost being mulcted out of so much money, for not hiring a separate room, for coming up to the factories at all. He raised his hand to his burning head and thought of Bob and Ella. He knew now that he hated them. He hated them! If he could see Bob now, he would kill him – he would lift him up and bash his head against the sidewalk.

He heard a clock strike. He tried to count the hours, but he was too confused. He knew it must be late. He knew he should go home, or else, tomorrow, he would be half dead. He wouldn't be able to even lift the tongs. When the hammer came down, he wouldn't be able to tighten up the way you had to. And the pounding would hit him in the belly, and maybe his insides would be sprung. Or the boss would come up and tap him on the shoulder, saying "go home". The boss would say, "Beat it, you're through." He cursed the drop forge. He raised his voice and cursed it out loud. Why did he have to work at a drop forge? Why did he have to live in one room? He suddenly crumpled to his knees. Sobbing, in a voice full of piety and longing, he prayed to God to make things different for him, to give his father some money, to let him go home, to give him a girl who would walk down the street on his arm. He laid his burning forehead down on the damp stone of the sidewalk. The night was soft, like a night in spring. There was a wind blowing in from the lake, like the wind that sometimes stirred through the valley where his home was, rustling the tassels on the shocked corn, making the young hogs raise their snouts to the sky and grunt quietly in surprised delight. But Leeman didn't feel it. He could feel only his pounding heart, like the pound-pound of the terrible drop forge. He rubbed his forehead on the damp stone and listened to it, the steam hammer beating at him, beating monotonously, terribly, like a pulse in his heart. And then, weeping, he stumbled forward on his way home.

The Way Things Are*

I

The mid-summer Louisiana sun was a red blotch in the hazy sky. To the three men in the open touring car it felt like a blowtorch suspended a foot above them. Two of the men lay sprawled out on the back seat with their coats off, with soggy handkerchiefs wrapped about their necks and with their mouths sagging open, as though they were a pair of strangled fish. The third man sat hunched over the wheel with a bandanna around his forehead to keep the salt sweat out of his eyes. The three men were a sheriff and his two deputies. They were out to bring back a prisoner – at least, that was what they supposed. They had really taken the twenty-six-mile drive over the sandy road because Avery Smallwood had put in a telephone call. He had said "Please bring two deputies, Mr Tuckahue", and Mr Tuckahue had brought the two deputies. Beyond that, they didn't know why they had come.

Now, as they passed beyond the broad, flat fields knee-high with cotton plants as far back as the eye could see, and passed beyond the last cluster of tumbledown shacks where the Negro sharecroppers lived, they came abruptly to the magnificent grounds which surrounded the Smallwood home.

After the long drive over the sun-baked sand, the house and the green grass and the tall shade trees that lined the road – cypress and sycamore trees and huge weeping willows with foliage like thick seaweed – all this seemed to the wilted men in the touring car like an oasis in the midst of a suffocating desert. The thin, freckled, studious-looking youth with the wire spectacles and the red bandanna, who was the driver, took a deep breath of the moist air, which had suddenly become fresh and sweet. The bull-necked young deputy in the rear seat sat up with a grunt and blinked his jet-black, handsome eyes like a baby awakening from sleep. His boyish, chubby, thick-witted face had a look of simple astonishment on it, as though never before had he encountered so pleasant a place. And the third man in the car, Sheriff Tuckahue, unhitched his immense angular body from the crooked position into which it had slumped and slowly raised his head from his chest, looking like some strange, spiny underwater animal rising from the sea.

The car was still a little distance from the concrete drive that curved up to the Smallwood home. Sheriff Tuckahue leant forward and jabbed the young driver in the shoulder with a bony forefinger. "Pull up a minute, Charlie," he ordered.

The car stopped under the shade of one of the overhanging willows. "We'll set heah a minute," the sheriff said. He had a dry, hoarse whiskey voice and a curious way of talking, with his thin lips pressed together and with the words sort of escaping from the side of his mouth: he spoke as though he begrudged the effort.

Harrison Towne, the barrel-bodied, bull-necked deputy, was twenty-eight years old and looked like an overgrown high-school football player. Now he laboriously mopped his porky, sweating face and swore softly with the exaggerated emphasis that boys use when they squat around in a circle smoking and spitting and magnifying their toughness in each other's eyes. "Jesus!" he exclaimed. "Jeeee–zus! Am Ah broiled? Do Ah feel baked? Sam," he observed to the sheriff, "you could fry an aig on me without crackin' the shell. Ah'm the clostest thing to a boiled porgy you evah seen." He turned around and slammed Charlie Rentle, the driver, on the shoulder with a beefy paw. "How are *you*, Charlie Wally?"

"Cut it out," Rentle said in a whining voice. "It's hot enough as it is."

"Charlie Wally's hot," Harrison said. "Charlie Wally's all bothered." He ruffled Rentle's thin, blond hair – his stubby forefingers dug hard into the youth's scalp.

"For Chrissakes, cut it out," Rentle said irritatedly. He jerked his head away.

Towne laughed. "Ah'm givin' you a free massage, Charlie. You don't want *all* that hair t'fall out?" He continued to laugh with exaggerated amusement. His laughter had a kind of snicker to it, a sort of loose, lewd quality, as though anything he found amusing possessed some secret smutty overtone. He glanced back at the sheriff to observe whether or not the clowning was appreciated. Sheriff Tuckahue was busy. He was uncorking his morning measure of rye whiskey.

During the ten years that Sam Tuckahue had remained Sheriff of Clarabell County, after giving up cotton-raising for the steady income of a government office, his monthly salary had gone one half in room and board to his widowed sister and one half to rye whiskey. No one had ever seen him when he didn't have any liquor inside of him, and no one had ever seen him completely drunk. He seemed to stay at a precise, well-calculated point of saturation.

Now, with a practised movement of his tongue, the sheriff dug a cud of tobacco from the pocket of his jaw and spat it accurately into the ditch. When about a quarter of the pint of whiskey had poured down his throat like sparkling water, he raised the bottle slowly from his lips and uttered a long, drawn out "Aaaaaaaah" of satisfaction. His upper lip puckered like the lip of a whinnying horse, and for a moment his yellow, snaggy teeth were visible. Then he clamped his lips together again.

The sheriff was a tall man, considerably over six feet, with arms and legs like hickory fence rails. He was forty-five years old, but looked fifty. Low down on his flat body he carried a round little pot belly, like a small beer keg. It looked incongruous in a man so devoid of flesh, but whenever Tuckahue referred to it, his horse face would wrinkle with pleasure, and he would explain carefully that there was six thousand dollars of good rye whiskey in that cooking kettle, if there was a single penny – and then he would thump on it.

Now, when he had corked the bottle, the sheriff bit off a chew of apple plug* and leant forward closer to the boy in the driver's seat. "Charlie," he said gently and amiably, through tight lips, "Charlie, you're the gawddamdest driver Ah evah seen. You make a car bounce like a mule with a bellyache."

"You told me to speed it up, didn't you?" Charlie argued with weary complaint in his voice. Whenever Tuckahue began this way, Charlie knew how it would continue.

"But Ah didn't tell you to choose out every hole in the road," the sheriff replied, warming up to the subject. "Gawddamn you, boy, you'd shake the best parts off a brass monkey."

"Ah'm sorry, Uncle Sam," Charlie apologized. He was new on this job, and anxious to avoid trouble.

"Uncle? Jesus Christ, Uncle?" Tuckahue paused to draw a deep, wheezing, astonished breath. "Ain't Ah told you nevah t'call me 'uncle'? What you tryin' t'do, embarrass me before mah chief deppity? Mr Rentle," he continued in an attitude of cold, pleasurable appraisal, "Ah'll tell you what you are: you're a sway-backed, castrated female bookkeeper. Mah good sister (may she die from a cancer in her private parts...)" – Deputy Towne haw-hawed – "mah good sister must have had you all by herself. Or else, by Gawd, you couldna turned out like you did." Tuckahue slammed his palm down on the upholstery. "That's it, by Gawd. An' if you'd take your pants off, we'd find out Ah'm dead right."

"How about it?" Deputy Towne suggested, in a rapture at the idea.

"Ah nevah thought," the sheriff reflected, "Ah nevah thought Ah'd have a female bookkeeper for one of mah paid deppities. If it wasn't for the duty Ah owe to mah kin..." He paused, unable to go on, gesturing melodramatically to indicate his misfortune.

"Ah reckon we better be goin' in to Mr Smallwood," Rentle said wearily. "He'll git fussed up if we're late."

The sheriff's face turned sour. "Let him *git*," he said. His upper lip puckered. "*Mr* Smallwood, Mr Avery J. Smallwood, prize bastard of the well-known Smallwoods." He spat contemptuously into the ditch.

"Hell, let's stay here," offered Harrison Towne. "Let's stay right here till next winter. Hell, *it's hot*."

"Sure is hot," Rentle murmured. "We don't git rain pretty soon, cotton'll burn right off the ground."

"Hot! You're hot, eh?" the sheriff said. "Listen to him," he smirked aloud to the empty air, "he's hot!... Mr Rentle, Ah reckon Ah'm just gonna fire you. Ah'm gonna fire you an' let you get a niggah job choppin' cotton all day. That'll learn you what's hot, Mr Rentle."

There was a brief pause, during which Rentle's peaked face became spotty with anger. Suddenly, as though arriving at a decision, he sat erect. He removed his wire spectacles. "Uncle Sam, Ah'm tired of your talk," he said firmly. "You ain't gonna fire me. No, you won't!" He took a deep breath. His pale lids were winking against the sun. "All this hogwash about helpin' your kin. Ah been talkin' to mah maw... Ah found out about that dicker* you made." His voice brimmed over with scorn. "You been gettin' free board since you took me on. An' that's the only reason you took me. You just favour that extra barrel of wild cat* each month... Well, Ah don't like you either, Uncle Sam," he said with sudden relish. "Soon as Ah get a job in mah own line, Ah'm gonna quit you. An' Ah reckon when Ah do, mah uncle Sam'll come crawlin' on his knees beggin' me t'stay – cos he wants his extra whiskey. But Ah reckon Ah won't stay." Rentle's thin lips curved in a pleased smile. "Nooo! Ah reckon Ah'll just tell you to go to hell. So you just stop your gassin', Uncle Sam, cos it don't make no difference..." This said, Rentle became occupied in polishing his spectacles.

Sheriff Tuckahue stared at the youth. For a moment his leathery horse face was expressionless. Then, slowly, it commenced to wrinkle with amusement. The small sharp eyes, which were green and set far back in their bony sockets, glittered like bright little stones. The upper lip puckered, showing the yellow teeth. "That's right, Charlie," Tuckahue agreed softly in a curious, pleasurable tone of assent, "it *don't* make no difference." His eyes sparkled. "An' Ah'll tell you somethin' else: when the time comes, Charlie,

Ah'm *gonna* crawl to you. Yessir! You know why?" He burst out into a short, fierce cry of pleasure and malice. "Cos Ah'm a smart man! When there's somethin' Ah want, Ah'll do anythin' t'get it – Ah'll even *crawl* for it. Yessir!" His voice boomed out: "Money talks, Charlie, money talks! An' a smart man crawls before them that's got it!" The sheriff reached for his whiskey bottle. He drank greedily. After a moment, he clamped his lips together in a tight, malicious smile. "Ah've kept mah job by givin' money to the right places. Yessir! An' Ah've used mah job t'*take* money from the right places. Yessir! Ah've licked the right boots an' had mah boots licked by them who depends on me. *Yessir!* Ain't that right, Mr Towne?"

"Sure is," Towne said laughing.

"You lick mah boots whenever Ah snap mah little finger – don't you, Mr Towne?"

"Sure do," the deputy laughed.

"An' that's the way it's gotta be," the sheriff concluded proudly. "That's the way of things! But it takes a smart man to know it. Ah know it!" he said, looking at the others in triumph. "Ah know it!" He gulped down another two fingers of whiskey. "Look at that," he ordered, pointing to the lawn in front of the Smallwood home, where half a dozen fat sheep were stepping slowly in the shade. "That's what the Smallwoods can do! The Smallwoods can keep sheep just to crop their gawddamn lawns. But we can't do that," he demonstrated in venomous triumph, "we can't do that!" He tilted his bottle and then started speaking while the liquor still gurgled down his throat. "'Bring two deppities, Mr Tuckahue!' he says to me. 'What's the mattah, Mr Smallwood?' Ah asks. 'About twelve o'clock,' he answers me." Tuckahue glared at his two deputies. "What kind of an answer is that?"

The two deputies didn't reply.

"So Ah goes out on a Sunday – on a Sunday, mind you – an' Ah drives all the way down heah with mah nephew Charlie Bonehead at the wheel, an' Mr Smallwood'll say to me, 'Mr Tuckahue,' he'll say, 'Ah want you to scratch mah back!' An' what'll Ah do?" The sheriff paused with his little eyes gleaming like bright stones. "Why, Ah'll scratch his back," he said with bitter relish. "Ah'll scratch any gawddamn part of him he wants," he finished off in triumph. "Because he's Mr Avery J. Smallwood, an' he owns ten thousand acres an' a thousand niggahs, an' Ah'll do just what he says like Ah was a niggah mahself – because mah good job depends on it. *Yessir!*" Tuckahue slammed his palm down with a smart crack on his bony knee. "Ah'll walk me up to Mr Smallwood an' Ah'll knuckle me down an' scrape mah belly, an' Mr Smallwood'll say: '*There's* a good man. He knows *his place* all right. Ah sure need him in that *sheriff*'s job!'" Tuckahue snorted happily. He pounded the upholstery. "By Gawd if Ah won't scrape me down just like a niggah sharecropper."

The sheriff jumped to his feet. He put on his long, black preacher's coat. "C'mon, Charlie," he bellowed, "bounce this car. Ah got a need t'do me some scrapin'!"

II

The Smallwood home was modern in style and elegantly handsome in its setting of green shrubs, leafy trees and delicately designed flowerbeds. It was the only house of its kind in a district where the majority of planters had not even been able to touch paint to their old homes for five years past, let alone build new ones. As such, it was both a showplace and a source of burning envy. By continuing to prosper through the lean years of the cotton market, Avery Smallwood had been almost unique in the owning class of his district. Malice dismissed him as lucky, but there was sound enterprise behind his success. His plantation was unusually large, for one thing; he ginned his own cotton, for another; and, most important, he controlled a weave mill in Baton Rouge which bought the cotton he himself sold. These things had enabled him to push ahead where so many others had gone under.

All of this – the house and the well-kept grounds, the fruit orchard which extended for a mile before the cotton fields began again, the new brick garage with servants' quarters overhead, the grazing meadows, the flowers, the trees – were a very special sight in the surrounding sea of tumbledown shacks and naked cotton fields. No visitor ever left Clarabell County without first driving past the Smallwood plantation.

Now, on this hot Sunday morning, as the open touring car with the three deputies swung up the long driveway, Avery Smallwood turned from his work on the veranda to see who was there. He had been hard at his painting since nine o'clock. When he caught sight of Tuckahue's dark, spiny figure jouncing in the rear seat, a grimace of disgust crossed his face, and he turned back to his canvas. Smallwood didn't like Tuckahue. He never had. With great care he stippled a spot of colour onto his canvas. He stepped away. Then he frowned. It was no good – it was no good at all. He sighed impatiently. Nothing he had done that morning was worth the time he had spent on it. He would have been much better off playing with the children. And now Tuckahue was coming.

Smallwood sighed again. He was a small man, only a little over five feet, with delicate, handsome features and a rather stern cast to his dark face. It was a bitter thing in his life, and it always had been, that he was physically so puny. He had never quite accepted it, as he had never quite accepted other aspects of his life. Unconsciously now, as though he were still a boy ashamed before other boys, the image of Tuckahue loomed up before him – a big, ugly, yellow-toothed ape, ostentatiously bending over, indicating by a sly little smirk that he was only trying to hear a little better... Aaaah, Smallwood thought, life had always been like that. It never seemed to offer a complete, a wholehearted satisfaction: success never came but it carried some gripe of defeat. As a boy there was his size. Now there was his work. And other things.

His work! What was his work? Smallwood asked himself the question now, as he had done many times before. Was his work business or painting? After college he had studied painting in Europe for a few years. He had returned home just before his father's death and taken over the management of the plantation. Taken it over successfully. Improved it, built a cotton gin, bought control in a mill. He was a successful man. He had a pretty wife whom he loved – he had children who were fine, bright, excellent youngsters... Was he happy? No. Had he ever been truly happy, truly satisfied with life? No. Never. And what was it? He didn't know. He never could find the answer. He only knew that something which pleased him on Wednesday would weary him on Friday. At the age of thirty-eight, when he had more responsibilities than he had ever had, and more success, he had gone back to his painting. Three days each week now he hurried home from Baton Rouge to spend all day on the shady veranda with his oils and his canvas. Well, he knew one thing: in those hours spent at painting he was able to forget what some people called "commerce" and what he knew to be a dirty business of "grasp and grab" – he was able to relax sufficiently to go back to that dirty business on the following week. Now, as many times before, Smallwood asked himself why he didn't retire. He smiled faintly to himself by way of answer. He knew why! He was afraid! Who could guarantee that painting wouldn't come to weary him as much as business? And, besides, he was frank enough to admit that he needed the success of his business life, he needed the sense of achievement that success brought him. Well, it was a compromise! His soul, God bless it, seemed to be divided – he might as well divide his life. Nothing was completely satisfactory: a man had to take what he could. If he'd been like other men, he might have turned to travel, or to women, or to drink. How many men he knew were doing that – trying to buy with money the satisfactions they lacked. No, that wasn't his way. There were too many pigs in the world already. He needn't add himself.

But this Bailey business... Smallwood shook his head, in a stir of irritation. Just when he wanted to be by himself, he had to put his mind to a stupid affair that never should have occurred in the first place. But there was Ed Bailey howling in bed over a broken jaw, and the nigrah boy Beecher under lock and key in the cellar.

Well, there was no way out of it – he could see that. But it had to be handled properly. No brutality. There was going to be no nigrah beating or lynch parties for a boy of his.

The touring car with the three deputies in it came to a stop. Smallwood turned his back and pretended to be absorbed in his painting. He pictured Tuckahue standing before him – a big, snaggle-toothed ape with his tongue hanging out and his little pig eyes hunting around for a mouthful of liquor. All right – he could look. He could look till he got blue in the face. A man had the right to expect the hospitality of a drink, but Tuckahue was a goddamned sponge. Give him a taste of some good liquor and he'd stick like a burr till he had sopped it all up. And Smallwood wanted to get back to his painting. If that damn fool Bailey had only kept his hands where they belonged, or if that Beecher boy had only been off somewhere in a card game... Aaaaaah, now the whole plantation would be in a bad humour for weeks, and work would fall off just when the cotton needed most care. The blacks were like that: get them upset over something, and they popped off like a lot of children... Smallwood heard the clump of Tuckahue's brogans as the sheriff mounted the steps. He wished he hadn't come so soon.

But it had to be done. You couldn't overlook it when a nigrah hit a white man.

III

Sheriff Tuckahue left his two deputies sitting in the car and went up to the veranda alone. Smallwood's back was turned to him. The sheriff smirked with contempt as Smallwood delicately applied a pinpoint of colour to the canvas. What a friggin' little rooster this Smallwood was – what a friggin' little ass, with his double heels and his "ain't I la-de-la?" painting... "Good mawnin', Mr Smallwood," Tuckahue said aloud in a practised, hearty voice. "It sure is a pleasure seein' you again."

"Eh?" Smallwood turned around. He affected surprise. "Oh!... Good morning to you. Excuse me, Ah didn't hear your car come in. How are you?" He held out his hand. He gave the sheriff's stringy, sweating paw a short, gingerish shake with his own small hand, and quickly withdrew it again.

"Jim Dandy," the sheriff replied... "Ah see you're doin' your pictures again," he observed, smiling.

"Why, yes!" Smallwood looked up at Tuckahue with a faint malicious curve on his full lips. "How do you like it?"

The sheriff's eyelids flickered. He knew this game. If he didn't step back fast, the little bastard'd have him floundering around like a horse in quicksand.

"Ah'd be grateful t'know what you think," Smallwood said softly. His voice was liquid, easy. There was no suspicion of irony in his polished tone.

Tuckahue studied the canvas. It was a highly impressionist representation of a cow with a young calf suckling at its teat. The sheriff blinked his eyes. He couldn't make head or tail out of the damn thing. Falteringly he turned to Smallwood with a smile that was meant to be ingratiating. "Pshaw, Mr Smallwood, Ah like it fine, but Ah reckon Ah don't know anythin' about sich matters..." "That oughta hold him," he thought. "He don't get no fish bait outa me."

"An' how do you like the colour of the cow, Mr Tuckahue?"

"The... the cow?" Tuckahue stammered.

Smallwood nodded.

Tuckahue studied the painting again. The cow was lemon-green on a blue background. He swore softly to himself. "Fine, Mr Smallwood, looks fine to me."

"Did you evah see a cow like that?" Smallwood enquired softly.

The sheriff cleared his throat several times before speaking. He wished he had a drink. "Reckon Ah didn't, Mr Smallwood. But, shucks, Ah don't know anythin' about pictures," he added hastily. "The bastard," he murmured to himself, "the little bastard."

"No, Ah guess it isn't very real," Smallwood observed, as though it had never occurred to him before. "Do you feel Ah ought to change it?"

"Why, shucks, Mr Smallwood, Ah don't know."

Smallwood looked up at Tuckahue's tight, uncomfortable face. His lips twitched with suppressed amusement. Then abruptly he tired of it. It was like baiting a hulk of wood. "Have a chair, Mr Tuckahue," he said. "We'll get to business."

A slight, uncontrollable sigh of relief issued from the sheriff's lips. He sat down quickly and folded his loose, stringy hands in his lap. He wished for a drink, but he knew it wouldn't do to take his own. He hoped Smallwood would offer him some.

Smallwood picked up his palette and began squeezing little dabs of paint onto the edge. He mixed the paint slowly with a small, fine brush. Finally he spoke: "We had some trouble out heah last night... A nigrah boy slugged Mr Bailey. Broke his jaw."

"You don't mean to tell me?" Tuckahue's voice was startled, but his lips remained tight. He sat up in his chair.

"Mr Bailey's bad off," Smallwood continued in his soft, even, polished tone. "I have a doctor on him. He'll have to chew milk for three months."

"You don't say?... Jiminy," the sheriff reflected, "that musta been a mean niggah. You don't break Ed Bailey's jaw easy. Or did the niggah use a rock?"

Smallwood shook his head. "Nooooo – no mean nigrah at all. An' he didn't use anything, cos Ah saw his hand. George Beecher's his name."

"Don't know him," the sheriff murmured.

"Well..." Smallwood paused for a moment with his dark, handsome head bent over the palette. "Ah reckon he had cause." He sighed wearily. "Mr Bailey got liquored up last night... went after a little yaller girl* ovah by the orchard... she didn't want him – guess she was too young anyway... well... that's how it started..."

Tuckahue sat back in his chair. A sly grin played at the corners of his mouth. He knew Big Ed Bailey – he coveted Bailey's job.

The man who was head riding boss for Avery Smallwood had the best spot in four counties. A thing like this might see Bailey out. "Ah reckon it ain't the first time," Tuckahue said slowly, enjoying himself. "When they start gettin' old as fo'teen, Ed don't like 'em no more." The sly, lewd grin crinkled the corners of his mouth. His little flinty eyes danced. He hooked a thumb under one suspender and looked closely at Smallwood, calculating the effect of his remark. "Nooo," he added as a kind of casual afterthought, "Ah reckon it won't be the last time either. Ed Bailey's just naturally got a taste for pullets."

Smallwood turned his head away. Tuckahue disgusted him. Licking his chops over a business like this. The leering and the nice, sly little pointers... Good God, the realization struck Smallwood suddenly – Tuckahue wanted the job for himself. Well... He smiled inwardly. Before he'd hire a sponge like Tuckahue for his personal manager, he'd give up cotton-growing. But it wasn't so funny. Getting too big for himself, that man... Smallwood squeezed a tube of paint delicately between thumb and forefinger... might be time he was kicked out of the sheriff's office. No... Smallwood checked himself – couldn't say he wasn't a good bloodhound. Well... let him stay there... so long as he kept in his place. He chuckled over the image. A bloodhound was correct. Give Mista Sheriff a pair of flop ears an' he'd look fine for a bloodhound.

Smallwood turned and presented a friendly countenance to the sheriff. His tone was suave: "Ah reckon it's too bad about Bailey. But he's the best manager Ah evah had. Keeps the riding bosses on the job, keeps the nigrahs from lazin', takes care of everything now Ah'm away so much... Ah reckon Ah ought to give him another chance."

Tuckahue licked his lips with the edge of his tongue. He leant forward. "Ah reckon Ah wouldn't be a good friend of yours, Mr Smallwood, if Ah didn't advise you that poor Ed Bailey just can't help himself. He'll promise all right – but you'll just have the same thing all ovah..." Tuckahue waited.

"Well... Ah suppose Ah'll be forced to get rid of him, then," Smallwood admitted regretfully. "But he's an awful efficient man."

Tuckahue ran his tongue around the outside of his lips again. Then he plunged: "Mr Smallwood, Ah don't mind sayin' frankly that Ah'd sure like to be in Ed Bailey's shoes. It'd be a real pleasure to work for you, Mr Smallwood."

"Well!" Smallwood's smile was friendly. "It's good to know that, Mr Tuckahue. Ah'll have to think it ovah."

"That's fine, Mr Smallwood – that's Jim Dandy." Tuckahue's little eyes sparkled. "By Gawd," he said to himself. "By Gawd, by Gawd!"

"Of course," Smallwood remarked with a worried air, "Ah understand you don't work any more unless you have your nephew, Charlie Rentle, on salary too... Ah'm afraid Ah couldn't afford the both of you," he submitted apologetically.

Tuckahue's face flushed a copper red. "Why, no sich thing, Mr Smallwood," he protested. "Wherever did you hear that?"

Smallwood shrugged grievingly.

"Why, no sich thing," Tuckahue repeated. "Ah put that boy on cos he's smart, that's all. Best deppity Ah've got. Just a lot of loose tongues flappin', Mr Smallwood."

Smallwood smiled. "Well, Ah reckon Ah better keep Mr Bailey on for a piece. At least he grows cotton for me. If you was mah manager, mah only crop'd be corn mash!" Smallwood burst into laughter. He found it impossible to contain himself. The sheriff's face was as long as a corn stalk. An incredible ass. Imagine him taking Bailey's job. And thinking he could do it too!

Tuckahue joined in the laughter. He forced a series of weak little chuckles out of the side of his tight mouth and then lapsed into silence. His eyes were brilliant with hatred.

Smallwood got over his amusement. "This is what I want done with the nigrah boy," he said.

Tuckahue listened with his long horse head turned away. He felt choked inside. He wanted to reach out. He wanted Smallwood by the throat for just one little minute. He'd break him in two. He'd break the little bastard in two.

"Ah want some of the starch taken out of Beecher," Smallwood said. "We just can't let him feel he can raise his hand like that and go free as a sparrow. For his own good he's got to be taught."

"It ain't the first niggah Ah've perked up with a little pistol whupping," the sheriff said sullenly. "Ah'll better him ovahnight."

"No you don't!" Smallwood's voice was sharp. "That's just what Ah don't want!"

"Well, say what you want, goddamit," Tuckahue raged to himself. "What the hell am I supposed to do, guess it?..." "You want him on the road gang for a spell?" he asked with terrific restraint.

"Noooo..." Smallwood pursed his lips. "Ah reckon not. Beecher's a good hand. Mah cotton needs a lot of carin' for right now. Sun's makin' the weeds shoot up smart. No-o-o, ah reckon if he's just scared some, it'll do fine. That's why Ah didn't want you down heah alone. It'll put a fear of the law in him to see some deputies."

So that was why! A sheriff and two deputies to come all the way down here to scare a lone niggah. Because Smallwood wanted it that way. Tuckahue squirted tobacco juice angrily over the porch rail.

"Be careful of them flowers, Mr Tuckahue," Smallwood said. "You'll have mah wife on your neck... Tell you what you do," he went on. "You take Beecher an' set him in the worst cell you got. Don't give him no bed to sleep on. Give him a plate of slop once a day that'll turn his stomach. And just forget about him. Ah reckon after he sits hungry and thirsty for a couple days, he'll come back heah and think it's paradise. He'll think twice before he hits a white man again..." Smallwood paused. "You know, Ah don't like to do this," he added earnestly. "But it's sure for the boy's own good. He don't learn now, he'll learn it bitter some other day. That's true, ain't it?"

Tuckahue nodded.

Smallwood took a key from his pocket. "Have one of your men bring him up heah, will you?" he asked. "He's in the cellar – around to the back. Ah want to speak to him first."

Tuckahue went down to the car and gave the key to Deputy Towne. They talked together for a moment. Towne lumbered off behind the house. As Tuckahue returned, he suddenly removed his hat with an exaggerated flourish. A woman stepped out on the veranda. It was Mrs Smallwood. She gave the sheriff a friendly but puzzled little "how do", which instantly enraged him, and he watched her with an acid twist to his mouth as she swung down towards her husband. She was a supple, athletic woman of thirty with a pretty, placid face. She walked firmly with neat haunches swaying and her ripe, prominent breasts jouncing softly beneath her knitted dress. "Hello, Avy," she said as she came up to Smallwood, "what have you done with George?" She bent and kissed him on the cheek. She was several inches taller than he. Her voice was charming, full and vibrant, with a singing lilt to it. It fitted her fine body.

Smallwood touched her shoulder in a light, caressing gesture. "Just get up?"

"Yes." She laughed deliciously. "Aren't I awful? Avy, you're not going to put him on that awful chain gang, are you?" she asked seriously.

Smallwood shook his head. "Mr Tuckahue's just going to let him cool down for a few days."

"Oh!" She swung around to the sheriff. "How do, Mr Tuckahue?" The sheriff bowed a little. It was obvious that she hadn't recognized him, and it burned him up. He had been introduced to her three or four times already.

"Promise me you won't hurt him?"

"Certainly not, ma'm."

"Ah'll nevah forgive you if you do," she said, smiling warmly at him, displaying her even, white little teeth.

"Don't worry, ma'm," Tuckahue assured her. "A niggah boy's like a setter dog. Train him right, an' he'll be all right."

"Ah think it's just awful what happened. Avy promised me he could be mah chauffeur when cotton season was ovah. Ah was countin' on it."

"Well, if he behaves himself," Smallwood said. "We'll see about it."

"Thank you, Avy. He's an awful cute boy. Ah'm countin' on havin' him."

"All right, dear." Smallwood touched her shoulder again in the same light, caressing gesture. The pleasure he took in her was patent on his face. "He's coming out now. Ah need to talk to him."

"Can't Ah stay?" She smiled prettily at him like a child begging for a favour.

"No, dear."

"Oh." She made a little grimace. Then she laughed. "Ah wish Ah was a man. Ah think it's awful bein' a woman – don't you, sheriff?"

Tuckahue grunted. He tried hard to find something gallant to say, but the words stuck in his throat. He grunted again.

Mrs Smallwood looked at the sheriff with veiled amusement. She gave a little bird laugh that trilled in her throat. "Now, don't you hurt him," she said. She swung down the porch with her soft, jouncing, beautiful stride.

The men watched her. They were silent for a moment.

She went inside.

IV

George Beecher stretched his cramped body and wondered what time it was. He was hungry, and he had been for several hours. The fine brown dust in the cellar, which had been blowing in from the dry fields all month, was thick in his throat. It ached him to swallow.

He stood up when he heard the heavy door being unbolted. "It's heah," he thought. A slight pain stabbed the swollen knuckles of his right hand. He waited nervously.

"Hey you!" Deputy Towne's voice boomed down into the cellar. "Hey you there – come on up!"

Beecher moved slowly with scraping shoes towards the shaft of light that slanted down the wooden stairway.

"Hey there, niggah – you deaf or you drunk? Come on, up."

"Ah'm comin'," Beecher said.

"You're mighty goddam slow about it."

"It dark in heah, boss."

Beecher reached the stairway and mounted it slowly. "It's heah," he said to himself again.

Deputy Towne stepped back from the doorway as Beecher came up. Then he laughed and dropped his hand from his revolver. "Shucks," he said, "Ah thought you was a man-eatin' tiger. You sure you the boy Ah want?"

"Ah reckon so, Captain."

"Well, come on then – Mr Smallwood wants to see you."

"It's heah," Beecher said to himself once more.

They walked side by side around the house.

"What the hell's the mattah with you, boy?" Towne asked curiously. "You drunk last night?"

"Nossuh, boss."

"You sure had *some* kind of devil in you."

Beecher didn't answer. His feet scraped the gravel. He put his swollen hand carefully into the pocket of his overalls.

"You don't give a damn, do you?" Towne said with amused contempt. "Just a ba–ad niggah, don't care what happens to you?"

Beecher saw Mr Smallwood on the porch talking to Sheriff Tuckahue. He saw the touring car parked on the driveway, with another white deputy in it. He walked forward, and a slow, throbbing flow surged up hot and bitter in his body. Inside him a voice was whispering, speaking to him. It didn't seem like his own voice. It was deep inside, buried deep down. It kept repeating itself like a record on a talking machine, over again, over again: "That's it, white deppity, that's it, that's it…" He felt strange. It was strange to have a voice inside you and you walking meanwhile, listening to it. "That's it, white deppity. Don't care whut happen. Got a belly full of carin'. Can't eat carin' no more. That's it, white deppity."

"Go on up, boy," Towne said. He remained on the gravel driveway.

Beecher mounted the steps. He walked mechanically, a little like a man abstracted. Deep inside him, the steady whisper kept repeating itself. He heard it, strange, like a buzz saw hidden in a wood. Then he saw the white men turn. They were looking at him. His head lifted a little. He didn't know it. He didn't know he had lifted his head. He walked slowly, facing them. "It's heah now…" He said it to himself quietly. "Heah now." His feet were heavy.

V

When Sheriff Tuckahue heard Beecher coming up the steps, he turned to look at him. He was surprised. He had expected a much bigger man. Beecher was middling in height, rather thin. He looked about twenty-two. His face and his naked shoulders and arms were coffee-brown. Tuckahue could see why the Mrs wanted him for a chauffeur. He had a nice, pleasing, smooth-skinned face, not one of those ape-looking fellers. Still, Tuckahue reflected, there was something bad about the boy's eye. By God, now if it didn't look like Beecher had a "notion" in his eye. Yessir. That was it all right. He could see it now. Well… Tuckahue stroked his nose. He felt a little upset. A nice-looking niggah boy like that with a notion in his eye. And you could always tell it. Dogs and horses were the same. You had to catch 'em quick, or they went bad. Well, he'd catch him. He'd take that notion out of him quicker'n a pig could whistle. It wouldn't be the first time.

"Come on ovah, George," Mr Smallwood said.

Beecher moved closer to the white men. Smallwood sat down and dandled one leg over the arm of his chair. He felt nervous now that the boy was standing in front of him. Punishing Beecher was easy. Too easy! Any brute could do it. What he had to do was make him understand what he ran into when he hit a white man. Like teaching a child what reality was like. It wasn't simple.

Smallwood surveyed the youth quietly for a moment. Then seriously, earnestly, in his liquid, even tone he said, "Well, George, how do you feel about what happened last night?"

Beecher didn't reply. His eyes were cast down a little. He was looking at Smallwood's leg dangling over the edge of the chair. The leg swung back and forth in a little arc, and Beecher followed it with his eye, following the white shoe. His throat felt choked with sand. He wondered if he could ask for some water.

"Did you hear me, George?"

"Yes, boss." The youth answered in a low, hoarse, guttural tone.

Tuckahue nodded a little. He knew the tone too. The tone and the eye went together. You could tell the stubbornness in them, like a hard wall that wouldn't be moved.

"Don't call me 'boss', George," Smallwood said. "Call me 'Mr Smallwood'." He paused for a moment, scrutinizing the boy. "Are you sorry for what you did, George?"

Beecher turned his eyes away from Smallwood's probing glance. He started to talk, stopped. Then he cleared his throat and swallowed. "Whut you *want* me t'do, Mista Smallwood?"

Quietly, inflexibly, Smallwood repeated his question. "Are you sorry for what you did? I want you to answer me, George."

There was a moment of silence. Then Beecher raised his head. Inside him there was pride and fear and fierce determination. "Nossuh! Ah do it again! Niggah get lynched for what Bailey done!"

"Niggah get lynched for what you do," Tuckahue broke in harshly. He sluiced a stream of tobacco over the porch rail. "What's the mattah with you, boy, talkin' like that? What you do an' what a white man does is two hell of a different things. An' don't you evah forget it!"

Beecher turned his head. His face was sullen, smouldering – all twenty-two years of his life were running hot and bitter into this one moment, pumping in his body like a flood tide. Inside him there was a torrent of rebellion, and blind, unheeding determination to speak out. He was engulfed by it. "You want

Ah let him force that little girl?" he cried in a passionate burst of speech. "She no more'n ten year old."

Tuckahue started to answer. Smallwood interrupted him. "Mr Tuckahue," he remarked acidly, "Ah'd like to remind you, for the second time, not to spit juice on mah wife's flowers."

"Excuse me," Tuckahue stammered. "By God," he raged to himself, "Ah'd give a month's liquor to drive a boar pig right through those goddam flowers."

"You shouldn't have hit him," Smallwood said to Beecher.

Beecher took a step forward. His face became distorted with emotion and pleading. "Whut *could* Ah do, boss? Ah *tell* him get away! He don't care *whut* Ah say. Ah gotta do *somep'n*, don't I? When Ah pull him off, he hit me, knock me down. Second time Ah hit him back. Whut you *want* me t'do?"

Smallwood jumped to his feet. "Ah want you to know enough not to hit a white man," he shouted angrily. "You should have run for help, or yelled, or done something like that – but you shouldn't have hit him!"

Beecher stood silent, trembling, face to face with Smallwood. His eyes were brilliant, blazing with emotion. A reckless, overwhelming desire to lash back at this white man was pulsing in his throat: to speak out once, to speak free, to raise his face once from the black earth and look free at a blue sky, to raise his head proud like a free bird flying – it choked him. He couldn't speak.

Abruptly Smallwood sat down. He wiped his brow with a handkerchief. He felt irritated with himself. He had lost his temper, and he shouldn't have. But, God... the boy was incredible. He couldn't see a step beyond his own nose. Where did he think he was – in Mars or in Clarabell County, Louisiana? By God, he didn't have the faintest recognition of a nigrah's position in the South. Talking like he was a nigrah chief back in Africa. Well, he wasn't – he was a black boy in a white man's world. He'd ruin himself for ever that way... And one thing was decided: Beecher would stay at farm work and stay close. A chauffeur's job would ruin him for good.

"George," Smallwood said more quietly, "you just forget about Mr Bailey. He's mah job, not yours. What you've got to see is what *you* did. Nigrahs have been lynched for hitting a white man – and you know it. Ah'll take care of Mr Bailey."

"How?" The word came in a whisper. Beecher's body was bent over, rigid – his burning, bloodshot eyes were fixed on Smallwood's face. He had lost control of himself. His whole being was engulfed by blind outrage at this white man's world. Through this one moment, his whole life was speaking. It was twenty-two years of being a sharecropper... it was the long rising water breaking over the levee... the deep, cumulative torrent hammering at last on the stone wall of flesh and custom, of gun and whip. "How?" he repeated. "How? How? How you take keer of him? You gonna send him to a chain gang? You gonna try him in a niggah court like you stand me up in a white man's?"

Smallwood flushed. His breathing became noisy. Then he gave a curious little laugh, and when his voice came, it was strange, with a kind of breathless restraint. "Bailey's not your business, George! Ah told you that! Ah'll tend to Bailey!"

"Sure you tend to Bailey!!!" Beecher's body snapped erect. The lifetime of scorn and bitterness, of suffering and injustice, poured out of him in a hysterical, reckless outburst. "You talk sweet, but you *do* like all the rest! You gone put me on a chain gang, but *he* ain't gone be there! You *know* he ain't! *You just lyin'!*"

Smallwood struck him in the face. Beecher reeled back a step, and then held his ground. "Go ahead," he cried hysterically, "you cain't hurt me. When Ah bust that white man on the jaw, Ah did the best thing Ah evah did in mah whole life. You cain't hurt me no more. Ah don't care whut you do!"

Smallwood stopped. His clenched hand was raised in the air. His dark face had turned sickly grey. He stood motionless, quivering, almost beyond self-control. But he stood still. He didn't strike again. And then, suddenly, a shiver passed through him, and in a quick, convulsive movement he brought his hand down to his chest. A look of strange, wild shame passed over his face. He was *wrong*! Jesus Christ, he was wrong! He *had* been lying. A nigrah boy had showed him for a liar.

Smallwood dropped into his chair. He clasped his head with both hands. His whole being felt agonized. Good God, how low he'd been to hit that boy. With all his fine words, how much like any other white planter, so quick to raise his hand, so keen for the rope!

He groaned. In that blind moment when Beecher had called him a liar, he had been dominated by an impulse to kill. Now the madness was gone, but in its place there was a sense of physical pain that shot through his body in long, burning streaks. Good God, had all the years of his life been a lie too? It couldn't be! No! *That moment* was a lie. Only that moment. He was different from the other planters. He had shown it. He had proven it.

The pain began to dwindle. He felt a little easier. Yes, he was calmer now... No, no, he thought soberly, it was obviously not true. He'd run this plantation for ten years, and he'd run it without the brutality and the gun rule that other planters used. And he hadn't cheated. God knows he admitted that his nigrahs didn't earn much more than their keep. They were poverty-stricken, and they'd never be anything else. They lived in sties, and they were herded around like cattle. But the price of cotton did that, not him. He had to compete or go out of business. The price of cotton did that. But by God he didn't cheat them the way the others did. He was no white Southern "gentleman" scaring up a lynching for a dull Saturday night. No, and he wasn't going to be!

Smallwood took a deep breath. He looked at Beecher. The boy was standing still, rigid, with his head slightly bowed and with a kind of blank film over his eyes. His mouth was open, and he was drawing great panting breaths.

Smallwood came to a decision: Bailey had to go! Yes, that was the first thing! Christ, how conveniently his mind had skipped over Bailey's part in the whole business. Bailey was useful to him, and so he had been prepared to give him another chance. Would he have given Beecher another chance if Beecher had tried to rape a white girl? Hardly. No, Bailey would go and go today. And it was only too bad he couldn't be put on trial. But there you ran up against the community. No other planter would stand for a white man on trial for the rape of a nigrah girl. It was out of the question. But Bailey would be out of a good job, and that was something. But Beecher? Beecher? It was hard... but Beecher had to learn. The world was what it was – and you couldn't get away from it. A nigrah boy who thought he could strike a white man with impunity would end up one day on the limb of a tree. Better to teach him now as you teach a child that strikes its parent. And you couldn't reason with him any more than you could reason with a child. Punish him, make it as mild as possible, but make him learn the code of the world before he got in the way – and the world ran him down. It was too bad, but it had to be done.

"George," Smallwood said in a low, restrained voice, "George, Ah want to apologize to you!"

Now, after the long, excruciating silence that had gripped the porch, as Sheriff Tuckahue heard what Smallwood finally had to say, he cringed physically under the wave of nausea that struck in his stomach. He felt he would burst with rage. A moment before, when he had been listening to Beecher, he had felt closer to clubbing him down than any other niggah he had ever heard. He had checked himself, he was thankful for that. Beecher was Smallwood's niggah. The quickest way he could find himself out of a sheriff's job, and right back chopping cotton, was to stick a snoot into Smallwood's business. And so he had waited for what Smallwood would do. And now – God Almighty, it was incredible – Avery Smallwood was apologizing to a niggah! Tuckahue straightened up. His thin lips tightened. He waited with cold contempt for what Smallwood would say.

And Beecher had stood waiting also! Inside him that strange voice, the voice that seemed to issue from a throat other than his own, that strange, low whisper out of another world which he had never experienced until that moment when Deputy Towne, the sheriff's deputy, the white man's deputy, had come with the law swinging on his hip to unlock the cellar door and bring him out for punishment, until the moment when the bitter flow of twenty-two years of a Negro sharecropper's life had surged up madly through his worn, nervous body – inside him that voice murmured final and bitter, over and over again: "It's done... heah now... finished now!" And Beecher had waited. His throat felt choked, and he had cried wildly to himself: "Don't care. Don't care. Ah don't care!"

And then Smallwood had sat down. The blow had not come – the whiplash had not ripped his back; the rope had not burnt; Smallwood had sat down. And Beecher had said it. Twenty-two years had burst out. In one great moment he had said it, and a thousand others with him. He had raised his head up proud like a free bird flying. It was all right now. It was all right!

"George," Smallwood said in a low, constrained voice, "Ah want to thank you for all you said. Ah was going to let Mr Bailey off, but Ah won't now. Ah'm gonna discharge him an' Ah thank you for speaking up."

Tuckahue gritted his teeth together. It was the most amazing thing he had ever heard a planter say to a niggah... But it was none of his business. An' he sure wasn't going to get mixed up in it.

"Do you hear me, George?" Smallwood said, with his head bowed and his eyes fixed on the floor. It was hard for him to look at Beecher. He had made up his mind, and he was carrying it through – but it was a hard thing to apologize like that, humble yourself, strip naked before an inferior. Yet, in spite of his shame, Smallwood had a curious feeling of happiness at the same time – a strange, troubled flush of pleasure at what he was doing. He knew it was right... he knew it was something no other planter would do – yet it cut hard... "Ah'm going to fire Mr Bailey, George."

Beecher was silent.

Smallwood raised his head. "But you, George, you can't go on thinking you can hit a white man an' not suffer for it." His voice became louder. There was a note of firm resolve to it. "Ah'm sorry, George, but you've got to learn that. You've got to learn what this world's like we live in. If you don't learn, you'll end up on the limb of a tree. Ah wouldn't want that happening to you."

Smallwood paused. He commenced to swing his leg over the arm of his chair again. "Ah'll see the judge," he continued more softly. "Ah'll tell him what happened. Maybe he'll let you off easy. Ah hope so. But you got to learn what the world's like before you come back heah."

Smallwood fingered his paintbrush. He picked absently at a loose hair. "All right, Mr Tuckahue," he said, and his voice once more found its even, liquid note, "you can take him now."

Sheriff Tuckahue jerked his head. "Get down to the car!" Beecher turned slowly and went off. He walked now as he had before, with his head down, his feet scraping mechanically, his bruised hand in the pocket of his overalls. Deputy Towne met him at the stairs and took him by the arm.

Tuckahue sidled over to Smallwood. "You mean that about the judge?" he asked out of the corner of his mouth.

Smallwood shook his head. "No! You just keep him in jail. Let him stew. If he asks about a trial, you tell him the judge is on vacation. Ah'll keep in touch with you. Ah reckon it'll take longer than Ah expected."

Tuckahue's upper lip puckered. "You give me a free hand with him, it won't take so long," he said.

Smallwood flushed. "Ah don't want you to touch him," he snapped. "You do as Ah say!"

"Certainly, Mr Smallwood, Ah won't lift a finger to him." Tuckahue's contempt was so strong within him that Smallwood sensed it. He sensed it, although the thin lips remained tight and the sharp bony face revealed nothing.

"Eh... just a moment, Mr Tuckahue." Smallwood surveyed him amiably. "About Mr Bailey's job..."

"Yes?" Tuckahue's little eyes lit up instantly.

"Ah'm afraid Ah can't give it to you!"

"Oh!" It was an involuntary grunt.

"No, Ah'm afraid not," Smallwood repeated smoothly. "But if you're tired of being sheriff, Mr Tuckahue, Ah reckon we could fix it. Might be your nephew could take it over."

"Why no, suh, no," Tuckahue stammered.

"Ah thought maybe you were tired of it."

"No sich thing, no sich thing, Mr Smallwood! Why... why... you can ask anybody," Tuckahue stammered. "Don't Ah do mah job? You ain't had any trouble with me, have you?" The big man floundered pitifully.

"Well, fine then," Smallwood said. He held out his hand. "See that you handle Beecher right." He gave Tuckahue's big paw the same stiff, gingerish shake as before and quickly withdrew his hand again.

"Ah won't touch a finger to him," Tuckahue swore fervently. "Ah'll bring him back so you don't even know him."

Smallwood picked up his palette and turned away.

"Well, so long," Tuckahue said heartily. He strode off down the porch.

Smallwood stood before his painting. He was listening to the clump of Tuckahue's brogans. After a moment he heard the car start. The powerful old motor roared and spat, and then the auto swung down the drive with its tyres humming. Smallwood turned around. He couldn't see Beecher. They must have put him on the floor. He sighed. It was a mess. But what else could he do? And if he said so himself, he had acted honestly. How many other white planters would have apologized to a black man?

He sighed again. The world was hard. It ground down on you like a hard wheel. It made you hard too.

VI

The old motor roared, and the tyres sang steady on the hardpan road. No one spoke. Charlie Rentle was busy at the wheel. Harrison Towne sprawled back, chewing the shreds of a dead cigar.

Tuckahue had told Harrison about Smallwood's orders, but the deputy knew better than to start in on Beecher himself. There were a good many ways of taking a notion out of a niggah, and Towne was no fool: his way was always the sheriff's way. The deputy smiled as he thought about it. He hadn't been so bright at school, but politics, by God, was a different matter. He wasn't turnin' out so bad at politics. You just had to know where the fat was – and stay close... He lounged back, waiting for his master's voice.

Sheriff Tuckahue was sitting stiffly erect. One long, hairy hand gripped the side of the car; his jaws were locked together, and a muscle in his cheek was working. He was frightened! He had been shaken all through by Smallwood's threat to his security – "Tired of being sheriff, Mr Tuckahue?..." Good God, he knew Smallwood! He knew the soft-tongued, friendly way with which Smallwood could finish a man – that upper-class, deadly politeness greasing the cut of the axe... "Sorry, Mr T., sorry" – as though it were breaking his goddamned heart. Christ Jesus, it was impossible! He'd been sheriff for ten years, and now this little barn louse would finish him with a word. Where was the fairness to it?... Jesus!... Tuckahue pictured himself chopping cotton again. No, it just wasn't possible. Smallwood *couldn't* play him a card like that. He couldn't be *that* low. Of course he couldn't.

The sheriff relaxed a little. He was beginning to feel easier. The more he thought about it, the more ridiculous it obviously became. It was just Smallwood as usual. Smallwood liked to do that – use his power, scare somebody. But still... still... Rentle! That was it, Rentle! Tuckahue fixed his eyes on the thin back hunched over the wheel. That was the ticket. Get his gawddamn nephew off the payroll right away. That would stop the tongues from flapping. Even Smallwood had joked about it – yes, the bastard – as if it made any difference to him. And Beecher! Yes. That too! Get Rentle off and bring Beecher back like a stiff shirt that's been through the laundry – bring Beecher back so he dripped honey like the humblest niggah evah lived. By Gawd, Smallwood'd have nothin' t'kick about, then!

"Hey!" Tuckahue shouted hoarsely at his nephew. "Pull up a minute."

The car stopped. Rentle glanced back over his shoulder. "Ovah to the side! You don't own the road. By Gawd but you're a bonehead!"

Rentle pulled over to the ditch and turned around sharply. He took off his spectacles. "Uncle Sam, you stop talkin' to me like that," he burst out in passionate resentment. "Ah ain't goin' t'stand for it – not a minute more, Ah ain't."

Tuckahue snorted.

"You heah me!" Rentle said. "Ah'm tired once an' for all of hearin' your tongue. You speak to me right or Ah'm goin' t'quit!"

Tuckahue burst out laughing. "Go ahead," he said. "Ah'm prayin' for it. You turn mah stomach till Ah want to vomit. You're makin' a sick man outa me. Go ahead, quit, Ah'm waitin'."

"Yes, you are!" Rentle said scornfully.

Tuckahue stopped laughing. He leant forward. "You quit, didn't you?" he asked softly. "What are you waitin' for?"

For a moment the youth looked at his uncle with a startled expression. Then he put his spectacles back on again. He removed his deputy's badge and undid the cartridge holster with the heavy revolver in it. "All right, Uncle Sam," he said, "you asked for it. Ah'm quittin' right now! But let me tell you somethin': by the time we get into town, you're gonna sober up some an' come crawlin' to me. But you ain't gonna get me back so easy. *Ah'm* gonna make the bargain this time!"

Tuckahue's mouth spread wide in a silent, venomous smile. "By the time *we* get into town, Charlie m'boy, *you're* goin' to be still hoofin' the road – that is, unless you can get some fellow niggah t'give you a ride."

"You goin' t'make me walk?" Charlie asked incredulously.

Tuckahue grinned.

Rentle got out of the car. "Uncle Sam," he said, "you're a son of a bitch!" He started off down the road.

"Watch yourself, Charlie," Tuckahue called after him. "Some young buck catch a pretty female like you walkin' alone, he's goin' t'do things to you! You come back all swollen up... your maw ain't gonna like it!"

Deputy Towne let out a loud, wet, laughing snigger. Rentle didn't turn around.

Tuckahue sat bent over. His immense body was shaking with suppressed laughter. He kept slapping a hand on his knee in a gesture of inexpressible amusement.

Towne sniggered lewdly. "You sure told him off, Sam," he said. "You sure told him," he repeated.

"An' Ah fired him five minutes ago," Tuckahue burst out suddenly. "Only, he didn't know it." He bent over again, slapping his knee convulsively. He was helpless with pure joy.

George Beecher, lying on the floor of the car, suddenly raised his head and looked off towards the fields. He had been lying quietly since the car started, with his head pillowed on his arms and with his face turned away from the white men. The racking, convulsive emotion which had stormed through him in the moment of speaking to Smallwood was gone. What remained was a feeling of weariness and hunger, and a vague sense of loss, as though something had been full in his body but had been drained away. The strange voice within him was quiet now – he only knew that his throat ached, and that it pained him to swallow. He didn't think of the future, but he felt it like a faraway pain, like a troubled nerve end buried and waiting in his flesh: the cell, the long days, the white man's court – and the road gang and the nine-pound hammer and the whip, the whip... how many black men come back? He lay quiet, wishing he had a drink of water. Then, drifting through the laughter of the white men, came the sound of singing from a church. He raised his head.

When Beecher got to his knees and looked around, Sheriff Tuckahue stopped laughing and eyed the boy closely. Beecher made him remember Mr Smallwood. He had almost forgotten about that side of the business. Getting rid of Rentle was only the simplest part. If he wanted to be right with Smallwood again, he had to damn well bring Beecher back turned inside out. And that was as easy as pulling teeth on a mule. The boy had as bad a notion in his eye as any niggah he'd ever seen... Tuckahue grunted and cleared his throat. "Where you goin', boy?" he asked with mock humour.

"Just lookin', boss."

"Aimin' to buy a piece of ground aroun' heah, maybe? Build yourself a house?"

"Nosuh, boss. Church ovah theah. Ah thought maybe Ah see someone."

A hundred yards in from the road there was a ramshackle Negro church. One of the door hinges had broken off, and the swelling note of a hymn came clear through the partly opened doorway. In front of the church there was a collection of dilapidated Ford cars and rickety wagons, but there were no people to be seen.

"Take a long look," Tuckahue said. He winked at Deputy Towne.

Towne grinned. "Yessir," he said, picking up the cue, "reckon you ain't nevah goin' t'see that church again. You just a poor, unfortunate niggah boy. Ah'm feelin' right sorry for you."

Beecher lay down in the bottom of the car and turned his face away. The white men grinned at each other. Tuckahue reached for his liquor bottle. "Here's to Avery J. Smallwood," he said. He spat over the side of the car. Deputy Towne sniggered.

The hot rye gurgled noisily down Tuckahue's throat. He drained the bottle and flung it into the ditch. He reached into the side pocket of the car, drew out another pint and fished for his jackknife.

"You sure put it down," Deputy Towne said admiringly.

There was no response from the sheriff. He drank again.

"Heaven's sake," Towne said, "where you put it all?"

Tuckahue grunted. He bit off a chew of apple plug and champed down on it hard. Then he exploded into violent, abusive speech: "Did he offer me a drink? No, by Gawd, no! Struttin' around on his double heels... 'Ah nevah dirty mah hands on mah own niggahs, Mr Tuckahue. That's what Ah'm payin' taxes for, Mr

Tuckahue. Ah only drink with gentlemen, Mr Tuckahue!...' The gawddamn bantam rooster!"

The sheriff spat violently over the side of the car. He erupted into sudden, unpleasant laughter. "That cow! Ha! Ha! That cow! Ha! Ha! Ha! He's a picture painter, Mr Towne. He's a friggin' artist. He stands on his front porch painting the asshole of a cow... 'How do you like it, Mr Tuckahue?' he asks me. 'Fine,' Ah says, 'real as life, Mr Smallwood...'" The sheriff shook with venomous, drunken laughter. "Gawd Almighty, Mr Towne, that cow looked more like the hind end of a trolley car than anything Ah evah seen. Put four wheels under it, and it'd roll right off down the veranda."

Deputy Towne joined half-heartedly in the sheriff's laughter. He was worried by the presence of Beecher. Beecher might report back to Smallwood. He winked at Tuckahue and jerked his thumb, but the sheriff waved his hand deprecatingly and gulped some more rye. His head was rolling around now. The new bottle was half empty. "Land sakes," Towne reflected, "the old buzzard's getting sure shot this time. Never saw him take so much in one stand before."

"The Smallwoods!" Tuckahue burst out suddenly. "Oh, the blue-blooded, blue-balled* Smallwoods. '*We* are the old South. *We* are the aristocrats. There's gentlemen's blood in us...' An' niggah blood too," he added, snarling.

Towne sniggered.

"'We don't do our own dirty work,'" Tuckahue continued. "'Oh no! We keep our hands clean. There's French per*fume* on us. We don't even wipe ourselves. Oh no. We *pay* for that!'"

"Hey!" Towne jerked his thumb towards Beecher. "Take it easy, will you?" he whispered.

"Aaaah! He won't talk!" Tuckahue dug his knuckles into Beecher's back in a gesture of drunken affection. "He won't talk. You like Smallwood less'n Ah do – don't you, dark boy? Sure you do!" He thumped Beecher on the back with the knuckles of his closed fist. "Sure you do," he repeated.

Beecher, lying on his stomach with his head pillowed on his arms, felt Tuckahue's fist like a faraway pound on his back. It was only half felt, vague, like a stray moth troubling his face at night. He was not aware of what the white men were saying. He had been lying in a doze with the hot sun comforting his body. His body seemed to suck up the sun, drinking it in to fill that hollowness inside. And his thoughts had drifted back to the noon hour in the fields, when his mother would come out with some black-eyed peas and a piece of cornbread, and he would stop for a moment to eat, and there would be a little breeze stirring the dead air. The white men's talk was a buzz in his ears, and he listened through their jawing for the sweet song from the church which rose and fell, and swung him up on a deep swell, and then died down again. It comforted him like the warm hand of a brush fire filling their room in winter, or like the deep, warm goodness of his mother when the mule kicked him and he had been sick with fever and she had pressed him soft to her breast.

Then he felt a hand tugging at his shoulder, and he heard the sheriff talking to him. "Turn around, boy, Ah want t'look at you."

Beecher turned his face to the white men.

Tuckahue was examining him with reddened, bloodshot eyes. "Pshaw – you're a nice-lookin' dark boy," he said. "What you want t'go gettin' yourself notions for?" Beecher didn't reply.

Tuckahue's face became crafty. He leant forward. "Listen, boy," he offered confidentially. "That Smallwood snake told me t'take you down to jail an' beat the hell out of you. But Ah ain't goin' t'do that, boy. Ah'm your friend... You heah me?"

The singing died out of Beecher's ears. The car came back, and the white deputies, and the nine-pound hammer, the jail and the whip. He heard the sheriff say it again: "Ah'm your friend, boy." And the deep, strange whisper inside of him began again: "No friend... he no friend... white sheriff no friend." Beecher raised his head. "Yessuh, boss," he said with familiar, practised humility. "Thank you, boss."

"But you got a notion in your eye, and that's bad," the sheriff said. "Bad for a niggah boy to have a notion in his eye."

"Say, Sam, how about movin' from heah?" Towne asked. "It's *hot*."

Tuckahue wagged a solemn bony finger at Beecher. "You got a notion in your eye, boy."

"No, Ah ain't, Cap'n," Beecher said humbly.

"Ah say you have!" The contradiction was stern. "Don't you talk back to me, George."

"Listen, Sam," Towne said, "for Heaven's sakes – it's *hot*. Let's get goin'."

"George," Tuckahue said, "why'd you hit a white man?"

Beecher was silent.

"Hey!" Tuckahue prodded him with his foot. "When Ah put you a question, you better answer."

Beecher sat up slowly. "You know why Ah hit him, boss."

"Well!" Tuckahue looked Beecher over with rising anger. "You're a sassy little bastard, ain't you?... Regular Smallwood niggah. Yessir! Always tell a Smallwood niggah by his sassy tongue."

Deputy Towne hitched his belt and leant forward. "Why'd you slug Ed Bailey? Was that yallah girl yours?"

"She warn't nobody's girl," Beecher replied sullenly. "She was just a little chile."

"What's the mattah?" Tuckahue laughed. "You want 'em to consent? Bailey don't want 'em to consent. Nossir, he don't like 'em to consent!"

Towne sniggered.

Beecher lay down suddenly and turned his face away from the white men. Tuckahue stopped laughing. He reached down slowly and grabbed Beecher by the strap of his overalls. He pulled him up to a sitting position.

The Negro youth and the white man stared at each other.

"Beecher," Tuckahue said softly, "Ah–don't–like–you. You're a Smallwood niggah! You got notions! Ah reckon Ah'm gonna have t'learn you somethin'. Ah'm gonna have t'learn you how to *crawl*, Beecher."

The slow, hot whisper began inside Beecher, the stubborn tide pulsed and swelled and rose up in his throat. "Ah'm tired of crawlin', white boss," he said. "Ah ain't gone t'crawl for nobody no more."

Tuckahue stared at him. His little flinty eyes were gleaming. "Beecher," he said softly, "Ah'm goin' t'teach you what this heah world's like you're livin' in! Ah'm goin' t'teach you the way of things. *Everybody* crawls, Beecher. Ah crawl for Mr Smallwood, Deputy Towne crawls for me, an' every niggah crawls for every white man. That's how it's gotta be!"

The Negro youth wet his lips. "Ah don't crawl no more," he said. "Ah got mah belly full!"

"Deputy Towne," Tuckahue said softly, without taking his eyes from Beecher's face, "get in the front an' start drivin'."

Towne stepped over the seat and started the car. The sheriff opened his hand slowly, releasing Beecher. The boy sank down to the floor. Tuckahue took another drink and corked the bottle. He was still staring at Beecher with bloodshot, gleaming eyes.

Beecher lay with his head pillowed on his arms. His face was turned away from the sheriff. The car jerked forward. The singing receded until he could no longer hear it. "Ah don't keer," the voice whispered inside of him. "Don't keer. Don't keer."

Sheriff Tuckahue lay back in the car. His head was swimming from the whiskey. He knew he had had too much, but he felt better for it. He felt fine. He felt full and free inside, strong and swollen like a running river, flowing and roaring inside. He felt like seeing Smallwood now. Put one hand on the back of his neck and squeeze just a little. Dig his fingers in! Gawd, he felt fine. He'd like to see that woman again. Christ Jesus, that big, bouncing, lovely bitch. She'd remember all right. She wouldn't forget him in a hurry. Put a hand on her where she was soft and juicy and make her yell just once. Make her yell. She wouldn't forget him that time. Tuckahue gripped the side of the car. He wanted a good niggah, did he? Smallwood was boss, wasn't he? And he wanted a good niggah, didn't he? All right! Before Tuckahue was through, that niggah'd be crawlin' on his hands and knees. He'd kiss the floor in front of every white man he saw. Mean bastard! Stubborn as a mule! Head full of ideas! Had a belly full, hey? By Gawd, a fine how do you do. Regular Smallwood niggah. All right, he'd iron him out. And nevah touch a hand to him. Nevah put a finger to him! Tuckahue suddenly burst out laughing. He smashed his hand down hard on the upholstery. His mouth opened wide, and his thin lips puckered back from the big horse teeth. "Harrison," he yelled, "Harrison, gawddamn you, stop at Shaney's when we get there! Ah want to buy me a bottle!"

"Say listen... you got some left, ain't you?" Towne called back. "Wait'll we come home."

Tuckahue laughed. "Stop at Shaney's, gawddamn you, Harrison," he said.

"OK!" The deputy assented, and swore exasperatedly to himself.

The sheriff leant back. He looked at the quiet body of the Negro boy, and his eyes glittered with pleasure. He felt marvellous. He felt like jumping up and yelling out loud. He wished he could see Smallwood now.

They came to a four-corners* where there was a gas station and a general store. Tuckahue lurched out of the car, winked broadly at Deputy Towne and strode inside. Towne knitted his brows and wondered what the hell the damn fool was up to. In another minute, Tuckahue came back. He ran down the steps of the store talking excitedly to Shaney, the storekeeper – a bald, fat little man of forty with a snub-nosed monkey face.

"By Christ," Tuckahue shouted, winking at Towne, "we gotta run for it! There's a lynch party comin' after George!"

Beecher jerked up violently into a sitting position. He stared at the white men with sudden, bitter fear in his eyes.

"Yessir," Shaney said, "I just got a phone call. Ed Bailey's friends are out after the niggah who beat him up. Is that him?" he asked, pointing. "Man, you're outa luck! Ah wouldn't change necks with you!" Shaney clapped his hand over his mouth to stifle his laughter. Towne caught wise, and his face split into an amused grin.

Beecher drew a deep, painful breath. "You gone t'let them take me, boss?"

"Hell, no!" Tuckahue said bombastically. He slammed his fist down on the upholstery in a melodramatic gesture. "They catch up with us, Ah'm gone t'defend you!"

"You bettah hide him," Shaney said. "Ah'll get you somethin'." He ran off behind the store.

"Is your gun loaded?" Tuckahue demanded excitedly of Deputy Towne. "Keep it on the seat! Keep it handy!"

Towne flipped his gun barrel ostentatiously. "Ah'll protect you with mah life, niggah boy!"

Shaney came running around the side of the store dragging a maggoty old mule blanket behind him. "Cover him with this," he said. "It stinks a little, but it'll hide him."

Tuckahue pushed Beecher down and flung the blanket over him. The white men shook with silent laughter. The sheriff leapt into the back seat. "Give it all it's got, Mr Towne," he ordered melodramatically.

"Stop at Benny Wilkerson's," Shaney advised. "Ah'll phone him when the mob passes heah."

"Right!" The car shot forward. Shaney stood in the middle of the road shaking with helpless laughter. Then he caught hold of himself and ran into the store to telephone his friends.

Beecher lay under the stinking mule blanket, sucking violently, painfully, for air, with his mouth gaping open. His fists were clenched, and his cramped body felt twisted into a thousand coils which snaked and writhed inside of him, begging to break loose, to snap out, to run free. The swaying, roaring, bouncing car kept hammering him cruelly on his knees, his elbows, his hip bones. His head seemed on fire with sudden pains – there was an unendurable buzzing in his ears, and his mind kept hammering the same thing over and over again like a wireless beating out a signal: "Whut they gonna do? Whut they gonna do? Whut they gonna do?" Then, deep inside, the voice began to whisper – it spoke to him coldly, cruelly, without pity: "They ain't gone help you. White boss don't help you. Turn you over. Done now. You done, George." Beecher listened, and his whole being wept in frenzy at what he heard. "They running!" he pleaded with the voice. "They not waiting! They ain't gonna turn me ovah!" But the low voice whispered again its cold, final warning, and again he thrust it aside, clinging bitterly, hysterically, to his shred of hope.

Then he heard the white man's voice close to his ear. Tuckahue had leant forward and raised the blanket. The voice was warm with comfort, but Tuckahue's face was sly and wrinkled with glee as he looked down at the boy. Beecher was scared all right. The niggah boy was scaring plenty. By Gawd, Tuckahue was goin' t'bring back a sharecropper like Smallwood never saw before. He'd bring him back dripping honey like he was a comb of beeswax, and he'd say, "Heah you are, Mr Smallwood – how do you like that? Ah done just what you told me, Mr Smallwood."

"Don't be scared, boy," Tuckahue said in a soft, sly, exultant tone, "you'll be protected! They ain't gone lynch you! Nossir! They said they was goin' t'cut off the hand that struck Ed Bailey – burn it before your eyes, they said – but they ain't gonna do it... nossir! Ah'll protect you, boy."

Tuckahue dropped the blanket back over Beecher's head. His upper lip puckered in silent laughter. He pulled out the bottle of liquor and finished off what was left. He flung it over the side. The car raced madly through the countryside.

Beecher lay on the floor sobbing from helplessness. He didn't know what to believe. There was nothing to believe. There was nothing to do. If he could fight... If he could run somewhere... If he could do something... The sheriff's voice came to him again, "Don't be afraid, boy – you don't need to be afraid."

"Ah ain't afraid," Beecher burst out in a wild cry, "but Ah cain't lay *heah*. Ah can't just wait *heah*."

"Sure you can... you got to," Tuckahue said. "Think of something, boy! Don't think of the lynchin'! They ain't gonna get you. They said they was goin' t'tie you to the back of a car – drag you till you scraped to death – but they ain't agonna do that, boy. Think of something! Think of your mammy. She loves you, doesn't she?

She wouldn't want anything to happen to you? Think of some nice, juicy... yallah gal, boy. You got a wife?"

"Lord Jesus, doan' talk like that," Beecher cried. "Let me go! Let me get out of heah! Let me run for it!" He pushed up on the floor. "Ah take mah chance, white boss! Let me run!"

"You're crazy, boy," Tuckahue told him gleefully. "You get caught sure that way." He pushed him down on the floor again. Beecher fell back, his body quivering frantically. The voice kept beating like a drum inside – "White man turn you ovah, George – turn you ovah, George" – and he crushed it down, stamped on it, trying with his whole soul to believe the white man was true.

"We'll get you through," Tuckahue said sweetly, comfortingly. "You just put your mind on some nice yallah girl. Tell yourself she's got no clothes on... make believe you're doin' things to her, makin' her yell, squeezin' her where she's soft. Those ridin' bosses said you ain't nevah gonna have a woman again, George. But don't you believe 'em. They said they was gonna cut off that black thing of yours an' give it to Ed Bailey to wear on his watch-chain – but they'll nevah do it, George." Tuckahue's face became exultant. "You heah me, George," he shouted, "they ain't gonna lynch you. They ain't gonna stick their jackknives into you. Ah ain't gonna let them burn *you*, George. Oh no! Ha! Certainly not, George. Ha! Ha! Ha! You just stay heah, George."

And then Beecher knew. He knew now. They weren't going to protect him. They were going to hand him over. God! Oh Jesus God! A cry of infinite horror convulsed the boy's whole body. It slashed through him inside – through his heart and lungs and belly, crying "God. Oh Jesus God!..." And then it was over. For one moment he drank down the fullest measure of horror and fear that he had ever known, and then it was over. It passed away. He was left free of it. And in its place there was something else. He felt it flaming up, burning and swelling in his body – hatred, pure burning hatred, and contempt – and over everything, like a cloth of silk on his soul, a sense of pride, of unutterable dignity and pride. He would die now, he knew it, but he was not afraid! He had said his say to Smallwood, he had struck his blow at Bailey – he would not be afraid now! Yes, sweet Jesus, he had spoken out! One black man had spoken out! They wouldn't see him afraid now!

Beecher lay quiet. He felt strangely, marvellously calm. He felt like a deep river rolling downhill. The roaring of the waterfall was strong in his ears, but the silk, the deep silk was folding him close.

Then Sheriff Tuckahue screamed aloud in mock fear: "Step on it, Harry, there's cars behind us." Deputy Towne let out a howl and drove the car forward. They were burning up the road at seventy an hour. "Christ Jesus, there's *six* cars behind us," Tuckahue cried. "Loaded up with men an' guns! Comin' after us!"

"Are they gainin'?" Towne laughed.

"Ah can't tell!... No, we're beatin' 'em! They ain't catchin' us," Tuckahue cried in mock triumph. "Keep your head down, George, we'll save you... Hey!" The sheriff caught his breath. "We're trapped!" He pointed ahead at the empty road. "There's six more cars up ahead! They got us, Harry. We'll have to hand poor George ovah. They're gonna lynch poor George. Slow down, Harry! They're blocking the road!"

Towne cut his gas. The car began to lose speed.

And then the wave of pride and dignity caught George Beecher and lifted him high. His heart was on fire with wild singing and defiance. Not for him! No rope for him! Never, never, never for him!

And in one violent movement Beecher leapt to his feet – and then fiercely, proudly, he flung himself over the side of the car.

VII

When Avery Smallwood put down his telephone, he stood like a man transfixed. He felt nauseous with horror. It was a terrible thing. It was simply incredible. And somehow he felt guilty. It was as though he were responsible for the death of that boy. But it wasn't true. He knew it wasn't.

His wife came into the room, and he told her, falteringly, what had happened. The tears came into her eyes, and her pretty face twisted with shock and pity. He wanted to comfort her, but he couldn't find anything to say. What on earth had made the boy do a thing like that anyway? Just a crazy notion about escaping. But so foolish, so damn foolish. And how could you foresee it? You couldn't know in advance about a thing like that. And he had had to do something in order to teach the boy.

"Oh Christ!..." Smallwood swore aloud. He sat down and gripped his head with both hands. What a hard world it was... What a bitter, miserable place... Poor Beecher lying on the road with his head crushed... A man just had to make himself hard, and then try to forget about it.

Smallwood got up. He went to the sideboard and poured himself a drink. He knew what would happen to him now: he would drift into one of his periods of depression. So damn confusing this life was... And now he wouldn't be able to go back to his painting till the middle of the week, or even later. It was hard. A man had to be hard to take things the way they were.

He got up and went out to the veranda. He didn't know what to do with himself. He hadn't felt so upset in ages. It was simply shocking... For want of something better, Smallwood started cleaning his paintbrushes.

Man on a Road*

At about four in the afternoon, I crossed the bridge at Gauley, West Virginia, and turned the sharp curve leading into the tunnel under the railroad bridge. I had been over this road once before, and knew what to expect – by the time I entered the tunnel, I had my car down to about ten miles an hour. But even at that speed I came closer to running a man down than I ever have before. This is how it happened.

The patched macadam road had been soaked through by an all-day rain, and now it was as slick as ice. In addition, it was quite dark – a black sky and a steady swishing rain made driving impossible without headlights. As I entered the tunnel, a big cream-coloured truck swung fast around the curve on the other side. The curve was so sharp that his headlights had given me no warning. The tunnel was short and narrow, just about passing space for two cars, and, before I knew it, he was in front of me with his big front wheels over on my side of the road.

I jammed on my brakes. Even at ten miles an hour my car skidded, first towards the truck and then, as I wrenched on the wheel, in towards the wall. There it stalled. The truck swung around hard, scraped my fender and passed through the tunnel about an inch away from me. I could see the tense face of the young driver with the tight bulge of tobacco in his cheek and his eyes glued on the road. I remember saying to myself that I hoped he'd swallow that tobacco and go choke himself.

I started my car and shifted into first. It was then I saw for the first time that a man was standing in front of my car about a foot away from the inside wheel. It was a shock to see him there. "For Chrissakes," I said.

My first thought was that he had walked into the tunnel after my car had stalled. I was certain he hadn't been in there before. Then I noticed that he was standing profile to me with his hand held up in the hitch-hiker's gesture. If he had walked into that tunnel, he'd be facing me – he wouldn't be standing sideways looking at the opposite wall. Obviously I had just missed knocking him down, and obviously he didn't know it. He didn't even know I was there.

It made me run weak inside. I had a picture of a man lying crushed under a wheel with me standing over him knowing it was my car.

I called out to him "Hey!" He didn't answer me. I called louder. He didn't even turn his head. He stood there, fixed, his hand up in the air, his thumb jutting out. It scared me. It was like a story by Bierce* where the ghost of a man pops out of the air to take up his lonely post on a dark country road.

My horn is a good, loud, raucous one, and I knew that the tunnel would redouble the sound. I slapped my hand down on that little black button, and pressed as hard as I could. The man was either going to jump or else prove that he was a ghost.

Well, he wasn't a ghost – but he didn't jump either. And it wasn't because he was deaf. He heard that horn all right.

He was like a man in a deep sleep. The horn seemed to awaken him only by degrees, as though his whole consciousness had been sunk in some deep recess within himself. He turned his head slowly and looked at me. He was a big man, about thirty-five, with a heavy-featured face – an ordinary face with a big, fleshy nose and a large mouth. The face didn't say much. I wouldn't have called it kind or brutal or intelligent or stupid. It was just the face of a big man, wet with rain, looking at me with eyes that seemed to have a glaze over them. Except for the eyes, you see faces like that going into the pit at six in the morning, or coming out of a steel mill or foundry where heavy work is done. I couldn't understand that glazed quality in his eyes. It wasn't the glassy stare of a drunken man, or the wild, mad glare I saw once in the eyes of a woman in a fit of violence. I could only think of a man I once knew who had died of cancer. Over his eyes, in the last days, there was the same dull glaze, a faraway, absent look as though behind the blank, outward film there was a secret flow of past events on which his mind was focused. It was this same look that I saw in the man on the road.

When at last he heard my horn, the man stepped very deliberately around the front of my car and came towards the inside door. The least I expected was that he would show surprise at an auto so dangerously close to him. But there was no emotion to him whatsoever. He walked slowly, deliberately, as though he had been expecting me, and then bent his head down to see under the top of my car. "Kin yuh give me a lift, friend?" he asked me.

I saw his big horse teeth chipped at the ends and stained brown by tobacco. His voice was high-pitched and nasal, with the slurred, lilting drawl of the deep South. In West Virginia few of the town folk seem to speak that way. I judged he had been raised in the mountains.

I looked at his clothes – an old cap, a new blue work shirt and dark trousers, all soaked through with rain. They didn't tell me much.

I must have been occupied with my thoughts about him for some time, because he asked me again. "Ahm goin' to Weston," he said. "Are you agoin' thataway?"

As he said this, I looked into his eyes. The glaze had disappeared, and now they were just ordinary eyes, brown and moist.

I didn't know what to reply. I didn't really want to take him in – the episode had unnerved me, and I wanted to get away from the tunnel and from him too. But I saw him looking at me with a patient, almost humble glance. The rain was streaked on his face, and he stood there asking for a ride and waiting in simple concentration for my answer. I was ashamed to tell him no. Besides, I was curious. "Climb in," I said.

He sat down beside me, placing a brown-paper package on his lap. We started out of the tunnel.

From Gauley to Weston is about a hundred miles of as difficult mountain driving as I know – a five-mile climb to the top of a hill, then five miles down, and then up another. The road twists like a snake on the run, and for a good deal of it there is a jagged cliff on one side and a drop of a thousand feet or more on the other. The rain and the small rocks crumbling from the mountainsides and littering up the road made it very slow-going. But in the four hours or so that it took for the trip, I don't think my companion spoke to me half a dozen times.

I tried often to get him to talk. It was not that he wouldn't talk, it was rather that he didn't seem to hear me – as though as soon as he had spoken he would slip down into that deep, secret recess within himself. He sat like a man dulled by morphine. My conversation, the rattle of the old car, the steady pour of rain were all a distant buzz – the meaningless outside world that could not quite pierce the shell in which he seemed to be living.

As soon as we had started, I asked him how long he had been in the tunnel.

"Ah don' know," he replied. "A good tahm, Ah reckon."

"What were you standing there for – to keep out of the rain?"

He didn't answer. I asked him again, speaking very loudly. He turned his head to me. "Excuse me, friend," he said, "did you say somethin'?"

"Yes," I answered. "Do you know I almost ran you over back in that tunnel?"

"No-o," he said. He spoke the word in that breathy way that is typical of mountain speech.

"Didn't you hear me yell to you?"

"No-o." He paused. "Ah reckon Ah was thinkin'."

"Ah reckon you were," I thought to myself. "What's the matter – are you hard of hearing?" I asked him.

"No-o," he said, and turned his head away, looking out front at the road.

I kept right after him. I didn't want him to go off again. I wanted somehow to get him to talk.

"Looking for work?"

"Yessuh."

He seemed to speak with an effort. It was not a difficulty of speech, it was something behind, in his mind, in his will to speak. It was as though he couldn't keep touch between his world and mine. Yet, when he did answer me, he spoke directly and coherently. I didn't know what to make of it. When he first came into the car, I had been a little frightened. Now I only felt terribly curious and a little sorry.

"Do you have a trade?" I was glad to come to that question. You know a good deal about a man when you know what line of work he follows, and it always leads to further conversation.

"Ah ginerally follows the mines," he said.

"Now," I thought, "we're getting somewhere."

But just then we hit a stretch of unpaved road where the mud was thick and the ruts were hard to follow. I had to stop talking and watch what I was doing. And when we came to paved road again, I had lost him.

I tried again to make him talk. It was no use. He didn't even hear me. Then, finally, his silence shamed me. He was a man lost somewhere within his own soul, only asking to be left alone. I felt wrong to keep thrusting at his privacy.

So for about four hours we drove in silence. For me those hours were almost unendurable. I have never seen such rigidity in a human being. He sat straight up in the car, his outward eye fixed on the road in front, his inward eye seeing nothing. He didn't know I was in the car, he didn't know he was in the car at all, he didn't feel the rain that kept sloshing in on him through the rent in the side curtains. He sat like a slab of moulded rock, and only from his breathing could I be sure that he was alive. His breathing was heavy.

Only once in that long trip did he change his posture. That was when he was seized with a fit of coughing. It was a fierce hacking cough that shook his big body from side to side and doubled him over like a child with the whooping cough. He was trying to cough something up – I could hear the phlegm in his chest – but he couldn't succeed. Inside him there was an ugly scraping sound, as though cold metal were being rubbed on the bone of his ribs, and he kept spitting and shaking his head.

It took almost three minutes for the fit to subside. Then he turned around to me and said, "Excuse me, friend." That was all. He was quiet again.

I felt awful. There were times when I wanted to stop the car and tell him to get out. I made up a dozen good excuses for cutting the trip short. But I couldn't do it. I was consumed by a curiosity to know what was wrong with the man. I hoped that before we parted, perhaps even as he got out of the car, he would tell me what it was or say something that would give me a clue.

I thought of the cough and wondered if it were TB. I thought of cases of sleeping sickness I had seen and of a boxer who was punch-drunk. But none of these things seemed to fit. Nothing physical seemed to explain this dark, terrible silence, this intense, all-exclusive absorption within himself.

Hour after hour of rain and darkness!

Once we passed the slate dump of a mine. The rain had made the surface burst into flame, and the blue and red patches flickering in a kind of witch glow on a hill of black seemed to attract my companion. He turned his head to look at it, but he didn't speak, and I said nothing.

And again the silence and rain! Occasionally a mine tipple* with the cold, drear smoke smell of the dump and the oil lamps in the broken-down shacks where the miners live. Then the black road again and the shapeless bulk of the mountains.

We reached Weston at about eight o'clock. I was tired and chilled and hungry. I stopped in front of a café and turned to the man.

"Ah reckon this is hit," he said.

"Yes," I answered. I was surprised. I had not expected him to know that we had arrived. Then I tried a final plunge. "Will you have a cup of coffee with me?"

"Yes," he replied. "Thank you, friend."

The "thank you" told me a lot. I knew from the way he said it that he wanted the coffee but couldn't pay for it – that he had taken my offer to be one of hospitality and was grateful. I was happy I had asked him.

We went inside. For the first time since I had come upon him in the tunnel he seemed human. He didn't talk, but he didn't slip inside himself either. He just sat down at the counter and waited for his coffee. When it came, he drank it slowly, holding the cup in both hands as though to warm them.

When he had finished, I asked him if he wouldn't like a sandwich. He turned around to me and smiled. It was a very gentle, a very patient smile. His big, lumpy face seemed to light up with it and become understanding and sweet and gentle.

The smile shook me all through. It didn't warm me – it made me feel sick inside. It was like watching a corpse begin to stir. I wanted to cry out, "My God, you poor man!"

Then he spoke to me. His face retained that smile, and I could see the big horse teeth stained by tobacco.

"You've bin right nice to me, friend, an' Ah do appreciate it."

"That's all right," I mumbled.

He kept looking at me. I knew he was going to say something else, and I was afraid of it.

"Would yuh do me a faveh?"

"Yes," I said.

He spoke softly. "Ah've got a letter here that Ah done, writ to mah woman, but Ah can't write very good. Would you all be kind enough to write it ovah for me so it'd be proper like?"

"Yes," I said, "I'd be glad to."

"Ah kin tell you all know how to write real well," he said, and smiled.

"Yes."

He opened his blue shirt. Under his thick woollen underwear there was a paper fastened by a safety pin. He handed it to me. It was moist and warm, and the damp odour of wet cloth and the slightly sour odour of his flesh clung to it.

I asked the counterman for a sheet of paper. He brought me one. This is the letter I copied. I put it down here in his own script.

My dere wife –

I am awritin this yere leta to tell you somethin i did not tell you afore i lef frum home. There is a cause to wy i am not able to get me any job at the mines. I told you hit was frum work abein slack. But this haint so.

Hit comes frum the time the mine was shut down an i worked in the tunel nere Gauley Bridge where the company is turnin the river inside the mounten. The mine supers say they wont hire any men war worked in thet tunel.

Hit all comes frum thet rock thet we all had to dril. Thet rock was silica and hit was most all of hit glass. The powder frum this glass has got into the lungs of all the men war worked in thet tunel thru their breathin. And this has given to all of us a sickness. The doctors writ it down for me. Hit is silicosis. Hit makes the lungs to git all scab like and then it stops the breathin.

Bein as our hom is a good peece frum town you aint heerd about Tom Prescott and Hansy McCulloh having died two days back. But wen i heerd this i went to see the doctor.

The doctor says i hev got me thet sickness like Tom Prescott and thet is the reason wy i am coughin sometime. My lungs is agittin scab like. There is in all ova a hondred men war have this death sickness frum the tunel. It is a turible plague becus the doctor says this wud not be so if the company had gave us masks to ware an put a right fan sistem in the tunel.

So i am agoin away becus the doctor says I will be dead in about fore months.

i figger on gettin some work maybe in other parts. I will send you all my money till i caint work no mohr.

i did not want i should be a burdin upon you all at hum. So thet is wy i hev gone away.

i think wen you doan here frum me no mohr you orter go to your grandmaws up in the mountens at Kilney Run.

You kin live there and she will take keer of you an the young one.

i hope you will be well an keep the young one out of the mines. Doan let him work there.

Doan think hard on me for agoin away and doan feel bad. But wen the young one is agrowed up you tell him wat the company has done to me.

i reckon after a bit you shud try to git you anotha man. You are a young woman yit.

Your loving husband,

Jack Pitckett.

When I handed him the copy of his letter, he read it over. It took him a long time. Finally he folded it up and pinned it to his undershirt. His big, lumpy face was sweet and gentle. "Thank you, friend," he said. Then, very softly, with his head hanging a little – "Ahm feelin' bad about this a-happenin' t'me. Mah wife was a good woman." He paused. And then, as though talking to himself, so low I could hardly hear it, "Ah'm feelin' right bad."

As he said this, I looked into his face. Slowly the life was going out of his eyes. It seemed to recede and go deep into the sockets like the flame of a candle going into the night. Over the eyeballs came that dull glaze. I had lost him. He sat deep within himself in his sorrowful, dark absorption.

That was all. We sat together. In me there was only mute emotion – pity and love for him, and a cold, deep hatred for what had killed him.

Presently he arose. He did not speak. Nor did I. I saw his thick, broad back in the blue work shirt as he stood by the door. Then he moved out into the darkness and rain.

FROM
AFTERNOON IN THE JUNGLE*
(1970)

FOR MY WIFE, ESTHER*

The Happiest Man on Earth*

Jesse felt ready to weep. He had been sitting in the shanty waiting for Tom to appear, grateful for the chance to rest his injured foot, quietly, joyously anticipating the moment when Tom would say, "Why, of course, Jesse, you can start whenever you're ready!"

For two weeks he had been pushing himself, from Kansas City, Missouri, to Tulsa, Oklahoma, through nights of rain and a week of scorching sun, without sleep or a decent meal, sustained by the vision of that one moment. And then Tom had come into the office. He had come in quickly, holding a sheaf of papers in his hand. He had glanced at Jesse only casually, it was true – but long enough. He had not known him. He had turned away... And Tom Brackett was his brother-in-law.

Was it his clothes? Jesse knew he looked terrible. He had tried to spruce up at a drinking fountain in the park, but even that had gone badly – in his excitement he had cut himself shaving, an ugly gash down the side of his cheek. And nothing could get the red gumbo dust out of his suit, even though he had slapped himself till both arms were worn out... Or was it just that he had changed so much?

True, they hadn't seen each other for five years, but Tom looked five years older, that was all. He was still Tom. God! Was he so different?

Brackett finished his telephone call. He leant back in his swivel chair and glanced over at Jesse with small, clear blue eyes that were suspicious and unfriendly. He was a heavy, paunchy man of forty-five, auburn-haired, rather dour-looking; his face was meaty, his features pronounced and forceful, his nose somewhat bulbous and reddish-hued at the tip. He looked like a solid, decent, capable businessman who was commander of his local branch of the American Legion – which he was. He surveyed Jesse with cold indifference, manifestly unwilling to spend time on him. Even the way he chewed his toothpick seemed contemptuous to Jesse.

"Yes?" Brackett said suddenly. "What do you want?"

His voice was decent enough, Jesse admitted. He had expected it to be worse. He moved up to the wooden counter that partitioned the shanty. He thrust a hand nervously through his tangled hair.

"I guess you don't recognize me, Tom," he said falteringly. "I'm Jesse Fulton."

"Huh?" Brackett said. That was all.

"Yes, I am, and Ella sends you her love."

Brackett rose and walked over to the counter until they were face to face. He surveyed Fulton incredulously, trying to measure the resemblance to his brother-in-law as he remembered him. This man was tall, about thirty. That fitted! He had straight good features and a lank, erect body. That was right too. But the face was too gaunt, the body too spiny under the baggy clothes for him to be sure. His brother-in-law had been a solid, strong young man with muscle and beef to him. It was like looking at a faded, badly taken photograph and trying to recognize the subject: the resemblance was there, but the difference was tremendous. He searched the eyes. They at least seemed definitely familiar – grey, with a curiously shy but decent look in them. He had liked that about Fulton.

Jesse stood quiet. Inside he was seething. Brackett was like a man examining a piece of broken-down horseflesh – there was a look of pure pity in his eyes. It made Jesse furious. He knew he wasn't as far gone as all that.

"Yes, I believe you are," Bracket said finally, "but you sure have changed."

"By God, it's five years, ain't it?" Jesse said resentfully. "You only saw me a couple of times anyway." Then, to himself, with his lips locked together, in mingled vehemence and shame, "What if I have changed? Don't everybody? I ain't no corpse."

"You was solid-looking," Brackett continued softly, in the same tone of incredulous wonder. "You lost weight, I guess?"

Jesse kept silent. He needed Brackett too much to risk antagonizing him. But it was only by deliberate effort that he could keep from boiling over. The pause lengthened, became painful. Brackett flushed. "Jiminy Christmas, excuse me," he burst out in apology. He jerked the counter up. "Come in. Take a seat. Good God, boy..." – he grasped Jesse's hand and shook it – "I am glad to see you – don't think anything else! You just looked so peaked."

"It's all right," Jesse murmured. He sat down, thrusting his hand through his curly, tangled hair.

"Why are you limping?"

"I stepped on a stone – it jagged a hole through my shoe." Jesse pulled his feet back under the chair. He was ashamed of his shoes. They had come from the relief originally, and two weeks on the road had about finished them. All morning, with a kind of delicious, foolish solemnity, he had been vowing to himself that before anything else, before even a suit of clothes, he was going to buy himself a brand-new, strong pair of shoes.

Brackett kept his eyes off Jesse's feet. He knew what was bothering the boy, and it filled his heart with pity. The whole thing was appalling. He had never seen anyone who looked more down-and-out. His sister had been writing to him every week, but she hadn't told him they were as badly off as this.

"Well, now... listen," Brackett began. "Tell me things. How's Ella?"

"Oh, she's pretty good," Jesse replied absently. He had a soft, pleasing, rather shy voice that went with his soft grey eyes. He was worrying over how to get started.

"And the kids?"

"Oh, they're fine... Well, you know," Jesse added, becoming more attentive, "the young one has to wear a brace. He can't run around, you know. But he's smart. He draws pictures and he does things, you know."

"Yes," Brackett said. "That's good." He hesitated. There was a moment's silence. Jesse fidgeted in his chair. Now that the time had arrived, he felt awkward. Brackett leant forward and put his hand on Jesse's knee. "Ella didn't tell me things were so bad for you, Jesse. I might have helped."

"Well, goodness," Jesse returned softly, "you been having your own troubles, ain't you?"

"Yes." Brackett leant back. His ruddy face became mournful and darkly bitter. "You know I lost my hardware shop?"

"Well, sure, of course," Jesse answered, surprised. "You wrote us. That's what I mean."

"I forgot," Brackett said. "I keep on being surprised over it myself. Not that it was worth much," he added bitterly. "It was running downhill for three years. I guess I just wanted it because it was mine." He laughed pointlessly, without mirth. "Well, tell me about yourself," he asked. "What happened to the job you had?"

Jesse burst out abruptly, with agitation, "Let it wait, Tom... I got something on my mind."

"It ain't you and Ella?" Brackett interrupted anxiously.

"Why, no!" Jesse sat back. "Why, how ever did you come to think that? Why, Ella and me..." He stopped, laughing. "Why, Tom, I'm just crazy about Ella. Why, she's just wonderful. She's just my whole life, Tom."

"Excuse me. Forget it." Brackett chuckled uncomfortably, turned away. The naked intensity of the youth's burst of love had upset him. It made him wish savagely that he could do something for them. They were too decent to have had it so hard. Ella was like this boy too, shy and a little soft.

"Tom, listen," Jesse said, "I come here on purpose." He thrust his hand through his hair. "I want you to help me."

"Damn it, boy," Brackett groaned. He had been expecting this. "I can't much. I only get thirty-five a week, and I'm damn grateful for it."

"Sure, I know," Jesse emphasized excitedly. He was feeling once again the wild, delicious agitation that had possessed him in the early hours of the morning. "I know you can't help us with money! But we met a man who works for you! He was in our city! He said you could give me a job!"

"Who said?"

"Oh, why didn't you tell me?" Jesse burst out reproachfully. "Why, as soon as I heard of it, I started out. For two weeks now I been pushing ahead like crazy."

Brackett groaned aloud. "You come walking from Kansas City in two weeks so I could give you a job?"

"Sure, Tom, of course. What else could I do?"

"God Almighty... there ain't no jobs, Jesse! It's a slack season. And you don't know this oil business. It's special. I got my Legion friends here, but they couldn't do nothing now. Don't you think I'd ask for you as soon as there was a chance?"

Jesse felt stunned. The hope of the last two weeks seemed rolling up into a ball of agony in his stomach. Then, frantically, he cried, "But listen, this man said *you* could hire! He told me! He drives trucks for you! He said you always need men!"

"Oh!... You mean my department?" Brackett said in a low voice.

"Yes, Tom. That's it!"

"Oh no, you don't want to work in my department," Brackett told him in the same low voice. "You don't know what it is."

"Yes, I do," Jesse insisted. "He told me all about it, Tom. You're a dispatcher, ain't you? You send the dynamite trucks out?"

"Who was the man, Jesse?"

"Everett... Everett, I think."

"Egbert? Man about my size?" Brackett asked slowly.

"Yes, Egbert. He wasn't a phoney, was he?"

Brackett laughed. For the second time his laughter was curiously without mirth. "No, he wasn't a phoney." Then, in a changed voice: "Jiminy, boy, you should have asked me before you trekked all the way down here."

"Oh, I didn't want to," Jesse explained with naive cunning. "I knew you'd say no. He told me it was risky work, Tom. But I don't care."

Brackett locked his fingers together. His solid, meaty face became very hard. "I'm going to say no anyway, Jesse."

Jesse cried out. It had not occurred to him that Brackett would not agree. It had seemed as though reaching Tulsa were the only problem he had to face. "Oh no," he begged, "you can't. Ain't there any jobs, Tom?"

"Sure there's jobs. There's even Egbert's job, if you want it."

"He's quit?"

"He's dead!"

"Oh!"

"On the job, Jesse. Last night, if you want to know."

"Oh!..." Then, "I don't care!"

"Now, you listen to me," Brackett said. "I'll tell you a few things that you should have asked before you started out. It ain't dynamite you drive. They don't use anything as safe as dynamite in drilling oil wells. They wish they could, but they can't. It's nitroglycerine! Soup!"

"But I know," Jesse told him reassuringly. "He advised me, Tom. You don't have to think I don't know."

"Shut up a minute," Brackett ordered angrily. "Listen! You just have to look at this soup, see? You just cough loud and it blows! You know how they transport it? In a can that's shaped like this – see? – like a fan. That's to give room for compartments, because each compartment has to be lined with rubber. That's the only way you can even think of handling it."

"Listen, Tom..."

"Now wait a minute, Jesse. For God's sake, just put your mind to this. I know you had your heart set on a job, but you've got to understand... This stuff goes only in special trucks! At night! They got to follow a special route! They can't go through any city! If they lay over, it's got to be in a special garage! Don't you see what that means? Don't that tell you how dangerous it is?"

"I'll drive careful," Jesse said. "I know how to handle a truck. I'll drive slow."

Brackett groaned. "Do you think Egbert didn't drive careful or know how to handle a truck?"

"Tom," Jesse said earnestly, "you can't scare me. I got my mind fixed on only one thing: Egbert said he was getting a dollar a mile. He was making five to six hundred dollars a month for half a month's work, he said. Can I get the same?"

"Sure you can get the same," Brackett told him savagely. "A dollar a mile. It's easy. But why do you think the company has to pay so much? It's easy – until you run over a stone that your headlights didn't pick out, like Egbert did. Or get a blowout! Or get something in your eye so the wheel twists and you jar the truck! Or any other goddamn thing that nobody ever knows! We can't ask Egbert what happened to him. There's no truck to give any evidence. There's no corpse. There's nothing! Maybe tomorrow somebody'll find a piece of twisted steel way off in a cornfield. But we never find the driver. Not even a fingernail. All we know is that he don't come in on schedule. Then we wait for the police to call us. You know what happened last night? Something went wrong on a bridge. Maybe Egbert was nervous. Maybe he brushed the side with his fender. Only, there's no bridge any more. No truck. No Egbert. Do you understand now? That's what you get for your goddamn dollar a mile!"

There was a moment of silence. Jesse sat twisting his long thin hands. His mouth was sagging open, his face was agonized. Then he shut his eyes and spoke softly. "I don't care about that, Tom. You told me. Now you got to be good to me and give me the job."

Brackett slapped the palm of his hand down on his desk. "No!"

"Listen, Tom," Jesse said softly, "you just don't understand." He opened his eyes. They were filled with tears. They made Brackett turn away. "Just look at me, Tom. Don't that tell you enough? What did you think of me when you first saw me? You thought: 'Why don't that bum go away and stop panhandling?' Didn't you, Tom? Tom, I just can't live like this any more. I got to be able to walk down the street with my head up."

"You're crazy," Brackett muttered. "Every year there's one out of five drivers gets killed. That's the average. What's worth that?"

"Is my life worth anything now? We're just starvin' at home, Tom. They ain't put us back on relief yet."

"Then you should have told me," Brackett exclaimed harshly. "It's your own damn fault. A man has no right to have false pride when his family ain't eating. I'll borrow some money and we'll telegraph it to Ella. Then you go home and get back on relief."

"And then what?"

"And then wait, goddamn it! You're no old man. You got no right to throw your life away. Sometime you'll get a job."

"No!" Jesse jumped up. "No. I believed that too. But I don't now," he cried passionately. "I ain't getting a job no more than you're getting your hardware store back. I lost my skill, Tom. Linotyping is skilled work. I'm rusty now. I've been six years on relief. The only work I've had is pick-and-shovel. When I got that job this spring, I was supposed to be an A1 man. But I wasn't. And they got new machines now. As soon as the slack started, they let me out."

"So what?" Brackett said harshly. "Ain't there others jobs?"

"How do I know?" Jesse replied. "There ain't been one for six years. I'd even be afraid to take one now. It's been too hard waiting so many weeks to get back on relief."

"Well, you got to have some courage," Brackett shouted. "You've got to keep up hope."

"I got all the courage you want," Jesse retorted vehemently, "but no, I ain't got no hope. The hope has dried up in me in six years' waiting. You're the only hope I got."

"You're crazy," Brackett muttered. "I won't do it. For God's sake, think of Ella for a minute."

"Don't you know I'm thinking about her?" Jesse asked softly. He plucked at Brackett's sleeve. "That's what decided me, Tom." His voice became muted into a hushed, pained whisper. "The night Egbert was at our house, I looked at Ella like I'd seen her for the first time. She ain't pretty any more, Tom!" Brackett jerked his head and moved away. Jesse followed him, taking a deep, sobbing breath. "Don't that tell you, Tom? Ella was like a little doll or something, you remember? I couldn't walk down the street without somebody turning to look at her. She ain't twenty-nine yet, Tom, and she ain't pretty no more."

Brackett sat down with his shoulders hunched up wearily. He gripped his hands together and sat leaning forward, staring at the floor.

Jesse stood over him, his gaunt face flushed with emotion, almost unpleasant in its look of pleading and bitter humility. "I ain't done right for Ella, Tom. Ella deserved better. This is the only chance I see in my whole life to do something for her. I've just been a failure."

"Don't talk nonsense," Brackett commented without rancour. You ain't a failure. No more than me. There's millions of men in the identical situation. It's just the depression, or the recession, or the goddamn New Deal,* or..." He swore and lapsed into silence.

"Oh no," Jesse corrected him in a knowing, sorrowful tone, "those things maybe excuse other men. But not me. It was up to me to do better. This is my own fault!"

"Oh, beans!" Brackett said. "It's more sunspots than it's you!"

Jesse's face turned an unhealthy mottled red. It looked swollen. "Well, I don't care," he cried wildly. "I don't care! You got to give me this! I got to lift my head up. I went through one stretch of hell, but I can't go through another. You want me to keep looking at my little boy's legs and tell myself if I had a job he wouldn't be like that? Every time he walks, he says to me, 'I got soft bones from the rickets, and you give it to me because you didn't feed me right.' Jesus Christ, Tom, you think I'm going to sit there and watch him like that another six years?"

Brackett leapt to his feet. "So what if you do?" he shouted. "You say you're thinking about Ella. How's she going to like it when you get killed?"

"Maybe I won't," Jesse pleaded. "I've got to have some luck sometime."

"That's what they all think," Brackett replied scornfully. "When you take this job, your luck is a question mark. The only thing certain is that sooner or later you get killed."

"OK then," Jesse shouted back. "Then I do! But meanwhile I got something, don't I? I can buy a pair of shoes. Look at me!

I can buy a suit that don't say 'Relief' by the way it fits. I can smoke cigarettes. I can buy some candy for the kids. I can eat some myself. Yes, by God, I want to eat some candy. I want a glass of beer once a day. I want Ella dressed up. I want her to eat meat three times a week – four times, maybe. I want to take my family to the movies."

Brackett sat down. "Oh, shut up," he said wearily.

"No," Jesse told him softly, passionately, "you can't get rid of me. Listen, Tom," he pleaded, "I got it all figured out. On six hundred a month, look how much I can save! If I last only three months, look how much it is... a thousand dollars... more! And maybe I'll last longer. Maybe a couple years. I can fix Ella up for life!"

"You said it," Brackett interposed. "I suppose you think she'll enjoy living when you're on a job like that?"

"I got it all figured out," Jesse answered excitedly. "She don't know, see? I tell her I make only forty. You put the rest in a bank account for her, Tom."

"Oh, shut up," Brackett said. "You think you'll be happy? Every minute, waking and sleeping, you'll be wondering if tomorrow you'll be dead. And the worst days will be your days off, when you're not driving. They have to give you every other day free to get your nerve back. And you lay around the house eating your heart out. That's how happy you'll be."

Jesse laughed. "I'll be happy! Don't you worry, I'll be so happy – I'll be singing. Lord God, Tom, I'm going to feel proud of myself for the first time in seven years!"

"Oh, shut up, shut up," Brackett said.

The little shanty became silent. After a moment Jesse whispered: "You got to, Tom. You got to. You got to."

Again there was silence. Brackett raised both hands to his head, pressing the palms against his temples.

"Tom, Tom..." Jesse said.

Brackett sighed. "Oh, goddamn it," he said finally, "all right, I'll take you on, God help me." His voice was low, hoarse, infinitely weary. "If you're ready to drive tonight, you can drive tonight."

Jesse didn't answer. He couldn't. Brackett looked up. The tears were running down Jesse's face. He was swallowing and trying to speak, but only making an absurd gasping noise.

"I'll send a wire to Ella," Brackett said in the same hoarse, weary voice. "I'll tell her you got a job, and you'll send her fare in a couple of days. You'll have some money then – that is, if you last the week out, you jackass!"

Jesse only nodded. His heart felt so close to bursting that he pressed both hands against it, as though to hold it locked within his breast.

"Come back here at six o'clock," Brackett said. "Here's some money. Eat a good meal."

"Thanks," Jesse whispered.

"Wait a minute," Brackett said. "Here's my address." He wrote it on a piece of paper. "Take any car going that way. Ask the conductor where to get off. Take a bath and get some sleep."

"Thanks," Jesse said. "Thanks, Tom."

"Oh, get out of here," Brackett said.

"Tom."

"What?"

"I just…" Jesse stopped. Brackett saw his face. The eyes were still glistening with tears, but the gaunt face was shining now with a kind of fierce radiance.

Brackett turned away. "I'm busy," he said.

Jesse went out. The wet film blinded him, but the whole world seemed to have turned golden. He limped slowly, with the blood pounding his temples and a wild, incommunicable joy in his heart. "I'm the happiest man in the world," he whispered to himself. "I'm the happiest man on the whole earth."

Brackett sat watching, till finally Jesse turned the corner of the alley and disappeared. Then he hunched himself over with his head in his hands. His heart was beating painfully like something old and clogged. He listened to it as it beat. He sat in desperate tranquillity, gripping his head in his hands.

Sunday Morning on Twentieth Street*

It was a fine day in early spring. Bright sunshine flooded the street, where a group of boys in Sunday clothes were playing ball. In most of the tenements the windows were up. Clean-shaven men in collarless shirts or in underwear, women with aprons or sloppy pink wrappers leant on the sills and gazed with aimless interest at the street, the sky, those who were passing below. Thus they would spend most of every Sunday morning through the coming summer, and now, in the first flush of mild weather, they had already taken up their posts. The street rang with the animated bickerings of the boys at their game, with the click of a girl's shoes as she skipped rope, with the muted sounds of a dozen unseen radios.

Into this familiar scene came a sudden intruder: an odd-looking ambulance with glazed windows. It turned into the street quietly, moved along slowly as the driver searched for a number, and then came to a stop before a rooming house – a drab four-storey building of yellowish, soot-stained brick. In the tenement windows above all eyes turned to the ambulance. On the street all games stopped, and, in an instant, the ambulance was surrounded by children.

Those who knew why it had come told the others. An hour earlier there had been a police car, and, still earlier, two men from the gas company. The odour of gas emanating from the building had been so strong that it had made churchgoers sniff as they passed by on the street.

The youngsters who clustered around the ambulance ranged from four to fourteen. Most of them were of Irish stock, the children of longshoremen and truck drivers, of subway workers and labourers. The boys were wearing their once-a-week suits, the girls had on decorous home-made dresses. Only one little Italian lad had on stained blue denim trousers as though it were any old day of the week. A few of the youngest children had begun giggling with excitement when the ambulance appeared, but most of the others had become rather quiet. They stood watching, neither shocked nor amused, their faces knowing and adult-grave. Yet, as the two drab men in the front seat of the ambulance stepped out and walked towards the door of the rooming house, the boys followed them with quiet, compulsive curiosity. The landlady said "Beat it" and shut the door in their faces, but they only wandered back to stare further at the ambulance.

Up above now, in the open windows of the surrounding tenements, new faces had appeared, and eyes were riveted on the doorway of the yellow-brick building. No one talked, no one moved away, and no one came down. Only two adults were on the street, and they had been there before the ambulance came: a dumpy elderly woman and the black janitor of a neighbouring tenement.

When the two men had gone into the house, one of the boys – a wiry, sallow-faced, blond lad – jerked his thumb and murmured softly to the others: "Oh, mamma, ain't they got the job?"

"They'll be carrying *you* down some day, Shorty," a stoutish lad commented with an attempt at humour.

"Knock on wood," the blond one replied, tapping his knuckles on his head.

"Here comes Big-Feet Mary," a third lad announced, pointing. Inspired by an idea, he doubled over with silent, exaggerated laughter. "Let's tell her we got a customer to play bingo."

The boys watched Mary's approach. They felt affection for Mary, because she was coarsely good-hearted, letting them play freely in front of her basement flat, occasionally treating them to a taste of beer. Yet their affection was blended with contempt, because Mary was a queer one, a funny-looking, offbeat gal. Widowed, and the mother of four little girls, Mary elbowed her way through life by turning a penny from the minor sins of her neighbours. She ran a private bingo party twice a week for all who enjoyed a game of chance and anyone else she could wheedle into coming. In addition, she augmented her penny profits by the illicit tax-free liquor she procured from time to time and sold to friends she could trust. She always was in danger of a collision with the law, but her four little girls were tolerably well fed and neat as a pin.

Mary clumped down the street, stomping as always like a big truck horse striking sparks from cobblestones. The nickname "Big Feet" did not come from the size of her feet, which were not out of the ordinary, but from the noise she made in walking. This in turn was the result of the metal cleats worn on her heels to preserve shoe leather. Now, with a genial, fleshy grin on her rubicund face, Mary clip-clopped towards the ambulance. She had stumpy legs like the supports of an old-fashioned sofa, her figure was barrel-round, and her bottom was gargantuan. At thirty-five she was quite a thing to see walking, and the boys met her, as always, with suppressed giggles.

"Hello," Mary chirped to them, waving her hand. "Hello, Tommy... hello, Dusty... hello, boys." Her voice had a warm, coarse, throaty quality.

Dusty, a stocky lad of twelve, winked at his fellows, shoved his hands into the pockets of his trousers and began the game: "Hey, Mary, we got somebody wants to play bingo."

"Yes?" Mary enquired, all alertness. She gazed from one to the other. "Where is he?"

"It ain't a man, it's a woman."

"Did you give her my address? Did you tell her when we play? Did you talk me up?" Mary enquired eagerly.

"No, but I'll introduce you when she comes down. She's right upstairs."

"For Heaven's sake," said Mary, "I don't need introductions. I just talk to people."

"You'll need an introduction to this dame," the Italian lad put in with a guffaw.

The boys laughed. Mary paused, looking alertly from one to the other – and then for the first time noted the presence of the ambulance. She asked quickly, "What's this here for?"

"Just somebody visiting somebody," Dusty replied with a straight face.

"You sure?"

Several of the boys nodded.

"Well, give your friend my address," Mary said, and then clip-clopped over to the two adults in the doorway of the next building. "Hello, dearie," she said to the woman, "I didn't see you in my place last night." The woman, who was chewing on a piece of thread, was in her late sixties, dressed in black, her eyes rheumy, a dark moustache on her pallid face. "No, I guess I wasn't there," she murmured. Then, with odd irrelevance, "Things is so dear."

"But bingo ain't dear," Mary argued sweetly. "You win at bingo."

"I don't win. And my husband wallops me."

"But you can't never win if you don't play," Mary persisted. "Bring your husband too."

"Well, I can't talk about it now," the woman replied with an air of great preoccupation. "Don't you know there's a suicide in there?"

"A suicide?" Mary exclaimed with intense dismay. "But there was one last week."

"That was only an old man – but this is a young *girl*. And they're going to bring her down right away."

"Right away?" Mary echoed. Her ruddy face had become liverish, and she suddenly looked ill.

"Some of them plans it for weeks," the janitor said reflectively. "This one had it all planned, I bet."

Sucking her thread, the woman in black replied with disdain, "Them that kills themselves is crazy."

"They ain't crazy," the janitor argued, "they's sorrowful."

One of the drivers suddenly appeared. He stepped into the front cab of the ambulance and leant over the seat. He pulled out a canvas tarpaulin, so folded that it looked like a market bag with handles at its top. Walking at an even pace, with no particular expression on his face, he re-entered the building.

"That's for to wrap the body with," the elderly woman exclaimed with animation. She chewed her black thread vigorously. "I wonder what she looks like now?"

"Oh, don't tell me," Mary cried, backing away. "A young girl! Oh, I don't want to stay here any more." She clumped off quickly across the street – but there paused, gazing up with pained wonder at the dark-shaded window of the rooming house.

"Hey, Mary," the stout boy called to her, "aintcha gonna wait for your customer?"

Mary didn't reply, but she looked over at him reproachfully.

"She's real crazy for bingo," Dusty jibed. "Only, you're gonna hafta lay her down to rest once in a while. She ain't so strong."

"And you ain't so funny neither," the blond boy murmured suddenly out of the corner of his mouth. "Why don't you let ol' Mary alone?"

"What's it to you?"

"You're a jerk," the blond boy replied sharply. "Shut up, or I'll slam you down."

The door of the rooming house opened again, and conversation stopped. Both men came out. They walked to the rear of the ambulance and opened the doors. Inside all was dazzling white, excessively sanitary-looking. Piled one on the other were several unpainted pine boxes without covers. The men lifted out the topmost one. The children became very still, even the youngest ones ceasing their chatter. The man who was holding the rear of the box rested it for a moment on his hip and thigh, while using his free hand to close the door. They went inside, with the smaller youngsters trailing after them. The landlady shut the door and leant against the jamb with folded arms. "Beat it," she said. She was a slatternly woman, with grey streaking her muddy-brown hair. "There's nothin' to see, so now get away," she told them with weary harshness.

The little ones scurried a few feet back. They gazed avidly at the shut door.

"Hey!" the stout lad announced humorously as he jerked his thumb at the ambulance, "It's nice in there."

The blond boy shook his head. "Oh, you jerk!"

"Oh, ashes to ashes," the lad in blue denim recited. "Oh, ashes to ashes, and ashes to ashes, and ashes to ashes…"

"I know that one," a red-haired girl burst out. "Ashes to ashes and dust to dust…"

"Shut your face, or I'll give you a bust," the Italian lad said. The boys laughed quietly.

"I wish they'd hurry up and bring her down," the stout one murmured. "I gotta go home for dinner."

The blond boy clapped a hand to his face. "Oh, mamma, he's thinking of eating. What a jerk!"

The other snickered. "This ain't the first stiff I ever seen. Maybe you never seen one, but I seen plenty."

"Bet you never saw what I saw," the Italian lad burst out excitedly. "I saw a man carved up like this" – he sliced his finger across his middle. "Oh boy, don't ask… did I have nightmares!"

"Listen…" another began.

The landlady opened the door. "They're coming," a little towhead of six cried out in an excess of excitement. He bounced up and down. "They're bringing the box." He scurried back, his fair skin flushed, his blue eyes feverish.

A hush descended on the street. The two adults in the next doorway moved out for a better view. The woman in black stopped chewing her bit of thread: it hung wetly over her lower lip. Those in the windows of the surrounding houses leant forward. Then, before the men could emerge, Big-Feet Mary uttered a curious, muffled cry. Her face became blood-red. She turned her back and started away furiously, clip-clopping down the street. She did not look back, nor did the others turn to watch her go. Her shoes pounded loudly until she stepped down to her basement flat and disappeared. Then the street became silent again.

The men appeared. The box had its anonymous occupant now in its dark canvas shroud. The younger children stared in eager fascination, but it was clear that they could not fully comprehend. The older boys, clumped together, looked on intensely, lips pressed together. The blond boy quickly crossed himself.

The man holding the front of the box rested it on his hip and thigh with practised ease while he opened the door latch with one hand. Without a word, both men strained in unison, lifting the heavy burden, sliding it in. The doors closed. With impassive faces, the two men walked to the front. The motor started, the ambulance pulled away.

The silence broke then, abruptly. On the sidewalk, where the younger children were standing, a small girl bounced her rubber ball, swung a leg over it skilfully, and commenced counting "One, two, button my shoe", as though the day were as usual again, and nothing had really happened. The towhead shrieked and burst into chatter.

The older boys, clumped together in the middle of the street, were still quiet. The intense looks, the strained eyes, had not wholly relaxed. They shuffled around, hands in pockets. "Oh, mamma," the blond boy murmured, "there she goes. Another stiff gone to hell!"

The stout one spat. "That's the way it is. I'm used to it."

"Who wants to play some ball?" Dusty asked quietly.

"OK," another murmured.

"Cripes, look!" the blond boy exclaimed, pointing to the door of the rooming house. "She don't waste no time, does she?"

The landlady had hung a sign behind the glass pane of the front door. It said "Vacancy".

The Italian kid clapped his hands together. "Oh, ashes to ashes… Oh, ashes to ashes, and ashes to ashes, and ashes to ashes…"

The blond lad spat and laughed softly.

Presently they began to play ball.

Afternoon in the Jungle*

Charles Fallon, aged thirteen, jiggled a hand grenade in his palm and waited for the traffic lights to change. When the Eighth Avenue bus moved off, he took cover behind a snow pile. At twenty yards he looped the deadly missile high into the air. It exploded squarely on top of the bus. Charlie smiled with satisfaction and scooped up snow for another grenade.

He progressed slowly up Hudson Street, killing time – a smallish, wiry, rather white-faced boy with tight lips. At the corner of Perry he found an envelope containing one million, two hundred and thirty-four dollars. He dropped his grenade and crossed the avenue to a pawnshop. It was Sunday, and there was a steel-mesh gate in front of the door, but Charlie made a wish and got inside. He helped himself to a flashlight, a pair of ice skates, a Boy Scout knife, binoculars, a picture of Mary in the Manger and a lot of other things. He left a hundred-thousand-dollar bill in payment.

At Twelfth Street he crossed the avenue again. He wandered down Greenwich, stopping to gaze at the pictures in the lobby of a movie house. He decided that Anita Louise was nicer-looking than a stuck-up like Norma Shearer.* He kissed Anita Louise. They sat on the edge of her million-dollar swimming pool, and he kissed her again. She was about to tell him how swell he was when the ticket taker came over and said, "Beat it, kid." He scuffed away.

At Eleventh Street and Seventh Avenue he planted himself before the window of a bakery. In rapid succession he ate a chocolate cake, a napoleon, a charlotte russe and two twenty-five-cent peach cakes with whipped cream. He was just about to buy the whole bakery when a lady came out and told him to stop leaning against the glass and move along.

Bored, he turned down Seventh Avenue and started home. Between Commerce and Morton he went into a candy store where he occasionally traded. The stout proprietress wheezed over to the counter.

"How much is the caramels?" Charlie asked.

"Two for a penny."

"And these?"

"Four for a penny."

"And the lollipops?"

"A penny apiece. Which do you want?"

"I'm going home and get some money. I'll be back in eight minutes."

He crossed the street again and walked down to Houston, wishing he could buy some candy. He knew a way to make one caramel last half an hour. You put it on your tongue and sucked it. It took will-power not to chew it right down, but the sweet taste stayed with you longer. And you avoided the toothache. He took off his soaking mittens and blew on his hands. He wished it weren't Sunday. His neighbourhood was like a cemetery on Sunday, because the factories were closed.

A bus approached, going south. Old Man Sheehy and his wife, who lived in Charlie's house, ran across Varick to catch it. The bus stopped. The old couple hurried forward, and, as Mr Sheehy took his hand from his pocket, a fifty-cent piece dropped to the sidewalk. He made a frantic grab for it, but the coin rolled onto the subway grille and dropped to the bottom of the pit. Muttering, the old man stepped up into the bus. He held the door back with his hand and shouted out to Charlie, who had run over to the grille, "If you find it, Charlie, I'll give you a dime!"

"Sure," said Charlie.

The bus moved off, and Charlie raced away. He would need chewing gum and a string to do the lifting. Fifty cents! He had retrieved pennies from subway grilles – once even a dime – but this was the first chance he had ever had at so much money. It would be the simplest thing in the world, of course, to tell Old Man Sheehy that he had not been able to find it.

He covered the distance to his house on Downing Street at a run. He was too excited to remember the broken step on the second flight of stairs, and his right foot slipped through, flinging him headlong and giving him a terrible crack on the shin. He limped up the remaining three flights with tears in his eyes.

His mother was sitting at the window, darning.

"Ma, can I *please* have three pennies?" he asked. Phrased as a question, his words expressed a command. He had learnt long ago that his mother always yielded to bullying.

"Hush, for goodness!" she said. "Your father's asleep. Now, why do you come in here with your wet rubbers and filthy the floor?"

"I'm going right out again. Just give me the pennies, Ma."

"I can't give you pennies. You had a penny for candy on Tuesday."

"Ma, I got to have them. Look, there's a dime that fell down in the subway place. If I had some chewing gum I could get it up."

"So that's it? You were trying to hold out on me, weren't you?" She laughed softly. "I'll give you one penny, not three, and you'll have to give it back."

"One's no good. I gotta have three. I can't do anything with one. It doesn't make a big enough piece of gum, don't you see, Ma?"

Mrs Fallon went into the kitchen and came back with her change purse. "I only have two pennies," she said. "Beside a dime for church tonight."

"Well, give me that. I'll..." He stopped to sneeze. "I'll change it. You'll get it all back, honest."

"No. I can't risk it." She gave him the two pennies.

Glumly Charlie accepted them. This would make his task harder, but he knew that his mother was inflexible about church money as about nothing else.

"And I expect the two pennies back," she said.

"OK." He was already busy in the kitchen, searching for a string.

"Ah, yes," his mother said, in the long-suffering whine he knew so well, "in the old days, if you'd come to your father or me for a penny, we'd give you a nickel. If you'd asked for a nickel, you'd get a dime."

Charlie found a ball of heavy cord, cut off a ten-foot length and stuffed it quickly into his pocket.

"But now your father's a cripple, poor man," his mother went on. "Limping where other men walk, working at night when other men work at day, he's grateful for the little he has."

"OK, Ma, I'm going," said Charlie. Without waiting for an answer, he banged out. He told himself that all mothers were a pain, and fathers worse. Catch the old man giving up a glass of beer to buy his kid a chocolate bar...

He ran down the block and around the corner to the candy store on Carmine Street. He bought two boxes of Chiclets and emptied them both into his mouth. The gum had to be moist and pliable, or else the coin wouldn't stick to it. He trotted across Varick, chewing hard, but on the right side of his mouth only, so that he wouldn't get a toothache. Near the bus sign he lay down full length on the icy grille. The concrete base at the bottom of the pit was covered with debris and snow and little puddles of water. Methodically he began to search for the coin, inching himself along from one spot to another on the grille. His heart pumped with excitement, and an image of the bakery window danced in his head.

Ten minutes passed with no result, and he stopped to blow on his hands. Then he returned to his task.

He located the coin. It lay half in a puddle of water, half on the concrete base – a difficult target. With a tight little smile on his lips he knotted the end of his cord several times and wound the chewing gum around the knot, giving it a broad flat base. A wrist loop at the other end of the cord prevented his losing it. Then, after thrusting the wad of gum into his mouth for a last moistening, he lowered it carefully to the bottom.

Working intently, he did not notice the man who had come up behind him – a small, shabby man of about forty-five, whose thin face was reddened by the wind but was liverish grey beneath the surface colour.

Charlie heard him before he saw him: the man's breathing was laboured, as though he were straining at a heavy burden.

The boy looked up briefly and went back to his work. He was concentrating upon the most difficult part of his job. The wad of gum was not sufficiently heavy to make a plumb line, yet he had to drop it with some force on the coin in order to make it take hold. It might take a hundred trials to achieve one accurate strike.

The man watched in silence for a moment. Then he dropped to his knees by Charlie's side, exclaiming in a hoarse tone, "Fifty cents, eh?" He peered down at the swaying length of cord above the coin. "Ah, it's hard that way, isn't it?" he asked softly.

Charlie didn't answer.

The man peered down to watch another trial. "Sure, the gum gets solid right away in this cold. It don't look to me like you'll make it, kid. And it's getting dark. You need real tools for this job. You'll never get it this way."

Without looking up, Charlie said loudly, "Who's asking you?"

The man got to his feet. Quickly he glanced all around. There was no one in sight. He stepped back a few paces and unbuttoned his overcoat. Secured to the inside of his coat by leather straps were four lengths of broom handle, whittled to reduced their thickness, each about three feet long, each fitted at one end with a rubber socket by which it could be joined to another length. With practised efficiency he connected them. At the tip of the final length there was a small rubber suction cup. He stepped forward, fitted the end of his pole neatly into the grate and, dropping to his knees, thrust it to the bottom. "I'll show you how a professional does it," he said lightly. He kept his eyes averted from the boy's face. "Now, this is one method. Another is cup grease. With cup grease you can pick up a bracelet. But when you spot some change a suction cup is—"

"What's the idea?" Charlie cried out in fury. "What do you think you're doing?"

"I'll show you how a professional does it, kid."

"Get out of here!" With his left hand Charlie tugged savagely at the man's arm. "Get out of here!"

The man fended him off, laughing in a hoarse tone that had no humour in it. "What's the difference? You wouldn't get it," he said. "Why let it lay there for somebody else?"

"The hell I won't get it!" Charlie cried. "You leave it alone. It's mine. Please, mista."

"I'll give you a nickel," said the man.

Charlie pulled up his string with decision and crammed it into his pocket. Then, rising, he stepped behind the man and kicked him viciously in the small of his back. The man cried out in pain. Instantly Charlie retreated a dozen feet.

"That's a hell of a thing to do," the man groaned, holding his back. "I'll break your neck, you little rat. You almost made me drop my pole." They glared at each other for a moment, motionless and undecided. There were thirty years between them, yet in a way they looked startlingly alike. Both were small, the boy as boy, the man as man – both were drawn, hardbitten.

The man knelt down again, watching Charlie carefully. He lowered the pole, but kept his head raised. Charlie stood indecisively. Then he ran to a snow pile by the kerbstone. The man shifted to face him. "You come near me and I'll break your neck," he said. "I'm telling you. Beat it. I won't even give you the nickel now. I'm mad."

Charlie grabbed a chunk of ice from the snow pile. He flung it with all his strength. It missed by a foot, but the man was frightened and jumped to his feet, pulling up the pole. Charlie retreated behind the snow pile. Trembling, eyes fixed on his enemy, he clawed under the crust of ice.

"You're looking for trouble, ain't you?" the man said bitterly. He glanced up and down the deserted, darkening avenue. "You think I like this?" he asked suddenly. "Do you think I like to fight with a kid like you over fifty cents?"

A snowball struck his knee just below the protection of his frayed overcoat. He shook his fist, his voice swelling with anger. "I'll give you trouble if you want it, you kid!" He stopped, panting for breath. Then he dropped the pole and hurled himself forward.

Charlie darted out of reach. A snowball, almost pure ice, struck the man full in the forehead. He slapped a hand to his head, half sobbing in rage and pain.

"How do you like that, you skunk?" the boy cried.

The man chased him, but Charlie was twice as agile and kept the snow barrier between them. Within a minute the man stopped, his mouth open, a hand pressed to his heaving chest. Without uttering a word, he went back to the grille and crouched down, lowering his pole.

Frantic, the boy varied his attack. He came past at an angling run, from behind, and slammed down a piece of loose ice. It struck the man at the base of his neck. His body quivered, but he didn't turn. He was raising the pole to slip it through another opening in the grille. Charlie made another rush, this time determined to use his feet. Swearing, the man leapt up to meet him, catching the boy's arm as he veered off in terror and swinging him in. He had him gripped by both arms. The pole lay on the grille between them.

"I ought to break your neck!" he cried, shaking him. "I ought to break your ratty little neck! But I'm not going to, see? You're a kid. But you listen..."

Charlie twisted hard, broke free, and at the same moment stamped on the man's foot. He ran to the security of the snow pile. The man stood looking at him blankly, his face twisted in pain. "Oh Jesus," he cried, "what a little gutter rat! Did I hurt you? Did I do anything to you when I had the chance? I was going to make you a proposition." A snowball struck him in the chest. "All right," he said. "I can't get it, if you don't let me. You can't get it, if I don't let you. We're both going to lose it. It's getting dark. I'll split with you. I'll give you twenty-five cents."

"No!" Charlie cried. "It's mine!" His whole body was shaking.

"Don't you see you can't get it without real tools?" The man was pleading now. "Your gum ain't no good in this cold weather."

"It's mine."

"Jesus, you found it, I'll admit it," the man said. "But I got a suction cup. I can get it for both of us."

"No."

"Jesus Christ, I got to have some of it!" the man cried, his voice corroded by shame and bitterness. "This is my *business*, kid. It's all I do. Can't you understand? I been walking all day. I ain't found a thing. You got to let me have some of it. You got to!"

"No."

The man flung out his hands. "Oh, you kid, you kid!" he cried despairingly. "If you was ten years older, you'd understand. Do you think I like to do this? If you was ten years older, I could talk to you. You'd understand."

Charlie's lips tightened. His white face, spotted by the cold, was filled with rage. "If I was ten years older, I'd beat your face in," he said.

The man bent painfully and picked up the pole. Limping slightly, his hand pressed to the small of his back, he walked away. He was crying.

Charlie stood trembling in triumph, his face turned to stone.

It had become dark.

Circus Come to Town*

At seven forty-five in the morning the two brothers reached the circus grounds to discover that the circus had not yet arrived. The immense grassy field was barren of tents, of ladies in spangled tights, of elephants and freaks, and all else that town lore associated with a circus. Alan, aged seven, permitted himself a frank wail of disappointment: "Maybe it isn't gonna come!"

Eddie, who was twelve, replied calmly, "The posters said Saturday, didn't they? Don't be a goof." He added after a moment's reflection, "It's good we're early: we'll be sure to get hired, see? First come, first hired."

"They'll hire *me* – won't they, Eddie?"

Eddie yearned to reply, "How many times you gonna ask me that, you goof? How do I know?" Instead, since he was himself acutely worried by the same problem, he answered, "I'll get you a job. You just let me do the asking."

"You sure there'll be clowns?"

"There's always clowns."

"How do you know?"

"I know, that's all." Eddie took his Boy Scout knife from his pocket and opened a blade. "Let's play mumbley-peg.* It'll kill time."

"The clowns I wanna see most," Alan murmured. "Them and the cannon that shoots people. It'll be awful if it don't come."

They sat cross-legged on the grass and began to play. The day was windy but fine, the sun was already warm, the air fragrant with the spring odours of turned soil, first hay cuttings and wild flowers.

Except for a difference in height and weight, the two brothers were much alike in appearance. Both were towheads, fair of skin and blue-eyed, with lean, delicately boned faces – both were slender, wiry and thin of body. Their family resemblance was further accented by their clothes: the same faded, worn and patched denim trousers; the sleeveless cotton shirts of identical cut, although different hue; the sneakers scuffed at the sides and patched with adhesive tape. They played their game and chattered about the circus – and secretly worried. Eddie had never seen a large circus, and Alan had not seen any circus at all, and there was great question in their minds whether they would see this one today.

They lived in a small Indiana hamlet in the centre of a farming area. It was a "play date" considered by circus people to be worth a visit only once in several years. When the posters that advertised the one-day gigantic spectacle had first appeared, the boys had rushed to their mother with the news. She had listened to them as she always did, and replied, as she so often did, "I'm sorry, kids, but two tickets cost a dollar twenty cents, and I just don't have it for circuses." There had been no argument from the boys. Since the day, three years before, that their father had deserted his family, the words "no" and "I'm sorry" had come to live with them and be accepted.

But shortly after this conversation Eddie had learnt something momentous from an older boy. If you came early, if you carried water or helped set up seats or did other work, you were given a free pass. And so here they were at seven forty-five, the two Campbell brothers with two peanut-butter sandwiches in a paper bag, both of them passionately eager to go to work. But their work had not yet arrived, and they had reason to be worried. With Alan it was the dark, gnawing question of whether a seven-year-old would be hired at all, but for Eddie it was something else. On days when their mother was away at work, he was responsible for his brother. She had permitted this expedition on the sole condition that he would not separate himself from the younger boy. He had promised – but he had an ugly premonition: that he alone would be hired and would therefore have to choose between the circus and his duty. To forgo the circus was unthinkable – but to let Alan manage himself for the day and walk the mile home alone would mean a licking and bed without supper. And so Eddie was playing mumbley-peg with a sense that no matter what he decided, some sort of disaster was lying in wait for him.

Eight o'clock became eight thirty, became nine. More and more boys appeared at the field. The Campbells stopped playing their game and circulated like spies in an enemy land. Each newcomer was asked whether he was buying a circus ticket or working to get in. And each new rival for employment, of whom there were a good many, was estimated as to age, strength and potential competition on the labour market.

Finally, at ten thirty, the first heralds of glory arrived, a line of trailers pulled by roaring tractors. The huge trailers were painted red and had "Berry Bros. Circus" inscribed in white on their sides. A great, ecstatic shout burst from the throats of all the waiting boys, and they raced down the length of the field yelling "I'll work... hire me... I'm strong." No one hired them, and no one paid any attention to them beyond shouting occasionally, "Look out there... watch out now... stand back." More and more trailers arrived and were dispersed to separate portions of the field. Then several station wagons appeared, and from them issued a swarm of men in overalls and jeans who leapt into feverish activity. Some lowered the sides of the trailers, disclosing great bundles of canvas and immense, varicoloured poles, others climbed upon the tractors to operate lifting winches and mechanical stake-drivers.*

The Campbell boys, like the others, scurried from one spot of activity to the other and called eagerly in thin boy voices, "You want some help?... Will you hire me?... You want some kids?" They were waved away or shouted away by men who were not unfriendly, but who were behind schedule and furiously preoccupied. And as more trailers appeared and more men – and then a fantastic, lumbering line of fourteen trotting elephants, each holding with its trunk the tail of the elephant ahead – and as the canvas was unrolled and spread on the ground, with even a few of the elephants put to work at pulling and hauling, despair gripped the brothers. Alan cried, "They ain't gonna hire us, you'll see... it's just a fakey story." Eddie, wanting to reassure him, needed reassurance himself, and could offer his brother no comfort. It seemed to both of them unaccountable and malicious that useful boys were not hired when there was so much activity on the field and so much work to be done.

And still the tractors roared off and returned with more trailers and more men. Presently the field became a dangerous place for small boys. They were warned loudly and repeatedly to beat it. In gloomy silence they wandered down to a quiet corner, where the non-working elephants had been lined up, side by side. There they found other boys and compared notes and learnt that no one at all had been hired. They sat down and watched the elephants and watched the activity on the field and became increasingly gloomy.

"I told you," Alan muttered after a while. "They don't want kids. Let's go home."

"Home? What for? This is more fun than home."

"No, it ain't. Not if we can't see the circus."

"We're seein' elephants, ain't we? Why don't you look at the elephants?"

"I'm tired of the elephants. I wanna see the clowns. If I can't see the clowns, I don't wanna stay."

"Well, you can't go home! I'll give you a bat on the ear if you go home."

Alan's voice turned shrill. "You don't dare hit me – I'll tell Ma."

"Aw, listen... don't be a baby. I'm not gonna hit you. But what do you wanna go home for? It's better here. There's still time to get hired, ain't there?"

"I wanna see the clowns," Alan muttered.

It turned eleven o'clock. Their paper bag was opened, and the two peanut-butter sandwiches were devoured. By now there were many more boys sitting with them on the edge of the field, and a sprinkling of adults also. Rumours passed along the line: the circus had arrived late, and for this reason there would be no afternoon show, and no boys would be hired. And, following this, a story exactly the opposite: in order to make the afternoon performance, extra help was needed. Every boy who wanted to work would be hired at twelve o'clock and would be paid a dollar in addition to his free ticket. "You see," Eddie cried triumphantly, "I told you to wait." Alan was cheered by this, but when twelve o'clock came and no one was hired, he began again to mutter about going home.

Presently a good-sized tent was raised at one corner of the field, and word passed that it was the cookhouse for the circus people, and that boys would be needed to set up tables and benches. But no one came to hire them, and when several of the older boys walked out on the field to enquire, they were waved off immediately. The menagerie tent went up, the walls billowing in the wind, and then the sideshow tent, and then, at one o'clock, the immense big top was raised, and a shout went up from the spectators, because it was an exciting sight – but there was no work for the Campbells or for any other boy. There was only the grim spectacle of several circus workers who came to drive stakes into the ground at intervals all along the edge of the field. They hammered the stakes and looped them with rope and walked away.

The brothers sat on the ground, close together, silent. For three weeks they had drenched their hearts in the glory and drama of this day. It had turned very sour. And when, after another half-hour of waiting, a boy sitting near them rose to his feet, announcing loudly that he thought he'd see if the sideshow was open for ticket buyers, they turned and looked upon his departing back as upon a personal enemy, and then turned and gazed at each other in bleak misery, each comprehending for the first time in his young life the full and terrible power of money.

And then they were hired. Suddenly, standing before them was a big, cheerful-looking man in a soiled blue-serge suit, his gay tie flapping a little in the wind, his straw panama hat pushed back on his balding head. He whistled shrilly with two fingers in his mouth, laughed as the line of boys started in surprise and bawled loudly, "Any you kids wanna see the circus?" Some eighty boys from five to sixteen jumped to their feet, all screaming "yes" at the same time. The man laughed, whistled piercingly again to bring silence, and then said, "I kinda thought so. Come around close." The boys ducked under the rope and thronged about him. He pointed suddenly at Alan. "You, sonny – how old are you?"

Alan stammered, quickly slipped into a lie: "Eight."

"That's good. I just wanted to be sure you were over two – we don't hire no kids under two."

A gale of appreciative laughter came from the boys. The man laughed with them, then abruptly sobered and whistled quickly for silence. He gazed at them with a measure of severity now, but with a lingering grin at the corners of his wide, thin mouth. "Listen to me careful, boys. No more joking." He held up a purple card. "When show time comes, I'm gonna give every one of you boys one of these tickets. That'll get you in free. All you gonna do for me is help pull a few ropes, cos it's a windy day, an' then set up some seats. You'll work maybe an hour, hour an' a half." He pointed at Alan again. "Now, nobody expects you to be as strong as a big boy. If you were all big boys, it'd be better for me, but you ain't. But so long as you do your share, you'll get a ticket."

"I'll do it," Alan cried passionately.

"I'll do it," a five-year-old echoed.

"OK. Now, you boys are lucky today – awful lucky. Some days we make good train connections an' we set up early an' we only have work for twenty or thirty. But today we're late, an' we're gonna use every one of you." He paused while the boys cheered. "But you listen to me. Square is square. I know all the tricks. I been sixteen years with the circus, and I been pushing boys for nine. That's my name: Pusher. You want to know anything, yell for Pusher. Now, there's some boys who'll work twenty minutes an' then duck under a tent flap. They come back later wanting a ticket, but they don't get it. There's other boys haven't got no fair play, an' they wanna quit before show time. They don't get a ticket neither. There's still other boys who ain't even here, but they'll show up two hours from now an' claim they worked like you did. Only, they don't know me. Square is square. I don't give free tickets for nothing. An' you know why I'm the pusher? Because I remember faces. I been studying every one of your faces, an' there isn't no boy gonna claim he was here unless I see him with my own two eyes right now. You got that?"

The boys shouted that they understood and were ready.

"Come on, then." Grinning a little, he started off at a dogtrot for the menagerie tent. The Campbell brothers, eyes shining with glory and delight, kept close together in the swarm of running boys. When they reached the tent, a distance of forty yards or so, Pusher's chest was heaving, and the sweat was rolling from his temples down the sides of his meaty face. He said with a cheerful laugh, "I sure can't run... like you boys... can. But you got it now... we're awful late. Bad rain last night..." He wagged a stubby forefinger at them and suddenly roared: "You get it? No show this afternoon unless you work hard and fast. I wanna see you go at the double." He thrust two fingers into his mouth, whistled piercingly and yelled, "Larry, where the hell are you on the guy ropes, Larry?"

A youngish man, unshaven, hair tousled, in dirty khaki coveralls, came running out of the menagerie tent. Pusher pointed accusingly at the flapping canvas and asked with anger, "You want it to blow down? I told you to start pulling ropes."

"Can't do everything," the other replied sullenly. "Joe said to spread hay for the antelopes."

"What's the matter with that Joe? Is he married to one of those antelopes? I wouldn't be surprised. Tight those ropes up before she blows away, goddamit. You kids here" – he gestured with both arms to a group of six boys that included the Campbells – "you stick with my friend, Larry. Do what he tells you."

"Wait a minute, how about some heft here?" Larry asked sullenly. There was a husky fifteen-year-old boy in the group, but the others were all younger. "How about some beef?"

"This ain't the only tent, an' I gotta start those chairs in. You think five thousand chairs move in by themselves?" He turned to the boys. "When you get finished here, come over to the big top, I'll give you your tickets... c'mon kids." Pusher ran off, the other boys dogtrotting behind him.

"Oh boy, oh boy," Alan whispered to his brother with swollen pride, "I told you I wouldn't be too little."

"Work hard now," Eddie advised. "We gotta keep on the good side of 'em."

Larry said with mingled acidity and humour, "All right, you day labourers, three on each side of that guy rope, smallest boys close to me." The group of boys took position and eagerly grasped the heavy rope. Larry bent over the low stake, deftly slipped the knot by which the rope, running from stake to tent wall, was fastened. He snagged the loose end in a hitch around the stake, held it with both hands. "All right, hit it!" The boys pulled hard and Larry jerked. "Hit it!" They pulled again, watching the tent wall become tauter. "Hit it hard! Hold it!" Quickly he looped the rope around the stake, tied it off. He moved to the next stake. As they waited for him to slip the knot, Alan whispered excitedly to Eddie, who was alongside of him, "Ask him if there's trained dogs in the show."

"Sh! We don't wanna bother him."

The command came, "Hit it!" They pulled. "Hit it... Hit it hard... Hold!"

They moved from the second stake to the third, to a fourth, a fifth. And rather quickly, for both brothers, the pleasure departed from what they were doing. It was work, hard work, to pull down mightily on a thick Manila rope with the tent wall snapping away in the wind. This was rope that had been weathered and beaten by sun and rain and time. Hempen barbs pricked and scratched their flesh, and their soft boy palms began to be chafed. Alan's arms commenced to feel heavy, his fingers to ache. The double line of stakes around the large tent seemed endless, and Larry's command kept up without pause: "Hit it! Hit it! Hit it hard!"

"My hands hurt," Alan burst out suddenly.

"Spit on 'em," Larry advised. "Don't let 'em get hot."

The boys all spat on their palms and went back to work with a heightened morale that did not last long. There was no magic in spitting on one's palms, they found. The flesh continued to redden and became increasingly sore, and they were pulling a little less hard and taking a bit longer with each rope. "C'mon, lean on it," Larry was beginning to say. "Hit it, will ya?"

They became lost in a jungle of ropes and stakes. Breathing became laboured, and lids blinked as salt sweat trickled into the corners of their eyes; thighs trembled with strain; soft young bodies accustomed to hard play but not to sustained work yearned for rest. "Hit it! Hit it hard!"

Eddie Campbell, panting and weary, began to worry. Knowing his own fatigue, he was afraid for his brother. If Alan stopped work, he would be fired. And if that happened, what would *he* do? Suddenly, although he was afraid of Larry, he asked boldly, "Mista, can't we stop for a minute?"

Larry straightened up, laughed a little, not unsympathetically, and said, "Only half around, kids."

The oldest boy amongst them, who was fifteen, spat on his square hands and said boastfully, "I'm not tired."

"Well, if you're not, I am," Larry told him. "Sure, take a breather." He threw back his head and stared up at the serene blue of the sky, and said with a laugh, "Anybody works in a circus oughta have his head examined. I sure hate a windy day – rather have rain than wind."

"How you doin'?" Eddie whispered anxiously to his brother.

"I'm awful tired," the latter confessed.

"I'm tired too, but you're not gonna stop workin', are you?"

"Oh no, I wanna see the clowns."

"That's the boy."

"Do *your* hands hurt, Eddie? Mine hurt awful. I'm gettin' blisters... look."

"Mine hurt too, but you won't stop workin', will you? We done half already."

"Oh no, I won't stop."

One of the other boys asked, "Mista, you know what time it is?"

"A little past two about. Let's go, kids."

"The show starts at two thirty, don't it?"

"Never has so far this season. My guess is today it'll start about four."

"You think maybe we can see the sideshow then, the freaks 'n' everything?" Alan asked eagerly. "Does the ticket give us that too?"

"I don't know, I ain't running this damn circus," Larry answered tartly. "C'mon, hit it! Hit it! Hit it hard!"

They worked, and Alan's weariness turned into fatigue, fatigue into aching exhaustion. He heard Eddie's whispered, panting encouragement – "C'mon, kid, only a few more, kid" – but he began to lose the power of response. Pride and desire could no longer weigh against burning hands and leaden arms. He stopped work.

"Oh, c'mon," Eddie pleaded fiercely, "*please*."

"I can't."

"You might as well sit down," Larry told him sullenly. "You ain't doin' no good anyway."

"You'll lose your ticket, Alan," his brother cried despairingly. "Let him keep working, mister, *please*."

"Oh, shoot, if that's what you're worried about, forget it," said Larry. "You think I'm gonna report you or something? What do you take me for?" He added to Alan, "You move along with us so Pusher don't spot you, that's all. C'mon, hit it, kids."

"Jeez, thanks," Eddie cried.

"Hit it! Hit it hard!"

The big tent was circled, finally, all ropes snagged tight, the canvas secure against the wind. "Amen," said Larry. "Finished, wrapped up." He chuckled softly as he looked at the boys. The fifteen-year-old had borne the work well, but the others were almost as deadbeat as Alan – all of them, including Eddie, had blisters on their hands. "Pooped out, yeah?" Larry said with his wry grin. "OK, hop over to Pusher an' get your tickets. I hope it was worth it."

"I ain't tired," the fifteen-year-old said boastfully. "I'm used to hard work."

"Well, good for you, sonny."

"Thanks, mista," Eddie murmured. "About my brother, I mean."

Larry reached out and poked him in the ribs. "You do the same thing for me some day."

Alan asked, "Can we get some water someplace? I'm so thirsty!"

"See over there, by that small tent? There's a water bag. If you find any beer in it, whistle for me." Larry grinned and went back into the menagerie tent.

Slowly, but feeling the triumph of their accomplishment, the boys made their way across the field. They compared blisters, and lied to one another that they were only a little tired. Alan whispered to his brother, "I did good, didn't I?"

"Sure you did."

"I wouldna stopped, but my hands hurt so much."

"You did swell. You did great."

"Are *you* tired?"

"Yeah, a little."

The water was warm, and tasted of the canvas bag, but they gulped it with pleasure and relief. And then, somewhat revived, they started off at a quicker pace for the big top.

"I wished you'd asked him about the dogs," Alan said. "Next to the clowns I wanna see dogs climb ladders an' things. I hope they have dogs."

"I'll ask Pusher," Eddie replied. "He'll know."

They found Pusher near the big top. He was standing before a trailer directing a line of scurrying boys who were carrying chairs. They went up to him in a group, the fifteen-year-old boy in the lead. He said, "Pusher, here we are. We fixed the ropes. You got our tickets for us?"

"Course I have," Pusher replied cheerily. "Just grab some chairs now an' run 'em in, two boys to a team."

Eddie said in a faint voice, "You mean we gotta work some *more?*"

"We gotta run those seats in, don't we?" Pusher answered jovially. "Can't have a show without seats. Only half in yet. Let's go, now, they ain't heavy."

"You said we'd get our tickets," the fifteen-year-old charged resentfully. "Why don't you give 'em to us?"

"Now, look here," said Pusher, with the smile vanishing from his face, "don't you tell me my business. My job's to get those seats in. I can't help it if there's a wind blows up an' we hafta pull ropes too. A little double duty won't hurt you. My job is seats. Whatsamatter, you too lazy to run a few chairs in? Well, yes or no – yes or no?"

"OK," the boy muttered.

"Well, grab a partner an' get in line. C'mon, you towheads. Brothers, ain't you? Get busy."

"We're tired," Eddie said. "Awful tired."

Pusher ruffled his hair. "Won't hurt you to get a little tired. You're a working man, ain't you?" He gave them both a little shove, pushing them into line before the trailer. "Circus gonna start in fifteen, twenty minutes."

Alan said to his brother in a wailing voice, "I can't do any more, Eddie, I'm too tired, my hands hurt too much."

"But it's only fifteen minutes. He said the chairs ain't heavy."

"I can't do *anything*, Eddie."

"Well, listen," Eddie whispered desperately. "You can make believe, can't you? I'll carry them by myself, but you hold one end, you make believe."

"Well... maybe I can do that."

"Let's go," Pusher bawled cheerfully, "hustle 'em in. Got crowds of people outside waitin' to see the show."

The chairs were stacked in flat piles in the trailer – wooden folding chairs attached in braces of three. A sweating circus worker stood inside the trailer and handed them down one at a time, rapidly, to a brawny sixteen-year-old. He in turn passed them to the teams of boys. Each team, with Pusher's cheerful tongue to whip it on, then ran on the double quick to the big top some twenty yards away.

"Let's get a little speed on. Awful late today. Wouldn't wanna miss the show altogether – would you, kids? Come on, brothers, your turn, grab a chair."

Eddie seized the chair flat in both arms, and Alan lifted one end as high as his exhausted muscles could manage, and they both ran at a dogtrot with Pusher's voice lacing their backs. Panting they made the interior of the big top. It was an immense confusion of moving figures, contraptions being hoisted to the roof, men yelling, seats banging and a uniformed band on a platform blowing discordant notes in tune-up. A voice called, "Well, don't stand there – move those seats, you kids." They followed the pointing arm of an assistant pusher to a rising tier of boards. They climbed the boards almost to the top, where men were setting up seats. They delivered their burden and scrambled back down, dodging other teams going up, ducking away from a tractor. Eddie said, "Walk slow, we'll rest goin' back." They slowed down, and the voice of the assistant pusher cracked a whip over them. "Hey, you kids, you workin' or loafin'? No loafers here." They began again to run.

There had been a jungle of ropes and stakes, and now there was a mountain of chair flats. The trailer was emptied, but another trailer was ready by its side. The work was not physically as wearing as the ropes had been, and they could always rest a little on the return trip, yet they sustained it less well because they were more fatigued. Alan kept saying that he just had to sit down for a while, he had to – and Eddie kept pleading with him. "You'll get fired if you sit down. Look, I'm doin' all the carryin'. You wanna see the funny clowns, don't you? Don't you, Alan?" But he himself was rapidly becoming as exhausted as his brother. The faces of both of them were milky white with fatigue – their taffy hair was sodden.

It was Pusher who carried them through. They hated him bitterly, and that helped – they could not shut their ears to him, and that also helped. "You see that feller? Wants a ticket for nothin'. He's tired, he says. Well, ain't that too bad? Wants to work, but don't want to get a little tired. Well, beat it, sonny. Just follow your nose an' beat it. You don't get no ticket from me. Now listen, you kids – the circus is gonna begin in another ten, fifteen, twenty minutes. If you want those nice little passes, you hustle them chairs. Only half a truck of chairs left now. Won't hurt you to work a little. It's good training, in fact, ha-ha. You hustle and I push, ha-ha – that's the way the world is. Move it, kids."

Eddie prayed. He prayed to dear God that Alan would not quit, that he himself would be able to hold out. He prayed that after all this hard work nothing, nothing would prevent them from seeing the circus.

When the last trailer was emptied and the last chair flat set up, it was five minutes past four o'clock. Inside the big top the sawdust rings had been cleared, and the band was playing. The boys stood in line before Pusher waiting for their passes, and the bigger ones crowed wearily, "Guess we did a little work today, huh?... I'd sure like to travel with this circus." The younger boys stood in speechless fatigue, yet in final pride and triumph, while Pusher said in his cheery voice, "Any you kids wanna come back tonight at ten thirty an' move those chairs out again, we'll give you a handful of change, a whole big handful of change. Well, here you are kids, just like I said – go right in an' have a good time... you've never seen a circus like it!"

As in a dream, the two brothers moved into the big top. The assistant pusher said, "Working boys, over there." They reached their section, and found their seats and sat side by side, huddled, with glassy eyes. The tent was filling up, the band was playing with noisy verve, the spotlights glared down on the sawdust rings. Alan murmured, "The clowns, 'n' dogs, 'n' cannon – that's what I wanna see."

"The trapeze," Eddie muttered in reply.

They didn't talk more, because they were beyond talk. They blinked their eyes against the lights and relaxed their spent bodies in the warmth of the sunbathed tent. Presently the band began to play softly, and an announcer's voice smote them from a microphone, but neither boy made much sense out of what he said. The band became brassy again, and some Hindu dancing girls ran out from the wings. For what seemed a long time they whirled around before them and moved their arms to and fro like weaving snakes. The elephants came out and did things that they tried hard to watch, but they had seen the elephants already, and the activity in all three rings was confusing. And presently, heads sagging on limp necks, the two brothers leant against each other and fell asleep.

Pusher said, "Look at 'em. It never fails. I bet there's five kids up there sound asleep an' ten more don't know what they're seein'."

The assistant pusher said, "Well, you pushed 'em hard today – we were late."

"I pushed 'em? I didn't blow up that wind. I got my job to do, don't I? They wanna see the circus so bad they just beg you to work."

"What the hell, we got the matinée on – didn't think we'd make it. Pretty good house, too."

The two brothers awakened at the cannon shot, with a terrible start, to see as in a nightmare the masked figure of a man sail out from the gun muzzle high, high in the tent and plummet down in a somersault into a net. There was a burst of applause, and then on all sides the spectators stood up. The audience began to go home.

Since there was no more to the show, the Campbell boys also went home.

With Laughter*

Tom Fennel snapped his fingers, sat up on the divan and burst into rumbling laughter. "Connie," he said to his wife, "I just realized that all evening I've been trying to put a jinx on you."

His wife interrupted her pacing to gaze at him with amusement. "How come?"

"We agreed we wanted a girl, but I've been a liar. I want another ball player in the family – I haven't got any use for a little old female with ribbons in her hair."

"Then I'll tell you something, pal – if it *is* a girl, don't you try making a tomboy out of her. I..." Connie paused, pressed a hand to the small of her back, then glanced at her wristwatch.

"You have one?" he asked.

"Yes – seven minutes."

"You certainly didn't stay long at eight."

"I'm advancing at a trot," she answered with a pleased smile. "You heard what Jake said: nature built me to whelp easy."

Tom stood up, frowning a little. "How about we call him again?"

"Not yet."

"Why not? You keep saying there's a definite rhythm..."

"Jake's like any doctor. He wants me to have some solid contractions before he decides it's the real thing. So far, there's only been these biddy cramps in the back."

"Then why are *you* sure it isn't false labour?"

"Because of the way I feel."

"Can't you tell Jake about it?"

"He's never had a baby – he wouldn't consider my ideas to be medically important."

"And your ideas are what?"

"I told you when you came home – that cowlike feeling I've had these last two months has gone. I feel so alive I could fly. I think it's nature's way of telling a woman her time has come."

Tom laughed. "Sounds like voodoo talk to me." He took her face between his hands, kissed her and said, "You're just working a racket to get attention."

"OK, go to bed. But don't be surprised if I wake you about three in the morning."

"I'll give you half an hour. Meanwhile, I'll go drink a beer to your perfect pelvis."

"It's time you did. You don't appreciate my anatomy enough."

"Yes?" he asked, and burst out laughing.

"And get me a glass of grapefruit juice, will you?"

Tom nodded and raised his voice as he went into the kitchen. "Say, I forgot to tell you about Paulie. When I was taking him over to your ma—"

"Nature calling," his wife interrupted. "Hold it."

"Sure."

Tom returned to the living room with a glass of juice and a beer bottle. He lit a small cigar, drank some of the beer and crossed to the television set. Then, rather abruptly, he strode into the hallway calling, "What did you say?"

The excitement in Connie's voice was unmistakable. "You can telephone Jake and tell him he guessed wrong. I've had a real contraction."

"You don't say... Good for you!" With some haste he dialled their doctor's number. When the elderly voice replied, he said quickly, "Jake? This is Tom Fennell. Connie says she's had a real contraction."

"Ask her where."

Tom called out the question, got the answer and said quickly, "It was low, in front."

"I guess she's starting."

"The rhythm's down to seven minutes now. Isn't it time she went to the hospital?"

"Yes. You get along and I'll meet you there. And listen, Tom…"

"Yes?"

"Please don't be one of those jerks who get all fussed. Connie's healthy, and the baby's in the right position with its head engaged. So just relax now and help her relax, will you?"

"Sure."

"OK. See you in about an hour."

"Connie," Tom called, "Jake says it's time to go. I'm calling Walt."

"Take it easy, you'll wake up the neighbours," Connie remarked with amusement as she returned to the living room. "There's no rush."

Tom dialled, shifted from foot to foot while he waited for a response and then spoke more loudly than he realized. "Hey, Walt, this is Tom. The baby's on the way."

"Good deal," his friend replied. "I'll be over in about fifteen minutes."

"Can't you make it sooner?"

"Man, you haven't called me since ten o'clock, so I just went to bed. I have to get dressed."

"Hop on it, huh?"

Tom hung up and said excitedly, "Is your suitcase ready?"

"All packed."

"What do we do now?"

Connie burst out laughing. "Go finish your beer."

Tom grinned, kissed her and said, "You're wonderful, sugar. Say – what did Jake mean when he told me the baby's head was engaged?"

"It means the cutie has moved down low so its head is between the bones of my pelvis… right here. It's the normal position for birth. Honey, it's a warm night – why don't we go down and wait for Walt outside?"

"OK, fine. I'll get your suitcase."

As they started down the stairs, he asked, "Was that last one seven minutes?"

"I'm still moving at a trot. We're down to six."

His face furrowed. "That Walt better come on time, or I'll break his neck."

"He'll come, Walt's dependable. Don't start worrying, honey, there'll be hours of this yet." They stepped out on the quiet street, and Connie took a deep breath. "Isn't it a beautiful night? I love it out here. It's like living in the country."

The spring moon was high, the night was very still, and it did seem more like a village street than part of a large city. Theirs was a new suburb of modest two-family homes with an amplitude of old oak trees and green lawns. At this hour most of the residents were in bed, front windows were dark, and the moon, unobscured by tall buildings, was flooding their side of the street with a clean blue-white light.

"Let's walk, it's good for me," Connie said. "We can leave the suitcase."

"You want your coat on?"

"I'm comfortable." She laughed as she took his arm. "But I'll sweat plenty in the delivery room, you can count on that."

He asked with curiosity, "Would you like it if I could be there with you?"

"I guess so. At the start, anyway. After that I wouldn't know you were there."

"What do you mean?"

She smiled. "Honey, when a woman is actually giving birth, her whole being is so concentrated on her own feeling – and on that terrific act of pushing out a mountain from inside her – that she wouldn't know if she was alone or in Yankee Stadium* with a hundred thousand people watching. She wouldn't care, either."

They walked in silence for a few minutes. Connie was thinking that elsewhere in the world other women were setting out with their husbands on the same errand of birth, and it gave her a sense of kinship that was strangely warming. And Tom was thinking, "If it's a little old gal, I sure hope she's honey-brown like Connie and got her straight hair. It wouldn't be kind if she took after me."

"You know..." he said.

Abruptly Connie's hand gripped his arm with a power that startled him. Her body had gone rigid, her jaws were clenched, and her eyes had opened so wide that her eyeballs gleamed unnaturally in the moonlight. He felt shaken to the roots. "Darling," he cried, but there was no response. She stood immobile. Then, after half a minute had passed, her rigidity dissolved in a heavy sigh. "Let's get the time," she said with a faint smile. She took a handkerchief from her pocket and began wiping her face and neck.

For a moment Tom was unable to make his cigarette lighter work. Then he blurted out, "Twelve twenty-four. My God, is that what the real pains are like?"

"That's them, honey. That was a beauty. The little lady is in a hurry. We've skipped to five minutes."

"What?" he asked with dismay. And then, with anxiety and anger, "Where's that Walt? Did he stop for a beer?"

"Now, relax. I had Paulie quicker than most women have a first baby, but I was four hours from the time of my first contraction."

"All right," he muttered, "but I'd sure like to see you and your perfect pelvis in the hospital. You're not trotting any longer, you're starting to gallop."

"Let's walk back. I want to put my coat on."

They waited in silence for another few minutes, and then Tom exclaimed, "There he is, I know the motor." He pressed Connie's hand and grinned with relief. Presently a Buick convertible swung around the corner and came up to them.

"Walt," Tom called as he picked up the suitcase, "don't get out, there's no time."

"OK, shove that in here," their friend replied.

He was an undersized, slender man, with a sharp-featured, coffee-brown face, and with a sly grin always twitching at the corner of his mouth. He and Tom had been fast friends since high school. "How you doing, Connie?" he called as he set the suitcase on the front seat.

Tom opened the rear door of the car, and Connie stepped inside. "I'm fine, thanks so much for coming."

"You gotten bigger since last week. You want to lay a little bet on twins?"

Connie didn't reply. In the act of sitting down she had gripped the front seat with both hands.

"What's the matter?" Tom called from behind her, and then stepped in quickly. He put an arm around her for support and covered one of her hands with his. He could feel the hot perspiration on her hand, and the rigidity of her body, and he groaned with sympathy and helplessness. A heavy sigh came then from Connie, her body relaxed, and he helped her back in the seat. "Get going," he said urgently to his friend. "Keep it smooth, huh?"

Connie's head was back on the seat, and her eyes were closed. She asked softly, "Did you time it?"

"Damn it, no!" Quickly he reached for his cigarette lighter.

"From the time the last one ended till this one began," she added. She began to wipe her face.

He studied the dial. "I can't be positive, but I'm almost sure it was five minutes again. Perhaps a shade under."

She opened her eyes and smiled at him. "Good." Then she took his hands in both of hers. "Tom, you're making too much of this. That was a healthy contraction, all right, but it's not as bad as it looks to you. I can take it – nothing's going to happen to me."

"Well," he answered in an effort at lightness, "I was way the hell off in Korea when you had Paulie. I'm inexperienced. Don't mind if I get a little flustered."

"You look as though you're sitting on nails. I'm just another woman having a baby."

"I love you so much," he muttered, "so much you don't know."

"I do know," she whispered, "and that's what makes this good and exciting, even if there is some pain."

"Hey, how am I driving?" Walt called.

"Perfect," Connie told him. "Just try and avoid any sudden stops, won't you?"

When the next contraction came, Connie muttered "Oh!" and bent forward under the force of it. It required an act of will for Tom to turn from her face to his watch. For a moment he felt bewildered – then, as he checked the minute hand, he became momentarily unstrung. He checked again.

Connie sat erect. She was panting a little, and her lids were half closed over her dark eyes.

"Connie," he muttered apprehensively, "that was only three minutes."

Her eyes opened. "You sure?"

"Yes!"

"It did seem shorter." And then, with keen distress, "Oh, Lord, don't tell me I'm going to have one of those taxicab babies?"

"Will it hurt you if we drive faster?"

"We better."

"Walt..."

"Right, I heard you," their friend replied. They were still on the outskirts of the city, and he pushed the speedometer to sixty. "Connie, is there any way to know how much time you actually have?"

"I'll know better when I get the next one." She was sitting tensely.

"What'll we do... I mean... we've still got twenty-five, thirty minutes."

"Maybe you can pick up a motorcycle cop," Tom said excitedly. "If a cop'd lead the way, we could go through lights. We'd make it in half that time."

"I'll keep my eye peeled."

Tom turned to his wife with naked anxiety. "What *will* we do if we can't make the hospital?"

For a moment Connie didn't reply. She felt such loss of equilibrium that she couldn't think. It was too shocking to accept – that she might be caught without assistance. Yet now it was a real possibility, and quite terrifying. Without forming her thoughts consciously, she suddenly answered the question with blunt harshness: "We'll have to let nature take its course... We'll stop the car and I'll have it!"

"Without a doctor?"

"*You'll* be the doctor!"

"Look out for that truck!" Tom yelled. "He's turning in."

"I see him," Walt answered, braking the car. "Take it easy, chum. There won't be any accidents tonight."

"What do you mean about me being the doctor? How can I..."

"You can do what's necessary!" Connie told him with determination. "If we get into that spot, you're the midwife."

"What do I do?"

She put her hands on his. "I'll tell you, honey – all I know, anyway. But Tom, listen... I'll really be in a bad way if you don't keep calm. If you realize you *can* help me, you won't get so nervous that you can't."

Tom's big body tightened, and his rugged face became very stern. "OK, sugar. Don't worry. Just tell me."

"We're making good time," Walt called. "I figure less than twenty-five minutes at this rate."

"Fine," Tom replied quickly, "but don't talk now. Connie has to brief me in case we don't make the hospital."

"We'll just have to hope there are no complications," Connie said tensely. She glanced quickly around the interior of the car. "Oh, Lord, there just isn't enough room in here. I'll need to hold on to something with both hands... and if you're going to help me... I don't know... maybe we can stop by a house where the people are decent... Well, we'll just have to face that wherever we stop..."

"How much time will we have? Will you have any warning?"

"I'll know in advance, there'll be time."

A contraction interrupted them. Tom flicked his lighter, fixed the time, and waited with set jaws until Connie opened her eyes.

"Three minutes again."

She nodded and sighed, and then smiled at him as she wiped her face. "I'm doing fine. It's like having an old-fashioned bellyache – nothing a person can't take. This handkerchief is soaked. Open the suitcase and pull out a diaper, will you? I'll baptize it for the baby."

He did so, hands and body moving very fast. Then he said urgently, "Get back to making me a midwife."

"Well... let's see..." she chuckled ruefully. "It's six years since I took that class for pregnant women. Well... I guess there's nothing at all you can do until the baby's head begins to be born. Just wait, and if I make some loud noises, don't think there's anything wrong. It's a woman's privilege to yell a little."

He pressed her hand. "Go on."

"Here's one thing I remember well, Tom. When enough of the head is in the clear, so that you can take hold of it, you have to support it with a hand on either side." She gestured. "Like this."

"OK."

"And what you do, honey, is to *lift* the head *gently*. In that way you help the head get born, and it makes it easier on me."

"All right, I'm clear on that."

"What next?" she wondered aloud. "Oh, yes... listen... when the baby's head appears, its face is turned down. But once the head is born, it'll start to turn up. Don't interfere with that."

"Go on."

They hit a rough spot in the pavement then, and the car jounced heavily. Walt called back "Sorry", and Connie said, "No harm done."

"We're in the city anyway," Tom muttered. "What else?"

"I'm thinking... Well... when the head is all born, the hard part for *me* is over. But you'll have to watch out then, because the body'll come out quickly – it sort of slides out, Tom, like those kittens we saw." She stopped talking as the car slowed down for a red light. Walt looked to both sides, saw no cars and stepped on the gas without waiting for the light to change. "What else?" Connie continued. "I must be forgetting..."

A contraction began, and her hand, which had been on Tom's knee, tightened like a clamp. "Oh, Lord," she whispered heavily when it was over, "that one surely paralysed me – it was fierce."

"Still three minutes," he told her.

Connie wiped her forehead and neck with the diaper. She said wanly, "Starting to sweat good."

"What do I do after the baby is born? I have to hold it upside down and slap it, don't I?"

"Wait," she whispered. She put her head back against the seat. Presently, with closed eyes, she began to talk again. "Yes, hold it upside down, but if it cries by itself, you don't need to slap it." She mopped her forehead. "Seems to me I must be skipping things you ought to know, dammit. Here's something... When the baby is fully born, you'll absolutely need your two hands to hold it. That's very important."

"OK." He was wondering how so many thoughts, images, fears, could be racing through his brain at the same time that his whole being was concentrated upon her instructions.

She opened her eyes and smiled at him. "And remember, a newborn baby is as slippery and wriggly as anything. I guess that's why a doctor always gets a grip on the ankles."

"Sounds like nothing at all," he told her in an effort to relieve his tremendous tension. "Catching a football on the run is much harder. Have I graduated? Is that all I have to know?"

"A baby gets born in three stages," she reminded him in a controlled way, but with fatigue showing. "That's only the second."

"Oh, God, yes! But how can I cut the cord?"

"Well... guess you won't be able to. Wrap the baby up and keep it warm. Let Walt find the way to call an ambulance."

"Will you be all right like that... and the baby?"

"Yes. Just let Walt be sure to describe the situation. Then the ambulance can come prepared."

"Walt, did you hear that?" Tom called.

"No."

Tom repeated it.

"OK, but we ought to be there in almost fifteen minutes now."

A low groan burst from Connie's lips, and Tom, without looking at his watch, knew that the rhythm had changed again. Under the lighter he saw that it was a fraction over two minutes. When he could speak to Connie again and had told her, she nodded, panting, and then whispered, "Tell Walt... I'm afraid we haven't got fifteen minutes."

"Are you sure? You feel that way?"

She nodded.

"Walt," he called urgently, "Connie doesn't think there's time."

"You want me to stop?"

Tom turned to his wife. "Not just yet," he called back, "but get ready."

"God Almighty!" Walt shouted excitedly. "What am I being so dumb about? There's a hospital on Franklin Avenue, it's only a few blocks." He slowed to take a corner. "We're going there."

"Do you know anything about it?"

"It's small... a denominational hospital. I pass it on my way to work."

"But do you know anything about it?"

"Don't know and don't care," Walt answered as he swung around a second corner, picked up speed and started back in the direction from which they had come. "This is an emergency, isn't it? We're there in a minute."

"Connie?" Tom asked, peering at her. "All right?"

"So far." She grasped his hand in both of hers. "Oh, I hope there's no trouble!"

Tom didn't answer. He was stroking her arm.

"There it is," Walt shouted. He was slowing down. "I'll run into the office and alert them. You bring Connie."

It was a rather new brick building, three storeys in height. Most of the windows were dark, but the entrance was lighted, and there were lights in one section of the ground floor, presumably the offices. It looked like the type of private institution in which there might be good equipment and service, even though there were only twenty or thirty beds.

The car stopped. Walt leapt out and ran for the steps.

"All right to walk?" Tom asked urgently.

"Yes."

He helped her out, both hands grasping her arms, and Connie said quietly, "I'm not counting on it, honey, I'm counting on *you*." She gave a low grunt, and her hands seized his arms. Her head fell forward.

"Oh, sweetheart, darling," he muttered. The weight of her head was on his chest, and he had a wild hunger to fling his arms around her and comfort her with his kisses, and at the same time he thought that he ought to be checking the interval since the last contraction – but he did nothing, because her hands were like clamps upon his arms, and he dared not move.

"Oh my!" Connie sighed. She was panting, her head still resting on his chest. "It won't be long now." With effort she straightened up. "Let's go."

"I didn't get the time."

"Never mind." She was breathing heavily, obviously needing the support of his arm around her.

"Can you manage the steps? You want me to carry you?"

"No... but go slow."

They were only on the second step when they heard loud voices from the other side of the entrance door, which had been left slightly ajar. Connie stopped abruptly. The door opened, and they saw Walt gesticulating, talking intensely – and opposite him a tall, lean white man of thirty-five who was standing with his legs wide apart and his hands on his hips. "But my God," Walter was crying rather incoherently, "he's a war veteran – how can you let a pregnant woman..."

"I told you already – there's no doctor on duty," the other man interrupted uncomfortably.

"There are nurses, you—"

"This hospital has a policy, and I'm not going to be the one to violate it."

A middle-aged nurse suddenly appeared behind them. She cried out, "But, Mr Clark, this is an emergency, it won't affect—"

"Don't interfere," Clark interrupted with resentment. "And don't tell me how to lose my job. I'm Night Supervisor, not you. I'm the one the Board'll hold responsible, not you."

Stunned, knowing the whole of it already while still unable to accept it, and feeling as though he were strangling, Tom cried out, "Are you saying my wife can't come in?"

"This hospital doesn't accept coloured patients."

A bull roar burst from Tom's throat, and he let go of Connie. "The hell you say, you son of a bitch. We haven't got time. She's going in, and you won't stop it!"

"You try to force your way in, and you'll be committing an illegal act," Clark replied without moving. "In my desk drawer I've got a pistol and a licence to use it. Don't make me."

"Tom," Connie cried, "*please, please.*" She caught his coat. "Take me back to the car."

He turned to her, putting his arm around her, his face contorted with rage, his mouth open and working. He wanted to beat this man to a pulp, to force their way in – but Connie's cry had cut through everything. There was no time for trial or error, and her voice had told him that. It was Walt who spoke out what was useless: "You think this'll read good in the newspapers? You think you still can treat us like cattle and get away with it? You stony-hearted bastard – I'll see that it gets out!"

For the first time Clark lost his composure. "Let it!" he snapped with passion. His eyes blazed, and he began to tremble with indignation. "Where do you get off insulting me? Nobody asked you here. This hospital was built by white folks for their private use. You've pushed your way into the schools and movies and restaurants of this city, but you won't get in here. Go to your own hospital. Go have your nigger babies in the damn Supreme Court."

"Oh... look!" the middle-aged nurse cried distractedly from the doorway. "Look at her."

The Fennells had taken only a few steps towards the car when Connie had stopped abruptly. With the awareness of a swimmer who is half drowned yet still can clutch at a piece of wood in the water, she had turned back. In front of the hospital there was an iron fence, and her hands were reaching out for it blindly. Her body was sinking into the ancient, primitive squat of a woman in labour.

"Oh!" the nurse cried. "She's having it now!" She disappeared inside.

Connie's hands, one of them still holding the diaper, found the rods of the fence. A grunt sounded deep in her throat – her body jerked forward, and then, as she strained and bore down, a low cry issued from her lips.

Walt ran over to Tom, his face twisted with rage, "What can I do?"

Tom, with one arm supporting his wife, did not hear. He was fixed upon her, and he looked frantic. After half a minute, the contraction stopped, but Connie did not let go of the railing. Her head was almost touching the bars, and she was panting heavily. She sank back suddenly, exhausted, the full weight of her body upon his arm. Her eyes were closed. In the spill of light from the hospital doorway, Tom could see the hot blood flush under her skin, and the running sweat on her face. He cried frantically, "Connie, let me get you to the car."

Her eyes opened, and she seemed to be having difficulty in focusing on his face.

"Let me get you to the car!"

"No," she whispered tiredly, yet with a self-possession that astonished him, "don't move me, darling. The baby's coming now."

"Oh, not here!" he cried out involuntarily. "Not on the street!"

In reply Connie gasped deeply for air. Then her body jerked forward, her hands seizing the railing again. A low, moaning grunt burst from her lips, and she bore down with the contraction.

"Let *me* hold her," Walt cried. "*You* have to help the birth."

Tom didn't reply. He was staring at his wife with anguish and desolation.

The middle-aged nurse ran out of the doorway. "I called an ambulance." Abruptly, with a small, meaningless cry, she ran back inside.

Connie sank back heavily on Tom's arm. She spoke with effort, as though she were half asleep. "Help me lie down." Then, as Tom lowered her to the sidewalk, she seemed to awaken. "Oh!... There are so many things I forgot to tell you."

"About the…" Her words turned into a gasp for air. She seized Walt's arms, and a low groan burst from her open mouth.

"Oh, Christ!" Tom cried, sobbing aloud. "Here on the street!" He dropped to his knees, his whole being sour with fear. His heart was hammering against the wall of his chest, and he told himself that he could not give his wife the help she needed, that something would go wrong and she would die, that his shaking hands never could hold a baby, that he had forgotten everything.

"Tom?" Her voice came weakly. "Tom?" He saw the look on her strained beloved face, and her aching need rose like fire within him, and he cried out to her in a clotted voice, "Yes, I'm here, I'll take care of you."

He became one with her, then. The world blotted out. There was only Connie and himself, and their child to be given life. He was not aware when a passing auto stopped and two white men got out of it to stand on the sidewalk and gape – nor did he hear Walt speak to them so savagely that they left. He did not see a light go on in one of the upstairs rooms of the hospital, or hear a window being open, or hear voices saying, "What's going on down there? *What?* Hey… that woman's having a baby!"

He heard nothing except the deep grunts and low birth cries of his wife. These possessed him, and it was as though his heart were inside her heart, so that he too was part of the rhythm of this birth, and the hands with which he would deliver became sure and steady. With fiery calm, he waited for each new contraction, for the moment when he would do for his wife what she needed. The moment came quickly. He heard a succession of low, deep cries from Connie that seemed to echo and re-echo in the hot stillness of his mind – and then he was supporting the tiny warm head between his hands and lifting it gently as he had been told.

A voice from the outside slipped into his consciousness then, angering him before he even knew what it was saying. He tried to shut it out, but he could not. "Don't bear down till I tell you, dearie. Pant, keep panting, that's the way." He turned to see a nurse – a young, blonde, *white* nurse – standing over his wife, and he burst out with a sob, "Get away! We don't need you."

"You certainly do need me," the nurse answered firmly, but without offence. "If the cord's not in the right place, the baby can strangle. Keep panting, dearie." And then, as she leant over by Tom to inspect the position of the umbilical cord, "You're doing fine, mister, but pay attention to me... Good, everything's fine. Bear down now, dearie. Another minute and it's over."

The head began to rotate with the next contraction, and, with that wondrous motion of birth, jubilation rose like a sweet sap within Tom's heart. The right shoulder appeared, and then the left, and he didn't hear his own cry when finally the tiny, exquisite body was lying on his arm and the warm, tiny ankles were between his fingers.

"Oh, wonderful, everything's grand!" the nurse said with delight. "Now keep holding the ankles, mister, and turn him upside down. He has to spit out before he can breathe. Oh, fine!"

The newborn cry sounded, and the new life wriggled and began to move its arms, and Tom didn't know that he was weeping. "My wife," he cried, "is she all right?"

"Why wouldn't she be? An easy birth if I ever saw one. Here... wrap the little fellow in this – we have to keep him warm." She glanced over at Walt, who still was kneeling behind Connie, unable to realize that his services no longer were needed. He looked exhausted. "Hey, mister, you... I dropped a sheet and blanket somewhere – there they are. She needs to be covered. Put the sheet under her."

"The cord," Tom said with excitement. "How..."

"Came down all prepared," the nurse interrupted. She was smiling with a kind of triumph that he could not understand – a thin, blonde, attractive girl in her early twenties who was giving the lie to all of the blind rage in his heart. "Got some cord ties," she continued, pulling a sterile package from one of her pockets. "Got scissors, got Kelly clamps* – that's all we need. I would've been down earlier, but it took time for the news to get to the top floor. It sure was a quick birth. I—"

"But my wife," Tom interrupted with anxiety, "she's so quiet."

"Just sleeping. She's had some hard work, mister – she'll wake up in a few minutes. Hold the baby nearer to me now. Isn't he a howler! Thinks he owns the world!" Her hands worked deftly. She cut the cord and said to Tom, who had shivered perceptibly, "Everything's normal, don't get worried. Cover him up now. He's ready to sleep a little."

Tom said in a low voice, "Can you take him for a minute? My knees are giving me hell, I need to stand up."

She did so, and he stood up slowly, rubbing his knees, and turned slowly towards the hospital steps with his shoulders hunching over and his thick neck swelling. "You would've let my wife die," he cried in a thick voice. "You no-good bastard... you were ready to see her die."

"No, Tom, don't be a fool!" Walt cried. He caught Tom's arm, was shaken off, caught it again. "Listen," he lied, "I hear the ambulance coming. There's always a cop with every ambulance."

Tom shook him off – and then suddenly burst into dry, wracked sobs. "Oh, my God, I'm glad I was born black! It's easier to be human." He stumbled towards his wife, crying out to the nurse, "Is she all right – are you sure?"

"Yes – she's waking up now."

"Out on the street!" Tom cried. The tears began running down his face. "She could've died."

A heavy sigh came from Connie, and her eyes half-opened. Bending over her, the nurse said quickly, "Everything's fine, dearie, the baby and you."

"Tom? Tom?" Connie murmured.

"I'm here." Still sobbing, he knelt down by her and kissed her cheek and forehead.

"Oh!" she said, and became fully awake. "It's normal? Everything all right?"

"All normal," the nurse told her. "A boy."

A slow smile came to Connie's face. "How nice. Let me see him... Oh, what a darling!"

"I hear the ambulance," Walt exclaimed jubilantly, telling the truth this time.

The nurse nodded. "Good. The birth's not over yet, you know." She opened Connie's dress. "Put him to suck. It'll help your contractions."

"Where did *you* come from?" Connie asked with surprise. "Did you deliver me?"

"I only helped. Your husband did the job."

"Oh, Tom, sweet Tom," Connie murmured, "I knew I could count on you." And then, as though her rapture could not be contained, she began to laugh – a tired, soft, joyous laugh that sounded in the night like a clear bell. It was a laughter that spoke of all that was good and healthy and hopeful in life, and it came from her like a bird song at dawn – and at the hearing of it Clark, the superintendent, entered the hospital and shut the door.

The Farmer's Dog*

Last year, in London, I went to a dog show with some friends – Hugh Stuart, a physiologist, and his wife Libby. While we were there, we met a man named Edmund Donat. Polish by birth, he was a chemist in the concern where Libby worked as a stenographer. When we were leaving at teatime, Libby invited Donat to join us. He accepted with such shy and manifest pleasure that it seemed evident he led a rather lonely life. He was a tall man, a bit stooped, nearly bald, with pleasant features and handsome dark eyes, but with an unhealthy pallor. He appeared to be about fifty-five, and I was surprised to learn later that he was ten years younger. Subsequently Libby told us that he had contracted typhus during World War II, when he was a prisoner in a concentration camp, and that he still was suffering neurological difficulties – just what, she didn't know.

When he had ordered tea, Hugh fell to ribbing his wife in an affectionate way about the limited intelligence of dogs. It had become clear as soon as we entered the show that Libby was a fervent dog lover and Hugh had tagged along reluctantly in a spirit of marital compromise. Whenever she expressed enchantment with a dog, he would mutter: "I've dissected the breed, darling – its brain is the size of a pea" – or, "Inbred for generations – has a wretched nervous system." Libby hadn't seemed to mind his remarks, although occasionally she would poke him with her elbow and say, "Shut up, fish lover" – and she regarded him now with a tolerant smile as he continued to needle her. Presently she said to Donat with a bubbling laugh, "You see what I'm married to? He doesn't like dogs because they're not something else." And, to her husband, "You idiot, can you herd sheep like a collie? I like a dog for what he is – even though you say an octopus is more intelligent."

"An octopus reasons, my dear, and uses a tool to open the clam he wants to eat. Dogs can be taught certain things, but they don't reason."

"If I may comment," Donat put in, "I believe there is a wide range in the intelligence of dogs, just as there is in the human being. At the upper level there surely are some dogs that *are* capable of intelligent reasoning."

"Have you concrete evidence of that?" Hugh asked.

"I think so."

"What?"

"I once saw a dog in a fearful predicament. I believe she reasoned about what was best to do. But I can't give you the evidence in a few words."

"We're in no hurry. Please tell us."

Donat gazed at each of us in turn, as though to make certain we really wanted to hear him out. When Libby said eagerly "Do tell us, please", he nodded, smiled in a shy way and began. He had a marked accent, but his English was fluent.

"The name of the dog was Pani – that means 'Madame' or 'Mrs' in Polish. But I must explain first that when Germany invaded Poland in '39, I was living in Warsaw. My father sent my mother and me to a farm he owned about thirty miles away. We never saw him again – he was called up to the army and killed. But that's another matter…

"There was a house on the farm where we used to spend our holidays. The land, about ten acres, was worked by a tenant family, and I was a good friend of the two sons. One of them was my age, almost seventeen, and the other, Antek, was a year older. Pani obeyed everyone in the family, but above all she was Antek's dog. Between Pani and Antek there was an understanding, and there was a love, that were quite extraordinary."

Until this point in his narrative Donat had been talking in a matter-of-fact way. However, when he referred to the bond between his friend and the dog, his eyes began to kindle, and from then on his face gradually became more and more animated.

"In December 1939, when the Germans had all of Poland under their control, they issued an order that every thoroughbred of certain breeds – Great Dane, Dobermann pinscher, German shepherd and a few others – was to be turned over to them. All other dogs were to be destroyed."

"Why destroyed?" Libby asked stiffly.

"Why not?" Donat answered with a smile. "It was a logical decision by an army command waging a ruthless war. They needed certain dogs for guard duty – all others were to them useless consumers of food. In fact, they regarded people more or less the same way. Well, so immediately Antek heard of it, he hid Pani in the barn. He did more than lock her in: he built a hiding place under the floor that would have been hard to find. He would take her out for exercise at night and visit her several times during the day."

"Didn't the dog bark?" Hugh asked.

"Oh, no, not even when Antek entered the barn."

"Because he muzzled her?"

"No, because he told her not to bark."

Hugh raised his eyebrows, and Donat, observing it, smiled a little, but offered no explanation.

"About a week later, early in the morning, an army truck came to the farm. There were three SS men in their black uniforms and, with them, a Polish interpreter, a turncoat from one of the border regions. Inside the truck there were two dogs chained to the sideboards. Well, the whole family was there, and the interpreter, an arrogant little weasel, said to the father, 'Where are your dogs?' It was young Antek who answered him: 'We only had one dog, and it died several weeks ago.' At this the weasel burst out laughing. He said, 'There's been a regular plague in this district – so many dogs have died recently.'"

Donat paused, ran a hand over his head and muttered, "You hate an enemy, but a turncoat makes you burn with special rage. Anyway, this weasel translated into German, and the corporal in charge snapped an order. Then that one, the corporal, walked up to Antek and aimed a pistol at his face. Antek's mother let out a scream and ran towards them, but one of the SS stopped her with such a shove that she fell down. The rest of us stood where we were, paralysed." Donat swallowed, and again ran a hand over his head. "The weasel said to Antek, 'I'll count ten. If you don't say where the dog is in that time, the German will kill you, and don't think he won't.' Well, before he even began to count, the mother screamed out from the ground, 'The dog's in the barn.'"

Again Donat paused, then spoke very softly. "I'll never forget the look Antek gave his mother – as though it was him she'd betrayed. It was a moment to freeze the soul."

At this point Hugh asked with keen interest, "Do you think Antek would have kept silent?"

"I don't know. When I asked him later, he told me honestly that *he* didn't know. But my feeling at the time was that the dog was as precious to him as anyone in the family, and he would not have spoken. Anyway, after the mother told, the weasel let out a guffaw and said, 'How clever you peasants are! Your dead dogs are always alive in the barn.' Well, so the father was sent to bring Pani out."

"*Was* she a thoroughbred?" Libby asked.

Donat shook his head. "A mongrel. We were certain the Germans would shoot her. Antek, naturally, was frantic. He began to plead with the interpreter, to tell him what a wonderful dog Pani was, to beg him to take her even though she was not a hundred per cent thoroughbred. He was carrying on awful, sobbing and half incoherent. His manner aroused the curiosity of the Germans, because they asked the weasel to translate. Well, presently Pani came into view. How shall I describe her? She was a big dog, larger than a German shepherd, with a tremendous chest, and with the muzzle and jaws of a Great Dane. She had short brown hair, a bushy tail and a wide black ring around her neck. We used to speculate about her bloodline. We knew nothing about her, you see. Antek had found her, a stray puppy. It was clear she had many strains in her – as though a larger Boxer had mated with a Labrador retriever, and their issue with a German shepherd, and down the line a Dane or even a mastiff. From all of this crossbreeding had come a dog that seemed to have inherited only the best from each of its sires. There was so much alertness in the way she looked at you, so much intelligence in her brown eyes, so much power and self-possession in the way she walked, that one almost could say she looked regal. There was no doubt the Germans were impressed with her. Antek, of course, never let up pleading. Through the interpreter he begged the corporal to show Pani to his superiors. He promised by all the saints that she'd learn whatever they wanted quicker than any other dog, and that she would be obedient to the death. Well, finally, that was how the corporal decided it. They took Pani away."

Hugh asked, "Did the dog fight to keep off the truck?"

"No, because Antek himself jumped on it and called her. He told the corporal she wouldn't need to be muzzled or chained like the others, but he insisted, and Antek did it. Then he put his arms around Pani and spoke to her a moment. He came down blubbering like a child."

Libby asked, "Was an arrangement made so Antek would be told what they did with Pani?"

Donat smiled. "Conquerors don't make arrangements. So far as Antek knew, it was farewell one way or another."

Hugh said, "But I judge it wasn't farewell?"

"No. Five months later we met Pani again. It came about because Antek, his brother and I joined an illegal Resistance group. Antek and I were arrested one night, when we were on a mission, because it was after the curfew hour and we had no pass. We were a month in prison in Warsaw, and then we were shipped to the concentration camp of Auschwitz. Fortunately for us, we were only there a few days – very fortunately. Together we were sent to a labour camp where there were about a thousand men. The work we had was to build a road from a new airfield to a main highway. It was killing labour, dawn to dark seven days a week, and the food was miserable and insufficient, but if a man was strong to begin with, he could survive – provided he had luck. By luck

I mean that he didn't get sick or hurt so he'd be shipped back to Auschwitz. We did have one blessed privilege: we were allowed to wash in some swamp water twice a week, so we could keep free of lice. Well, so Pani wasn't at the camp when we arrived – at least we never noticed her. But one morning in June Antek saw her with another work commando."

Donat paused, ran a hand over his head as he seemed to do every time he felt special emotion, and there was a slight hoarseness in his voice as he went on. "I wish I could describe to you how Antek behaved that night. I myself didn't see Pani, and although Antek and I were in the same commando, we couldn't speak at work. It was not until we were in the barrack that he could tell me. He came up to me like a man who had just buried his child. His eyes and face were wild. He said, 'Pani's here, and she doesn't remember me!' Well, after some questions, I got an account from him. But first you must understand something important about our conditions there: every work commando had about forty men and was guarded by two capos, two SS men and three dogs. A capo was a prisoner who carried a club and acted as an overseer, and who got special food and privileges for the filthy work he did. Usually they were men with a criminal background, brutes who had lost their humanity. But in spite of them and the SS guards with their rifles and tommy guns, it would not have been impossible for determined men to sometimes escape. Some would have been killed or caught, but others would have gotten away, and many of us were desperate enough to try. It was the dogs that prevented us. You have no idea how those dogs had been trained to ferocity towards us prisoners. All of us looked the same, by the way – the same striped clothes, the same shaven heads. At every worksite one dog remained with an SS man, and the other two guarded the perimeters – that is, the outside line permitted us. If a man came within ten feet of the line, the dog on that side would be on its feet with a snarl that would curdle your blood, and also would alert the guards. At five feet, without warning, the dog would attack with an absolutely insane fury. In only our second week there, during a rain, a man slipped in the mud and rolled down an embankment over the line. By the time a guard ran up, he was dead, his face unrecognizable, his throat mangled. It didn't take more than that to make us all tremble before those horrible dogs. We knew that even if we bolted into the woods without getting shot, those dogs would be at our throats sooner or later. Well... this explains to you why Antek was so heartsick. That morning, when our commando was being counted, he was standing in an outside file. Another commando moved up alongside ours. He saw Pani not two yards from him – a guard had her on a chain leash. Naturally he didn't dare call to her. What stunned him then was to see Pani suddenly turn her head and look at him. He said she gazed at him steadily for about thirty seconds, but without any sign of recognition, just staring at him the way a man might. Then her commando moved off. Yet, as Antek said, Pani was a dog, not a man, and unless she had forgotten him completely, it was impossible she wouldn't react to him."

"And she had forgotten him?" Libby asked intently. "I don't see why. An intelligent dog shouldn't forget its master in only five months."

"Wait, you'll hear," said Donat. "What troubled Antek most was the thought that the SS had transformed his beloved Pani into the same kind of wild beast the other dogs were. 'I would have preferred her dead,' he said to me. 'I didn't dream they would do this to her.' I remember what I answered him. I meant it to be a comfort, but it wasn't. I said, 'If they can turn a schoolboy into a murdering SS man, why isn't it easier with a dog?' All Antek did was look at me and walk away... Well, about a week later, our commando had a change of guards. With one of the new SS came Pani. The first time I saw her assigned to a perimeter of our worksite, I feared her and hated her like any other dog. And yet it struck me by the second day that there was something strange in her behaviour. Because each time Antek's work brought him anywhere in her view, I had the feeling she was quietly watching him."

Hugh said, "Are you telling us that she *had* recognized Antek, but was not letting on? That's hard to believe."

"Antek noticed the same thing, and neither of us knew what to believe."

"How did Pani act with you?" Libby asked.

"It happens I rarely was close to her, either on the march or at work. Once, when I did come close, she looked at me exactly as she had at Antek the first time. I didn't know what to make of it."

"And how did she act with the other prisoners?" Libby asked.

"Like the other dogs."

"Did she ever attack one of them?"

"I'll tell you about that in a moment. Well, so after a week of this, Antek said to me one morning, 'I didn't sleep last night. I'm convinced Pani *does* know me. I'm going to find out.' I asked him how. He said he didn't know – he would think of a way. Two days later he made an opportunity. It was after our midday meal – the bread and some of that lovely nettle soup they gave us day after day. When the whistle blew, Antek jumped quickly and picked up his wheelbarrow. As he passed Pani, he tipped it over – it was a load of sand. Then he ran for a shovel, meanwhile getting a kick for his clumsiness from a capo. Well, I was in a position to watch him shovelling up the sand, and to watch Pani also. It was a hot day, and she was lying down in the shade of a bush with her big tongue lolling out. The sand had fallen on hard earth about four yards away from her, but some of it spilling closer. As Antek shovelled it, he moved nearer to her. Meanwhile, although I didn't know it until later, he kept saying her name in a low tone. When he reached the danger line, Pani jumped up. And then something astonishing occurred: she didn't snarl at him or get ready to spring, but she looked over at the guard who was *her* guard – and then she turned back to Antek and watched him without making a sound. Immediately that happened, I looked over at the guard also – he was a distance away, relieving his boredom by throwing stones at some birds. When I looked back at Pani, Antek had one leg no more than three feet from her. Of course, he was taking the chance of being seen by a capo or a guard, but with all the work going on he wasn't noticed. And Pani still did nothing – she didn't even snarl at him. Then, when he moved away, she lay down again."

"So, you *are* telling us she knew him but was concealing it," Hugh said.

"What else?" Libby exclaimed. "It's perfectly clear."

"Not to me."

With a luminous glow in his dark eyes, Donat said, "You'll be able to draw conclusions better in a moment... That night Antek was in a fever. He'd gotten an idea, and nothing could shake it. Not only was he convinced Pani knew him, like you say, but something more. He swore to us that Pani knew *she* was a prisoner of the Germans just like him. 'I'm forced to build a road for them,' he told us, 'and she's a prisoner forced to do guard duty. But she knows she's a prisoner.'" Donat paused, smiled and shook his head.

"Nothing could convince Antek otherwise. It was not only I who told him that *no* dog could have such logical understanding, but others told him also. There was a group of us who relied on one another – we were good comrades. One was a farm boy like Antek, a second was a young priest, and the third, interestingly enough, was a veterinarian. It was he who insisted more than any of us that Antek was loony on the subject of his dog. 'No,' Antek kept replying, 'I could see it in her eyes. I know what she was telling me.' Well, the next morning Antek called us together again. He said, 'Pani and I are going to escape. I'm telling you so you can be prepared. When I run, it may be a chance for you. I can't tell you when I'll do it. Keep your eyes open.'"

Donat paused for a moment, stroked his head, then sipped some tea. "Our arguments had no effect. We pointed out that even if Pani didn't attack him, the two other dogs would be after him right away. To this Antek answered that he would run with a tool in his hand, and Pani and he could handle them. When the veterinarian begged him to test Pani further, Antek answered that he simply had to seize the first opportunity – perhaps Pani would be changed to another commando. So that morning, even though

I hadn't decided what I would do, I followed Antek's example: I put my ration of bread inside my shirt instead of eating it... Well, an hour after work started, I gave up any idea of escaping. By accident I threw a shovelful of gravel so that a small stone struck a capo in the leg. He clubbed me so hard across the back that he knocked me down. Then he fell to kicking me. By the time he let up, I knew running away was not possible – it took all my strength and will-power merely to lift my shovel. A little while later something else happened that made me feel sure Antek also would have to give up the idea of escape. One of the prisoners – I learnt later he was sick with a high fever, but was trying to hide it – became delirious in the hot sun. With a shovel in his hand he started to walk like a blind man directly towards Pani. She jumped up with a terrible, warning snarl – and at the same moment the man reeled and fainted. What Pani would have done if he had fallen towards her instead of away from her, I can't actually say, although my belief is she would have done what she was trained to do. Anyway, when Antek passed me a moment later, I whispered to him, 'Don't run!' He didn't answer me – his face was like stone – and a few minutes later he ran."

Donat smiled faintly, and said in a quiet, tremulous way, "Now I will explain our geography. Our commando was breaking stone from a hillside to use for the roadbed. We were spread out for maybe seventy-five yards with one SS man at the head of the line and the other at the rear. The hillside rose quite steep and was barren, so no dog had been stationed there. On the other side of us, commencing only thirty feet or so away, there was a big field of sunflowers. I think maybe you have not seen such a field. The plants grow seven and eight feet tall before the seeds are ready for harvest. A man can run into a field like that and be lost to view in a second. However, there were two dogs stationed on that side – Pani close by and a Dobermann pinscher about thirty yards ahead. Well, the capo nearest us ordered two of the prisoners to carry the man who had fainted to one of the trucks we were loading. While his eye was on them, Antek dropped his wheelbarrow. He picked up a crowbar he had put in it beforehand and suddenly he was running at full speed for the shelter of the sunflowers. He was about five yards to one side of Pani, and I heard him yell 'Pani, come!' – that was all, not another word."

"And Pani?" Libby burst out.

"For one moment my blood froze," Donat answered. "Pani bounded up with a terrible snarl. With one tremendous jump she was right at Antek's heel. In the next second I expected her to leap on his back. And then, as though some chain had suddenly pulled her up short, she stopped where she was. I—"

"She caught his scent!" Libby interrupted excitedly. "She reacted before knowing it was Antek."

"Yes, I think so," Donat agreed, "but it was more complicated than that. By this time a whole series of things were happening at once. Antek disappeared into that thick forest of plants. At the same time the guard behind us, about thirty yards back, started shooting. He had a sub-machine gun, and he sprayed the area in Antek's direction. He shot off a whole clip – I don't know how many bullets, but many. Meanwhile, the guard in front had yelled a command at the Dobermann pinscher near him. That dog ran into the field directly opposite where he was, and he was followed by a black German shepherd that the guard had loosed from his chain – and then that guard himself, with a rifle, ran into the field. I can't tell you whether all of this happened in five seconds or ten or thirty – but meanwhile Pani remained where she was, half crouching, absolutely motionless. I didn't have time for any thoughts then, but later I felt I understood her behaviour – she was paralysed by opposing forces. Antek had been only partially right about her. She knew him and wouldn't attack him, but the discipline of her training under the SS prevented her from running with him. She was a prisoner in a deeper sense than he knew. And it is my belief that in those few moments that she remained motionless there was a terrible struggle going on in – what? – her feelings, her soul, her intelligence? I think all of it, a struggle such as a man would have."

"Oh, come now," said Hugh. "Why attribute—"

"But you haven't heard yet," Donat interrupted emotionally, "because in the next moment Pani let out a howl that made me think she had been wounded by one of the bullets. It wasn't a snarl or a bark or anything except a kind of wounded howl, as though she was suffering pain. And in the very next second she disappeared into the sunflowers." With a nervous gesture Donat wiped some beads of perspiration from his forehead. "If it is possible for a man to continue living although his heart has stopped beating, then my heart stopped when I lost sight of Pani. Was she running to escape with Antek or to tear him to pieces with the other dogs? I didn't know. Everything was confusion – a blur, a nightmare. What direction was Antek taking? The field of sunflowers was perhaps six hundred yards deep. It ran on a decline away from us, so that I could see on the other side, where it ended, a pasture with cows and some farm buildings. In back of the pasture* the land rose to a wooded hill. Antek surely would try to go there, I thought. Then, suddenly, from off in the field, there was the most savage howling of dogs. 'They've caught him,' I thought, and I heard myself beginning to scream without my wanting to and without being able to stop. The howling kept up, and then there were rifle shots – half a dozen, maybe. And then, suddenly, there was the most awful quiet, like the quiet of death. It lasted, that quiet, lasted and lasted, until I felt entombed, but later I knew that it could not have been more than two or three minutes. And then I saw Antek."

Donat's dark eyes were glowing luminously. He seemed almost unaware of our presence as he relived the moment of seeing Antek alive. "I saw him running near the farm buildings. Everyone saw him, including the SS man who had remained behind. But he couldn't do anything, because his sub-machine gun had no effect at that distance. Antek ran behind a barn, and, when we next saw him, he was climbing the hill towards the trees. I didn't actually see him enter the trees, because right then happened a tragedy. My two other comrades, the veterinarian and the priest, had not run. But suddenly now – what made him do it? – the young priest bolted for the field. It was madness. The SS man had stationed himself so he could command the area between us and the field. He cut our friend to pieces."

There was a moment's silence. Then Libby asked, "And Pani? Was she with Antek?"

"No. Presently out of the field came the other SS man. His left arm was bloody, and the front of his uniform was ripped open. Hobbling by his side was the black shepherd – one of its forelegs was dangling, bloody and bitten through. I didn't know German, but there were others who did. They made out what the guard yelled – that Pani (he called her by a German name) had gone insane... ripped open the throat of the pinscher, crippled the shepherd, and then, when the SS man came upon them, attacked him also. He had shot her."

"Ah," Libby exclaimed, "it's what you said when you began. In a most terrible predicament..." She didn't finish, but turned to her husband and murmured, "No flip comments, please. I'm not in the mood."

"I don't feel flip," Hugh said quietly. "I'll admit to being impressed. By any chance, do you know what happened to Antek?"

"Yes, I do. He made his way to a group of partisans. He survived the war, and he's a farmer again. Occasionally we write."

The Cop*

Before he lost his legs, Enzo must have been an impressive man, one of those six-foot, burly Italians of the north. He was about fifty when I met him, still handsome in a craggy way, with only a sprinkling of white in his black hair. He always sat dominatingly erect in his wheelchair, his powerful hands on the stumps of his thighs, a lusty glint in his dark eyes. The trattoria he owned, which was near my rooming house, was largely patronized by factory workers. Since the food was good as well as cheap, I took to eating there daily. About a week after I had become a regular patron, Enzo wheeled his chair over to my table and asked abruptly, "You American or English?"

"American."

"It's plain you're not a tourist or a businessman. You eat here and not around the Via Veneto, you wear the same shoes and suit every day. You look a bit old to be a student. An artist maybe, but I don't think so. I've been scrambling my brains to guess what you're doing in Rome."

The puzzled look on his face made me laugh aloud. "Why didn't you ask me?"

He laughed also. "I like to figure things out. But now I'm asking."

"In the mornings I teach school."

"Impossible! Your Italian is as crippled as I am."

"I teach English in a private school."

Enzo struck his formidable nose with a thick finger. "Ah... Still and all, if the pay is low, why not go home and teach there? You'd earn more, no?"

"I want to live a year or two in Italy."

He looked amused. "At your age it must be the girls. Ours are warmer than yours, eh?"

"The girls and your pasta."

"From my pasta you'll never get sick," he said with a chuckle. "The girls you better pick with care. Penicillin is afraid of what some of our girls have."

A day later Enzo wheeled up to me and said sharply, "What's up with you, anyway? Those men who just left – you were listening so hard to their talk I could see your ears stretch. What were you writing down? If you weren't a foreigner, I'd think you were working for the police – but not experienced at it... a hell of an amateur."

I felt somewhat embarrassed, so I took the notebook out of my pocket and offered it to him. "I make notes because I'm a writer. I put down the way people talk – the expressions they use."

For a few minutes Enzo examined the notebook with intense concentration. Once he muttered, "You spell Italian worse than you speak it. You need lessons." But when he gave it back to me, his manner became cordial. "So that's why you typewrite every afternoon?"

"How do you know that?"

"One of my kitchen girls is a relative of your landlady. Well... so you're a writer as well as a teacher, eh? For newspapers?"

"No."

His interest in me seemed to increase. "You write books maybe?"

"So far I've only written stories."

"Ah, I see. Stories, eh? Very interesting."

Thereafter Enzo came to my table rather frequently. He asked a good many questions about life in America, but primarily he seemed interested in me because of my writing. It was puzzling, because he was a man who had read little outside of newspapers and popular magazines – and yet the questions he put were of a semi-technical nature: how a writer got his ideas, what part true facts played in stories, whether it was easy or hard to write, and why. Every week there were several new questions, as though he were pondering the matter, but whenever I asked why he was so interested, he would only shrug and laugh.

THE COP

When the school year ended and I told Enzo I was leaving Rome in a few days, he invited me to be his guest at a late supper. I had other plans for my remaining evenings, but he was so oddly insistent that I finally accepted. Around midnight, when we were alone in the restaurant and were starting a third bottle of wine (Enzo having drunk two glasses to each of mine), he said rather shyly, "I have a proposition for you. You're a writer, and there's a story to my being a cripple. It's a story about..." – he hesitated as he groped for the right words – "the human heart, let's say. What I mean is... a man has his needs, he's selfish – all men are, they're born that way. But still... a man pays a terrible price for thinking only about himself. It's a contradiction... How should a man live?... And why doesn't his heart tell him in the first place how to live?" He hesitated again, with an embarrassed look. "This story... I don't mean I'm important – just another man – but maybe that's why... Do you understand me, maybe?"

"Yes," I said, "of course."

"Good. So my proposition is: I'll tell you what happened to me – you put it down so people can read it. What do you say?"

"If I can, I'll be glad to."

Obviously pleased, Enzo smiled, but in a restrained way, and I could see tension instantly rising within him. He reached for the bottle of wine and refilled our glasses. Then he muttered, "To tell this I need the help of the grape... I'll begin with... let's see... Well, my family was of the poorest: no father, he was killed in the First World War. When I was sixteen, my mother got me into a seminary so I could eat and there'd be one less hungry at home. I liked to eat, naturally, and I had love for the Madonna, but to be a priest wasn't for me, and at eighteen I left. I lived on the edge of nothing for three years – there were millions without work – and I was so hungry sometimes I could have eaten the Devil without salt. When you're on the bottom, my friend, your eyes see nothing good. I decided, 'All right, that's the way the world is: it's every man for himself in a jungle.'"

Enzo drank, then moved his chair closer to mine. "But when I was twenty-one, my luck changed – I got the chance to be a cop. That was in the capital of a province up north – hilly country, not many hours from Milano. I liked being a cop – the uniform, the position it gave me, the way it made girls look at me. But mostly I liked the chance to feather my nest. You know how it works... the pimps, the racketeers, a businessman doing something slippery – they all pay off. The higher you are in the police, the more you get. So I took all I could and waited my turn to move up."

"That was in Mussolini's time, of course?"

"Yes." Mockingly Enzo gave the Fascist salute, then spat on the floor. "A cop like I was doesn't care who sits in the saddle. You take their pay whoever they are, but work for yourself." He refilled his glass, drank it off, filled it again. "Take the way I was with women. I'm telling you exactly, no sugar-coating. A woman is to give a man pleasure, I said, and to hell with the moonshine and poetry. Let's say when I was a detective, let's say I caught some good-looking farm woman breaking a regulation, like black-marketing eggs in the war years. Did I want her to go to jail? Not especially – what for? First I'd take the basket of eggs as evidence – plenty of omelettes for me there. Then I'd put my arm around her and say, 'Well, now, little chicken, you don't want to go to jail, do you?' Most times they were too scared to do anything but curse me out a little. I didn't care about that so long as they laid down for me... Well, so that's the kind of man I was. I was satisfying myself and making my way in the jungle... But now I come to the year that did me in. It was 1943, the middle of the war, right after the Allies had taken Sicily. You remember what happened after that?"

"Not exactly," I said.

"It was complicated as hell. First, Mussolini was kicked out of the government. Then, when the Americans and British invaded down south at Salerno, the new government surrendered to them. But there were German armies in Italy. They took over by force, disarmed our army, occupied the whole country. Right away then a kind of civil war started. There were Fascists still supporting the Fritzes, and everywhere partisan groups sprang up to fight for the Allies. I admired those partisans, but I wished 'em in hell. The way I looked at it, if the Fritzes were going to be beaten, it was the Allied armies who would do it, nobody else. What could these partisans accomplish? Nothing, it seemed to me – kill a few soldiers, attack a supply column: fleas biting a tiger. But what trouble they would make for the rest of us, especially me! You see, I knew some German from my seminary, so I'd been assigned to the Gestapo to interpret. I liked those Gestapos the way a man likes typhus, but it seemed to me there was only one thing to do: wait it out, pretend I was friendly, win their confidence. But every time those fleas hopped, the tiger snapped his tail – and I sweated. Those Gestapos were suspicious of every Italian – and I knew what went on in the cellar of their headquarters. God's blood, I was scared to death they'd turn a fishy eye on me."

Enzo drained his glass and sat for a moment in brooding silence. His rugged face seemed to soften as I watched him, and, when he spoke, his voice had an undertone of sadness and nostalgia. "I lived in a small hotel on the main square. The owner had a daughter, Grazia. I'd seen her grow up, a kid full of spirit, always running and laughing with her long hair flying. All of a sudden she was sixteen, a woman, and I wanted her. Any man would have. You should have seen that girl – deep-blue eyes like the sea... wheat-coloured hair down to her hips... a face so pretty and shining your heart would melt – yet with a body so ripe a man ached to put his hands on her. I was thirty-three, seventeen years older, but a difference like that doesn't mean anything if a man and a woman spark each other. Grazia liked me well enough, and I would have been planning day and night to be the first with her one way or another, if it hadn't been for one thing: her father. He wasn't a special friend of mine or anything like that, but it happened that he had once saved my life. For me that was the only thing on earth that made one man have a blood obligation to another. It tied me to him, so that I couldn't play tricks with the girl. She had to be willing. So in my spare time I hung around when she was tending bar or doing work in the hotel. There was no mother in the way when I wanted to pay Grazia a compliment, or tease her a little... You know the way a man does with a virgin to pave the way. I didn't realize then how much she was in my blood – I just wanted her to start thinking about me instead of anyone else. Of course, every Fritz in town stepped into that hotel bar when he was off duty, but with them Grazia was like ice. She was no blind little kitten about men either... What Italian girl is? She always wore a pin in her hair that was three inches long. 'Any man tries to force me,' she told me once, 'I'll blind him!'"

The bottle of wine was empty, and Enzo wheeled behind the counter for another. He returned, opened the fresh bottle, filled his glass and seemed not to notice that I had stopped drinking. "The trouble that came started with her father," he continued with some bitterness. "He went to Milano and didn't come back for a week. One morning I said to Grazia, 'When's your old man coming back?' She was scrubbing the floor in the lobby, and she stopped and looked around – there was no one there except the desk clerk, and he was half deaf – and then she stepped up close to me with a strange look on her face.

"'I just heard last night,' she told me. 'I've been waiting for you to come down. Poppa's not coming back.'

"'Why not?'

"'He sent a message. He said he expects you to watch over me while he's gone.'

"'Where's he gone to?'

"'He's in the hills. He's joined the Garibaldis.'*

"'Blood of the Virgin! I could break his neck!' I said.

"'Is that how you feel about it?' she asked me with a very disappointed look.

"'How else? He's an imbecile. He'll get killed for nothing.'

"'In that case, you won't help?'

"'Help who?'

"'Poppa said you can tell me things you hear around Gestapo headquarters.'

"'Your old man's got fried eels in his head instead of brains,' I told her. 'In the first place, I don't hear anything. They don't trust me. In the second place, even if I did, what will happen if I tell you? You'll get word to him – he'll tell those other heroes, and then one day soon some of 'em will be caught and vomit out everything. Where will I be, then? My feet off the ground and my neck in a noose!'

"'Oh, I see,' she told me, 'you're a coward.'

"'Don't use words you're too young to understand.'

"'You've forgotten the day you were drowning and my father saved you!'

"'Who's forgotten? Your old man wants me to watch over you. I will gladly. If you want the protection of a marriage, I'll even marry you. But I'm not having anything to do with the Garibaldis.'

"She looked at me then as though I were garbage. 'Oh,' she said very scornfully, 'I see. For my father's sake you're willing to marry me. Thanks, I'll remember. When I want to marry a bootlicker of the Gestapo, I'll whistle.'"

Enzo paused to drink a glass of wine, and then half of another. He said wryly, "It never before meant a pig's ear to me what anyone called me. A stone weighs, a word doesn't. But when Grazia called me 'a bootlicker of the Gestapo', I felt like whipping her behind with a wet rope. Maybe it wasn't the word, though, but the look in her eyes. It hurt my manhood to have her look at me that way. And I kept wondering about myself. Why in the name of all the saints had I said I'd be willing to marry her? I hadn't intended to say it… the words just popped out. I'd never told any woman before that I'd marry her… it made me feel queer. Well, all the next week Grazia didn't talk to me unless she had to, as though I were a stranger or one of the Fritzes, but then something happened. The Garibaldis had been getting more active – they'd even captured an SS colonel in a road ambush. The Germans put up posters offering a big reward for information about them. I said to myself, 'Aha, that's enough money to put the evil eye on them.' Then some special squads with dogs were added to the garrison in town, and I said 'Aha' a second time. It was plain there was going to be a drive to clean out the hills. It happened then I got the grippe. It left me weak in the legs, so I spent several days sitting in an armchair in front of my window, listening to the radio and looking out. One evening, just after dark, a man bicycled up to Gestapo headquarters on the other side of the square. It was raining hard, and he had his head pulled down into his coat collar, but by the light over the doorway I spotted him right away – Gianfranco the pedlar, a hunchback. He used to buy odds and ends in town – needles, thread, cooking things – and bicycle into the hills to sell to the farmers and sheep-herders. I knew him well, because years ago I'd fooled around with a niece of his. When I saw the guards take him inside, I remembered something: he always was a Mussolini lover, used to strut with the Blackshirts in every parade. So I thought to myself, 'Money doesn't stink, eh, Gianfranco?' After twenty minutes he came out, looked around carefully, then bicycled over to the hotel. Soon as he went inside, I forgot my weak legs and went downstairs. Like I expected, he was at the bar. The place was full of Germans, so I watched from outside. Gianfranco had three quick drinks in a row. When he was paying his bill, I went out to the lobby. I waited until he was outside, and then took a look. He was bicycling in the direction of the hills. So then I sat down to think it over. It was perfectly clear what was up. The only question in my mind was: should I tip off Grazia? I knew it would sweeten her towards me a lot if I did – but I wanted to be sure there was no way it could make trouble for me. It seemed to me there wasn't any, so I decided. Grazia was serving some soldiers at the bar. I couldn't be sure one of 'em didn't understand Italian, so I tapped her on the shoulder and said, 'There's a phone call from Milano, I think it's your old man.' I walked back to the lobby, and a minute later she came running out. I said, 'There's no phone call, but something's up. We have to talk private.' Grazia was suspicious, but she led me down the hall to her room. When I closed the door, she said, 'Don't try locking it.'

"'And don't you be such a scared virgin. What do you take me for?' I told her, almost yelling. It burned me to have her speak like that. 'What was that pig-faced Gianfranco drinking?'

"'Grappa. Why?'

"'Has he been in your bar before this?'

"'What are you trying to do,' she asked very coldly, 'make a police spy out of me?'

"'I'm remembering your old man saved my life. Maybe now I'll do the same for him, the imbecile. Answer my question.'

"She looked at me with big eyes then, suddenly scared. 'Gianfranco's come in now and then, not often.'

"'Those other times – did he drink grappa?'

"She thought for a second. 'No, ordinary wine, never more than one small glass.'

"'So for him he spent big tonight, hey?'

"'Yes.'

"'When he paid you, did you see how much money he had?'

"'No.' She put her hand on my arm. 'Enzo, what's this got to do with my father?'

"'Nobody knows the hills better than that son of a whore, Gianfranco. Just before he bought himself that grappa he was in Gestapo headquarters.'

"Grazia said '*Madonna mia*' and started to tremble. 'So what do you think?'

"'I think he got a first payment on the reward. If I'm right, I don't believe the Germans will lose time. I think they'll move troops during the night and attack as soon as it's light enough to see.'

"'*Gesummaria*,'* Grazia said, 'may I be split in four parts if I don't put a knife in his dirty heart one day.'

"'Never mind that now,' I told her. 'Have you got any way to send a warning?'

"'Yes,' she told me. She was white as paper.

"'In time for them to get away?'

"'I hope so.'

"'Now look,' I told her, '*leave me out of it!* Nobody has to know who tipped you off.'

"'Sure, Enzo,' she said, 'of course.'

"As I was opening the door, she kissed me on the cheek. I didn't realize then what the kiss meant to me. All I thought was, 'Fine, I've sweetened her up – I'll be quits with her old man, there'll be nothing in the way.' I went back to my room and sat down in the dark to watch the square. The rain had stopped, there was nothing stirring. Ten minutes later there was a knock on the door. It was Grazia, and she was shaking. She said, 'I can't send anyone. I called the only two contacts I have. They're not home.' And then she gave me one in the belly. '*I'm* going. I know where they are. Will you give me a gun, Enzo?'

"In that moment I saw the handwriting on the wall. Grazia would be captured and the Gestapo would learn the part I'd played in her going. But how could I stop her? I wasn't thinking of her, you see, only of myself.

"'Will you give me a gun?' she asked me a second time.

"'Don't talk nonsense,' I yelled at her. 'I only have one gun, and the number's registered. You wouldn't know how to use it anyway.'

"'But just listen why,' she begged me. 'The Germans might get there before me, but if it's still dark, I can shoot in the air as a warning.'

"'I can't give it to you!'

"She started out, but I caught her arm. I said, 'Grazia, maybe I can help. How far do you have to go?'

"For a second she stared at me in a way I can see yet... a look of hope in her eyes you couldn't put into words. I saw what she was thinking... that *I* would go. 'It's about twenty kilometres by road,' she told me. 'But who knows how roundabout I'll have to go to avoid patrols?' She kept looking at me with her heart in her eyes, but I closed my mind to her the way you shut a door. I was too afraid to go, and I cursed the Garibaldis, and I only wanted to find a way to stop her from going.

"'It's crazy,' I told her. 'It's already eight o'clock. To get there in time you've got to arrive by four in the morning at the latest. How can you cover twenty-five or thirty kilometres on foot in eight hours – when it's dark, when you'll have to cross fields, climb over fences, maybe hide?'

"'I'll run part of the time.'

"'Without using a flashlight?'

"'I'll use a small one when I have to. I've got to try, don't I? Is there any other way?' She waited for a moment, and then, when I didn't say anything, she pulled her arm loose and started for the door. I felt so sick and scared that all I could do was yell at her, 'So at least put on a black dress, you little fool. Take a piece of charcoal to rub on your face if you get in a spot. Take a club against dogs. And some food to keep up your strength – sugar, cheese, bread... especially sugar.'

"She didn't say anything. She just looked at me with a stony face and left."

For a moment Enzo interrupted his narrative. He peered intensely at me with eyes that had become bloodshot. He was leaning forward, his hands gripping the arms of his chair. "I let her go like that – a sixteen-year-old girl. My mind wasn't on her: I was scared only for me. The minute she was gone, I sat down and tried to make a plan for myself. The only really safe thing was to run. With my credentials I didn't have to worry about curfew: I could move at night. Who could give me a safe hideout? From my police experience I knew that to stay in hiding for months took very favourable conditions – the right place, friends willing to risk their own necks, even the right neighbours, often. I couldn't think of anyone. To keep moving from one city to the next was no good either: there was too much danger of being nabbed in a bus or railroad station, where they were always checking papers. Something occurred to me after a while that seemed first-rate. The Swiss border was only sixty kilometres away. On a bicycle I could be there in good time. I'd go direct to the border guards with my credentials and my interpreter's card. I'd tell 'em I was after an underground leader who was expected to cross. I felt absolutely confident that after a bit of talk I'd know where their guards were stationed – and where I could cross safe. I'd be in Switzerland before daylight."

Enzo laughed softly, ironically, and, in a curious gesture, slapped one of his stumps several times with the back of his hand. "So," he said, "I had a plan... I felt safe enough to breathe easy – and right then I began to think of Grazia. I imagined her running through the night, that little kid. I gave her one chance in a hundred of not being caught. And then, like somebody had hit me on the skull with a hammer, I began to think what would happen to her in the cellar of the Gestapo. I broke out in a sweat... I got so sick to my stomach that I almost vomited. I told myself again and again that I ought to start moving, but my legs stayed where they were. I could see Grazia's eyes as she'd looked at me, waiting with so much hope for me to say I'd go in her place. She knew that as a cop I could have gone by bicycle. It would have been risky, but a hundred times less than for her. Why had I shut my mind to it? I began to curse myself. I looked into the mirror and spat and told myself I deserved to live blind and hungry for ninety-nine years. For the first time in my life, y'see, there was someone who meant more to me than my own skin. I wanted Grazia to be safe – God, how I wanted it! It wasn't that I wanted her for myself: I just wanted *her* to be safe. So, even though I told myself again and again that I ought to start moving, I sat all night long like a paralytic. Like I'd expected, at four in the morning the Germans were on the move in the direction of the hills – motorcycles, armoured cars, trucks with infantry. At six thirty a staff car came back and drove into the closed yard alongside Gestapo headquarters. I could see only the driver. Then, at seven fifteen, *I* got a call – whether I was sick or not, they wanted me at headquarters right away."

Enzo's bloodshot eyes were staring at the empty darkness of the restaurant. He had stopped drinking. His hands were gripped together, the fingers were working. "I was sick all right," he muttered, "but not from the grippe. Did they have Grazia or didn't they? As I crossed the square, I felt as though I wouldn't make it to the other side. My knees were weak – I had such pain in my temples I almost couldn't keep from groaning out loud."

For a few moments Enzo fell silent, but then he shook himself out of his reverie. He said painfully, "I was sent in to the commissar, Brandt. He'd been a cop like me before he got into the Gestapo, but high up, chief of detectives in some city, a man about sixty. He was sharper than I was, and I knew it – one of those who never show what they're thinking or feeling, with a face like granite. I hated him, and I was afraid of him. First he asked me how I was feeling (not that he cared a damn), and I said I was a little shaky in the legs. Then he asked, 'Did you hear the troop movement this morning?'

"'Yes, Herr Commissar,' I answered. 'It woke me up.'

"'That was a raiding party,' he told me. 'We had information about a partisan hideout – a cave in the hills.' He stopped talking then, keeping his eyes on me, and I almost jumped out of my skin. I was so scared I got a strange, crazy thought – I wished I had a bag of salt so that I could sprinkle the floor with it for good luck the way some peasants do in a new house. It was completely crazy. Anyway, Brandt went on talking. He said, 'The approach to the cave was kept under observation last night by three men friendly to us...'

"'Gianfranco and his two brothers,' I thought to myself.

"'These men,' the commissar said, 'were stationed thirty metres apart along the bank of a small stream. The cave was about two hundred metres on the other side. Our troops were to reach the area at five o'clock. Twenty minutes before they arrived, the partisans were given a warning and got away.'"

Almost whispering, Enzo said to me, "When I heard that, I thought I'd explode with excitement at what little Grazia had done. But a second later I felt like Brandt had shoved a towel down my gullet and I was strangling. 'The warning came from a girl,' he told me, 'the bar girl in your hotel.'

"I pretended surprise as best I could. 'Grazia? I never would have guessed her out of the whole town.'

"'Why?'

"'She's a kid. How did she get involved?'

"'Yes, how?' Brandt asked sarcastically. 'Just a pretty, innocent little girl – good Catholic too, I'm sure. She was jumped by one of the men when she got near the stream – and she put a bread knife into his chest so hard she couldn't get it out. When the others came at her, she ran into the stream – screaming to the partisans that German soldiers were coming. She screamed quite a number of times before they shut her up... Well, Enzo?'

"'Well what, Herr Commissar?' I asked.

"'What do you conclude from this?'

"I took off my raincoat to gain a moment's time. Then I said, 'Seems like the partisans have a group in town... and a good intelligence service.'

"'Agreed.'

"'But isn't it strange,' I went on, 'that they'd send a girl on a mission like that?'

"'She got there,' Brandt said, 'so maybe they knew what they were doing. Anyway, she's our key. I've already questioned her, but she's being very patriotic. As you know, my Italian is not so good. I'm not sure she understood me entirely. Right now she's getting some special attention. When she comes back, you talk to her. I want her to know what her situation is without any mistake. If she'll give us the names of everyone in the group, she can go back to tending bar. If she doesn't, I won't leave her alone until she's in little pieces.'"

Sixteen years had passed since Brandt had said this to Enzo, but, as he repeated it to me now, his tone became a whimper. "'Until she's in little pieces,'" he said a second time. "You can't know what those words did to me... how frightful I felt, how guilty. I *had* to ask what was being done to her. It was a risky question: I was not supposed to know what went on in the cellar, or ask what 'special attention' meant. My tongue felt big as a sausage – I could hardly wag it. I said, 'Herr Commissar... I know this girl well, and I have an idea how to handle her... but first... if I may ask... it will affect what I say... what's she getting... the attention, I mean?'

"Brandt gave me a long, cold look. 'What's the matter with you?' he asked. 'You're sweating, your voice is trembling...'

"'I'm still not over the grippe,' I answered as easily as I could. 'It's not important.'

"He looked at me a moment longer, then he said, 'I'd like the girl to work for us from now on, so I thought I'd try giving her a shock as a first step – nothing that would stop her from being in the hotel as usual tomorrow. I told the boys to line up and have some fun with her.'"

A twisted, sad little smile came to Enzo's lips as he told me this. Gazing at me, he said softly, "Now, pay attention to what can happen to the human heart. For a few moments I thought I'd go out of control. But why? I already knew she was being tortured. Was it any worse for poor Grazia to be raped by half a dozen men than to be beaten with clubs, or have her nails pulled out? Perhaps not as bad. You might say because I loved her I was made wild by just thinking of it. No, it was something worse. It was like I was having a nightmare where many things were happening at the same time. I felt as though I was inside Grazia's flesh, inside her heart, that I was weeping her tears and feeling her shame – and yet at the same time *I saw myself as one of the men who were raping her.* Hadn't I taken women who didn't want me – not by direct force, maybe – but by other ways that amounted to the same? And if not for Grazia's father, I would have played any trick to have her. Right then I saw the man I was – no different from those pigs in the cellar! Ah, Mother of God, it's impossible for me to explain to you, to put into words what happened inside of me then – like a volcano vomiting everything out of its belly. But I remember every thought, every feeling. And I remember saying to myself, 'All right, you coward, you stinking swine with sewage in your veins, you have one thing: a gun. When they bring in Grazia, you'll shoot Brandt, and then her, and then yourself.'"

Again the twisted, sad little smile came to Enzo's lips. "As you see," he said, "I didn't shoot myself, or them either. After a while two SS men brought Grazia into the office. She was walking, but like in a stupor, and she was crying... my God... that crying... not loud, but every part of her body crying to Heaven. They put her down in a chair, and she fell off it and lay like a rag doll that a child throws away."

Enzo paused. He was weeping now, silently, the tears running down his craggy cheeks. "She was wearing a black skirt and sweater... I remember some buttons on the side of the skirt were missing. Her legs were bare... and streaked with blood. Brandt saw the blood and smiled like with surprise. He said to the SS men, 'Don't tell me an Italian girl her age could still be a virgin?' Both of the men laughed, and one said, 'We were surprised too.' Brandt waved them out. To me he said, 'She'll talk now, I think. Go ahead with her...' It was then I changed my mind about what to do. I said 'Yes, Herr Commissar' and walked over to Grazia. I raised her up and sat her against the wall. I said 'Grazia, this is Enzo' over and over again. Her crying started to die down, and her eyes began to see me. I asked Brandt for some water. When he brought it, I put the glass to her lips and ordered her to drink. She took a little, then suddenly drank it all down like she was parched. I said, 'Grazia, look at me. Do you know me?' She looked and gave a little nod. I said, 'Watch me!' I took my revolver out. 'Do you see this?' She nodded again. 'Watch carefully now,' I said – and I snapped up and pointed the gun at Brandt."

There was a moment's pause while Enzo's fingers worked in his lap. "You'll see," he told me, sadly and bitterly, "I did everything right... I thought every next step out fine – except for one thing. I said to Brandt, 'I'm so close to shooting that if you make one little move I don't order, you're finished. Get over there.' I put him to one side of the door, so that if it opened, he wouldn't be seen – facing the wall with his hands on it. When I frisked him, I found a knife in a belt sheath as well as his Luger. Then I backed off so I could see Grazia while I watched him and the door. She was sitting up stiff now. I said, 'Listen, Grazia, I'm taking you out of here. Do you understand me? Answer!'

"'Yes, Enzo,' she said. It took effort for her to speak. 'I understand, Enzo.'

"'Can you walk? Stand up.'

"She got herself up, but then had to catch hold of the back of the chair. 'Are you dizzy?' I asked.

"'A little,' she said. 'But I'll be able to walk, Enzo. Oh, Enzo, *please* take me out of here. If you can't, then shoot me, *please*. Promise to shoot me, Enzo. Swear by the Virgin.'

"'Yes, I promise,' I told her, 'but be quiet now.' It was almost more than I could bear to have her saying 'Enzo, Enzo', as though I was her saviour instead of the coward who had gotten her into this. I went for my raincoat and hung it over my arm so it would hide the pistol. Then I went over to Brandt. I said to him, 'Listen with care, as one cop to another: you want to live, and I've got no reason to do you in. I'm no partisan, but I want this girl. If you act sensible, you'll be free in half an hour. You want to strike a bargain on that?'

"'Sure,' he said. 'What do you want me to do?'

"I told him then: he was to stay three steps in front of me and the girl. We'd go straight to the courtyard and get into a car. He'd drive. Once we were in the hills, I'd let him out. But if he tried anything at all, I'd plug him.

"'Don't worry,' he said. 'I'm no fool.'

"And that's how it went," Enzo said. "I put my left arm around Grazia and kept my gun arm-free. From the office to the courtyard was not far – down one stairway, through a door. We passed only one SS man and the guard in the lobby. There was a platoon of men in the yard, but Brandt hollered for a car, and there were no questions. I put Grazia in the back and said for her to lie down. I got in with Brandt and told him to start easy until we were a block away and then go fast. In fifteen minutes we were outside the town, and twenty minutes after that we were high in the hills, and I told him to stop. I was feeling so good, so damn excited, that I couldn't help making a game of it. I said, 'Tell me the truth. You think I'll plug you now?'

"'We had a bargain,' he answered. 'Like you said, we're both cops. I'm sure you won't.'

"'That's right,' I told him, 'but maybe Grazia feels different. You want to shoot him, Grazia?'

"She answered... I tell you she answered like a bride at the altar saying yes... I took the Luger out of my pocket, cocked it and held it out to her."

Enzo gazed at me and smiled bitterly. "So there we were... in a German staff car parked in the hills... a neat little target for any partisans who were around... the one thing I hadn't given mind to. So a tommy gun hit us from one side, and grenades from another. When I came to, I was in the partisan camp and everybody was sorry – but how did they know who was in the car? I had no legs... Brandt was dead... and my little Grazia was dead too."

Enzo turned away from me and stared at the empty darkness of the café. He said slowly, "So there you are, my friend – that's my story. It seems to me... how much I've thought about it!... that... well, take insects now... whatever it is insects have (instinct, they say)... they know how to live their lives. But we who are human beings... we have such awful mixed-up hearts... and what things they make us do, eh?"

UNCOLLECTED
SHORT STORIES

The Gentleman and His Son*

Mrs Vivian's tone remained calm, and her roundish, pretty face, still pretty in spite of her age, retained its usual composure – but underneath she was frightened. "What are you going to do?" she asked. She could see the extent to which pure rage and profound shame, bitterness and terrible anxiety were all furiously mingled in her husband's emotions. He was, and had been, such a gentle, cordial being, such a truly decent gentleman down to the bottom of his heart, that it made her sick to see him suffer this way. He stood, holding the forged cheque in his hand, gazing down at it with an agonized, stricken look. His heavy shoulders were bowed, his sturdy body appeared soggy, as though all of the muscles had turned flabby in an instant, his ruddy face had suddenly become mottled, spotted with bluish patches. "Tom, *dear*, you mustn't take it this way," Mrs Vivian cried suddenly, with great intensity. "I don't care what happens, *you* mustn't be so unhappy about it."

Vivian answered her as though his throat were constricted by something tight, making his voice small and hoarse. "Aren't *you* unhappy, Ann? How can I help being unhappy?"

"Listen, darling," Mrs Vivian said, "you listen to me!" She stepped up close to him, facing him, peering into his eyes. "I'm going to tell you the truth, whether it sounds becoming or not. Francis is our son – we love him. We've done our best for him, and we'll continue." She paused, drawing a deep breath. "But Francis, as a man, isn't worth the nail on your little finger. No, listen to me," she cried passionately. She grasped the lapels of his coat. "He isn't – not to me or to life or to anyone!" She flung her arms around him. "Tom," she said, "Tom, you're the finest man alive! Do you hear that? You're the finest person I've ever known. I'm not going to let you be unhappy!"

Vivian put his head on his wife's shoulder. He raised one hand slowly and pushed back the fold of her dressing gown. Then he pressed his face to the warm flesh of her throat, seeking comfort, expressing gratitude, in a gesture made more intimate for them by its very repetition, and the familiarity of years. They stood like that, quietly, for a full minute. Vivian felt drowsy, almost drugged. He would have liked to lie down on a bed by his wife's side, with his face and eyes pressed to her warm, sweet-smelling flesh, and sleep. He remembered the forged cheque. It awakened him, painfully, with a sense of physical shock. He raised his head. Ann saw again the stricken look, almost animal-like in its pure, abject suffering. She thought: "He looks old, suddenly. This strips him down. I wonder how I look? At our age there's no resilience." She took his hand and led him to a chair. She sat down, close to him. "What are you going to do?" she asked for the second time.

"What do you think I should do?"

"I don't know... I only think of the obvious things."

"We've been trying them for five years."

"Yes."

"I too..." Vivian listened to a bird piping sweetly on the roof outside their bedroom window. He could hear Pet, their fox hound, running way off somewhere on the grounds, baying as though he had struck a fresh rabbit scent. "I'll tell you, Ann," he said musingly, in a flat, unhappy tone, "I'd like to know what a psychiatrist would say about the fuss I'm making. He'd probably call it a low order of self-preservation. Francis has been raising hell, or going to hell, for five years. Now, suddenly, I'm more than worried; I feel as though my whole life were shaking around me. Why? It's too obvious. Now my pride is involved, my reputation in the eyes of my circle."

"But of course," Ann said, "why shouldn't it be that way?"

Vivian thrust his hand through his hair. Where hers had turned grey, his was still jet-black, strong and glistening. "Because it shouldn't," he said. He rose impatiently. "I should be thinking of Francis, not my petty reputation."

"Darling," said Ann gently, in her calm tone, "that's just nonsense."

"Why?" He paused, waiting for her answer.

She smiled. "You're a normal human being, aren't you?... If that isn't enough, you're fifty-six, not ninety. You've got a wife, another son, and an important position in an important world! Now let me ask *you* something: you're thinking of Francis – is he thinking of you?"

"No, by God, he's not!" Vivian exploded. "He isn't – he never has! And, by God, he ought to!"

"That's something to know!" Ann remarked quietly.

"But where does it get us?" Vivian asked in that constricted tone again. "Tell me that! He's still our son."

"I don't know where it gets us," Ann replied, "but I think right now the most important thing is to know what we really feel about Francis."

"I can't talk any more," Vivian said. "I've got to see him or I'll burst."

"Do you want me to come with you?"

"What do you think?"

"I think not."

"I too, but I don't know why."

"Never mind. Trust your feelings – with him too... I think he's still asleep."

"I'll manage to wake him!" Vivian went to the door.

"Tom..."

He turned, hearing once again the sweet piping of the bird on the roof.

"Never mind... I'll be downstairs if you want me."

Vivian went out.

Their son's room was on the floor above. It shouldn't have taken him so long to climb one flight of stairs. He knew he had lingered because he was afraid. He had always been cowardly about facing things out with Francis. He had not known how. As he paused before the door, his glance caught the forged cheque in his hand. It turned him wild inside, making him frantic to lash out – yet it burdened him at the same time with a depressed, suffocating sense, as though something foreign had lodged in his breast and would remain there for ever, constrictive and heavy. He flung the door open.

Francis was awake. He was lying in bed, smoking a cigarette. His thin face looked unwashed, unattractively pallid. Vivian marked with sudden astonishment, as though he had never seen his son before, that it was not the face of a boy of twenty-five. It was years older. It was the face of a man of thirty-five or more, with pockets under the eyes and a mouth that was creased at the sides, as though the man had lived through years of bitter struggle instead of the easy, pleasant life that Francis had always had. He felt astonished, and somehow hurt, as though he himself were to blame. He wondered if he was.

"Good morning," said Francis. He sat up, smoking. Vivian walked over and dropped the cheque on the blanket. "Ah!" said Francis. Then, calmly, "Sit down, Father."

"You signed that, of course?" Vivian asked.

"Sit down, Father."

"The devil with that. I want to talk to you."

"Please sit down, Father."

Vivian detected the mockery in his son's tone. This was baiting the bull, he supposed. Well, he wouldn't be baited – and Francis could have things on his own terms if he wanted to play at strategy... He pulled up a chair.

"Now you'll be comfortable," said Francis. "Yes, I signed it."

"Were you drunk?"

"No."

"I had hoped you were."

"No, it was quite deliberate." Francis's eyes were smiling. He had jet-black, handsome eyes that contrasted strangely with his thin, rather badly featured face. "I was serving notice that I can't get along on the allowance you give me."

Vivian felt the suffocating sense in his chest. "Serving notice by forgery?"

"It won't be forgery unless I'm prosecuted."

"How do you know you won't be?" The blue patches appeared on Vivian's face again.

"I'd be extremely surprised." Francis paused to light a fresh cigarette. "You intend to cover the cheque, don't you?" he enquired lightly.

"I haven't made up my mind."

Francis shrugged.

"Francis, for God's sake, are you soft in the head? What's the matter with you? You forge the name of my chauffeur – a *chauffeur*, Francis. Doesn't it even involve your pride?"

"Oh no," replied Francis mildly, "I don't have any pride about such things, Tom."

"Well, I do," Vivian told him savagely, "and I won't have it."

Francis's voice became cold and very quiet. "You can't stop it, Tom. I told you I am serving notice. I want you to give me an allowance I can get along on. If you don't, I'll have to raise the money I need by any means that occur to me. That'll probably include borrowing from your friends, as well as signing cheques in the name of your chauffeur. You force me to do it."

Vivian sank back in his chair. He hadn't expected it to be this way.

"Listen, Tom," said Francis earnestly, "you've got to stop judging me by your standards, and get new ones for me. If you do that, we can all be quite happy together."

"The cheque you forged was for six hundred dollars," Vivian said. "Would you tell me what you did with the money?"

"I have about a hundred left. I blew the rest of it over the weekend impressing a girl."

"Some floozie, I suppose?"

"No. This one had manners and went to Barnard."*

"Was it worth it to you?"

"No. But I'll probably go on doing it."

"Francis, what's inside of you?" Vivian asked pleadingly.

"I don't know, Father, not much. Appetites."

"Don't you want to work?"

"No."

"Is this going to be your life?"

"Why not? I rather like it."

"But it depends on me!"

"Now listen, Father, it's not the money you're worrying about. Even with what I want it's only a drop in the bucket. It won't even dent your income."

"But you can't live like this – you can't!" Vivian cried. "A man has to do something with his life. I'm not trying to dictate to you. Do what you like. But be useful!"

"Those are *your* standards again."

"They're life's standards."

Francis leant forward intensely. "What are these standards?" he asked. "You trade on the stock market. You make money by gambling in munition stocks. A man dead is a penny in your pocket. You gamble in bonite* stocks. They pay interest on child labour. Why does that make you better than I?"

"What is this?" Vivian cried in astonishment and outrage. "Some radical bug?"

Francis laughed. "Oh, no. I'm merely pointing out that by doing nothing, I'm perhaps doing less harm than you."

"I've never heard anything so silly," Vivian said explosively. "Do you want me to retire to a mountain peak? Why make me responsible for the evils of the world? How about the charities I support?"

Francis laughed. "Don't worry, Tom. It isn't important. I didn't say I wouldn't spend your money, did I? But since you brought up the talk about standards, I'm merely pointing out that everything in this world seems to have a small streak of slime about it – and you're not any more free of it than I am… But it doesn't make any difference. Excuse me."

Francis lay back and closed his eyes. When he spoke again, his tone had suddenly become brooding and weary. "Tom, you don't know me very well," he said. "This year we haven't talked much. The last two years I've been abroad – before that I was at college."

"If it's my fault, I'll undo it," Vivian pleaded. "I thought you wanted to be alone."

"I did. It's not your fault." Francis's eyes were still closed. "Listen... I'm not always happy. But I've discovered the way in which I can get along best. I've got to have money for it. You double my allowance! I need about twenty thousand a year. I'll go along quietly in my own way. I'll try not to scandalize your name." He opened his eyes. "If you don't do that, Tom, I'll sign cheques or do anything else I have to! I can't change what I am! If you put me in jail, I'll stay there! If you throw me in the gutter, I'll lie there!... That's all, Tom. You have another son, and he fits. You concentrate on him."

"But what is it?" Vivian whispered. "What is it?"

"I don't know," Francis replied, "maybe the blood is running thin."

"Francis, one word," Vivian cried, "won't you even *try* to do something with yourself?"

"No."

"I beg you, Francis, if you have any feeling for me."

"No."

"Not even for your mother?"

"No."

Vivian looked at his son. He saw the thin, sharp-featured face. It appeared suddenly to be a cruel face, a depraved, vicious face. "I won't have it," he burst out. "This is cheap, it's mean! You're blackmailing me like the lowest scoundrel! I don't have to stand for it, and I won't!"

"You will," said Francis. His handsome black eyes were very calm. "Your place in society means too much to you. You wouldn't dare to do anything."

"I hate you. I hate you," Vivian cried. "I despise you... Oh, no, listen," he cried, frightened, "I don't want to hate you. I mustn't. Please, Francis, give me a chance. I don't hate you."

Francis smiled. "It's all right."

"I won't be blackmailed," Vivian muttered brokenly. "I won't."

"I'm sorry to hurt you," Francis told him gently.

Vivian glanced up once, then stumbled from the room. He walked down the corridor blindly, then the first stairway, then the second. He kept repeating: "I mustn't hate my son! I mustn't hate him!"

Ann was downstairs. She saw him coming and ran to him. Then she saw his face. "Dear," she said quickly, taking his arm, "it's lovely out in the garden: come out for a bit." She guided him. He stumbled over the lintel, and she had to hold him. It was like holding a bag of meal. They walked over towards the pond, where the sun lay like gold leaf on white lily pads. "But, darling," she burst out suddenly, "there's no need to cry like that. You mustn't cry, my darling."

"I should *do* something," he said. "Why don't I *do* something?"

They stumbled forward, holding on to each other.

The Piece of Paper*

For a moment, by deliberate effort, Captain Wheatley shook himself out of his reverie. "I must be calm," he said to himself. "I will achieve nothing unless I am calm."

He started down the long stairway, walking slowly, his left hand gripping the banister, his right hand, misshapen by bandage, dangling loosely at his side. His lined face, with its mechanical smile, was in bitter contrast to the radiant, well-fed countenances of the men who followed him, Dr Asa Wheatley, his brother, and Lynn and Jeffry Thomas.

At the turn of the stairway he saw his wife and sister-in-law looking up at him. The two women were standing side by side in the parlour doorway, their hands tightly clasped. He saw them – he did not see as well the sharp anxiety on their faces. "Hello, Ruth," he called to his sister-in-law, and in the same instant his soul turned inward again, frightened of what he would presently tell these people. "How are you?" he added mechanically. He was not aware that to them his manner was not calm, but terrifyingly stony.

A few minutes before, waiting for him, his wife had turned in tremulous desperation to her sister-in-law, pouring out her fears, begging for reassurance. "He's almost like a stranger, Ruth. Soldiering doesn't change a man this way – it didn't when he was here last year. To call for outsiders on his first night home! And the Thomas brothers, they're not even relatives like you."

"Are they here, too?" Ruth asked in astonishment.

"Yes…" Martha wept. "Oh, Ruth, you don't… you…" She was afraid to finish.

Ruth laughed at that, knowing what would be in Martha's mind. "He's been at war, darling. I doubt if there were any women at Port Hudson."*

"But he stayed a week at some house in Louisiana on his way home. I know there must have been someone there."

Ruth hugged her, laughing again. She was a tall, sinewy woman, the very opposite of Martha. Frankly and helplessly, she had always envied Martha her husband, her children, her soft femininity – and, feeling guilty, had become her staunch friend. "No, honey," she said, "something must be upsetting Richard, but it isn't that. Tell me what happened after he was captured."

"He wasn't captured."

"But the newspapers—"

"Yes, but when Vicksburg fell, and they knew Port Hudson would have to surrender, Richard got through the Yankee lines at night."

"Then he's been all these weeks making his way home?"

"Yes, and..." Then she had stopped, clasping her sister-in-law's hand feverishly. "He's coming down. Oh, Ruth, watch him, tell me what you think."

Wheatley came over to them, the mechanical smile fixed on his lips. He was a dark-faced, handsome man of thirty-six, standing a little under middle height, slim and very erect. "It's good to see you, Ruth." His sister-in-law flung her arms about him, kissing him unashamedly on the mouth. "Oh, you darling. I'm so happy you're safe."

Wheatley patted her shoulder. Secretively he glanced at her, trying to estimate her. So, in the first moment of greeting, he had tried to estimate each of the others, even his wife – needing to know one thing only: not whether they loved him, but whether they would understand, whether they would support him in his purpose.

"We were so afraid you'd be in a Yankee prison camp by now." Ruth cried happily. She winced as he looked at her. His greyish pallor, the hollows in his sensitive face, made her heart ache.

Lynn Thomas tapped his own empty right sleeve. "In three years Richard still hasn't been able to match me," he exclaimed with perverse delight. "What are a couple of fingers?"

"Darling, sit down and rest," his wife urged.

"Yes," Wheatley said. "Asa, Jeffry, my thanks to all of you for coming so quickly."

They sat down. The room became awkwardly still. Wheatley felt the singleness of their glance upon him, and he quivered under it. He had summoned them there for a purpose, and now they were waiting. For weeks he had gone over this scene in fantasy, repeating what he would say, feeling confident in advance of the strength that could come from bitter pride. Now he felt only weakness, and a dreadful trembling in his breast. Now, in the old room, with the old faces before him in living reality, with the sense that outside was the garden he had only dreamt of in camp, that beyond were the real slave cabins and still further beyond the actual expanse of his land – now he felt imprisoned by the spiderweb of the old life. He had forgotten this web, he had forgotten the hold it might have on these loved ones who had remained at home.

The silence lengthened. Only the wheeze of Asa Wheatley's breathing punctuated the stillness. All knew that what Martha had told them earlier was true. Wheatley was like a stranger, indefinably apart from them. He sat slouched in his chair, his old gaiety gone, the warm radiance absent from his face, his good hand pressed curiously to his chest in the gesture of a man who is ailing.

"Richard," his wife said nervously, trying to make conversation, "did you have to leave your precious Plato at Port Hudson? I haven't dared ask about my picture yet."

Wheatley looked up. He touched his breast pocket. "You'll find the picture upstairs in my uniform, darling. But the Plato fed a winter fire."

Lynn Thomas laughed. He was at the sideboard with a drink in his hand. "Many things have been lost in this war."

"Darling," his wife asked again, "do you hurt there? You keep pressing your hand there!"

"Eh?" said Wheatley. He took his hand away from his chest. "Oh, no…" But a moment later the hand automatically returned.

There was silence again. Asa Wheatley cleared his throat and scratched uneasily at the ruddy flesh of his cheek. "Well, it's not hard to judge what your diet was at Port Hudson," he observed professionally. "Well, that's war, I guess – but we'll fatten you up before you go back, Dickie boy."

Wheatley said nothing. He was seeking a way to begin, but his mind felt muddy. It had been so different in fantasy.

Lynn Thomas laughed again. "The Lord fights on the side of the army with the most shrapnel and the least wormy potatoes, eh, Richard?"

"Wormy?" Ruth exclaimed. "You mean that?"

Lynn guffawed with masculine superiority.

"But you really mean food with worms in it? What do you do?"

"Why, pick out the worms and eat the food," Lynn laughed. "What else?"

Jeffry Thomas clenched his fist. He was a burly, rather coarse man, but a good-hearted neighbour and friend. "However hard it is, we'll win," he observed darkly. "We're fighting for the independence of the South, by God, while all those damn Federals* are fighting for is the right of factory owners to hire cheap labour. We're going to show these meddling abolitionists that the South wants to stay the way it is, that their damn Mr Lincoln can sign all the damn pieces of emancipation paper they want him to – but the old South is going to *keep* staying the way it is, now and for ever."

"Amen!" murmured Asa.

"Listen," said Wheatley, getting up suddenly. "Listen..." His voice trembled. The others fixed upon him, and again he was shaken by the sharp singleness of their glance. He crossed to the fireplace, turning from them, staring down in silence at the empty, clean-swept hearth. The abrupt, nervous hush in the room was almost physically painful.

"Oh, my darling, my lover, my wounded one," his wife called mutely to him. "What has happened? Even if there is someone else, let me help you. Come back to me." But she sat still, her hands folded in her lap. And Asa, his brother, thought: "Whatever it is, Richard, you must learn that you know too little of the comfort God can give. You need God now, and I can help you find Him." And the Thomas brothers, too, passed judgement. Jeffry said, "This looks like funk. He always was a little soft. He's had too much, poor man." And young Lynn, gazing down at his empty sleeve, he, who beside Martha was the dearest person there to Wheatley, thinking of the lost hours when they had argued the *Symposium** and Socrates, when they had probed Lear* and quoted Keats, times of most poignant pleasure, because they were alone of their kind in the community... Lynn thought with soft bitterness, "The poetry is gone, and that's the whole of it! In you and in me both, Richard. It will never be again!"

Wheatley stood before the fireplace, his hand pressed to his chest, his mind trembling. For this moment he had chanced the Yankee lines around Port Hudson. For this he had driven his exhausted body hundreds of miles. These people were the closest to him in the world. Either they would understand... or no one would. And if they did not, then this truth he had come to tell would rot in his breast... You, Martha, he cried silently, you are my wife. You love me, but will you understand? Will you win the mind of one other Southern woman for my purpose now? And Ruth? You kissed my mouth. You are fifteen years younger than my brother – you would go with me in adultery if I asked – but will you understand this? Asa! You are a God-fearing and a humane man. You are a physician as well as a planter. When it becomes necessary for you to whip a slave, you cannot do as Jeffry does. Instead you hire an outsider, you shut yourself in your house until it is over. A man like you won't want the killing to continue without purpose – will you, Asa? But will you understand? Will you help me with Jeffry, who is stubborn and hard-fisted, like so many in our South?...

Slowly, he turned to face them. "Asa... Jeffry," he said. His face was white. "All of you, listen: *we're finished*. The South is finished!"

They stared at him, but they did not speak. Jeffry Thomas clenched his fist. "No, by God," he burst out. "No! You've been fighting, and I haven't. But I say no, no!"

"Listen to me," Wheatley pleaded. "I beg you. It isn't what you think. This war has changed. We fought one war for two years, and we could have won that war. But it's a different war now, and we're finished, Jeffry!"

Again there was silence.

"Well..." said Lynn softly, "tell us..."

Wheatley looked from one to the other. His eyes were feverish. "I didn't call you here aimlessly. I have a purpose. And if you love me at all, I beg you to listen honestly. I've got to try and make you experience what I experienced... because then maybe you'll understand what I understand."

"Of course, Richard," his brother said gruffly. "Talk it out. We'll understand."

Wheatley pressed his hand to his chest. He wondered if they were aware of the terrible trembling in his breast, the trembling that had begun with the attack on Port Hudson and had not left him since. "We should have won at Port Hudson! It wasn't just another battle we lost: it was control of the Mississippi. And by Jesus Christ we would have smashed the Federals..." He stopped and stood staring at them. "Except for one thing."

"Yes?" asked Lynn softly.

The answer came slowly, in a curious tone. "A piece of paper, Lynn. A little damn scrap of paper with some words scrawled on it." The others exchanged glances. Wheatley saw it and burst into an unpleasant laugh. "No, I'm not loony. Listen: the first Yankee attack was on May thirteenth. To reach us they had to come out of their cover in swamps and magnolia woods and cross three hundred yards of naked ground. We were ready for them. We had seven thousand men in rifle pits that were buttressed by logs and great gabion baskets.* We had a six-yard abatis of wooden spikes before the pits. We had twenty-one heavy guns behind high revetments, as well as light artillery. I was praying that they would attack. I know how our Napoleons could cut them down." He stopped and pressed his hand to his chest.

"Richard," said his wife.

Wheatley's voice seemed to burst from his throat, "*They're using slaves*. The Federals have recruited slaves!"

"*What?*"

"Yes, Jeffry, yes, Asa, slaves! From the first moment of the attack we knew something was wrong. You know what a battle is like, Lynn. We heard their cry before we could see them. And it wasn't the Yankee huzza. It was different, it was their own, and I tell you it rose over the musketry and over the guns, and I thought it would fill the whole earth. It was 'Ah-h-h-h-h', like that... 'Ah-h-h-h!' And it was a cry of such fury that I felt as though a great hand had taken hold of my chest and was shaking me." He stopped and drew hoarsely for breath. "And then we saw them! They burst through the smoke, running, yelling – two brigades of slaves in Federal uniform. They were from New Orleans. And leading them, running ahead of the entire line, was a giant black carrying the flag of the United States!"

"My Heavens!" Asa muttered. The others said nothing. Jeffry Thomas began to pound on his knee with his clenched fist.

"I tell you I couldn't speak! I couldn't give a command. There was only one thing in my head: those slaves had guns. And with guns every one of them *was my equal*!"

Jeffry jumped up with an oath.

"It's true," Wheatley cried wildly. "What can stop any man on a battlefield? A gun only. With their guns they could kill me equally as I could kill them."

"Oh damn, damn, damn," Lynn cried. "Damn Abe Lincoln, damn Stevens,* damn them all to hell."

"By God, a bullet stops *them*, too, doesn't it?" Jeffry cried violently.

Wheatley threw up his hand in a curious, passionate gesture. "But if I didn't think it was insane, I'd say those slaves needed three and four bullets each. They wouldn't stop, Jeffry. We opened on them with such a blast of canister and grape and musketry that the air itself turned to lead. But they kept coming. They dropped by scores, but they kept coming. I saw that colour sergeant hit three times, but he never stopped. He was bleeding in the head and the arm and the chest, but he kept running. And he didn't go down until he ran into the abatis like a blind animal, and I heard that last yell, that 'Ah-h-h-h-h' – and then all day he hung there with the flag of the United States hugged to his breast..."

"Oh, Richard, Richard, Richard," said his wife. "Richard, Richard."

"You've got to understand," Wheatley cried to them. "You've got to know what this means. They attacked six times that day. It was madness, because they had no artillery support. And I tell you that, slaves or no slaves, they were the bravest soldiers I've ever seen. They turned the tide. In the weeks of siege it was they who pushed their saps closer and closer to us. And we hammered them and we hammered them, but we couldn't stop them. And Port Hudson fell... and Vicksburg fell... and the South is lost, my friends, it's lost, it's lost!"

"No, Jesus, no!" Jeffry Thomas cried. "You're hysterical. This is nonsense."

Wheatley raised his head fiercely. "I'm hysterical all right, but it isn't nonsense. Ah, Jeffry, listen to me: I saw those dead bodies on the battlefield. I recognized some of them. They were slaves from our work battalions at New Orleans. We kept losing them by hundreds before New Orleans fell. Every mile the Federals came closer, we lost more slaves."

"What of it? We've had the problem of runaway slaves for a hundred years. The Yankees give uniforms to a few thousand, whip some, liquor up others – and then send them into battle. And you think the war is lost?"

"They weren't whipped, and they weren't drunk," replied Wheatley passionately. His eyes had begun to blaze, and the pallor was leaving his cheeks. "Can't I make you understand that? No more than Fred was drunk!"

"*Fred*," cried his wife. "Our good Fred?"

"Yes," said Wheatley, "our good Fred. Two nights before the attack, an officer caught Fred reading. Did *you* know he could read, Martha? I didn't. He learnt secretly, knowing he could be branded and cropped for it. And what was he reading? A handwritten piece of paper, my friends, that has been passed through the work battalions of every Southern army. A copy of Mr Lincoln's piece of paper, Jeffry. Mr Lincoln's 'Emancipation Proclamation'." He stopped and looked at them. "We put Fred in the guardhouse. During the night he escaped. And twenty other slaves dusted away with him. Now he probably has a gun in his hand…" – he turned to Jeffry – "and with that he's your equal and my equal, my friend."

"Equal, is he?" cried Jeffry. "I'd show him equal. If I caught him, I'd whip him till the hide peeled off."

"Yes," said Wheatley, "but meanwhile he's gone, and there are thousands and tens of thousands like him. Don't you see what it means? That colour sergeant fell on our spikes, and he held that flag to his breast like a man…" His voice choked. "God, it was like a man holding his beloved! And the reservoir of such men! The Federals wouldn't use them for the first two years. But now they are. They're recruiting entire brigades wherever they hold territory. And they're swamping us with their manpower, because the slaves will fight for them, but they won't fight for us." His hand gripped his chest. "And I tell you that wherever that 'Emancipation Proclamation' reaches there are thousands who sift away overnight like sand through your fingers. They're going from the plantations and the munition factories and the riverboats and the work battalions. The South is built on slavery, and the foundation is leaving us."

"Well, *my* slaves won't run away," said Jeffry violently. "Maybe it takes a *man* to hold them in line, but mine won't run away."

Wheatley laughed. "Yes, they will, my friend. If the Federal armies come anywhere within fifty miles of us, yours will run away and ours will too."

"Not ours, Richard," his wife cried. "Why, ours are devoted to us!"

"Like Fred?" Wheatley asked. "Like *Fred*, Martha?" His whole body commenced to shake. "Slaves are devoted to being free! That's what I know now! That's what I'm trying to make you understand. And it's right. It's right, by Jesus. Men who will fight like that for their liberty *deserve* to be free. Do you hear me? They deserve it!"

"Wheatley! Do you know what you're saying?" Jeffry Thomas cried hoarsely. "Damn you, you're talking like a Northern abolitionist."

Wheatley's dark face became coppery. "I'm talking like a Southern officer who has learnt a truth. With a gun like mine, every black man is my equal. *And I won't keep such men in slavery any longer!*"

There was an instant of terrible silence. "What do you mean?" his brother Asa asked in a whisper. "What are you saying?"

"I'm going to free my slaves. And I'm asking you, I'm beseeching you, to do the same. This war is over. A piece of paper has decided it. And I'm saying let's end it now. There's no purpose in a hundred thousand more dead. Let's free our slaves and have peace. Because that's how it will end anyway. Slavery is finished."

He looked at them. No one spoke. "Asa... Jeffry..." he pleaded softly, "we three are the most important planters in this part of Carolina. What we do won't be lost. Peace must begin somewhere. It can start in this parlour. I don't know if what we do will go further. But I have confidence it may. And we will at least be able to walk with our heads up, my friends. We can make a peace with God that I know now we should have made before." He stopped, his face flushed, his eyes glowing. He held out his hand. "Will you do it, Asa? Jeffry, will you? Don't you know in your hearts that I'm right?"

Jeffry Thomas walked over to Wheatley and stood before him, towering over him, his fists clenched. "Mr Wheatley," he said, "you've been a neighbour and a friend, but the only honest thing *my* heart tells me is that you've turned corrupt and cowardly. You ask us to follow you? In this *insanity*? In this betrayal of all we stand for? Why, God damn you, *I* won't free my slaves, and your brother won't free *his* slaves, and *neither will you*."

The grey pallor returned to Wheatley's face. "But I will, Jeffry," he whispered. "I didn't know whether you would. I merely hoped. Apparently I've failed. But I must do this thing, and I will."

"No you won't. I can have you arrested tomorrow morning as a traitor and a Yankee spy. And if you don't think so, you're even more insane than you seem."

Wheatley stared at him for a long time. Then, deliberately, he turned his back. "Asa..." he said.

Powerfully, his face distorted, Jeffry Thomas swung him around. "Do you hear me, damn you? You think I'm going to let you put dynamite under the slave cabins on every other plantation in this county – under mine? Do you, you damned fool?"

"Take your hands off me," said Wheatley. He turned again to his brother. "I'm waiting to hear you, Asa."

Asa's plump face was ghastly. "Richard," he said falteringly, "Richard, boy, you're not well. You've been through too much. You're not in proper mental condition to make such a decision."

"Oh!" said Wheatley. "Then you're threatening me too?"

"No, no, Richard," Asa begged. "I'm your brother – but I'm a physician too. I can see what I can see."

"Then you *are* threatening me! And you, Ruth? Do you think I'm insane too?"

His sister-in-law wrung her hands. "I just can't understand this – I can't, Richard."

An expression of bewilderment crossed Wheatley's face. He turned from one to the other. His tongue felt strangely thick. "But look... look," he said.

"You'll just be a leper," Lynn Thomas said softly. "Don't you realize that, Richard?"

Wheatley crossed the room and gripped Lynn's wrist. "But it's right!"

Ruth raised her hand quickly. Jeffry, who had been about to speak, stopped. He looked at the two men and then fell silent.

Wheatley's eyes were on his friend's face. "I repeat the word, Lynn: it's 'right'. There was a time when that word was important to both of us. Isn't it now?"

"Right?" Lynn asked softly. "If an illiterate black has been taught to fire a gun, he may be your equal on a battlefield. But is he your equal otherwise?"

"Why is he illiterate, Lynn? Who kept him so?"

"He is, nevertheless."

"Fred is no longer."

Lynn shrugged. "Even so, is Fred your equal? Is he mine?"

"Lynn, Lynn," said Wheatley, "I can't answer. These questions came to my mind too. I'm confused. I only know that I have this trembling in my breast. I only know that men who will accept death as those men did must not be in bondage to me any longer. Don't you at least understand that, Lynn?"

"Good," said Lynn. "You speak of 'right'. Other men have freed slaves in the history of the South. But now? In wartime? If you free yours now, what about Asa's? Has he no rights? We're in a death struggle. Which side are you on, Richard?"

Wheatley raised his bandaged hand. He was deathly pale. "This shows the side, doesn't it?"

"Not if you free your slaves now. If you do that, you betray the South. Do you hear me? You betray your friends, your family, your class."

Wheatley pushed him away, crying out in the voice of a man who is being strangled. "And this truth? If I betray that?" He stumbled across the room to his wife, calling aloud the anguish of his loneliness. "Won't anyone remain with me? Won't you, Martha? Darling... out of our whole... even if you don't understand me... don't you repudiate me too."

She was silent, weeping. He shook her. "Martha!"

"Ah, my God, Richard," she cried, "but Lynn is right. He is, he is. I love you, but please, my darling, don't do it. It *will* be a betrayal."

Wheatley groaned. "So be it," he said. He fell to his knees by her side, and they heard him sob deep down in his throat. He thrust his hand against his mouth and bit at the flesh. Then, without a sound, a word, a backward glance, he got to his feet and stumbled blindly from the room. They heard him mount the stairs.

"Ah, Christ," Lynn Thomas said, "so many things have been lost in this war. Mr Lincoln and his damn piece of paper! Ah, poor Richard, poor Richard. It will never be the same again. Will it? Will it? Will it?"

"No," Ruth whispered, twisting her hands.

Martha rose. She crossed the room slowly, weeping. "Excuse me," she said. But at the door, at the terrible crash from the floor above, she reeled back sickeningly.

On the bedroom carpet, by Wheatley's body, there was a note: "With these words, I free my slaves."

Husband and Wife*

Although it was fifteen minutes before show time, May Alberti still was wearing a robe, and she was knitting away on a man's woollen sock like any housewife on her own back porch. As Forel, production manager of the circus, came up to the steps of her dressing room, she smiled at him cordially and waited in silence to see what he had on his mind. Forel asked, "Where's your old man?"

"Up front somewhere."

"I'll wait for him." He paused and then added lightly, "Meanwhile, I'll enjoy looking at you."

May glanced at him briefly and turned her eyes back to her knitting. She said amiably, "I'm an old married woman, pal, sixteen years."

"Imagine that! Can I ask you something personal?"

"You can ask."

"Thinking back to my own marriages, all four of 'em, after sixteen years things must get awful routine. Where's the kicks?"

May stopped knitting. Her manner was not unfriendly, but it was definite. "Pal, we got six months together in this circus, so let's get the sex angle straight. I don't play around."

Forel laughed without embarrassment. "OK, May."

"There's something else on your mind, isn't there?"

Forel nodded, started to say something, then stopped. As she looked at him closely, he muttered, "Well... I suppose it's easier to tell you than him."

She stopped knitting, "What?"

"You're a professional. Do I have to tell you Rudy's act has slipped?"

May flushed. A delicate, uncomfortable trembling began in the pit of her stomach, as though a thin piano wire had been set vibrating there, and she snapped back at Forel with open belligerence. "What are you talking about? I know he hasn't shown his best yet, but you're forgetting he got hit by a grippe the first week of rehearsals. And what about the weather? It's been stinking. The wire sweats, and the damp air blurs his eyes. You know how much a wireman* depends on his eyes."

Forel was quiet for a moment. Then he responded softly, "No dice.* The weather's just been average for any spring."

"He's just as good as he always was," May said passionately. "I know he's been missing the front somersault, but we've only been playing a week. He needs to warm into it."

Again Forel shook his head. He was wondering to himself, a bit wistfully, what it took in a man to make a stunningly beautiful woman like this so loyal to him. "You're blind, baby. Rudy's slipped a lot from the man I saw in the Garden* four years ago. He's uneven – he doesn't have the same fire, and he's missing the hard ones too often. He's gone downhill. I saw it at the first rehearsals, but I gave him the benefit of a doubt. Now I know! He isn't the outstanding act I thought we were getting."

There was a long silence. May's face was flushed, and her deep blue eyes were glowing with resentment, but inwardly the piano wire was vibrating. She could hate Forel for what he had been saying, but she couldn't dismiss it: he was too good a circus man.

Forel asked suddenly, "How old is Rudy – about fifty-five?"

"He was forty-seven last month."

"C'mon, baby – you're not talking to the press."

"I haven't got any reason to lie to you."

Forel studied her for a moment. "*I'm* forty-five. When I joined the Sells Floto as a kid flyer, Rudy was there in a teeterboard* act. He was a good deal older than me, and he was just beginning to learn the wire in his spare time."

"I don't get it," May exclaimed with bewilderment. "I ought to know how old he is."

"OK..."

"Why, he's got the body of a man of twenty. He's never out of training."

"That's why he's lasted so long. There isn't anybody in the profession won't tip his hat to Rudy – he's been a real artist."

May locked the fingers of both hands together to still their trembling. She said abruptly, "So let's get down to cases. What do you want?"

"Number one: he has to cut out the front flip."

It was the answer she had expected, but it was cruel to hear it. She said painfully, "That's what he's most famous for. It's the high point of his act."

"It used to be. We opened six days ago, and he's made it only five times in twelve shows. What did he do this afternoon? It's not only he missed three times, but he took so long getting set for each try that the audience got restless."

May said in a low voice, "He came back looking like hell. You don't know what it did to him."

"When the doctors told me I never could fly again, what do you think *my* face looked like?"

May was silent. There was nothing here she could deny or excuse. Rudy *had* been missing, and it *was* bad showmanship. All along she had taken for granted that it was no more than a slow start at the beginning of a season. But what if he had slipped and would never climb back?"

"Listen," Forel said, "since Rudy's your guy, you ought to have something else on your mind. A front flip is not only damn hard to do on a tight wire, but it's dangerous. How many wiremen have had the guts even to try it? At his age, missing the way he is, he's going to get hurt bad one of these days."

It was the truth, and May knew it, and the resentment within her suddenly died. She said in a subdued, unhappy voice, "OK, I'll tell him. I guess I'm even glad of it. What the hell – a backflip looks just as good to a crowd. They don't know what's hard and what's easy."

The spotlights that were strung around the back-lot area came on suddenly, piercing the twilight, and Forel glanced at his watch. Inside the big top the band had begun a lively tune. Fifty yards off, the elephants were being lined up for the opening procession.

"That isn't all," Forel said. "We've got a pretty good show, but so far we aren't making money. We're up against the same competition from television that's made most outfits fold. But I figure there's still room for a tent circus – provided it's got real class."

"What are you leading up to?"

"Come Saturday, when we play Lafayette,* I'm changing the routine. There's a new troupe coming in, a high-balance act. I'm using them as the last number in part one."

May stared at him. "That's Rudy's spot. Where'll you put him?"

Forel answered softly, but with unmistakable firmness. "I'll give him centre ring between the cycle act and those Belgian jugglers. The band'll play Rudy's music, so it won't foul him up any."

She had not expected this, and it was an absolutely stunning blow.

"There'll have to be a salary cut, too," Forel added. "Forty per cent."

Many feelings came to a sudden boil inside May's heart, but resentment was the first to burst out. "If you think Rudy'll work under those conditions, you're an idiot."

The reply was cold. "Don't call me names, baby. The show hasn't failed Rudy – he's failed to deliver. Nobody gets cushioned in this game."

For a long moment May's lips worked and trembled. Then she muttered, "I shouldn't have said that. I know you're being straight about this. I'm all shook up."

"OK, no grudges... Naturally, I've had it in mind that Rudy might quit. He's been a headliner so long it'll be rough to step down."

She said nothing. She was not looking at Forel now.

"Anyway, you've got till Saturday to think it over."

Out of her own turmoil, without intending to communicate an intimacy to this man, May suddenly cried out, "God, we can't afford to quit!"

An ironic, somewhat sad smile came to Forel's lips. He asked softly, "After all those years of good money, aren't you well fixed?"

"No, we're not!" She turned to him suddenly, not intending to beseech, but doing so in spite of herself with eyes, voice and the misery on her face. "This'll break Rudy's heart. He's not prepared for it."

"You know," Forel said with compassion, "I think you've both been living in the clouds. Didn't you know Rudy couldn't keep up the same pace for ever? A lawyer or a doctor hit their prime at his age, but not a man who uses his body. He's got to start slipping."

May remained silent. Her eyes were glistening with tears. She felt unhinged, unable to think.

Inside the big top a burst of laughter indicated that the clowns were at work with the incoming crowd. Now, trunk tied to tail, the line of elephants came lumbering down to the stage entrance. A bit further off performers were issuing from the pad tent to take their places for the opening spectacle.

Forel said, "You better get dressed. Spec starts in five minutes." His eyes lingered on May's face, and then, in a gesture that was purely friendly, he stepped up to her and patted her shoulder. "I'm sorry, baby, I really am." He strode off down the path of straw towards the stage entrance.

May sat still for a few moments with the tears beginning to flood out of her eyes. Then she rose, walked up the several remaining steps to the door of her dressing room and went inside. As she placed her knitting in a hamper, she thought to herself, "If I don't stop this goddamn crying, I'll ruin my make-up." With that she clapped both hands over her face and began to sob bitterly. The Great Alberti cut down into just another act – even the European circus world would hear of it in a month. Of course Rudy wouldn't take it! He'd walk out.

Only, after he walked out... what? They'd been counting on a full season's work. It was the end of April – everything good would be booked up. They'd be begging their agent to pick up a theatre date, a county fair. But whatever they got wouldn't be enough.

May slumped down on a chair. She reached for a tissue on her dressing table, wiped her eyes and told herself that getting in a panic wouldn't help her think this through. The truth was that they *had* handled their money like dizzy kids! She knew run-of-the-mill performers who were better off now than they were. Other circus people holed up in some little motel in Florida in the off-season, or put money into a trailer that now belonged to them – but only first-rate hotels had been good enough for the Albertis. Yet the hell of it was that Rudy always talked a lot about financial security. Only, how did any man develop his cock-eyed ability at making bad investments? He had sunk three thousand in a machine that would revolutionize the book-binding industry – except that no company wanted it. After that had come the clothespin that every housewife would need, and the plastic arch support that no one ever bought – and how many others? She couldn't remember! It would be like trying to remember all the silly hats she'd ever bought, all the dresses scarcely worn and then given away to friends. *She* was no bargain at saving money, either.

So now here they were – without enough savings to tide over until next season. And there was something else Rudy didn't know: that a piece of expensive surgery was scheduled for his wife as soon as the circus closed. If they quit this show, it would be madness. Before the year was out, they'd be the usual pair of stony-broke entertainers borrowing from relatives and friends. It was her job to see that Rudy didn't quit. They'd been dreamy kids about money long enough.

May wept, feeling terrified of the anguish in store for her husband. Other men were performers working two shows a day for a buck, but Rudy was an artist, and he needed to perform with every eye on him like a violinist in a concert hall. When the big top rocked with applause, she felt pleased – but to Rudy the applause was vital: it was sunlight to him, he needed it because it told him that yes, he *was* an artist – yes, he was tops. It was rotten enough to take a salary cut, but to have it known everywhere that Alberti no longer rated a solo…

Hearing footsteps outside, May quickly dried her eyes. She began to wonder why Rudy hadn't returned for the opening procession.

No performer had the right to skip Spec. As he reached the doorway, Rudy paused to peer inside. She had not turned on the lights of her dressing table, and the only light in the room came from a work lamp beyond the doorway. She said quietly, "I'm here, sweetheart."

He came in slowly. "What are you sitting in the dark for?"

"Just thinking."

"You been worrying about me? I decided to skip Spec whether Forel beefed or not."

May could not see the expression on his face, but the heaviness in his voice made her say instantly, "You sound upset!"

"Yeah, I am." He paused for a moment. "I went into the animal tent to see that new spider monkey. A young couple passed by me. From a side view the boy looked so exactly like Gregg that I had an actual... what's the word?... hallucination." He paused again, and May could feel his unhappiness like cloth between her hands. "I was *positive* it *was* Gregg. Then the boy turned, and I got such a dizzy feeling I thought I'd keel over. I felt just as bad, just as sore at life, as the night we lost him."

May stood up, put her arms around her husband and pressed her face to his.

Rudy said wistfully, "You know, I haven't cried since I was a kid. But sometimes I think it must be a relief to be able to cry."

"That's right," she replied softly, "your feelings don't stay knotted up in your belly." She kissed his face. "Rudy, dear, a part of me is always going to be missing because of Gregg, but I don't feel the same way I did three years ago."

"A night like this I feel exactly the same."

"I know you do, and I wish you could change. Gregg's dead, and we have to accept it." Her thoughts turned to Forel's ultimatum, and she added deliberately, "The way all people have to accept sickness sometimes, or growing older. What would be the use of complaining that each year makes us older?"

"Well, sure, of course," Rudy exclaimed bitterly, "but Gregg was just starting his life. God... if only I hadn't bought him that damn motorcycle!"

May's arms tightened around him. "It's so terribly wrong to blame yourself. He could've died of polio or in a plane accident. I agreed to his having the motorcycle – it wasn't all *your* responsibility."

"What an act we were developing!" Rudy muttered. "Six months more and we would've shown the circus world something they never dreamt could be done on a wire."

"I know, darling. All those years of planning and training... I know how cheated you feel."

He reached for a chair, swung it close and sat down. May stood by him, pressing his head to her body, caressing his hair. She knew, although they never talked about it, that there was something else behind Rudy's grief over their son: the fact that Gregg was the child of her first, bad marriage, and that their own marriage, so deserving of children, had been barren.

A roar of laughter from the big top rolled over the wagon. They could tell from the band music that the elephant act had finished, the clowns were on, and the Iron Jaw was about to go. Rudy said, "I'm feeling easier now. I'll start to warm up."

May came to a sudden decision: to postpone the more serious part of what Forel had told her until after the show. She said with effort, "I got bad news for you, sweetheart."

"What?"

"Forel wants you to cut out the front... right away, tonight."

He didn't react as she had expected: his response was a ripple of disdainful laughter. He jumped up and switched on the overhead bulb. "What do you know? Old Forel..." He stopped, gazing at her splotchy make-up. "You've been crying... sitting here worrying about how I'd take it, weren't you?"

"Yeah."

"Ah, sweetheart, I'm sorry. There's no reason to be upset."

"Doesn't it upset you?"

He laughed. "Hell no! Now that Forel's a manager, he's forgotten what a performer's up against." He moved a bit away from her and began a circular bending movement with his torso. "Forel's forgotten how hard a top performer has to press himself. When you're good, you make the hard ones look easy to an audience – but that doesn't mean they don't take every ounce you've got. Sure, I've been missing the front – and worrying about it has affected the whole act. But now I know *why* I've been missing!" He paused in his exercising, and a flashing smile lit up the rather stern expression his face usually wore in repose. His smile was a beautiful thing to May, and her heart leapt to see it.

"I've been doing two things wrong," Rudy said as he went back to his exercise. "You'd think after all these years I wouldn't make mistakes, but you fall into 'em. It clicked for me the minute I hit bad this afternoon. First of all, I've been bouncing too long. It makes me heavy on the wire, and I lose a shade of the height I need. Tonight I'm taking off fast, I won't give myself time to get tight. And second... I haven't been following through with my eye. That's the chief reason."

"Following through when... in the air?"

"That's it – the old Alberti trade secret... I've been goofing on it."

"How come?"

Rudy grinned at her. "That's what I've been asking myself since this afternoon. Oh, I didn't altogether forget it, but I haven't been concentrating on it the way I need to. So stop worrying, sweetie. Forel won't have any complaints tonight."

He changed his exercise to rapid knee bends, and conversation stopped. May sat down at the dressing table and began to rub cold cream on her face. She felt excited by what Rudy had said – it made sense. A front flip was much harder than a back somersault, because a performer couldn't see where he was landing: his feet had to hit before his head came around. On the wire it was incredibly difficult – there was no margin of error. Long ago Rudy had explained how taking a visual fix, while he was upside down in the air, enabled him to keep control: he could shift his weight a hair's difference in completing the turn. It always had seemed incredible to her that he could do this, because the whole jump only took a second. But that was Rudy – it was why he had become

"The Great Alberti". And if he hadn't been following through with his eye, that *could* be the answer to his bad performances.

"Listen," she said, "we'll have to tell Forel you're not cutting the front tonight."

Rudy nodded. He stopped exercising and began to unbutton his shirt.

Out of a sudden need to be reassured still further, May said, "Forel thinks the act as a whole has slipped a little."

Rudy had stepped to a wall hook to hang up his shirt. He swung around with his dark eyes blazing, his face hard with anger. "Forel's a fool! What makes him a smart circus man – the fact that he did the triple when he was a flyer? He did it for a couple of years and then what? Missed his rhythm – you heard him tell it – and fell into the net wrong side down like any other jerk who doesn't know his business. Does that give him the right to judge Alberti?"

The wonder May felt was answered – and it brought a lump to her throat. Rudy always was generous in his estimate of other performers, and they both knew that Forel had been magnificent. This outburst of anger conveyed a great deal: that Rudy himself was worried about slipping. And yet, at the same time, his very intensity made her yearn to believe that it was Forel who was wrong – that Rudy would be his old self tonight, and that he wouldn't lose his solo spot. With a burst of emotion, she said, "Rudy, old boy, I have a notion you'll make 'em yell tonight."

He replied with his flashing smile and his body relaxed. "Time to get ready. Tend to your face, sweetie – you're a sight." He began taking off the rest of his clothes.

May turned back to the mirror. She was thinking that if Rudy *had* lost confidence, no amount of technique would help him. What he did on the wire required confidence above everything else. Troubled, she watched his reflection in the mirror. His face was more stern than usual, and she could see how determined he was. He wasn't really a handsome man, she knew, and yet how much she loved the way he looked – the bony, masculine cast of his features, the tight olive skin, the wide mouth with the sharp, grooving lines on either side. She sighed and thought, "How lucky I've been to have him."

Mechanically she began to wipe the cold cream from her face, but she continued to observe him in the mirror. Rudy was of medium height, not very broad, his lean torso tapering to narrow waist and hips. Only the development of his thighs and legs gave any indication of his physical power. As May watched him put on his plastic cup and tights, she reflected that she always had had a reverence for his body – the way the wife of a violinist might feel about her husband's hands. No one became a top violinist without being so dedicated that he could accept the practice and discipline involved, and Rudy was dedicated in the same way. To guard his vision he never would read on a moving train, he rarely went to the movies or looked at television. His diet was even more spartan than that of most performers: fruit juice and tea for breakfast, a poached egg and a cup of milk at midday, only a modest meal at night. Never a dessert or a glass of beer, or a drop of the brandy she loved after supper. And even in the off-season, when most performers let down, he did his three miles of roadwork daily. It was no accident he was great. The publicity they handed out said he had been born to a circus family in Argentina and had been trained on the wire from the time he could walk – but that was a tale for the birds. The Latin in his appearance came from an Irish grandfather, and he was the son of a New Hampshire farmer. Water boy in a mud circus was how he'd begun! It was not until he had had years of experience that he'd even begun to try the wire. And the dances he did on it were his own creation – no one had developed an act like that before. There were others who were effective stuntmen on the wire, but Rudy's act was music and poetry.

Smiling softly, May began to make up her face. And then, abruptly, Forel's voice and Forel's ultimatum were echoing in the room: "A lawyer or a doctor hit their prime at Rudy's age, but not a man who uses his body. He's *got* to start slipping..." Forel was no fool. Was it possible Rudy had lied to her about his age?

It was true that his hair would be quite grey now if he didn't dye it. Yet what reason would he have had to deceive her?

There was a shout from outside the wagon. "Mr Alberti... first call... Roman Chariots going on."

Rudy was seated on a rug on the floor, legs spread apart. He was warming up hard now, turning and twisting his torso, touching his forehead to the floor, starting what he called "the flow of oil in his joints". He sang out, "OK, you can skip the five-minute call." The voice outside called back "Thanks", and Rudy said to May, "Slowpoke,* stop dreaming, get dressed."

"I'll be ready," she answered comfortably. "You're the one who's taking your time tonight."

"Just a minute more. I'm not sweating enough."

May blotted her lips and stood up. She took off her robe. Gazing at herself in the mirror, she decided that she had gained a pound, maybe two, and she'd have to cut down on desserts. And then, for the first time, it occurred to her that the operation she was going to have would leave an ugly scar. The idea made her wince. She never had had an operation before, and the thought of a surgeon's knife cutting into her body was rather terrifying. She sighed, and her lips moved in silent speech, and she said to herself, "C'mon, baby, stop feeling sorry for yourself. You're thirty-nine, and these things happen."

She began to dress. Her costume was an adaptation of gaucho clothes, and she loved it. The blouse was gold-coloured silk, and the skirt was black with a flaring swirl; there was a tight black bolero, and a spangled comb for her thick hair. As she checked her appearance in the mirror, she thought to herself, "You're not so bad for your age, old girl, and maybe the scar won't be so big."

Rudy got up from the floor and wiped his face and neck with a towel. He said intensely, "I feel good!" He began to put on the clothes with which he started his act – a wine-red blouse and tight black gaucho trousers. Both garments had special zipper arrangements, so that he could remove them when he was on the wire. Over them went a faded bathrobe to conceal his costume while he watched the setting-up of his rig.

May asked, "Raincoats?"

"Sky's clear." He slipped his feet into the webbing of the wooden clogs they used from dressing room to tent. "I'm ready."

She picked up a small bag and peered into it. "Your shoes, my shoes, the towel. OK… My make-up all right?"

He took his gold cape from a wall hanger and looked her over. "Sweetie, you're better-looking now than the day we got married."

May puckered her lips at him. "For a lie, it sounds great."

He bent down and kissed her throat lightly, and May said, "You busy after the show? Can I date you up after your spectacular performance?"

"It's going to be a hell of an act tonight, if I say it myself. Let's go."

Neither of them speaking, they crossed the thirty yards of straw to the entrance of the big top. Inside there was the good feeling that a capacity audience gives, and they could tell at once that the crowd was warm. The acts in the three rings were coming to a close, and the applause was generous. May asked, "You want to tell Forel or should I?"

"You! I don't even want to see the jerk." He gave her his cape and tightened the cord of his bathrobe. "Don't let him argue with you. Just tell him and turn your back."

She walked over to a group of clowns clustered around a miniature fire wagon. "Anybody know where Forel is?"

One of them pointed. "In the audience, second row."

"Thanks."

The acts came to an end. The clowns moved out to cover the interval, and Rudy slipped into the centre ring to supervise the setting up of his rig. May walked down to Forel and touched his arm.

"Hello, May."

She raised her voice so she could be heard above the crowd laughter. "Be a pal, will you? Rudy wants one more chance at the front."

Forel responded with a sour grimace.

"You know how you'd feel in his spot."

"I already told the band and the MC."

"You can untell 'em... Please!"

He looked at her, and his lips twisted. "All right, but only once! And if he misses, he better have something in mind for a substitute climax."

"You're a peach... thanks."

"What's he decided to do on Saturday night?"

"I haven't told him. I didn't want to upset him before the show."

She walked off quickly to meet Rudy coming out of the ring.

"Those damn fools keep stringing my wire higher on the right than the left," Rudy snapped irritably as he took off his bathrobe. "This circus is full of morons... What did he say?"

May took their shoes out of the bag. "Said good luck, and he thinks you're ready to sail."

He grunted, and they both were silent as they changed. Rudy put on his cape. The clowns came off, and the band beat out a drum roll. The master of ceremonies went into the familiar introduction: "We present to you now the fantastic master of the art of walking a single thin wire... the performer whose name is known all over the world... the Great Alberti!"

The band swung into a tango, and May and Rudy walked rapidly towards the centre ring. She was wearing her performer's smile, and Rudy had the stern, imperious look that the onstage walk always brought to his face. They stood in the centre, turning and bowing to the audience. Then Rudy said, with wonder in his voice, "Had to swallow a lump – hasn't happened in years."

"Doesn't mean a thing," May replied quickly, but it did mean something to both of them. All performers knew what it meant to have a lump of anxiety form in the throat before going on, and they weren't ashamed to speak of it. But just tonight it shouldn't have happened to Rudy.

With his usual flourish, Rudy took off his cape and handed it to May. She moved to the side while he ran up the steps to the starting platform, seven feet above the ring. He scraped his slippers on the rubber mat to remove any particles of sawdust, picked up the weighted balance rod and poised before the wire. The music halted for two beats, and then, as it began again, he was on.

The tango was slow, seductive, and his feet moved with sensuous grace. He danced slowly to the opposite platform, reversed and glided back. "Oh, it's good, it's beautiful," May thought fiercely. She was trying to see his performance with new eyes, to estimate it as Forel would. She felt positive that Rudy never had been any better than this – his feet deft, his body moving in sweet harmony with the music.

Rudy paused at centre. He bent forward slowly, balanced the rod on the wire, and then, at a heavy beat in the music, swung into a handstand. It was a stunt that looked much harder than it was, and it brought applause. The return to the wire was more difficult, but he did it smoothly – sinking into a half knee bend, wobbling a little as part of his regular showmanship, and pretending that he needed the bar for balance. It was good – it was fine – but, as he rose, a shiver ran through May: for an instant he had seemed to sway and to *need* the rod. It had happened so fast that she couldn't be sure, and she watched him anxiously. He was dancing again, working down to the platform by which she stood. As the number ended and he stepped up to applause, he gazed down at her and said with his teeth clenched "Had a wobble", and there was an expression of dismay on his face that was appalling to her. "Forget it!" she called quickly. "You haven't been so good since we started – listen to the audience!"

The band went into the next number, another tango, but fast and hot. Without the rod now, Rudy launched himself upon the wire. With the first few beats, May saw that he was too intense and ahead of the music. He slowed down and recovered his rhythm a moment later, but she thought, "Damn Forel!" Then it was going smoothly again, his feet nimble and fast, working the wire from end to end, his reverses perfect. It came time for him to take off his shirt, and he did it well, dropping to his crotch, bouncing back to his feet and ripping off the shirt with a flourish. He tossed it to her as the crowd applauded. He danced for a bit, and then it was time for his trousers — and this, too, went smoothly, although it never was easy, even for him.

Now he was down to white shirt and tights. The music became more intense and rose to a crescendo. Rudy lost a beat, and had to double a step to catch up — and May suddenly began to feel hollow inside. As she thought back, every one of his performances had been uneven like this. It was what Forel meant in saying the act had slipped. All top stars missed hard ones occasionally, but their basic work never was ragged. Rudy's never had been before — or had it? For all she knew, he had been on a slow downgrade for some time without her seeing it.

The music was Spanish flamenco now, throbbing and wild, and she thought his dancing lacked zest, as though he were physically weary. It couldn't be that, she knew: it could only mean his mind was elsewhere. Like her, then, he was worrying about what was to come.

The flamenco was broken by a drum roll. Rudy took centre, steadied himself, bounced three times on the wire, and then — as she caught her breath — did a back somersault. Both feet landed, but she saw at once that he was fighting desperately not to fall. It was not the fake unsteadiness he sometimes used for effect: it was a body-wrenching effort to prevent himself from toppling. Applause swelled from the audience as he kept his footing, but it had been too close for May to feel any triumph.

The flamenco ended. Another drum roll began. On the far platform, Rudy was stepping up on stilts. He turned sideways and began the slow crossing. His eyes were fixed upon the wire in deadly concentration. It was a stunt that always excited an audience, although it was less difficult to master than his rhythmic dancing. Nevertheless, it involved the danger of an uncontrolled fall, and May watched him with an anxiety she had not felt in years. It went well. He stopped at centre, and she waited for him to go into the balance on one stilt alone. Nothing happened. He remained still, frozen, and she knew he was fighting a lump. The pause lengthened until it became uncomfortable. Then, slowly, the stilt came off the wire and applause broke out. The stilt came back – there was a moment of unsteadiness, but then he was moving again. Watching him, May cried out inwardly, "Darling, don't try the front tonight – let it go!" Without willing it, she moved closer to the platform. She reached it as he did, and the appeal was trembling inside her. But then she looked at his sweating face, intense and savagely determined, and she cried to him beneath the applause, "You'll make it, lover, you're hot tonight." He didn't reply – he didn't look at her – and she couldn't even be sure he had heard her. His arms were extended mechanically to the audience, but his eyes were fixed on the wire.

The master of ceremonies spoke through the microphone: "You will now see the most difficult feat ever achieved on a single strand of wire – the dangerous front somersault. I'll ask you to keep silent, please, while the Great Alberti makes his attempt."

The band went into the slow tango it had played first. Rudy danced out on the wire and stopped in centre. With his arms out, he balanced himself. Once again, the music gave way to a drum roll. The audience was hushed and expectant, and it seemed to May that the blood had stopped flowing through her body, so cold and clammy had her flesh become. Rudy began bouncing, and she counted with him – once, twice, three times, a fourth – and then he leapt. "You did it!" her heart cried as he landed, but he was wobbling and working desperately to keep his footing – and then he fell. He landed easily to appreciative applause, but May saw the furious disappointment on his face as he ran for the platform. Only then did she realize that she had forgotten to warn him to try it only once. Forel would have bad faith to charge against them. Rudy was on the wire, and the drum roll began again. He bounced once, a second time... and paused to steady himself. He bounced once... and again stopped. Then it was once, twice, a third time, a fourth, a fifth – and the moment he took off she knew it was bad. She saw the shudder of his body in mid-air as he tried to correct the error – and he came down with his feet at an angle and was flung chest forward against the wire. There was a gasp from the crowd as his body struck the ground. With a cry, May ran to him. He was lying on his back, eyes and mouth open, his blanched face contorted with pain. She dropped to her knees by his side, calling to him wildly. She felt disembowelled by the fear that his spine was broken. Several stage hands ran over. One took hold of his shoulders, and May screamed at him violently, "Don't move him – get a doctor." Abruptly, Rudy's chest began to heave. He gasped for air like a swimmer emerging from the depths. "Knocked the air out of him," one of the hands said, "that's all it is!" Colour was coming back into Rudy's face, and the look of pain was departing. A moment later, he raised his head and began to struggle to his feet. May helped him up, crying with anxiety, "You all right? Is your back hurt?"

"I'm not hurt," he gasped, with his chest heaving. He took a step away from her.

"No more tonight!" she cried fiercely. "You'll kill yourself. Take a bow."

Rudy hesitated... and then a look of awful sadness came over his face. Slowly he extended his hands to the audience. As they listened to the respectful applause, she saw a shiver go through him. The band, which had been playing wildly throughout, suddenly stopped. The master of ceremonies announced that the first half of the programme was over, and there would now be an intermission of twenty minutes.

They went off. May's arm was around Rudy's waist, and she could feel the nervous quivering of his body. The front of his jersey was torn, and there was an ugly purple welt where the wire had seared his chest. "Was it only your wind?" she asked anxiously. "Don't you want a doctor to look you over?"

He shook his head.

The prop man guarding their things said sympathetically, "Sure glad *I* ain't a performer. You guys have to *work* for your lettuce."

Rudy said nothing. He took the towel out of the bag, wiped his face and neck and slipped into his bathrobe. Members of the audience began to file past them with glances of curiosity. As they changed to their wooden clogs, a teenage girl ran up with a programme in her hand and asked eagerly, "Can I have your autograph, Mr Alberti?" Giving an autograph was something Rudy enjoyed and always was gracious about, but he turned to the girl with a frown and snapped, "What for? It isn't worth anything" – and turned away again.

"Not tonight, honey, I'm sorry," May whispered to the bewildered girl.

Rudy muttered "Let's go", and started out. May snatched up their bag and followed.

They were silent on the way to the dressing room, Rudy with a frozen face and May with tears blurring her eyes. Inside the wagon he stood for a moment staring at the floor, and then muttered, "For the first time in my life, I feel like getting drunk."

"You want a shot of cognac, honey?"

"I need something – I'm shaking to pieces inside."

She took a flask from the drawer of her dressing table and poured a small drink into a paper cup. Rudy tasted it, grimaced, then downed it. He cleared his throat and said wryly, "Has a nice taste, I guess, doesn't it?" He sat down. "Makes you feel warm inside. I can use some more."

May poured another small drink. "Let me see your chest."

He shook his head. "It's just a bruise. We'll put some hot towels on it when we get back to the train."

"Does it hurt you?"

"Only a little."

"I'm so sorry, sweetheart. I know how much you wanted to make it tonight."

He said nothing. He was staring at the floor, and the light from the overhead bulb was cruel to his face, making it look drawn and old. Abruptly he raised his head, drank the cognac at one gulp and threw the cup away. He coughed and said softly, "May, sit down... close to me, huh?"

She pulled a camp chair over to his, and he took hold of her hand, gripping it tightly. "I've gone downhill this year, haven't I?"

Her first impulse was to evade. She said with a little stammer, "You *have* been missing the hard ones more than usual."

"It isn't just the hard ones," he replied intensely, "it's my whole act, isn't it? Those wobbles tonight! Even the backflip almost went wrong."

"It's just a slow start at the beginning of a season."

"It's more than that," he said, with his voice rising. "I've *lost* something! I don't *own* that wire the way I used to. It's standing me off now, fighting me like it did when I was a beginner – every time I started a practice session, I never knew how I'd do."

"Rudy—"

"I've slipped, haven't I?" he interrupted. "Isn't that the truth?"

"Maybe... Oh, I can't tell, I'm too close to you... Yes, maybe you have, darling – I'm afraid you have."

"But I was damn good last season, wasn't I?" he asked with a cry. "You remember how I finished off in Rio?" He turned away from her. A twitching began in his cheek that she remembered with pain: his face had twitched like that the night her son was on the operating table. "I've passed my peak, that's the story... But, God, how could it happen between last season and this? It's only been a few months."

They were silent for a moment. Rudy's cheek was twitching spasmodically, and May was trying to restrain her tears.

"Those drinks've made me a little dizzy," he muttered. "But I needed 'em. This was a bad night for me, honey. It hurt my confidence. I felt so good when I started – but that first wobble shook me. I can't buck Forel now. I'll cut the front out and work on it between shows. Maybe I can get it back."

May said falteringly, "Darling, I got awful bad news for you."

He looked at her intensely.

"Starting Saturday night, Forel's got a new act coming in. If... if we want to stay with the show, you've got to... well... you can't do a solo any more."

The twitching of his cheek stopped abruptly. His eyes blazed. "Forel told you that? When?"

"Before the show. I didn't want to upset you."

"He wants to use Alberti as just another act? With a money cut, too, I suppose?"

"A big one, forty per cent."

Rudy jumped up. His bony face had turned pallid with anger. "We're quitting tonight!"

"Are you sure you don't want to think it over?"

"What's there to think over?"

"The rest of the season…"

"I'll send a wire to Ralph – I'll tell him to get another booking."

"Now, at the end of April?"

He suddenly had no answer, but his eyes remained hot.

May said bluntly, pressing him despite the anguish she felt, "You'll get some in-between bookings, but we won't have a season – nothing like it."

"So we won't! But I can't take this, can I?"

"Rudy, darling, we don't have much of a bankroll to fall back on. How we going to get along?"

The fury in his eyes began to give way to dismay. When he spoke, it was with bewilderment. "*You* want me to do it – tell the whole world Alberti's on the skids?"

It was acutely painful for May to say it: "You just told me yourself, two minutes ago, that you'd passed your peak. Nobody gets cushioned in this game."

A stunned look came to his face. Slowly he felt for the chair and sat dow.

"Rudy, sweetheart," she said, knowing the size of the wound that was opening inside of him, "you're forty-seven. A doctor or a lawyer are in their prime at that age, but not a man who uses his body. You can't go on for ever."

The twitching began again, and he pressed a hand to his face. "Yeah, of course," he muttered, "I've always known that some day… but only last year in South America…" He fell silent.

May put her arm around him and kissed the hand that was pressed to his face. "We haven't had our eyes open, dearest – not you, not me.

Now I'm trying to see things clear. It's four years since you played the Garden. Why? Because Ringling* didn't make any offers. Sure, you've played the whole world since then at good money, but not what the Garden would've paid. And do you realize this was the only circus call we got this year? Nothing from Europe."

"Well, sure," he muttered with intense uneasiness, "but we played Europe only two years ago – they like to change their acts."

"I think it's something else." She paused, and her lips trembled. "I hate to say it, but I think you've probably been slipping a little for several years, and we haven't seen it."

"But I *can't* take Forel's offer!" Rudy said with a cry. "Once I lose my solo spot, it'll all be downhill. Five years from now it'll be a mud circus in the Dakotas playing for keep and twenty dollars a week. That's how it'll end. Performing is all I know – I can't clerk in a shoe store."

"Oh, no, darling," she said passionately, "don't look at it so black – you're still wonderful. If you'd ended up with the stilts tonight, that audience would have been plenty satisfied. You may have to step down from being a headliner, but that isn't the end of everything. We'll work every angle. If you start next October booking country fairs and theatres, we can have a swell season. But right now we're in a pickle. We need money. We can't lay off."

Rudy pressed a knuckle of his clenched fist against his teeth. He groaned and said nothing.

"Lover, we've got a special need for money that I haven't told you."

"What?"

"When the season's over, I've got to have an operation – a pretty expensive one."

The expression on his face changed in the instant. The twitching stopped, his brow furrowed, and May saw with gratitude that his thoughts had turned solely to her. "Since when? Why haven't you told me?"

"Since I saw the doctor in Pittsburgh. You were just starting to rehearse... I didn't want to worry you."

"What's wrong?"

"A lot of women my age grow tumours inside, honey."

"Oh, May!" His hand caught her arm. "Is there any worry it could be..." He didn't finish.

"A cancer? No! The doctor was quite sure."

"Is the operation dangerous?"

"Not with a good surgeon. It's major, but nothing a healthy woman can't take. Only, I certainly want it done right, dearest."

Rudy flung his arms around her. "Of course it'll be done right! We'll get a top surgeon. You'll have everything you need, and a long rest afterwards – in Miami, say, or Bermuda."

May smiled at him. "You're talking a lot of money, pal."

"Oh!" he muttered.

"A good surgeon... a week in the hospital... the cost of the operating room and the rest... it won't be peanuts."

He got up and began to pace the room. "Yeah... I got the habit of talking big, haven't I? Can the operation wait till the end of the season?"

"He said it could, but not too much longer. He gave me the name of a doctor he knows in Des Moines, so I can get checked there."

"Money," Rudy muttered, "money, money! We're sure in a squeeze!" His cheek was beginning to twitch again. "You're right, we can't quit! When you're on the skids, you take what you can get... You can't have a solo act all your life... Plenty of performers never even have one at all."

He said this, and then a dry, forlorn, almost childish sob burst from his throat – and to May it seemed as though he were having a nervous breakdown before her eyes. The wild twitching of his face, the spasmodic, tearless sobs that seemed to erupt from his throat, were accompanied by bursts of disconnected talk. "What a hash I've made of things! What's ahead for us now? Oh, what a jerk I've been! Swell-headed and stupid! When I think of all the money I dropped on those damn investments... God, I should be able to retire now... nobody would ever get the chance to say, 'That old stumblebum once was good on the wire!'"

"Rudy," she cried, "don't talk nonsense! We'll get along fine."

"I'm talking facts," he retorted wildly. "I started out as a water boy, and I'll end up that way. You're married to a stupid jerk – don't you know that yet? I even lied to you about how old I was – I was afraid you'd be scared to marry me. I'm not forty-seven – I'm fifty-four... now you know it. But you're only thirty-nine – you don't have to drag downhill with me... you can shake loose... you won't have any trouble getting married again. Why, you're still young enough to have children. But this time pick a man with some sense."

His bitterness, the loss of self-respect, his unnerved, unmanly talk, were stunning to May. She perceived with great pain that they never had fully understood each other. Rudy hadn't known that she loved him for himself – and not because he was a high-paid or famous performer – and that she would love him whatever he was. And she never had appreciated how much fear and worry there was behind his self-discipline, and his immense skill, and his success – so that now, when he was losing position, he was feeling utterly worthless. It was a torment to her to see him like this, completely wretched and needlessly despairing, and her yearning to help him was so keen that she said something she knew was a lie – yet a lie that contained within it a painful grain of truth. She jumped to her feet. "You never really loved me, did you? It's coming out now!"

The remark, and her tone of voice, stunned him.

"Oh, you needed something in skirts for your act," she went on harshly, "but you never had any *respect* for me – just a good-looking prop for your act."

He put up his hand as though to defend himself from the cruelty of what she had said. "What do you mean? What's got into you?"

"If I caught polio tomorrow and was left crippled, you'd leave me right away, wouldn't you?"

"You're crazy!" he shouted. "How can you talk like that? May... I love you with all my heart, don't you *know* that? I'd love you no matter what happened to you!"

The grain of truth behind her lie came out now. She sank down on a chair and began to weep. "Then why do you insult me? Why do you tell me to marry someone else?"

"Oh, dearest, I didn't mean it. I was just talking wild."

"You did mean it, or you wouldn't have said it! *You* think I've stayed married to you only because you were a success! You don't believe I've really loved you! You think I'm a tramp!"

"Oh, May, no!" he cried. "I *didn't mean* it that way. Darling, don't cry like that. I can't bear it!" And then, as she continued to weep, he dropped to his knees before her and flung his arms around her. "You're my whole life, May. I'd go to pieces if you ever left me."

"Then it's time you learnt what I'm like," she told him passionately. "You think I care whether I wear a damn mink coat or whether you're forty-seven or fifty-four? And let's say it... did it ever occur to you that I never in the world would blame you because we didn't have any kids together?"

"Oh, May," he cried, "May!"

She caught his face between her hands. "You stupid, goddamn fool... when are you going to learn that I took you for my husband because I loved you? I haven't been living with you for a price!"

"Oh, May," he cried, "May!" and began to weep. He held on to her desperately while convulsive sobs racked his body. She put her arms around him then and cradled him, murmuring, "Darling, darling." She didn't speak or try to stop his weeping, but, by her arms enfolding him and her lips to his forehead, she tried to make him feel how much she cherished him. Once he muttered through sobs, "Oh, I can't stop crying... what's happening to me?" And another time, "What a weak man I am! I always thought I could take anything." And a bit later, "Gregg was such a nice boy..." She held him, and soothed him, and kissed his face, and joined her own tears with his, knowing that this man of hers, who had not cried since childhood, was now weeping for everything at once – for the mistakes he had made in life, for the death of their son, for the fact of ageing, for the uncertainties of the future. And she was glad when he muttered, "Oh, I want to cry, there are things you *have* to cry about!"

It was a long time before his sobbing quieted. As it did, he began to sigh heavily, and his tight, shaking body relaxed, and he pressed closer to her. She had, then, a keen, exquisitely joyous sense that somehow they had turned a page in their life together – that they had come closer, and looked more deeply into each other's hearts. With bursting love for him – for all that he was in strength and in weakness, in skill and in false pride, and in self-pity also – she said softly, "Rudy, darling, listen to me. Are you listening?"

He said nothing, but she knew he was.

"You know what I think we need to do most of all? We have to forgive ourselves for being human!" She laughed just a little, lightly and tenderly. "I'll forgive myself for being a spendthrift, and for the dizzy things I did with men before I met you – because they shouldn't make me ashamed any more. And you'll forgive yourself for being everybody's pushover in business matters. We sure weren't always smart – but who is?" She was quiet for a moment, and then her arms tightened around him. "And mostly I think we need to forgive ourselves for getting older – you with your grey hair and me with the wrinkles that are coming around my eyes. I want us to get comfortable with everything we ever did, and everything to come. And I know how we can do it. You know how, Rudy?"

He said nothing, but moved his face against her throat.

"Just by loving each other – that's all. Just being sweet with each other – even in a mud circus at twenty bucks a week."

His arms pulled her closer, and his lips kissed her face softly, and a sigh of deep release sounded in his throat.

"Oh!" she thought suddenly, with exultation. "How much I love him! How good it is to be in love!"

To Climb the Pyrenees*

As Jacquet waited for the apartment door to open, he reflected that in similar circumstances no Frenchman would have invited him to dinner. He had met his host only five days before, and, aside from passing chatter about Paris, their talks had been confined to business. In Jacquet's code of behaviour, their relationship did not warrant dinner with the family, but perhaps this was a custom among German businessmen – he would ask his wife when he got home.

The door opened, and Jacquet was agreeably surprised by the woman confronting him. Frau Beck, who appeared to be in her middle thirties, was tall, auburn-haired, handsome, with a trim, splendid figure. She held out her hand and greeted him with a simple cordiality he liked, although he winced a little as she took note of the scar tissue on his neck. He had been severely wounded in 1943. Plastic surgery had accomplished a great deal, but his natural good looks had been somewhat marred. He still suffered over it, especially in the presence of a pretty woman.

Frau Beck took his topcoat and led him from the foyer to the living room while telling him that her husband had not yet come home. Their son, who was attending the university in Göttingen, was arriving for the weekend; Alfred had gone to the airport to meet him.

Thinking that she must be forty at least, Jacquet said the expected thing: "It's hard to believe you have a son of university age."

She murmured "Thank you" and went on to other matters. "Alfred told me only this morning that your wife is German."

"Yes."

"If he had mentioned it a day sooner, I would have cooked Swedish for you – I do it quite well. As it is, you'll know every dish I've prepared."

"I doubt it. My wife is a busy physician who hates to cook. When we don't dine out, she reads her medical journals while I prepare supper. Our friends consider it rather droll, but we find it agreeable."

Frau Beck laughed. "I'm relieved... Is your wife from Bavaria, by any chance?"

Jacquet nodded, smiling. "I've been told before that I speak German with a French-Bavarian accent. It must sound queer."

"No, very pleasant. Now I'll ask you to excuse me while I run back to the kitchen. Can I give you a drink?"

"Thank you, not just yet."

"There are some magazines in that rack." She smiled and strode from the room, and Jacquet thought, "What an attractive woman!" He was glad of the invitation now. No evening would be dull with Frau Beck on view.

He gazed around the room. The bookshelves, the half-dozen prints and paintings on the walls bespoke a cultured household, and the new, modernistic furniture indicated money. As he moved to examine a painting, he thought wryly, "The conquered have risen from the ashes." Even with his earnings as a textile designer and his wife's salary from a children's clinic, they couldn't afford an apartment like this. Paris was the loveliest city man's imagination had created, but it was also old and crowded, and there were too many buildings like his without a lift or central heating.

"Modigliani," his mind said automatically – and then he stood rigid and unbelieving as he stared at the canvas. It was, like so many Modiglianis, a portrait of the artist's wife. This time he had given her black hair, very large, mysterious eyes, a sad, abstracted face, an elongated, swan-like neck. After a bewildered moment Jacquet thought, "Many artists have repeated a study." Quickly he bent forward to find the date... 1919. The canvas that had hung in his mother's apartment had been painted in the same year – he absolutely remembered that, because of the story attached to it. Was the frame the same? He closed his eyes, trying to recall. He found he couldn't.

Normally, Jacquet had a ruddy complexion, but there was a pallor in his cheeks now as he tried to weigh the possibility of two studies not only similar, but exactly alike… the size of the canvas… the fascinating look in the woman's eyes… and the peculiar chair on which she was seated, like the chair of a clerical dignitary, with armrests and high back. He lifted the painting off the wall and strode to the piano, on which there was a bright lamp. Holding the frame with one hand, he took hold of the lamp with the other. As he did so, he caught sight of a Renoir on the wall beyond – and he gasped. He circled the piano and stepped up to the painting. His heart was beating rapidly; his brain was in tumult. He stared and closed his eyes, and stared again, It was a small, lovely study of varied field flowers – poppies, nasturtiums, cornflowers – the colours ever so delicate, and so indelibly imprinted on his memory. The date, if any, was hidden by the frame.

Profoundly shaken, almost doubting his senses, Jacquet raised the Modigliani and placed it alongside the Renoir. He knew then, immediately, that he was not mistaken. Although he had not seen these paintings since 1939, he had gazed at them throughout his childhood and youth. It was possible that Modigliani might have painted an exact duplicate of the canvas he sold Jacquet's mother one night in the Rotonde* – it was possible that Renoir had duplicated the particular canvas Jacquet's father had bought at a charity bazaar – but it simply was not possible that both of them had done so. The question, then, was how Alfred Beck had acquired them. The German officer who had occupied his family apartment during the war, and who had looted it of everything valuable when he left, might have sold these paintings to a gallery in Germany – where Beck later found them. It might have happened that way, yes. Unless Beck had been that officer – unless Beck himself was the thief!

He heard a door open in the hallway beyond. Moving rapidly, he put the Modigliani back in its place. Then he stood waiting, his hands gripped behind his back, his slender, wiry figure under rigid control.

As Beck entered, followed by his son, Jacquet produced a smile and advanced to meet him. Beck was in his early fifties – a tall man, athletically trim like his wife, with only a little grey streaking his black hair. His handshake was strong and welcoming. He said gaily, "Monsieur Jacquet, I've brought home the finished contract, as I promised, and also my son, Reinhardt." His manner made clear that he was not only fond of the boy, but proud of him. Reinhardt was taller than his father, perhaps six feet three, but softer in physique, with thick spectacles over nearsighted eyes.

"Do sit down," Beck said. "Will you have some port, or whiskey?"

"Whiskey with a little soda, please."

He began making conversation like any urbane guest, but inwardly he was on fire. If Beck *were* the man, he was thinking fiercely, what about the furniture that also had been stolen from his apartment? It was more than twenty years since the Germans had fled Paris, and furniture didn't last for ever, but perhaps there would be a piece or two left in one of the other rooms? How could he see the rest of the apartment?

But no, the thought came instantly, that was unnecessary. The paintings were staring at him: he needed nothing more. He had only to find out how Beck had acquired them. "Thank you, just right," he said as he sipped the highball. In fact, it was stronger than he usually liked a drink to be, but he welcomed it now as a sedative.

Sitting down beside him, glass in hand, Beck said, "I'm really delighted that you and Reinhardt and I are able to have a little chat together. Let me tell you why." With enthusiasm he began to explain that he was a long-time, profound admirer of French culture, the French intellect and what might be termed "the soul of France". Reading French more easily than he could speak it, he knew many French thinkers, poets and novelists. He added that he was not deprecating German culture or the German mind. To the contrary, he felt that both cultures were complementary, and that in the future they would nourish the world.

As Beck continued, Jacquet smiled at him cordially and grew more and more irritated. His host, who obviously was trying to please him, didn't seem aware that he was parroting the Nazi propaganda line of 1941. But *he* remembered it damn well, and he was neither flattered nor impressed. It was the same offensive filth French collaborators had spouted while watching German boots goose-step up the Champs-Élysées every day.

"All of this is to prepare you for a question," Beck said. "My son and I have a difference that you, as a Frenchman, can resolve."

"Please tell me," Jacquet murmured, and wondered whether this were not the reason for the dinner invitation.

"Father has offered me a year at a foreign university," young Reinhardt said. "He wants me to go to the Sorbonne. But I've heard that the Sorbonne is so overcrowded that some students can't even get into lectures."

"I'm afraid that's true in some faculties," Jacquet replied. "Which one—"

"Literature."

"I don't know about conditions there, but I can find out and write you in a few days."

"I would appreciate that, sir."

"Oh, come now, Reinhardt," Beck said indulgently. "Whether you go to the University of Florence or Uppsala, or any of the others you've been mentioning, the most important part of your year will not be the lectures. It'll be what you learn about another people, about the air they breathe. You'll absorb..." He stopped as a pretty, bright-looking girl of thirteen entered the room. "Ah, Ursula, dear," he said fondly. He introduced her to Jacquet, jocularly, as "the second of his most important achievements in life", kissed her cheek and continued talking with his arm around her. "You'll absorb more from your friends than your professors. So why don't you come out with the real reason for your reluctance to visit France?"

Reinhardt hesitated, then spoke with a simple candour that made Jacquet rather admire him. "Monsieur, if I go to France, I wouldn't like to be regarded as one of yesterday's conquerors or made to feel unwelcome because I'm German."

"It won't happen, I know!" Beck insisted. "The French are a deeply courteous people. Except for a few old cranks, the war is forgotten. Our two nations are allies now."

Yes, Jacquet said to himself, this *is* why I was invited – it's why the boy came home this particular weekend: he was summoned to come. A feeling of laughter rose inside him. A father's devotion had brought Jacquet to an apartment in Dortmund where he had found, by incredible coincidence, what had been missing for over twenty years.

"I'm not so sure," Reinhardt said doggedly. "Father, only last week I heard a story. Two friends of mine were in France in August. In Lyons they asked a woman to direct them somewhere. She was about forty-five, they said, and she answered them in German – not very good German, but better than their French. After she had told them how to go, one of them – to be polite – asked where she had learnt to speak German so well. Her manner suddenly changed. She said to them with real venom, 'In Bergen-Belsen, in one of *your* concentration camps.'" Reinhardt paused, and then said to Jacquet, "I wouldn't like to meet up with that sort of thing. Personally, I've done nothing to deserve it."

"Quite right," Jacquet murmured, "you haven't."

Thirteen-year-old Ursula whispered in a tone loud enough for Jacquet to hear, "Father, what's a concentration camp?"

"I'll explain later," Beck muttered, and turned to his son. "I've been to Bordeaux twice in the last four years. I've never met any hostility. Monsieur, what's your opinion? Be frank."

Jacquet addressed himself to Reinhardt. "I don't doubt the story you were told. Wounded people react in a wounded way, and such things can happen. What I do doubt is the likelihood of your encountering anything like it. You'll be moving in university circles, among people who think. You'll be judged by the way you conduct yourself. Only an idiot would regard a student of your age as one of yesterday's invaders."

"Exactly!" Beck exclaimed.

"Besides," Jacquet said, turning to Beck, "as the years have passed, even old soldiers have come to see things in perspective. Enmities fade away – isn't that so? Or weren't you in service during the war?"

"I was, of course. And you're absolutely right... Well, Reinhardt, what do you say now?"

"I'm very glad to hear Monsieur's opinion."

"If you do come to Paris," Jacquet said, "I can help you find quarters."

"That's extremely kind of you."

"What branch of the service were you in?" Jacquet asked Beck. His manner was easy, but his pulse was racing.

Beck laughed. "In the sinecure service – the legal department of the army. I'm an attorney, you see, although I haven't practised Law for the past ten years. For me it was a war without bullets, my opportunity for a love affair with Paris."

"Ah, you were stationed in Paris!" Jacquet exclaimed a bit hoarsely. He drained his glass.

"Will you have another drink?"

"Please, but milder this time."

Beck took Jacquet's glass and went to the bar. He began to talk of the first impression Paris had made upon him – of his first walk from the Place de la Concorde up the Champs-Élysées – surely one of the noblest city vistas of the world.

Frau Beck came into the room, smiled at Jacquet and sat down by the side of her son. She asked her husband for a drop of vermouth, and told them that supper would be ready in a few minutes.

"What part of Paris did you live in?" Jacquet asked.

"I've forgotten the name of the district. It was only a few minutes' walk from the Arc de Triomphe."

"Ah, yes," Jacquet murmured, "l'Étoile." His throat felt parched. He drank deeply.

"I had a charming apartment on a boulevard lined with trees. There was a lovely one near my apartment. Rousseau, I think it was called."

"Parc Monceau," said Jacquet, speaking more loudly than he intended. "The Boulevard de Courcelles passes right by it."

"Le Boulevard de Courcelles, of course, that's where I lived," Beck exclaimed with delight. "And every morning—"

"How long were you in Paris?" Jacquet interrupted.

"Almost two years, from '42 until the summer of '44."

Jacquet had his answer now, fully and completely and without possibility of error. Yet, in the same moment that a cry rose in his throat – "It was No. 66, you thieving pig, third floor!" – a paralysing thought came, and he remained silent. His mind had leapt to his return to Paris. "Business is business," he could hear the directors of his company saying. "Why didn't you keep your mouth shut? We all have our war wounds – why did you play the sentimental child over some paintings you haven't seen in twenty years?"

Jacquet pressed a finger to his right temple, where a nerve seemed suddenly to have gone wild, throbbing and jumping. They would say that, and what answer could he give? None! There wasn't even room for deceit, because the negotiation had been handled by the directors themselves. The only reason he had been empowered to sign the contract was that Beck wanted to discuss changes in some of the patterns. Now the patterns had been agreed upon and Paris notified. The contract involved a third of the production of his company for the next two years, a sizeable matter. He had an obligation to the directors – and to his own position. Why were these paintings so important to him? How often had he thought about them in the last ten years?

He heard Frau Beck say "Won't you come in to dinner?", and rose to his feet. There was a grimace on his lips that he intended to be a smile, and he was not aware that she was eyeing him with curiosity. The moment they entered the dining room, his eyes flashed around, but he saw nothing from his old apartment. He took the seat his hostess indicated, nodded a response to something Reinhardt was saying and told himself bitterly that it was not the paintings that enraged him so much as the indignity of allowing this thief to get away with his theft. And yet he knew already that he couldn't say anything. This dinner and his gall would be swallowed together.

An elderly maid carried in a soup tureen and placed it before Frau Beck. Reinhardt circled the table with a wine bottle and poured. Aware that he had to break out of his silence, Jacquet said "Superb" to Frau Beck when he had tasted the soup. "*Formidable.*"

"Monsieur," said Reinhardt, "would it be intruding to ask what happened to you during World War Two? It's a curiosity of mine – I ask everyone of your generation. But if you don't—"

"Not at all." As Jacquet spoke, his words began to come more and more slowly. "When the war came, I was in the south with an anti-aircraft unit, although there was no fighting in our area. After the defeat in the north and the Armistice, my unit was demobilized. But a few comrades and I..." – he paused as the nerve in his temple began to jump wildly "made our way to the Spanish border, our idea being to cross the Pyrenees..." He suddenly was unable to go on. A cold sweat had broken out on his forehead, and he was gripped by a kind of paralysis. He sat very still, staring at the tablecloth, and for some moments was utterly oblivious of the eyes of his hosts upon him and of their distress. He was listening to words – words spoken by whom, by what? By his soul, his bowels, his dead comrades on that journey? He didn't know. He only heard: "And what sort of a man are you now?" Now you're like everyone you once despised! You're not the man who dodged patrols and clawed his way over the Pyrenees and suffered five months in a Spanish prison in order to get to England, in order to say, "Here's a Frenchman ready to fight." The man you are now would have been a collaborator!

It was a truth not to be evaded, a truth like sour vomit in his mouth. He felt dirty inside and out, soiled by the excrement of practicality, by all those venal considerations he had spat upon in 1940 when he was young and brave and what mattered to him was France and freedom and clean hands. "I am corrupt," he thought with anguish – and became aware of Beck's hand on his shoulder and Beck's agitated voice saying, "Monsieur, what's wrong? Are you ill? Can I help you?"

He saw then that the eyes of the whole family were upon him, and he muttered, "Excuse me... It's nothing..." Beck's hand was still on his shoulder – he felt it there like hot lead – and he suddenly straightened up in his chair and forced a smile and began to talk rapidly in a frenetically convivial manner. He told them that he had a mild disability which produced a type of seizure. He had inherited it from his father... it was not epilepsy, and not serious – a momentary chemical imbalance. He was fine now – he begged them not to be disturbed: it might be another year before this would happen again, certainly not again tonight.

As Beck returned to his seat, Jacquet quickly drank a glass of wine, then turned immediately to Reinhardt. "I didn't finish my story. My comrades and I wanted to get to England. We were three days walking and hiding in the Pyrenees before a Spanish patrol caught us, and then we were five months in jail. We weren't mistreated, merely underfed and overrun with vermin. When they let us out, we made it to Gibraltar and then to North Africa. I fought against your General Rommel,"* he said to Beck, "and in '44 in Normandy."

"Were you wounded in the neck?" young Ursula asked.

Her mother looked at her reprovingly, but Jacquet smiled at the girl and said, "Yes, my neck and one toe."

"Ah, how awful war is," Frau Beck murmured.

"Yes, awful," Reinhardt exclaimed with a certain excitement, "but, for those who survive it, an experience of such intensity that it must develop a man unbelievably."

Jacquet regarded the young man for a moment. Then he commented quietly, "I assure you that war can also diminish the stature of a man unbelievably." He leant forward, his dark eyes very bright. "Would you like to hear the single experience of those years that made the most impression on me?"

"I would very much."

Now, ostensibly speaking to Reinhardt, Jacquet kept glancing at Beck. "I was in the Allied army group that entered Paris first in the summer of '44. That same day I got a jeep and raced to my family apartment. My father had died before the war, but I hoped to find my mother there. The apartment was empty. Later I learnt she'd gone to some relatives in the country when Paris fell. When I say the apartment was empty, I mean that its wartime occupant, a German officer, had taken everything with him when he left."

Beck's face suddenly became tight, and his eyes riveted upon Jacquet.

"Except for a few items," Jacquet continued in an easy voice, "everything had been moved out – beds, tables, sofas, linen, books, paintings. Unfortunately the concierge couldn't tell me the name of the officer. She was new – the old one had died."

"War is awful in every way," Frau Beck murmured. "Those horrible bombings of our cities…"

Gazing at his hostess, Jacquet decided that she knew nothing. Likely Beck had sold everything except the paintings. A man of taste! Without looking at Beck, he could feel his eyes – he almost could smell the tension in the man.

"Bombings are a part of war," Reinhardt said to his mother, "but I can't understand how a German officer could steal the effects of a French family – a common soldier might, perhaps, but not an officer. He must have been a degenerate."

"But you're mistaken," Jacquet said. "War is an animal business, and, speaking frankly, there has been more than one regime in history that encouraged its citizens to be animals. France was looted both officially and unofficially – why should individuals lag behind their government?"

The maid served Jacquet a plate with filet of trout and new potatoes, and Frau Beck asked, "Have you had boiled trout before, Monsieur?"

"I have to admit it – it's a French dish also."

"What a shame! I wanted everything to be special."

Beck was standing by Jacquet now, pouring a different wine, and Jacquet said to Reinhardt, "In my district many people left Paris in 1940. Their apartments, like mine, were occupied by German officers. The same thing happened to their possessions."

"Where did you live?" Beck asked suddenly, in a hard, aggressive tone.

"Place des Vosges, where the Victor Hugo Museum is. Do you know it?" He sipped his wine.

"Of course, I visited it," Beck replied animatedly. The tight look departed from his face. "Your trout, Monsieur. Don't let it get cold."

Picking up his fork, Jacquet said pleasantly to Reinhardt, "I wouldn't want you to misunderstand my point of view. My wife is German, and her brother is my beloved friend. Both of them, however, resisted the corruption of the Hitler period – they left Germany for political reasons. If Goethe or Brahms had lived in my apartment, they wouldn't have stolen my paintings. But if they had been indoctrinated members of the Hitler Youth…"

He shrugged, and his eyes flicked momentarily to Beck. "People are malleable – it is their history, their education, the moral atmosphere of their land that make them decent or corrupt… Ah," he exclaimed as he tasted the trout, "this is delicious."

Beck said, slowly and pointedly, "For those of us who were anti-Nazi, the years under Hitler were dreadful."

"I'm sure," Jacquet responded with a nod. He began, then, to tell them an amusing story of the war years, and followed it with a tale of comic scandal among French film stars. He was an engaging raconteur when he put his mind to it, and the excitement he was feeling lent zest to his chatter. In the course of a few minutes, the mood in the room became light-hearted, and Beck himself began to talk with convivial gaiety. After the trout came venison with Swedish lingonberries, and Jacquet exclaimed "*formidable*" more than once, and drank a good deal of wine in an effort to contain his racing spirit. He wanted the dinner to be at an end. It was, finally, with a cherry *torte** and coffee, and when Beck offered a cognac, Jacquet asked – begging his hostess's pardon – whether he might not enjoy it while reading over the contract. His plane, he explained, left early in the morning, and there might still be need for revisions. Frau Beck said "Of course", and Beck ushered him down the hallway to his study.

It was a small room lined with bookshelves, the furniture comfortably old, and there Jacquet recognized his own desk and, upon it, a porcelain seashell that had belonged to his mother. He smiled thinly, and reflected that possibly he had misjudged the handsome lady of the house. She had remained quite placid during the conversation, but perhaps her hands were dirty too, and it might well be that she and her husband, in conceiving their pretty post-war children, had rocked pleasurably together on his parents' bed. He would never know, and he did not really care.

"No, thank you," he replied to Beck's offer of a cigar, and sat down at the Empire desk he had used as a student. He began to read the contract. It was neither a long nor an involved document, and presently he looked up with a smile and said, "You must have been an excellent attorney for your army. This is clear – everything is covered. I don't even have a comma to suggest."

"Thank you," Beck said with manifest pleasure, and offered his pen. "I've already signed for my firm."

Jacquet paused to sip his cognac, then pretended to notice the porcelain for the first time. He exclaimed, "Why, what's that?" and leant across the desk to pick it up. "How astonishing! You got this in France?"

"During the war, in some little antique shop."

"Do you know what it is? It has a name, 'Porcelaine de Sèvres'."

"I thought it was just a pretty ceramic. You make it sound valuable."

"Oh, no, not this piece. There are some from the eighteenth century that are, but one only finds them in museums. What interests me so much about this one is a peculiarity…" – he pointed to the portrait of a young girl in the centre of the shell – "the combination of her dark blond hair, her white blouse and the blue rosette at her neck. I've only seen one other exactly like it in my life – my mother's. She kept it on her dressing table. She used to put her wedding ring right there when she went to bed at night." Glancing at Beck, he saw with satisfaction that the man was looking at him with stiff uncertainty.

"An interesting coincidence," Beck said in a muted voice.

"Isn't it?" Jacquet exclaimed, with a smile. "She's one of my clearest childhood memories – this girl's face, I mean. What dreams I made up about her! She was my first love! At that time my family lived on the same boulevard you did during the war." Still smiling, his eyes on Beck, he added with the air of a man reminiscing, "66 Boulevard de Courcelles, third floor." He watched Beck trying to think back – and then saw that the number had echoed in his memory, and saw the blood drain out of his face until his cheeks became a milky grey. Jacquet went on lightly, "When I returned to our apartment, this was one of the family possessions I missed most of all. Ah well..." He signed his name to the first copy of the contract, picked up the duplicate – and paused. "Could I ask an enormous favour, a matter of sentiment? Would you give me this little porcelain? I promise to send you another from Paris."

Beck's face was still pallid, and there was an uncertainty in his eyes that filled Jacquet with savage pleasure.

"I'd be delighted. There's no need to reciprocate."

"Oh, but I will. And you don't know how I appreciate it." He signed the second copy of the contract, folded it into his wallet and stood up. "There, our little business is done, and I hear music."

"My daughter."

"How well she plays!" He picked up the porcelain and put it with care into a side pocket of his jacket. "A thousand thanks."

"Not at all," Beck said with a wan smile.

Just before they entered the living room, Jacquet paused. He turned around in the hallway and said softly, "I want to congratulate you on your splendid children. And the respect they have for you is obvious."

"Thank you."

Jacquet's eyes began to glitter. "I know it would hurt you to lose their respect. That was why I said my apartment was on Place des Vosges. It wasn't. It was No. 66 Boulevard de Courcelles."

Beck became rigid. His fists clenched, and he looked down at Jacquet with naked hatred.

"Now, pay attention," Jacquet said, "and use your intelligence before you make a mistake. When my mother left Paris, she took her valuables and documents. I still have today, as a family memento, the bill of sale my father received for the Renoir – date, sum, description. If I make it a court matter, you won't have a bill of sale to show."

Beck's breathing was audible – his neck and face looked swollen now, engorged with dark blood. Jacquet didn't know whether the next moment would bring a physical attack. He was on guard, but he didn't give a damn. Without a pause, he said, "Neither of us has a bill of sale for the Modigliani. But what you don't know, since you never changed the frame, is that he personally inscribed it to my mother on the back of the canvas. I know what he wrote, and I can prove it. I'm leaving now, and I'll take the paintings with me. You can tell your family you sold them to me – or perhaps that you wanted to make reparation for what others, who were not anti-Nazi like you, did during the war."

Jacquet walked into the living room. He thanked Frau Beck for her hospitality and her superb dinner, apologized for needing to leave at once and kissed the hand she offered him. He shook hands with Reinhardt, and said he would write to him soon. Ursula stopped playing, and he touched her shoulder lightly, while telling her she had a lovely tone. Then, as the family watched with an astonishment that turned into stupefaction, he took down both paintings and started out of the room. There was a spicy aspect to his gambit that especially elated him – he had no bill of sale for the Renoir, and Modigliani had been too drunk that night to sign a canvas for anyone.

Beck was standing in the doorway, blocking it. There was a moment's pause as Jacquet came up to him. Frau Beck called out, "Alfred, what's happening? Our paintings!"

"I'll explain," Beck muttered, and, ashen-faced, stepped out of the way.

It was not until Jacquet was in a taxi on the way back to his hotel that the satisfaction began to drain out of him. He was travelling through streets with new and shining buildings – testaments that this city, like so many others, only lately had been mutilated by war. He began to wonder why human beings, so innocent at birth, grew so often to be basely vile, and were so easily pushed and gulled into becoming what a man should never be. Was it this, perhaps, that had made poor Modigliani paint endlessly his sad, contemplative faces?*

Notes

p. 1, *The Way Things Are and Other Stories*: A collection issued in 1938 by International Publishers, New York, with a short introduction by communist journalist and novelist Michael Gold (1893–1967).

p. 3, *Margaret*: The American writer and activist Margaret Maltz (née Larkin, 1899–1967), whom the author married in 1937 and from whom he was divorced in 1964.

p. 5, *Season of Celebration*: First published in *Story* in September 1937 under the title 'Hotel Raleigh, the Bowery'. The story also appeared in *The Flying Yorkshireman* (1938), a collection of novellas by five authors, and was dramatized by Philip Stevenson (1896–1965) and published as a play in the *One Act Play Magazine*, Vol. 1, No. 6 (October 1937), under the title 'Transit'.

p. 7, *Bowery*: A street and neighbourhood in Lower Manhattan in New York City.

p. 9, *ptomaine*: Food poisoning.

p. 13, *tinhorn*: A "tinhorn" was originally a low-stakes gambler who nevertheless acted in a showy manner; by extension the term refers to any person who pretends to have money, ability or influence. Here the term may therefore simply mean "braying" or "arrogant". Alternatively, it may be a lapsus for "tinny" – the way the bum's voice is described later in the story (Chapter IV).

p. 15, *ol' Beantown*: Boston.

p. 18, *J.P. Morgan*: The American financier John Pierpont Morgan (1837–1913).

p. 19, *All people... and rejoice*: The first stanza of 'All People That on Earth Do Dwell', a hymn by William Kethe (d. 1594) based on Psalm 100 and sung to the tune of the 'Old Hundredth'.

p. 20, *Van Dyke beard*: A style of beard named after the Flemish painter Anthony van Dyck (or "Van Dyke", 1599–1641).

p. 20, *The Lord... He doth us take*: The second stanza of 'All People That on Earth Do Dwell'. The word "flock" is replaced by "folk" in the original hymn.

p. 20, *Abide... eventide*: The first line of the hymn 'Abide with Me' by the Scottish clergyman Henry Francis Lyte (1793–1847), sung to the tune 'Eventide' by the English organist William Henry Monk (1823–89).

p. 21, *The birds... shall ne'er*: The first three lines of the second stanza of 'The Lord Will Provide', a hymn by John Newton (1725–1807).

p. 22, *At the cross... rolled away*: A blasphemous adaptation of the well-known hymn 'At the Cross', by Russell Kelso Carter (1849–1928).

p. 22, *No strength... goodness*: The beginning of the last stanza of 'The Lord Will Provide'.

p. 22, *Scissor Bill... missing link*: From the 1913 song 'Scissor Bill', by the Swedish-American labour activist Joe Hill (1879–1915), sung to the tune of 'Steamboat Bill'.

p. 22, *a couple Jenny Linds*: A reference to the famous Swedish opera singer Jenny Lind (1820–87).

p. 24, *the Rialto*: A nickname for the Theater District in Manhattan, New York City, from the name of the Rialto Theatre (located at 1481 Broadway, at the north-west corner of Seventh Avenue and 42nd Street), which opened in 1916.

p. 26, *"Pan, razuma Popolska?"*: Cod Polish for "Do you understand Polish, sir?"

p. 29, *crabs*: Pubic lice.

p. 31, *speaking in the tongue*: That is, "speaking in tongues" (glossolalia), or the ability to speak in a language one doesn't know through divine inspiration, one of the beliefs of Pentecostalism.

p. 37, *roll*: Rob.

p. 53, *backhouse*: An outdoor lavatory.

p. 63, *Count your blessings... God hath done*: The refrain of 'Count Your Blessings', a hymn by Johnson Oatman, Jr. (1856–1922).

p. 65, *Goodbye*: First published (as 'Good-by') in *New Masses*, Vol. 22, No. 12 (15th December 1936), with the strapline "The falling of a steel beam made all the difference to Olga, who up to then had not felt that she must escape."

p. 67, *Bessemer furnace*: A furnace using the process developed by the English inventor Henry Bessemer (1813–98) for the mass production of steel from molten pig iron.

p. 77, *Incident on a Street Corner*: First published in the *New Yorker*, 19th November 1937.

p. 85, *The Game*: First published in *Scribner's Magazine*, Vol. 100, Nos. 4–6 (October–December 1936).

p. 93, *A Letter from the Country*: First published in *New Masses*, Vol. 24, No. 8 (17th August 1937).

p. 93, *vittals*: Victuals.

NOTES

p. 93, *chinning*: Talking to.

p. 95, *the Legion*: The American Legion, an association of US war veterans.

p. 102, *forty-four*: That is, .44.

p. 102, *store teeth*: False teeth.

p. 103, *The Drop-Forge Man*: First published in *The Way Things Are and Other Stories*.

p. 109, *straw boss*: A lower-level supervisor or foreman.

p. 112, *a phrenologist's head*: That is, a model head used by phrenologists to discern a person's character. Phrenology is a now-discredited pseudoscience which claimed that personality and intelligence could be determined by the size, shape and "bumps" of the skull.

p. 119, *The Way Things Are*: First published in *The Way Things Are and Other Stories*.

p. 122, *apple plug*: A piece of apple-flavoured tobacco.

p. 123, *dicker*: Bargain.

p. 123, *wild cat*: That is, wild-cat (illicitly distilled) whiskey.

p. 130, *yaller girl*: A black or mixed-race girl with light-brown skin.

p. 150, *blue-balled*: A jibe alluding to a supposed discomfort ("blue balls") attributed to prolonged, unreleased sexual arousal.

p. 154, *a four-corners*: A crossroads.

p. 161, *Man on a Road*: First published in *New Masses*, Vol. 14, No. 2 (8th January 1935), reprinted in *Proletarian Literature in the United States: An Anthology* (New York: International Publishers, 1935), *The Best Short Stories, 1936* (ed. Edward J. O'Brien) and the Soviet journal *International Literature* (French and German editions).

p. 162, *like a story by Bierce*: The celebrated American satirist Ambrose Bierce (1842–c.1914) was also the author of several ghost and horror stories.

p. 166, *mine tipple*: An above-ground area of a mine where coal is tipped from wagons and then sorted, cleaned and prepared for transportation.

p. 171, *Afternoon in the Jungle*: A selection of stories published in 1970 by Liveright, New York. In addition to the stories reproduced in this section, the book included 'Man on a Road' and 'The Way Things Are', which had already appeared in *The Way Things Are and Other Stories* (see note to p. 1).

p. 173, ESTHER: Maltz's third wife, Esther Engelberg (née Goldstein, 1913–98), whom he married in 1970.

p. 175, *The Happiest Man on Earth*: First published in *Harper's Magazine*, Vol. 177 (June–November 1938), and reprinted in *The*

Best Short Stories, 1939 (ed. Edward J. O'Brien). The story was the winner of the 1938 O. Henry Memorial Award.

p. 183, *New Deal*: A raft of economic measures introduced in 1933 by the Democratic president Franklin D. Roosevelt (1882–1945) in an effort to combat the effects of the Great Depression. It included public-works projects, social security, regulation of banking and job-creation programmes.

p. 187, *Sunday Morning on Twentieth Street*: First published in the *Southern Review* (Winter 1940).

p. 195, *Afternoon in the Jungle*: First published in the *New Yorker*, 11th January 1941.

p. 195, *Anita Louise… Norma Shearer*: The American film and TV actress Anita Louise (1915–70) and the Canadian-American actress Norma Shearer (1902–83).

p. 203, *Circus Come to Town*: First published in *Masses & Mainstream*, Vol. 3, No. 7 (July 1950). The story won the Normandy Pen Award for Literature in 1952.

p. 203, *mumbley-peg*: "A children's game in which each player attempts to make the blade of a knife (in some places a fork) stick in the ground when thrown from a series of positions, the loser being required to draw out of the ground with the teeth a peg which has been driven in with a certain number of blows with the handle of the knife" (*OED*).

p. 205, *stake-drivers*: Hydraulic machines used to hammer stakes into the ground.

p. 219, *With Laughter*: First published in the *South-West Review*, Vol. 45, No. 2 (April 1960) under the pen name Julian Silva.

p. 222, *Yankee Stadium*: A baseball stadium located in the Bronx in New York City.

p. 234, *Kelly clamps*: A type of haemostatic forceps.

p. 237, *The Farmer's Dog*: First published in the *Saturday Evening Post*, 13th July 1968, under the title 'The Prisoner's Dog'.

p. 248, *In back of the pasture*: At the back of the pasture.

p. 251, *The Cop*: First published in *Afternoon in the Jungle*.

p. 256, *the Garibaldis*: The "Garibaldi" partisan brigades, named after Giuseppe Garibaldi (1807–82), the leader of the Italian Risorgimento.

p. 259, *Gesummaria*: An Italian exclamation of surprise or fear (from "*Gesù e Maria*", "Jesus and Mary").

p. 271, *The Gentleman and His Son*: First published in *New Masses*, Vol. 33, No. 4 (17th October 1939), with the strapline "Albert Maltz contributes a short story of bourgeois family life in America today."

p. 275, *Barnard*: Barnard College, a private women's liberal arts college in New York City.

p. 276, *bonite*: Francis means "bornite", a high-grade copper ore.

p. 279, *The Piece of Paper*: First published in *Direction*, Vol. 5, No. 4 (Summer 1941).

p. 279, *Port Hudson*: The site of a famously long siege (22nd May–9th July 1863) during the American Civil War (1861–65). After an initial unsuccessful attack (13th May 1863), the Union forces led by General Nathaniel Banks (1816–94) laid siege to the stronghold of Port Hudson, Louisiana, on the lower stretches of the Mississippi, while those led by Union general Ulysses Grant (1822–85) were besieging Vicksburg upriver. The port was eventually surrendered by the Confederates (with whom Captain Richard Wheatley was serving) following the fall of Vicksburg.

p. 282, *Federals*: Unionists.

p. 283, *the Symposium*: A Socratic dialogue by Plato.

p. 283, *Lear*: Probably the character of King Lear in Shakespeare's tragedy, rather than the English artist and poet Edward Lear, author of *A Book of Nonsense* (1846). Keats famously wrote a sonnet 'On Sitting Down to Read *King Lear* Once Again'.

p. 284, *gabion baskets*: Wicker or brushwood baskets, cylindrical in shape and open at both ends, designed to be filled with earth or stones, and used in military fortifications.

p. 285, *Stevens*: The American politician and lawyer Thaddeus Stevens (1792–1868), a fierce abolitionist.

p. 293, *Husband and Wife*: Written in 1961, this story was unpublished during Maltz's lifetime, but was adapted for television in the United States in 1962 under the title 'The Great Alberti'. It is published here for the first time.

p. 294, *a wireman*: That is, a tightrope walker.

p. 294, *No dice*: No chance.

p. 294, *the Garden*: Madison Square Garden.

p. 294, *teeterboard*: An acrobatic apparatus that resembles a playground seesaw.

p. 296, *Lafayette*: A town in Indiana, around sixty miles north-west of Indianapolis.

p. 304, *Slowpoke*: Slowcoach.

p. 314, *Ringling*: A leading American travelling circus company.

p. 319, *To Climb the Pyrenees*: This story, originally written under the pen name Julian Silva, was rejected by the *Saturday Post* in 1961. A revised version, with a slightly different ending, was submitted seven years later to the same magazine, where it was published with the title 'The Spoils of War' (5th October 1968) and the strapline "Jacquet hated this Nazi with all his soul. But how could he destroy him without destroying himself?" In this volume we are using the text of the 1968 version and restoring the original title. The alternative ending can be read in the final note to this story.

p. 321, *the Rotonde*: The Café de la Rotonde on Boulevard du Montparnasse, the haunt of many famous writers and artists in 1920s and 1930s Paris, among them the Italian painter Amedeo Modigliani.

p. 328, *General Rommel*: The German field marshal Erwin Rommel (1891–1944).

p. 330, *torte*: Cake (German).

p. 334, *contemplative faces*: The 1961 version ends with the following additional paragraph: "Raising the painting, which was obscured by the night, Jacquet peered at it with tender melancholy. But then, after a few moments, he shrugged and said to himself with faint pride, 'If it comes to it, I'll climb the Pyrenees again.'"